The Secrets You Hide

KATE HELM

ZAFFRE

First published in Great Britain as an epub in 2018
This edition published in 2019 by

ZAFFRE
80–81 Wimpole St, London W1G 9RE
www.zaffrebooks.co.uk

A CIP catalogue record for this book is
available from the British Library.

ISBN: 978–1–78576–474–5

Also available as an ebook

1 3 5 7 9 10 8 6 4 2

Typeset by IDSUK (Data Connection) Ltd
Printed and bound in Great Britain by Clays Ltd, Elcograf S.p.A.

Zaffre is an imprint of Bonnier Books UK
www.bonnierzaffre.co.uk
www.bonnierbooks.co.uk

'Sin is a thing that writes itself across a man's face. It cannot be concealed. People talk sometimes of secret vices, there are no such things. If a wretched man has a vice, it shows itself in the lines of his mouth, the droop of his eyelids, the moulding of his hands even.'

Oscar Wilde, *The Picture of Dorian Gray*

Suzanne, September 1997

The key turns in the lock.

Must be Pip, messing about. Again. Didn't he learn anything from what happened before?

On my canvas, my little brother's face is crinkled up in a Cheshire cat grin. And I bet it's the same on the other side of my bedroom door.

'Pip, unlock the door and let me out. You're in enough trouble already.'

An hour ago, he was sheepish and sorry, but he can't keep that up for long. I picture him on the landing, his paint-stained fist stuffed into his mouth, trying to keep quiet. He can never keep it up. Laughter always fights its way out. *Silly Pippin.*

I wait for the giggles but hear nothing.

I try to return to the painting I'm doing of him and Mum on Porthcurno beach, but the silence won't let me. How long have I been in here? Long enough for the sun to move round and turn my room into an oven.

'Pip, come on.'

Then I see it. My *own* key, on my window ledge. It can't be Pip who locked me in because only my parents have the spare.

I put down my fine Filbert brush. Goosebumps spring up along my spine.

When I came up to my room, the house was full of the usual Saturday sounds drifting up the stairs: Pip strangling blue-black scales out of his recorder; Mum's Moulinex grinding raw beef into pink, wormy mince; a DJ mumbling dedications on Radio 2.

But now there's nothing.

I focus on my easel. I promised Miss Hamilton I'd try a landscape, but as usual, people crept into the picture. I love the stories faces tell, and all the colours I can use to bring them to life. Mum's pale cheeks turned Madder Rose by the Cornish sunshine. her hair dripping with salty water. Pip's eyes forming wicked crescent moons: he'd just told a joke. The sand is Winsor Yellow, the sky Cerulean, flecked with fat gulls in titanium white.

OK, my birds look as clumsy as dinosaurs but Miss Hamilton says practice makes perfect. She's the best thing about moving to secondary school. She thinks I could be a proper artist one day.

I hear a deep, adult sigh from the landing. Not my brother.

'Dad?'

'Suzanne. Listen to me.' My father's voice is tight.

'Pippin was only playing, Dad, I can save up for new turps—'

'It doesn't matter now.'

Hope surges. Sometimes Mum manages to stop one of his moods developing.

'So, we can still go to see *Men in Black*?'

He mutters something I can't hear – as though he's talking to someone else. Then, 'Suzanne, this is important. You must promise me you won't come out straightaway.'

'Daddy, what's wrong?'

'Just be a good girl and wait fifteen minutes. No, twenty.'

'Has something happened, Daddy?'

I'm nearly too old to call him that, but sometimes it calms him down.

'Don't try my patience, Suzanne.' I hear anger in his voice. It sounds like Cadmium Red. 'Promise me you'll do as you're told.'

'I promise.'

My mouth has a strange taste, greasy like the oil paints.

A flash of silver appears at the bottom of the door, as he pushes the spare key to my bedroom through the gap. It rests on the dense threads of the new carpet, where Pip spilled the turps and Saturday started to go wrong.

'Daddy, it's OK. I already have a key.'

'I know.'

'But . . .'

I stop. My father always has a reason.

'It's ten past twelve now, Suzanne.'

'Yes.'

Except my clock radio says 12:15. Mum sets it five minutes fast, because I'm allergic to mornings, like Snoopy on my duvet cover.

'At half past – no earlier – unlock the door, and go straight downstairs, don't open any doors. Go to number 26 and tell Len to phone 999.'

He and Len used to be friends. Now Dad says Len is an interfering old sod.

'Are you hurt, Daddy?'

A pause. 'No.'

'I'm scared.'

'Don't be, Suzanne. Repeat back what I said.'

'At . . . at half past, I unlock the door and go downstairs and get Len to call 999.'

I step away from the easel. The floorboard creaks.

'Suzanne! Don't move.' The anger deepens. *Lamp Black*.

I stop. Did he hear me – or is he watching through the keyhole?

'That's better. Good girl, Suzanne. I know I can trust you. And . . . remember, you're my best girl.'

'Daddy? Daddy, wait—'

Light shoots through the keyhole, falling on the carpet in the shape of a Ludo piece. He's gone.

I listen to the house, but all I can hear is my own rapid breathing. I breathe through my nose to slow it down, like the asthma nurse taught me, but now the resinous smell of the spilled turps makes me dizzy.

Have I done something wrong? Telling on Pip, making Dad cross? He is never cross with me.

I close my eyes, focus on the sounds of the avenue: lazy birdsong; the clatter of two skateboards; a soapy sponge sloshing against Len's beige Ford Sierra. But inside, nothing stirs. There are three other hearts beating in the house – four if you count our dog Marmite's, and, of course, I do – but the silence is total.

I'm afraid.

I open my eyes. The red twenty on my clock radio turns to twenty-one. Nine minutes left.

Something is happening on the other side of the door. Voices on the landing, footsteps on the stairs. Male voices. Murmuring, disagreeing.

I strain to hear but the thump of my heart drowns them out.

'Pip? Daddy?' I call, even though it's not his voice I hear. 'Who's there?'

Silence.

Dad has been acting strange for months. Has something happened? Images of what might be beyond that door fill my head.

I blink. Did I imagine the voices? I must have. There are no other sounds, not one.

On the carpet the metal key glows in the sun. Should I unlock the door now?

I mustn't. I'm his best girl, and I promised.

And eight minutes won't make any difference to whatever is on the other side.

Georgia, March 2017

1

I can't remember this man's name, but he kisses better than a stranger should. We stagger along the seafront, leaning against the turquoise railings to catch our breath before kissing again. After a while the gulls become bats, silhouetted against the blinding moon, and the pier winks at me over my stranger's shoulder.

'I'm up here.'

I point towards the square, wishing I lived further away, so we could kiss-walk some more.

'Wow. You live in a wedding-cake house. I've pulled a rich chick.'

We climb the chequerboard steps, holding on to each other. Hungry. Every time I try to put the front door key in the lock, he kisses me again. But finally we're tumbling into the flat, and . . .

Shit.

The door to the living room is ajar – he can't go in there.

'Not that way.' I pull the door closed. It slams.

'What are you hiding?'

'Six children and a bad-tempered pit bull. So don't go in there unless you want to be savaged while the kids sing "The Wheels on the Bus".'

'I'm a teacher. Kids don't scare me.'

I step back, staring at this man I've brought home. I sensed he was safe, and just that bit drunker than I am. But can I be sure? I've covered enough cases where victims felt exactly the same thing.

Suddenly this seems a bad idea.

'Look, I—'

'Is that uncool?' he says. 'Are we meant to know nothing about each other?'

I laugh. 'It's not a quirk or anything. It's just . . . simpler. I'm not looking for a relationship.'

'Well, that's a coincidence, because neither am I.'

He smiles, and I step towards him.

It's OK. He's OK.

Alcohol has softened my focus a little, but my instincts are always sound. This man is harmless.

He follows me into the bedroom. We kiss – sour apple, bitter hops – and begin to undress each other. It's slow, frustrating, him fumbling with the buttons and zips of my stuffy courtroom clothes.

Without a word, we agree to undress ourselves. But my ochre blouse is still a battle, the too-tight buttoned cuffs catching at the end of my wrist. The fabric rips as I pull it past my knuckles.

'In a hurry, are we?' he says.

I answer him by unhooking my bra and letting it fall on the floor. Daring. Confident. It's easier to pretend to be something you're not with a stranger.

'Race you!'

The teacher is wearing less than me, so wins the game, naked now while I'm still wrestling with my tights. He pushes me back into the bed, lies down beside me, and pulls my pants and tights off my legs in one inelegant, effective move.

'You're bloody beautiful.'

I pull him towards me. He reaches down to his discarded jeans for a condom. I like him more for not having to ask. But not enough to want to learn his name.

He pushes into me, and I don't even care what my own name is anymore.

2

It's two in the morning and I can't sleep because of what's hidden behind the living room door.

I move away from the teacher's body. He runs hot as a radiator, and when the cool silk of the kimono touches my skin, it tingles.

I tiptoe into the front room and shut the door behind me.

The shutters are open, and I work by the violet moonlight. The canvas is still tacky, so I cover it with a light tarp, and manoeuvre it behind the folding screen. I pick up my acrylics and tidy them away too.

Sketches and notes litter the honeyed parquet floor. When I first saw this flat, the bay took my breath away: the view, and the clean light that pours through the floor-to-ceiling windows. But the floor space has proved just as valuable. Where Victorians used to dance and flirt, now my notes on killers, rapists, dealers and cheats jostle for position.

I tidy up quickly, glancing at each handwritten sheet to file it in the right place, but trying not to let the details linger. My work-in-progress shows a husband and wife screaming at each other like tetchy toddlers fighting in a sandpit, faces mottled pink with outrage.

I imagine for a second what the teacher would say if he came in now, saw the portrait. This grisly pair were briefly infamous, not even for fifteen minutes, but long enough that he might remember their bland, cruel faces. They were convicted for manslaughter of their infant son. It should have been murder. I wonder what the man in my bed would think: what kind of person paints pictures of the worst humanity has to offer?

I scoop up my original sketches, the court reports, the photograph of the child unlucky enough to be born with them as parents. In my portraits, I build up the layers, to reveal people as they really are, the secrets they hide even from themselves.

The sketches go in the dove-grey armoire, next to past cases. A cupboard full of people I've condemned with a smear of pastel, from a fire-starting teenager to a poisonous pensioner. I have to wrestle the cabinet doors closed: there's too much crammed inside, I should have a clear-out.

As I straighten up, my thighs ache. I want to go back, wake the teacher up for more, forget about the pictures, the stories, the *evil*.

Too late. I'm already contaminated by what I've remembered about the case.

I fetch a glass of tap water, then climb into the huge armchair that always makes me feel child-sized. Through the window, the sea is indigo, separated from the sky by a ribbon of velvet-black horizon. Above it, something flashes white: a star, exploding millennia ago? Or perhaps just a gull's wing catching moonlight.

My eyes are playing tricks on me from lack of sleep. I let them close.

3

'*Hello, sleepyhead.* I made you coffee. I couldn't find tea.'

The touch on my arm makes me flinch. But now I remember. It's the teacher, so close that I can smell my toothpaste on his lips.

I open my eyes; outside, the sky is 5 a.m. grey. I know this time of day. But I am not used to sharing it with another living thing.

'Hello.' My voice is croaky. 'Yeah, I don't drink tea. It reminds me of funerals.'

A question creases the teacher's forehead, but he stops himself voicing it. He has strong, open features that would be difficult to sketch. Usually, I can see through good-looking people, find a crack that shows their secret weaknesses. But this man is hiding nothing. It's so rare that it's remarkable.

'Where did you hide the pit bull and the six kids, then?' he asks.

'In the cupboard. All my dirty secrets, locked away.' I reach out to take my mug; steam rises from the black surface. 'I'm Georgia, by the way.'

'I remember. What's *my* name?'

I blush. 'Sorry. The cider . . .'

He laughs and holds out his hand to shake mine, his skin warm.

'I'm Niall. Pleased to meet you.' He sips his own coffee, looks round the room. 'It's an amazing flat. And you live here on your own?'

I nod. 'Where do you live?'

'Kemp Town. This room is probably bigger than our whole flat. And there are five of us, sharing.'

'I'm very lucky. I'm . . .' I am about to tell him the usual half-lie, that I lost both parents as a child, but I don't want the sympathy and the questions that'll bring. 'I came into some money, a couple of years ago.'

'Good on you.' He shrugs, to show he doesn't resent my luck. 'I ought to get off in a minute. Can't show up at school in the same clothes. They notice everything, the kids.' He grins. 'Wasn't exactly how I expected the Monday pub quiz to turn out.'

'Me neither. A school night. Aren't we terrible?' A memory of last night passes between us. 'But you can finish your coffee.'

He walks towards the window and I watch him take in the view: the sea, the promenade, and closest to us, the genteel garden square. *No ball games. No barbecues. No dogs allowed.* Someone should tell that young fox, brazenly crossing the grass.

The sky begins to lighten. Niall's broad shape is silhouetted against the glass and part of me wants to reach for him again.

Movement on the grass catches my eye. The fox again? No. The shape is wrong. It's a person. A child. A boy, dressed in the reddest pyjama top I've ever seen.

I catch my breath. Rough sleepers sometimes camp down there for the night, before they're moved on, but there's no sign of a tent or a sleeping bag. And the kid can't be older than four or five, plus he's only half-dressed, in pyjamas . . . No, it's a child's football strip.

Thank God Niall is here. A teacher will know what to do.

'Should we go down there?'

Niall looks at me. 'Sorry?'

'The boy. He shouldn't be on his own.'

'What boy?'

I stand up and point towards the kid, statue-still in the centre of the lawn. His red clothes make him glow against the emerald grass. Who knows how many of my neighbours must have seen him already, but decided he was someone else's responsibility. People make me sick.

'I hope he's not been there all night. He must be frozen.'

Niall leans forward, so close to the window his breath frosts the cool morning glass. Then he looks back at me, laughs nervously.

'I can't see anyone.'

I tap the window impatiently.

'*There.*'

I glance at Niall: perhaps he's short-sighted.

But when I turn back towards the green, the boy *has* gone. How? There wasn't long enough for him to reach the pavement or disappear behind the shrubs that fringe the gardens.

Niall says, 'There's a fox down there. Maybe that's what you saw.'

The animal stares me out.

'I'd seen the fox already, but . . .' I stop. There really is no one else there. 'You're right. My hangover must be worse than I thought.'

'Long night, eh? I really should go, before it's light.'

He reaches out to touch my hand and I feel his blood, pulsing. I am lonely, suddenly, at the thought of him being gone.

I take a deep breath.

'You know, you get a great view of the sunrise from the bedroom, on a clear morning like this.'

His eyes widen. 'Really? Well, I wouldn't want to miss out on that, would I?'

I take his hand. However hard I try to convince myself, there are still times when I really don't want to be alone.

4

'When he asked you if you wanted to have sex, what did you say?'

'He didn't ask. It . . . Things were moving faster than I wanted them to. But when he was about to . . . When I realised what he was about to do, I said no.'

'And that's the word you used?'

Oliver Priest, for the prosecution, leans in towards the young woman, his voice kind and courteous. It's one of his tactics. He already knows the defence will try to portray her as a slut or gold-digger who knew exactly what she was doing when she went into the footballer's bedroom. It's Oli's job to make the jury remember that she is somebody's daughter, somebody's friend. Somebody like them.

'Yes. I told him to get off, that I didn't want *that*.' His witness speaks softly. She's brave, this one. No TV link, no screen to prevent her having to see the accused. 'And when it . . . happened, when he forced himself . . . I said no. Three times.'

Her cotton dress is demure, neckline high, hemline below the knee. *Tea roses,* I write, *flesh-tint pink, with viridian leaves. No thorns.* Her name is Julie Tranter though, of course, the law bars journalists from identifying women making an accusation of sexual assault. The reasons are sound, but the ban does mean the public can struggle to see victims as real people.

Perhaps I might use a blur of that floral fabric to suggest how vulnerable she must feel.

'You said it out loud? You didn't just *think* it?'

'I *screamed* it the third time. He heard me. But . . . his expression didn't change at all.'

I glance up at the footballer in the dock, his face flinty. He hasn't looked at the witness box since the girl took the stand. That must tell its own story.

I write: *in denial.* Try to commit him to memory, because while the court is in session, I'm not allowed to sketch a single line. Instead, I have to rely on my notes, jot down word portraits of the characters I must bring to life after the court adjourns. Court artists are yet more proof that the justice system is a relic, unfit for the twenty-first century. But then again, if the judges ever *do* decide to let the cameras in, I'd lose my job, and the little power I have to make the guilty pay.

'Why did you feel you had to shout?'

'Because he wasn't stopping. I was . . . terrified but still, I had to try to make him hear me. To stop it. To stop *him*.'

'And do you think he *did* hear you?'

'Your Honour.' The footballer's barrister is on her feet. 'My learned friend is asking the witness to speculate on things she can have no knowledge of.'

The defence barrister is petite, with silky blonde curls poking out from under her wig. I know what the jury will be thinking: surely no woman could defend a guilty man?

But 'Cruella' gained her nickname for playing dirtier than any male lawyer would dare. She will dwell on intimate details – contraception, underwear, periods – that mean nothing, but taint the young woman for the rest of the trial. And I bet she'll hint at a fondness for rough sex, to explain away the bruises mentioned in Oli's opening address. By the time she's finished her cross-examination, Julie Tranter won't even be sure herself if she consented or not.

'I agree,' Judge Ronaldson says. 'Do tone it down a little, Mr Priest. But I think we'll leave it there for today in any case.' He stifles a yawn. 'Ten tomorrow, members of the jury. Thank you for your attention today.'

'Court rise.'

The timing of the adjournment is a small victory for Oliver: the jurors will fall asleep tonight with the woman's testimony in their minds.

As soon as the judge leaves, I quickly sketch the defendant's sharp suit, the full pout of his lips, before he's taken back down to the cells.

'Get my good side, will you, Georgie?'

Oli passes alongside the press bench as the court empties.

'Wow,' I say. 'I think that's the first time you've admitted you even have a bad one.'

He smiles. 'OK, my *better* side.' He leans in, so no one else hears. I smell the sharp, grapefruit tang of his moisturiser, the one he has sent specially from America. 'How are we doing with this one?'

'Bribing the judge is working,' I whisper.

'Shh.' He leans in even further; his wig has slipped and I glimpse a fresh crop of white along his real hairline. He'll be happy with the added gravitas. 'Seriously, how are we coming across?'

I smile at the barrister habit of calling their witness *we*.

'She's likeable. Believable.'

I put my notebook in my bag, and we walk out of court together. Of course, I won't tell him how I plan to give the prosecution a helping hand.

Oli frowns. 'You think? Allowing yourself to be groped in a steam room, without knowing who was doing the groping? It's not exactly Jane Austen.'

I sigh. 'She knows what to expect from Cruella?'

'As much as any of them do.'

We've spent hours discussing this. Despite his single-sex public-school upbringing, Oli is one hundred per cent the feminist when it comes to rape trials. He specialises in cases where the victims need someone to speak on their behalf, and the Crown Prosecution Service instruct him because he is bloody good at it.

'How's Imogen? Can't be long now.'

The frown on his face melts away.

'Three weeks. Maybe. They say first babies are always late.'

'Yours will be bang on schedule, I bet you.'

'I'm bloody terrified, Georgie. Control issues. You know.'

I smile. 'Fatherhood will suit you. You've waited long enough.'

It's one of those rare moments when Oli doesn't seem to know what to say.

'Georgia! I need to talk to you about your ideas for the six.'

Today's TV producer, Toby, shouts at me across the corridor. Neena Kaur, the reporter, is already heading outside to do a live broadcast for the rolling news channel. My sketch of the afternoon's proceedings will go into a more polished report for the flagship bulletin at 6 p.m.

'Duty calls, I see,' Oli says. 'My best side, remember? And when the jury's finally out, let's grab a coffee.'

'I'd love to.' I remember something. 'Actually, it'd be great to chat through some of your old cases. I've been asked to do a commission for an art book. I might need some contacts.'

'A book, eh?' Oli's eyes light up. 'I always knew it was only a matter of time until your talent was recognised—'

'Georgia, we really do need to get this in the bag,' Toby says, pushing himself into the conversation.

Oli raises his eyebrows at me.

'Can't stand in the way of the public's right to know. We'll make a date, right? Toodle pip, Georgie.'

'*Cheerio*, old thing,' I say, watching him as he heads towards the robing room. He turns at the last minute to blow me a kiss.

Toby is staring.

'Are you chummy with all the barristers?'

'Only the ones I nearly married,' I say, walking out of the courtroom, down the grand staircase. 'What's the hurry with the sketch?'

'They've a lot of late-running stories tonight. Want our package sent asap. What are you planning? We want Sam Carr in it, obviously.'

It takes me a moment to remember that Carr is the footballer's name. I had stopped thinking of him as a person. But I already know what I want to draw.

'Did you catch the moment when he scowled at the prosecutor over the evidence about the girl's clothes being ripped?'

'So long as it doesn't imply he's guilty.'

I shake my head. 'I'd *never* do that.'

'You must have a hunch, though?' He smiles. 'All these years staring at crims in court. Can't you tell whodunnit?'

For a moment, I feel like telling him the truth – who I really am, what I'm trying to do – just to see his reaction. But instead, I scoff.

'Of course I can't. You can't judge a book by its cover.'

5

Daylight blinds me as I step through the courthouse doors.

A few steps ahead, the footballer and his entourage punch their way through the paparazzi. He's headed for the limo parked on double yellows.

Whirr, click, whirr.

The cameras flash and the pack members call out. 'Over here! Mate, mate, look this way. Play the game!'

The footballer blinks in the glare of the sun, gropes for his Aviators. *Arrogant?* Tick. *Obscenely wealthy?* Tick.

Guilty? Almost certainly . . .

'How'd it go today, mate? You in the clear?'

Above us, the flat blue sky fills with flapping wings. The gulls plunge down from the Gothic turrets, their eyes focused on the swelling crowd, looking for food.

I cross the busy road. When I look back, more people are piling out of court: lawyers too rushed to remove their raven-black robes; scruffy, plain-clothes detectives; finally, the spectators, swapping notes after their free day out.

Neena is brushing her hair in the satellite truck mirror, ready for the live two-way. She's the only reporter I consider a friend – the rest are chummy enough, but they'd sell their granny for a front-page lead. I wave, and she waves back, and then I shoulder my way into the Barely Legal Cafe.

'All ready for you, Georgia.'

Manny, the owner, greets me with a smile and a double espresso.

'Cheers.' I yawn, think of last night. 'I need it!'

The beaded curtain flicks across my face as I walk through to the storeroom. Whenever there's a trial in Brighton, I use Manny's as an impromptu studio. My pastels case lies open on the chest freezer. The aluminium easel has a sheet of 360 gsm card pinned to the board, angled to catch the light from the yard.

I sharpen my pencil, test the point of the lead against the flesh of my little finger. Sharp enough to pierce the skin. I step back from the easel and . . .

The fear makes me freeze.

Fear of the blank page, fear of getting it wrong, fear that a guilty man will walk. I am always scared of failure, but some cases feel more personal than others.

'Got all you need?'

Toby steps into the room. He clearly thinks he should be in a war zone, not slumming it at a seedy sex case in the provinces.

'Yup. Except peace and quiet.'

'Remember. It doesn't have to be great art. Just has to be there on deadline,' he says, as though it's him, not me, that has spent the last thirteen years on the press bench.

I'm not an 'artist' to the people that hire me – I'm just another hack. So long as my drawing of the footballer is cartoonishly recognisable, it'll do.

Toby is waiting for me to reply, but I turn sharply back to the easel and he slopes away.

Anger fuels me. Pencil touches paper. In a first, fast movement, I sketch in the oak boundaries of the court, then the shapes of the defendant, the prosecutor, the judge.

I could draw the regulars in my sleep. Oli, still too bloody handsome for his own good. The eternally tetchy Judge Ronaldson, whose eyebrows resemble little hamsters scrabbling up his forehead. Cruella, girlish, but pulsing with bottled-up venom.

Now the accused. The reason I do this.

As my hand sketches his shape, I replay the evidence in my head.

Once I've made a man look guilty, there is no way back. Jurors are told to avoid news coverage when they're on a case, but most can't resist a quick google during the big trials. And the cliché is true – my pictures paint a thousand words, none of them good. Facial expression, composition, even the vividness of the pastel colour I use can create an impression of evil, if that is what I intend.

Have I ever changed a verdict? There's no way of knowing. But I try my best to see justice done. And it's a consolation to know that even if a guilty man is acquitted, my picture – and the question marks it seeds in people's minds – will follow him for the rest of his life.

'You're late.' Toby pokes his face through the curtain. 'I've promised to send it by half past, and if there's a problem, I need to know now!'

'I never miss a deadline.'

He tries to push past me to see the picture.

'Where's his bloody face?'

'Toby, I was doing this job while you were still doodling Ginger Spice's cleavage in the margins of your exercise book. Trust me, it'll be there.'

'But—'

'Just go . . .'

I pull out my notes, try to focus on them, not the rumble of the coffee grinder, the hum of the post-court rabble. The words swim; either my handwriting is getting worse, or I need reading glasses. I squint.

Lazy posture, my very first note reads, *makes his Savile Row suit look like a sweaty nylon off-the-peg.*

An image comes to me: when the girl first spoke, Sam Carr sat up straight for the first time. He must have realised all that sponsorship money wasn't going to buy his way out of this. The pout left his lips and . . .

I saw evil.

All doubt leaves me. Carr deserves all he gets. I lean in and he comes to life with slick black hair, and lips straight as tramlines, bloodless next to his sunbed tan.

Two minutes to deadline.

I position myself so I can work without looking directly at the face I've drawn. In court, I never make eye contact; I learned how dangerous that can be in my first ever case. But there's still something stopping this image coming alive. On instinct, I add two dots of Prussian blue to his pupils, smudge the blue with the black.

The footballer stares right back, arrogance tempered by alarm.

I smile: *Yeah. You're not getting away with this if I can help it, you piece of shit.*

'Done,' I call out.

Toby pushes past me to grab the easel and carry it into the street where the cameraman is waiting.

As I make my way through the crowded cafe, I feel the weight of what I've done. It's never easy, but it is needed. Outside, the cameraman is zooming in on my sketch. From this distance, I can see it's not my best work, but at least it's there on time.

Neena waits for the tape.

'Cutting it fine, George.'

'What can I say? I'm a perfectionist.'

6

Day three, and it's time for Cruella to cross-examine the alleged victim. I wish I could skip this part, I already know how it always goes . . .

'What *was* going through your mind when you entered that steam room?'

The barrister's robe casts a shadow across the court. She licks her lips: it's one of her tells, a sign she's about to go for the kill.

'That it was *hot*,' Julie Tranter says, only just managing to stop herself adding 'duh'.

I wince.

'That it was *hot,'* repeats Sam Carr's barrister. 'Steamy, I presume.'

'Yeah. Because it's a steam room.'

I can't quite see from this angle, but I am pretty sure she rolled her eyes.

'And you were in there with three men you didn't know.'

The young woman sighs and straightens the skirt of her crimson dress. The wrong colour. But the jury would have judged her just as harshly for wearing the floral one two days running. *She hasn't been home. Perhaps she is* that *kind of girl.*

'I knew them. We'd been chatting right before. In the spa pool.' She sounds sulky.

'Ah. So you knew their names?'

'I knew who *he* was.' She nods towards the footballer without looking at his face. 'Not the others. But they seemed like nice lads.'

'Nice lads. Yes. And who left the spa pool first?'

'They did.'

'Mr Carr and his two teammates? And then you followed them in?'

'Yeah. I like steam rooms.'

'You liked the idea of getting close to a famous footballer, too, didn't you?'

Silence. The young woman realises she's walked into a trap. I've been where she's been. In the witness box, you feel like the star attraction in a travelling freak show. And utterly alone.

Oli is on his feet.

'Your Honour—'

Cruella gives a magnanimous wave.

'Fine, I'll withdraw that last question. Now, tell me about this steam room. Can you give me an idea of the space? Was it, say, the size of the jury box?'

'No. Much smaller. A third of that.'

'So there you are, an attractive young woman, wearing virtually nothing, stepping into a *very* confined space where it's hard to see anything, knowing there were three male strangers inside. Weren't you worried?'

'Not really.'

'Is it not the case that by going into the steam room, you were sending the defendant a message?'

'What message?' Miss Tranter says, defiance in her voice.

Out of the corner of my eye, I see Oli has gone very still.

'That you were *up for it*. That you wanted him.'

Oli is on his feet again.

'Your Honour, my learned friend is putting words in the witness's mouth.'

Judge Ronaldson sighs.

'Yes, I think we ought to leave discussions of the steam chamber before we become even more overheated.'

The defence barrister nods.

'Of course. So let us move on to when you accompanied Mr Carr to the bar, alone . . .'

Oli sits down again. I feel for him – of course, he had to put the young woman on the stand. Without her, there is no case. But it's always a risk.

Cruella is smiling.

'What did you say to your friends? When you left?'

'I said . . .' The young woman hesitates.

'Remember, you're under oath.'

'I said not to wait for me. I said . . . I was going to have some fun.'

I lean over the long line of porcelain basins, putting in eye drops. The fierce heating in court makes everything dry out, and my head throbs.

'Georgia. Are you OK? I've been worried about you, after last night.'

Maureen Lomax is behind me in the mirror, face set in an expression of fake concern. But her bifocals magnify her gleeful eyes.

'Hello, Maureen.'

'Your producer was in a real tizzy. And, artist to artist, you won't mind my saying, the sketch did lack finesse. Sam Carr would never have got all the sponsorships and modelling jobs if he looked like a rabid bulldog.'

'I'm not in the business of vanity portraiture.'

'Just constructive criticism!' Maureen takes a tissue; her damson lipstick has feathered into the smoker's lines around her mouth. 'Take my advice, make them prettier.'

'So I can flog them to the criminals when they walk free?'

'They pay for a couple of good cruises every year.' Her thin lips stretch across her teeth as she reapplies her make-up. 'I'm hardly going to hang them on my walls. No wonder you look so tired if you take your work home with you.'

I look away. 'I study them. I want to get better.'

'Oh, darling. Tomorrow's chip paper, that's what our work is. Though this *Art of Justice* book will have a slightly longer shelf life, eh?'

Bloody hell.

'I didn't realise they'd asked you too.'

She laughs. 'I gave them *your* name, actually, Georgia. I like to support young talent. Even when it is still a tad . . . raw.' She pats my hand, her fingers dry as snakeskin. 'You just need to stop taking it all so seriously.' She zips up her bag and tip-taps out across the tiled floor.

I wait a few seconds before following her out into the stuffy corridor, where the press pack waits for the afternoon session to begin. I stand slightly apart, hearing laughter, knowing the hacks will be swapping some sick joke or other. Neena insists the graveyard humour keeps the nastier evidence at arm's length, so it doesn't contaminate our 'normal' lives.

I realised when I was eleven that there's no such thing as normal – at least for me.

I turn my back on the journalists, and head for the window, for a last glimpse of daylight before we go back into court.

Shit.

A boy in a bright-red shirt is standing on the other side of the road.

That boy, the one I saw in the square. His bare feet teeter on the edge of the pavement, his arm swinging a purple soft toy so high it almost hits the passing cars.

It's a Teletubby. *Tinky Winky*, I think; that show had a cult following when I was an art student.

The kid stares straight up at the window. Straight up at me.

There's something familiar about him: could he be one of the barristers' kids, off sick from pre-school?

No. Because barristers' kids don't generally hang around in garden squares in the middle of the night.

Still, at least I know I wasn't imagining him.

Did he follow me from the square?

But I saw him there two nights ago. Where has he been since?

I wave frantically at him, trying to signal that he should get away from the edge of the pavement. But he keeps staring, his toy lifted into the air by the side wind from speeding cars.

No one else is helping him.

I push past the clusters of lawyers and witnesses, run two steps at a time down the marble staircase, through the metal detectors, launch myself at the wooden doors, out into the street.

Thank God. He's still there, on the other side of the road, his back to me now, so I can read the back of his crumpled pyjama top.

11 REDKNAPP

Redknapp hasn't played for years.

The kid turns back and sees me. There's something wrong with his face. A birthmark, or a scar, runs down his cheek, red as a ripe strawberry.

He takes a step towards me. One leg of his pyjamas is hitched up, and his knee is black, as though he's taken a tumble playing football.

He takes another step . . .

'No! No, stay there, stay where you are.' I launch myself towards him. An elderly woman pounds on a horn as I miss walking into her car by centimetres. 'I'm coming—'

A flash of beige and burgundy metal thunders in from my left. The number 7 bus from the County Hospital. So fast. *So close.*

'No, stop!' I hammer on its metal chassis.

The bus is gone. I stare at the pavement, at the empty space where the child was, three seconds ago.

My heart doesn't beat. The world is silent. I force myself to look down at the road, expecting to see a lifeless form . . .

There is nothing on the tarmac. No child, no toy. No blood.

I run towards where he was standing.

'Kid, where are you? Come out, I don't want to hurt you.'

The only place he could have gone is the alleyway ahead of me. But he can't have run that far, that fast. There's nothing to hide behind.

Unless he went into Manny's?

I push the door open, scan the empty tables. Nothing.

'You still hungry, Georgie?'

Manny emerges from the kitchen, his hands and thick forearms sheathed in camellia-pink rubber gloves.

'Did you see a kid?'

I push past him, into the back room. Check under the sofa, behind the storage crates, even inside the bloody chest freezer. Frost coats the shrink-wrapped buns, burgers, mince. There's no room for a child. The door to the yard is locked and it's crammed with crates full of empties. Nowhere to hide.

'A kid?'

'A boy.' I think about what else I saw. 'Four years old, maybe? In pyjamas that look like a football strip.' I remember the old name on the back. 'A hand-me-down. He was outside and then he disappeared and this is the only place he could have come to hide.'

'No kids here.' He pulls off one of his gloves with a sucking sound and places his hand on my shoulder. Fatherly. 'I worry about you, Georgia. You always look so serious.'

Adrenaline makes my hands shake and my head pound.

'There *was* a kid, Manny. I saw him.'

Manny shrugs. 'Plenty bastards come and use my toilet, without buying nothing, then sneak away. Block my Saniflo. But, Georgia . . .' He gestures towards the clock on the wall. 'You late for court now, right?'

Six minutes past two. Toby will be flapping.

'He was on his own, Manny. A little kid.'

'Well, if he's in trouble, he'll be picked up pronto. Round here's crawling with police. Here.' He produces two soft amaretti biscuits from his apron pocket. 'Sweets, for your blood sugar. Now, back to work, your pictures won't draw themselves.'

I take the biscuits and head back to court, with one last glance down the alleyway. The kid, whoever he was, is long gone.

7

'We couldn't be more thrilled to have you on board.'

The book editor – *my* editor now – takes me into a room with the best view in London. The window frames the Thames, which shimmers in the late afternoon sunshine.

'I was thrilled to be asked. It sounds like a fascinating book.'

For once, I don't have to fake enthusiasm. The project features artists in the criminal justice field: those who reconstruct faces from human remains or create scale models of crime scenes. Each one of us will be commissioned to return to a case that stayed with us and create a new piece for a full-colour hardback. The money is terrible, but the prestige can't be bought.

'A passion project, for me,' Benjamin says, making intense eye contact. He's older than me, but he still thinks he's a charming boy who can get away with anything if he flirts enough. 'The bosses let me off the leash occasionally, so long as I keep the reality star autobiographies in the bestseller lists.'

His latest commissions are laid out on the long, glass table. Maybe he expects me to ask about the notoriously demanding singer, or the TV presenter more famous for his fluid sexuality than his talent. I don't care about either.

Instead, I place my portfolio on the table, feeling unexpectedly nervous. I haven't had to present my work for years – my reputation brings me all the court gigs I can handle. But this is new.

'My own greatest hits,' I say.

He unzips it, leafs through a few of the pages, then gives me another lingering look.

'I love your style. And your colour palette is so vivid. It's much more expressive than the other court artist's ... What's her name? Marjorie?'

'Maureen.'

I wonder if he pretended to forget *my* name when he spoke to her. She'd have liked that.

'Are you friends or enemies?' he asks, with a twinkle.

'Neither. She's my main competition. When a case is big enough, we're usually hired by rival organisations, though these days she tends to be hired by the Press Association, to serve the papers, and I'm mostly exclusive to the BBC.'

'The BBC made the right call,' he says. 'You've got way more talent – your colours *sing* ... Would you consider oils for this commission?'

Goosebumps form on my skin and I can smell the tarry stink of turpentine.

'I prefer pastels for my sketches. Acrylics for something longer term.'

'OK. Let's see how it balances out.'

'Who else is involved?'

'There's a guy who does e-fits as the day job but draws Manga in his spare time. And a forensics boffin who rebuilds corpses but trained as a sculptor. People love to know about the people behind the investigations. Who is the *real* Georgia? What motivates her?'

I bristle. 'I thought the focus was on our work. Not us as people?'

'Oh, the art is definitely what will sell the book,' he backtracks seamlessly. 'We all remember the best courtroom sketches – they have a way of working their way into the public consciousness. Far more than photos, I'd say. But readers will love to get a window into that world, and the minds of the artists themselves. When did *you* first realise you had a gift?'

'I wouldn't call it a gift . . .'

'Come on. There must have been a moment when a teacher spotted your talent in a sea of dreadful stick men?'

Miss Hamilton.

I haven't thought about her for years.

'I started to get serious about my painting at secondary school. I certainly wasn't a prodigy.'

He nods. 'And did you consider other careers in art before focusing on the underbelly? Maureen told me she came to the courts because she had a thing about men in uniform.'

I pull a face. 'Really?'

'Disturbing, right? But what about you? Do your parents work in law?'

'My parents are dead.'

'Shit. I'm sorry.' Benjamin flinches. 'Well, of course, it's not just your story. It's the stories your images tell. Which cases would you like to revisit?'

'The Daisy Moritz case was my best known.' I lean across to show him the sketches I did of a film actress accused of paying two thugs to attack a rival and destroy her looks. 'A real Hollywood tale. She got out last year. I'd love to see how prison changed her. She'll do it, I'm sure. I bet she's missing the spotlight.'

But Benjamin is shaking his head.

'Maureen got in before you, I'm afraid. Two peas in a pod, her and dear Daisy. Any other ideas?'

I take the portfolio back and point out some of the more notorious figures I've sketched: a drummer accused of supplying drugs that killed a groupie; a political power couple convicted of blackmail; a miserable coward who shot seven students but lacked the guts to turn the gun on himself.

'Hmm. Perhaps.'

'Is there a case you have in mind, Benjamin?'

He smiles. 'Am I that transparent? We *did* have a thought, actually. Remember the Christmas Eve arson case? I believe it was quite early in your career. We might see a real change in your style, between now and then.'

'Daniel Fielding?' His name makes the goosebumps prickle up again. 'Yes. He was my first big case. But no one wants to see a portrait of him, surely?'

'No, we'd want you to paint his father, Jim. Between you and me, we're even considering it as a possible cover. What he did really resonated with people. Unless you prefer painting villains to heroes?'

'I can make an exception.'

Instantly, I see Jim Fielding more clearly than the man across the table from me. Bulky, rough around the edges, but a hero for sure. He'd fought his way through his own burning house to rescue two children he'd been babysitting. But he was too late to save his wife from the fire his own son had started. It was the cruellest act with no clear motive.

'He was an unforgettable witness.'

Benjamin nods. 'Readers would love to know how a person can survive something so devastating. Have you got the sketches from that case with you?'

I turn to the back of the portfolio and take out the relevant folder. Benjamin inspects them, and my scribbled notes from court.

'I'd love to include these too. I still can't believe this is all you have to work from? You must have an amazing memory.'

I shrug. 'I almost got done for contempt before I knew the rules. I was at art school, doing a project inspired by Lombroso – he was an army doctor who thought you could recognise criminal tendencies from facial features. I decided to go to the Bailey to sketch criminals myself. It was a journalist who saw me drawing and warned me to stop. But he liked what I'd sketched and asked if I could work from memory. That's how it all started.'

It's not, of course. But it's the story I've concocted for Georgia.

'Fascinating.' Benjamin puts on his reading glasses and squints at a lined page. '*Looks like a firm but fair chief of police, or a godfather with a heart of gold.* I love it!'

'I don't know if Jim Fielding would want to do it, though,' I say. 'Who would want to revisit the worst time in their life?'

'You'd think that, but most of the people we've approached to sit for the book so far are flattered. There's something special about a portrait. Especially if the painter looks like *you* do.'

I don't react to the smarmy compliment.

'I don't know . . .'

'Look, I'll get in touch with Fielding, it always comes better from us. People love the letterhead, the London address. Though as he's not a celebrity, there'll be no sitting fee. Daisy bloody Moritz has already taken most of my contingency budget. And he's only in Gloucestershire, isn't he? Should keep your travel costs down.'

'OK.'

I smile sweetly, thinking of the huge bouquets in reception, and what this glass palace must cost in rent. I don't miss the daily deceits London requires of people. I can't wait to get home.

'Brilliant, brilliant. And don't worry about having to reveal too much about yourself. Maureen has already given me chapter and verse on her life story, but you're the more serious artist and, if you don't mind my saying, the more talented one. It'll be a nice contrast to let your work speak for itself.'

8

The train home is quiet, and I find a table to myself, plonking down the heavy bag of free books Benjamin gave me.

'We can't pay much, but you'll never be short of ghostwritten memoirs to gift to people you don't like at Christmas.'

I pour red wine from a mini bottle to celebrate my first ever book commission. Maybe he was bullshitting about the cover, but I let myself imagine Maureen's face when she finds out *my* painting is the one they choose.

Most of the time, it doesn't bother me that I am alone, but tonight I wish there was someone to join the celebration. I consider calling Oli, but he'll be home by now, and I don't want to intrude on the time he and Imogen have left before the baby arrives.

Who else could I call? My foster-parents, maybe, but I cut ties too long ago for things ever to be the same. And no one at art school stayed in touch after I dropped out to do the court sketching full-time.

I wonder if Miss Hamilton would remember me. The image of her in the meeting was so vivid: her eyebrows shooting up past her tortoiseshell specs as I showed her my work in my first art class at secondary school. The first person to notice that I could *really* draw.

'Your faces are wonderfully expressive, Suzanne. Such bright colours – you're going to love using oil paint. Your pictures make me feel happy when I look at them. That's an extraordinary gift.'

Has she ever seen the miserable sketches I draw now, and felt a sense of déjà vu? Though she wouldn't have recognised the name – I left Suzanne behind years ago.

My plastic cup is empty already so I pour the last of the wine. Through the window, the shimmer of London gives way to terracotta suburbs, and then the chartreuse glow of Sussex fields. The countryside here reminds me of home.

Don't go there.

I take the *R v Fielding* folder out of my portfolio. Inside are copies of the ten finished drawings I did for the Press Association during the trial.

My first image shocks me. It's thirteen years since I've seen it. Sometimes, the papers do use the later sketches when they dredge the case up again, on the anniversary of the fire. But they never use this picture, because in it, Daniel Fielding looks innocent.

He's slender, like a young David Tennant, flanked by two bulky prison guards. What stands out in this image are his nervous chalky-blue eyes. I remember how they'd dart around the courtroom, as though he was looking for something.

Until they settled on me.

We were both eighteen, the youngest people in the court. What he couldn't have known was that I'd been alone in court too, once. I felt his fear. More than that. I felt unsure he was guilty. As he stood in the dock, he didn't look capable of stealing a car, never mind killing his stepmother. And that is what I drew: a lost boy.

The reporter gave me a bollocking when he saw the sketch, and I thought my new career was over before it had begun. It didn't fit the story, 'having him look like butter wouldn't melt.'

It only took a day for me to realise how wrong I'd been about Daniel. I hadn't slept the night before Jim Fielding gave his evidence. I was terrified I'd screw up, because everyone already knew what the grieving hero looked like. His face had become synonymous with heroism. A local photographer had taken a picture of him moments after he rescued the children from a fire. It made every single front page.

I forgot my fear as soon as Jim stepped into the witness box. His evidence was so compelling I could almost smell the smoke and hear the hungry lap of the flames consuming his house. There are faults in my sketch, sure. It's overworked – the chequered pattern on his chokehold tie is fussily drawn, his hair too dense. But still, I can't take my eyes off the image of Jim reading out a Christmas card, tears falling down his cheeks.

I drain the wine, my ears already buzzing from the alcohol. Thirteen years on, and it's still the most dramatic testimony I've ever witnessed.

The QC had asked the jury members to look at copies of a Christmas card written by Jim's wife Tessa. It seemed manipulative to me, and I'd even shot Daniel a sympathetic glance.

'Mr Fielding, would you read out the message written by your late wife?'

As Jim spoke, his fingers gripped the outside of the card, a huge, padded thing with a gilded fir tree and nativity scene. I caught a glimpse of the text on the front: *Merry Xmas to the Best Mum and Dad in the World.*

Jim took a deep breath, his fastened suit straining against his chest.

'To Mum and Dad. Wishing you the very best Christmas ever, all of us together.' Jim's country vowels were soft and long and

his voice never faltered even though he was already crying. *'With lots and lots of love from Tessa, Jim, Amy – and baby makes four! Isn't that the best pressie ever??? I'm pregnant! You're gonna be grandparents!!!'*

Jim held up a flimsy printout clipped to the inside of the card: a snowy scan of an unborn child.

I realised what it meant before the jury members did.

'Did your son know your wife was pregnant, Mr Fielding?'

Jim sighed. 'I've asked myself that question so many times. Whether he might have guessed and started the fire to kill both of them. We'd planned to tell him that evening, invited him back home, a second chance. But maybe he found out and that's what made him do this.' He turned to face the dock. 'Please, Daniel. Tell me. Is that what made you do it?'

But Daniel stared straight ahead.

'And did the police explain why your son is only charged with your wife's murder?'

Jim nodded. 'They said the baby didn't count. That because he wasn't capable of living outside Tessa's body, that he couldn't be murdered.'

'It was a boy?'

'Yes. They found out at the post-mortem. Tessa never knew. She'd wanted it to be a surprise.'

'Baby killer!' someone shouted from the gallery.

Two of the jury members were already in tears. But I felt wired – in that moment, I understood what my real job was. My hand zig-zagged notes across the page, as though possessed by something. Perhaps the same thing that kept dragging me back to the Bailey, even though being in court brought back terrible memories.

My 'gift' meant I could help the guilty get what was coming to them.

As soon as the court adjourned, I drew two fast images in succession: one of Jim, and then a new sketch of Daniel.

I look at it now, and remember how every line was designed to damn him. No longer a lost boy – he stands in defiance, not fear. His fists are balled, not in self-defence, but with a killer's pent-up rage.

That's the sketch the paper still uses, when they find some spurious reason to mention the case. I made sure that Daniel Fielding would not be forgotten. Sometimes I even wonder if that's why he changed his plea: my picture showed him he couldn't hide what he was.

'The next station will be Brighton, where this train terminates.'

Already? I tuck the drawings back into the plastic sleeve, but an article falls out, onto the floor.

I pick it up: it's the double-page spread from the last day of the trial.

The papers went to town when Daniel unexpectedly pleaded guilty on the day his defence was about to begin. There's a photo of Tessa and Jim Fielding on their wedding day, the summer before she died. The picture has the sunshine filter turned up high, their faces bleached out by happiness. Jim's daughter Amy, just about to shed her puppy fat, wears a pale-pink dress. She holds the hand of an adorable little bridesmaid, and at the edge of the frame is a pageboy, or rather half a pageboy, unable to keep still. The children are Jodie and Charlie O'Neill, the kids whose lives Jim saved only months later.

Daniel skulks on the edge of the family group, in the same baggy suit he wore to court, as uncomfortable as any teenager would be at his father's wedding. To start with, the lawyers said, he tolerated his new stepmother. But he was harbouring resentment that turned into a terrible rage.

At the centre of the article, as always, is the photo that made Jim Fielding famous, taken in the moments after he rescued those kids. I barely glance at it as I pick up the clipping, but something catches my eye . . .

No.

I lean in close.

That's not possible.

It's like I'm seeing the image afresh. Jim Fielding is outside his house, flames filling the window behind him. He's dressed as Santa Claus, but instead of a white beard, his face is sooty like a miner's, his eyes scarlet. He has one child under each arm. One is the girl from the wedding photo, the bridesmaid, in a blackened sleepsuit with bunny ears.

But it's the other child who transfixes me. It can't be. Surely?

It's Charlie, the pageboy. Half his face is obscured as he leans into Jim's body, tears running stripes down his filthy cheeks.

He's wearing Liverpool football pyjamas.

The back of his shirt has partly melted, so it's hard to tell the fabric apart from burned skin. But I can make out the lettering.

11 REDKNAPP

9

I hold the image closer to my eyes. The newsprint dissolves into tiny dots, then sharpens again.

It *is* the child I saw on Brunswick Square, and outside the court.

The carriage is unbearably hot, completely airless. Struggling for breath, I scramble out of my seat, towards the doors, gasping, willing the train to stop now.

Breathe, Suzi-soo, breathe.

My mother's voice in my head.

When the train finally stops, I jab at the door-release three, four times, and jump out. I run to the barriers, my hand shaking so much I drop my ticket. A ragtime rhythm fills my ears as I sprint past a man playing the station piano.

Out of the building. Down the hill. In the distance, the sea is turning purple. People block my path and I try to skirt around them, running, not looking at their faces, in case I see someone else who can't really be there.

My breath gets shorter. My brain races. The boy I've been seeing is definitely Charlie O'Neill, the little kid in Liverpool pyjamas. Except he probably doesn't hero-worship Jamie Redknapp anymore, because now he must be . . . what, *seventeen years old.*

Cars brake, horns blare as I race across King's Road. The sea is so close now. I don't even know what I'll do when I get there.

I collapse against the railings for a moment, trying to catch my breath to cover that final four hundred yards. I grip the metal so hard that turquoise paint flakes off in my hands.

Run. Run again, across the shifting pebbles, to the shoreline. I rip off my shoes, step into the sea in my bare feet, needing the shock of the cold to bring me to my senses.

That boy can't be real.

The water laps up to my ankles and my breath slows. Abruptly, I stop feeling hot, and begin to shiver, though the rose madder sunset is still warm. Part of me wants to chase it, past the lagoon, past the cranes and silos of Shoreham, the pier at Worthing. I never want to stop moving.

But you can't outrun madness when it runs in your family.

Is this how it begins? I've tried so hard to protect myself and others from harm – turned my back on friendship, and love. Lived alone. Lived a lie. Obliterated all trace of the girl I was, to get away from what my father was and what he did.

I drop down onto the pebbles, my shins grinding against the cold stone. There has to be an explanation for this.

The water is lapping away, the tide going out.

I hear voices: a party of lads, splashing in the water next to me. Beer spilling out of open cans, the smell of weed drifting over. They're the age Charlie O'Neill must be now. Getting drunk, pulling girls.

'Fancy a puff, gorgeous?' one of them calls out to me. The others laugh.

The menace has gone and everything seems normal again. Even me.

'Does your mum know what you're smoking?' I say, and they laugh again.

I'm just . . . *tired*. From the night with the teacher, maybe. I got drunk, took a stranger home, lost sleep, felt discombobulated afterwards. And the portrait commission has made me look back at some of my bigger cases.

That's all.

I scramble to my feet, seawater dripping from my trouser hems, feet stinging as I push them back into my sodden shoes. I turn away from the shore. This can't have anything to do with my father, or what he did.

And if I am wrong?

The sea is only two minutes from my flat. I've always known what I have to do if I begin to lose my grip on reality.

They say drowning is a gentle thing, once you stop struggling.

10

As I walk to court next morning, I can't shake the feeling that I'm being followed.

I turn around to check: the first time, it's a cyclist, scowling because I've strayed into the bike lane. When I get the feeling again, I don't turn. There is nobody there.

The case continues. Oli calls one of Julie Tranter's friends, to talk about why they'd gone to the hotel. A girls' weekend, supporting a third friend who had just split up with her fiancé. The young woman paints a picture of pampering and early nights, titanium white robes, soft shoulders to cry on.

'Miss Henry, you're @proseccogal on Twitter, am I right?' Cruella asks, when she begins her cross-examination.

The girl nods.

'And can I just check, you've never suffered any hacking, compromising of your account, that sort of thing?'

'Nope. I work in IT. Change my password every week.'

'Good. So we can assume that all the postings and photographs from your account on the weekend of the *alleged* incident, were yours? Because I'd like to show you some of those.'

She reaches down for a file and passes a pile of papers across to the judge, the witness, the jury. I can't read Oli's face but his shoulders are hunched up, a sure sign of stress.

A sudden movement in the public gallery catches my eye. I glance up at the box suspended above the court. Today the double row of pull-down seats is only half-full: during a juicy murder trial, the public have to draw lots.

I recognise the footballer's mother, his brother, his manager. But when I look past them, I flinch.

A child – it's Charlie, of course – sits in the corner, legs swinging in the air because his bare feet won't reach the lino. He's yawning.

He's not real.

So why does he look more alive than anyone else in court?

I blink.

Charlie has gone.

'Did you post these tweets, Miss Henry?' Cruella asks, as the judge and jury members study the papers.

I glance up at the public gallery again, holding my breath. Three people again. Mother, brother, manager. No child.

Thank God.

'Yeah. But before it all went wrong for Julie. Before we knew what. . . he was capable of.'

'That's for the jury to decide,' Cruella says, dismissively. 'But perhaps we can look at each one in turn and you can tell me about the moment you took it. Let's start with the one that reads: "look at who we've just seen checking in." Can you read it out?'

The witness sighs. '"Look at who we've just seen checking in. Sam Carr. Our girlie weekend just got a lot more exciting. Things are looking up."'

'And you took that picture? Of Sam Carr? Or to be more specific, of Sam Carr's groin region in a pair of tight gym shorts.'

A wave of laughter passes through the court.

The witness nods and the footballer glances up at the gallery. Before I can stop myself, I look up again. Charlie is back, laughing, though he can't know what this means. Perhaps he admires the footballer.

Stop it. He's not real.

I blink. Make him disappear. He's just there because Fielding and his story are on my mind.

Except I saw the boy *before* I knew the editor wanted me to focus on Jim.

As the witness continues, I can't focus on her. I am too busy looking for the child who doesn't exist.

Cruella destroys @proseccogal using the smiling selfies with the alleged victim, and the tweets about the mega bar bill they're running up.

Oli doesn't re-examine. It's not a knockout blow, but it doesn't help his victim's credibility.

After the judge adjourns early for the weekend, Oli approaches me.

'You got time for a coffee?'

'Shouldn't you be going off to paint the nursery or something? Take your mind off all this.'

'We've had it ready for weeks. Organic eggshell in primrose spring, or possibly spring primrose. Imogen spent months mulling the paint charts. Now she's busy stockpiling gadgets and nappy rash cream and God only knows what else.'

'You'll know what it's all for soon enough.'

'Maybe. Though we have a maternity nurse booked to help us out at first.' He looks slightly shamefaced. 'I'll do the fun stuff though. Rugby training. Whether it's a girl or a boy. Anyway, the traffic back into London will be hell so I won't try to drive back yet. Manny's after you're done? Forty minutes?'

I shake my head. 'I need some fresh air after that evidence. The pier? And make it an hour, I'm getting slower at drawing these days.'

In my sketch, I blur the witness as she looks down, and place the footballer in the foreground, so he's bigger, more powerful. It's as far as I dare go without risking making Toby or Neena suspicious.

Neena glances at my drawing as she mumbles her piece to camera, committing it to memory.

I wait. Has she seen through me, realised what I am trying to do?

'Is the sketch all right, Neena?'

'Yeah, I just . . .' But she just sighs. 'Forget it, I'm being picky. It's been a long day, right, George? We'll all be on better form once this week is over.'

11

Oli is standing at the entrance to the pier, framed by candyfloss-coloured signs, and cascades of bulbs.

'Sorry to keep you waiting,' I say, kissing him on both cheeks. 'Last minute queries.'

'It's fine. I like staring at the sea. Enjoying the calm before the storm.'

'Are you excited?'

He smiles. 'I'm utterly terrified. I can't really admit it to Imogen. She's the one who has to be in the trenches, as it were.'

As we pass through the entry gates, a sudden breeze hits us sideways. Oli puts out his hand automatically to stop me falling.

'She's probably guessed how you're feeling.'

He nods. 'I do have an awfully transparent face. So, how about you, Georgie? What news?'

I'm almost tempted to tell him about Charlie. My kind-hearted ex approaches every problem – in or out of court – with a mixture of critical thinking and empathy. He'd take my odd hallucination in his stride.

But he has more than enough on his plate.

'All good. Getting lots of work. Crime still pays.'

The pier isn't busy yet; the schoolkids haven't arrived. Manic jingles get louder as we walk closer to the amusements. To our right, the burned-out West Pier glows copper, skeletal and elegant as an ageing catwalk model.

'And it's working out, being down here?'

'I like it. The light is beautiful. And my neighbours are nice. I no longer worry that I could die all alone in my flat and not be discovered for several months.'

It was meant as a joke, but Oli gives me *that* look, the *I worry about you* one that floors me every time.

'And you're making friends?'

'Oli, don't fuss.'

But I smile, to show I don't *really* mind. When I'm with him, I remember how much I liked knowing someone cared. Until I began to hate myself for all the lies I told.

'I only want you to be as happy as . . .' He stops.

'As you and Imogen are?'

Oli shrugs. 'Is that wrong?'

'No. It's nice.'

I walk faster, looking anywhere but at Oli, so I won't splurge out everything that's wrong with my life.

He catches me up. 'I fancy doughnuts.'

'You don't want to get grease on your suit, Oli.'

'I feel like living dangerously.'

There are white-painted benches running alongside this section of the pier, and I sit facing Kemp Town. Oli walks back towards me, cradling a large paper bag, oil from the doughnuts already bleeding through.

'Naughty but nice,' he says, and his grin reminds me so much of the man I met thirteen years ago.

'I'm hoping to do the Fielding case,' I say, as I take a warm doughnut, 'for this art book.'

'Really?' Oli frowns. 'That's a blast from the past.'

'Going to see Jim Fielding on Saturday, to try to talk him into it. He called the publisher back straightaway, so maybe that's a good sign.'

I explain the idea behind the book, as we head towards the rides.

'Fascinating concept. Why did you pick *that* case?'

'You think it's for old time's sake? Actually the publisher suggested it. But obviously I remember it very clearly for other reasons.'

He nods. 'You and me both.'

We laugh. Is this what being grown-up is? Being able to remember the pleasure before the pain, and feel nostalgic?

'I'm nervous, though. It's one of those cases that got under my skin.'

Without thinking, I glance back along the pier, half expecting to see Charlie. No one is there.

'Yes. Bloody awful case but that Christmas card was a knockout blow. Daniel Fielding knew his number was up, right then.'

'Still took him another week to change his plea.'

Oli bites into the doughnut and smiles.

'Fat and sugar and a salty sea breeze. Bliss. Yeah, I still remember the defence team's faces when he said he was guilty, they weren't expecting it. Fielding was an odd kid. I know we went heavy on the jealousy motive, but there was no history of violence. A bit of drunk and disorderly, but only after his mother committed suicide.'

I stop. 'I knew Sharon Fielding was dead but not how she died.'

'I imagine the defence would have brought it up, if they'd had the chance.'

'How did she do it?'

'She jumped off the Clifton Suspension Bridge in Bristol.'

The doughnut has solidified in my mouth, a choking thing. I force myself to swallow.

Oli doesn't notice.

'Who knows what grief did to him? You captured his vulnerability in that first sketch; I remember seeing it before I even met you, and it really hit me. He looked lost.'

Daniel's face *is* the one that I see sometimes before I go to sleep, when I replay old cases in my head. I assumed it was because he was my first commission for the PA, the one that made me.

But maybe it was because we were both as lost as each other.

I glance down, through the gap in the decking boards. The grey-green water roils beneath us.

'I can't imagine jumping. Why did his mother do it?'

'Difficult childhood. In and out of care, I think. Plus, there were rumours about Jim not exactly being the perfect husband.' Oli wipes the sugar off his fingers with a napkin. 'Not that it's any excuse for what Daniel did.'

We get up, walk past the Haunted House, the screaming faces so badly chipped they're more pathetic than scary.

'Sometimes people do things that have no explanation,' I say, finally.

I hear shrieks. The first kids are arriving after school, running towards us, feet clattering along the planks, pale legs exposed by hitched-up skirts.

Oli stops next to the dodgems, frowning. He takes my hand, and I feel that electric charge, momentarily. Then I remind myself he is my friend. No more, no less.

'Georgie, are you sure about going back to *that* case? I've never seen much sense in revisiting what can't be changed.'

The way he looks at me, I could almost convince myself he knows who I really am, and what I did. Even though I never told him about my past, he knew there was *something*. We spent the last six months before I broke off our engagement in a tug-of-war, him trying to make me trust him, me holding back.

I let go of his hand.

'It's a commission. That's all.'

We're near the end of the pier now, alongside the Crazy Mouse, the loops and curves silhouetted against the grey clouds.

'You are all right, Georgie?'

'Never better.'

'Only you seem . . . distracted. I know we're not together but you'd still tell me if I could help you with anything, wouldn't you?'

I look out at the horizon, the end of the world. I think of Charlie, in the garden square, on the road, in court.

'Was there anything else about the Fielding case that didn't come out in court?'

'You're not going to come over all *Law and Order* on me, are you? Daniel's probably out on licence by now anyway, if he's been a good boy. Justice has been done.'

I nod. 'I suppose.'

'Don't get me wrong, the book is a great opportunity for you. And the countryside near where it all happened is beautiful, in a

Gothic, Brothers Grimm sort of way. Word of warning, though. Jim Fielding will try to chat you up. He might be a hero but he also has an eye for the ladies. Watch yourself.'

I smile. 'All right. I'll pack my chastity belt.'

'Good. You don't want to end up being the third Mrs Fielding. Not when you remember what happened to the first two.' He takes the empty doughnut bag from me, rolls it into a ball, and drop-kicks it into a waste bin. 'Now, how about we sneak in one game of air hockey before my train home?

12

I watch Neena as she broadcasts live outside Bristol Crown Court. A new day, a new set of violent criminals for me to draw.

Pretty much everyone who was covering the Brighton rape trial has headed west today for the sentencing of two bank robbers. Oli's witnesses weren't due to deliver anything headline-grabbing so the circus has come to a different town.

Usually, I refuse to come to this court – the memories are too painful. But I steeled myself this time, made an exception because the Forest of Dean is less than two hours' drive from here. There, tomorrow, I have to persuade Jim Fielding to relive the worst time of *his* life, for a picture.

'As he sentenced the brothers, the judge remarked on the CCTV which showed the guilty men laughing as they beat their victim. He told them, "You were also laughing at civilised society, at everyone who believes in right and wrong."'

Neena is in her element: trial reports are her speciality, delivering juicy evidence in grave BBC tones. A rent-a-quote MP rages next to her, calling for the return of capital or corporal punishment, I can't hear which.

When she wraps up, she walks over to me.

'How was that?'

'You looked the part, as always.' I turn to her. 'Look. Sorry about the sketch. I know it wasn't my best.'

She shoots me a nervous look, caught out by my admission.

'It did the job. It was there on time.'

I saw Charlie again, in court. And later, when I had to recall the faces of the guilty men, and the unfamiliar circuit judge, all I could picture was the small boy in the red football shirt, standing next to the dock, kicking the oak frame with his bare feet.

'Come on, Neena. The robbers looked like cartoons.'

'I'd be worrying more about the judge if I were you. He looks at least three stone heavier in your picture, and he's very touchy about his weight.' She laughs half-heartedly. 'Look, are you OK, George? Only you don't seem yourself.'

Not myself.

When I caught a glimpse of my reflection in the windscreen of the outside-broadcast truck, I didn't see Georgia, the cool, professional court artist.

I saw Suzanne. The tragic victim, the unreliable witness.

'George?'

Could I tell Neena about the visions? She's my closest female friend, and she was there for me when I split up with Oli, deliberately not siding with either of us.

But she's also employed by my main client. I daren't let her doubt me, not until I work out for myself what's going on. I smile.

'Didn't sleep much, knowing I had to be up early to drive here.'

She sighs. 'Ugh. Sleep. What's that?'

'The twins?'

'It was supposed to get better when they went to nursery. But they chatter to each other until past midnight and then they cry because they're too tired to sleep. Honestly, I used to look forward to weekends but I am almost hoping for a traffic jam on the way home.'

I smile. 'You wouldn't give them up for the world.'

'No. You're right. I'll see you back in Brighton on Monday, OK?' She puts her hand on my arm. 'And try to get some rest. I'm worried about you.'

'No need. We all have off days.'

'Yes, but—' She stops herself.

'What?'

'I'm not supposed to tell you, but . . . The news editors have noticed the drawings are a bit rough. One is already trying to replace court drawings with graphics, to save money. Your work this week hasn't done you any favours.'

'Oh. Right.' I want to throw up.

'Just . . . go home and enjoy that lovely seaside air and come back on Monday ready to do your best work. Because when you're on form, there's no one else who can capture the drama like you do.'

She squeezes my arm again, and I nod.

'Thank you for the warning.'

As she walks back towards the truck to check the newsroom have given her the all-clear, I try to think positive. The meeting with Jim is an opportunity. It's no longer just about putting Maureen's nose out of joint. If I can get Jim to sit for me – even paint a picture the publishers use on the cover – it will surely shut those producers up. I *know* I'm good enough.

And maybe seeing Charlie is just a manifestation of how important this is to me. It can't be a coincidence that I'm seeing the boy *now*.

Or it might just be my usual obsession with guilt and victims. Perhaps what I need is to draw a hero for once.

Either way, painting Jim could build my profile, and help me get my head straighter.

And hopefully send Charlie away for good.

13

As soon as I get back behind the wheel of the hire car, I put my foot down. Once I leave Bristol city centre, I can relax a little. I love how driving makes me feel.

In control.

I started learning the day I turned seventeen. Trevor taught me in his big old Jeep, even though my feet barely reached the pedals. We'd do endless circuits of the boggy field at the back of the farm, and he took the mickey, but in a kind way, joking about *lady drivers*.

Marion and Trevor saved me. My grandfather – Mum's father, widowed and as brittle as old leaves – was the only relative who could have given me a home after the *incident*. My social worker tried so hard to persuade me, but I knew by then: family meant nothing. Worse than nothing. Family meant danger.

So instead, I went a hundred miles east, to this couple who had a gift for working with difficult older kids. They took in Suzanne – wounded, stubborn, defiant – and gave her the space to become Georgia.

Of course, they were being paid to do it, and in my first days there, I threw it back at them constantly.

'You've only got me here because I'm taking care of your fucking mortgage on your fucking ugly house.'

I never swore when I was Daddy's girl.

They didn't swear back. Instead, they soaked up my anger like sponges. And their house wasn't ugly, just ramshackle, a series of beige bungalows adapted originally for their disabled son, who died when he was six. They knew pain, understood you couldn't take it away from someone.

I couldn't help but heal there, just like their two butter-soft rescue Staffies, and the flock of former battery chickens who stopped pecking each other, grew rust-coloured feathers and learned to lay again.

I stayed for six years: for the first few months, I refused to go to school, or leave the farm at all. When my father's trial began, I locked myself in my room, and it was Trevor who coaxed me out.

'You'll regret it if you don't take the chance to tell the jury what happened. For your brother's sake. And your mum's.'

They took me back to Bristol in the mud-spattered Jeep, and Trevor circled Small Street and Quay Street once I was called to give evidence, so he could take me home the instant it was over. It took less than forty minutes.

I confirmed who I was, and a little about our lives before. But I wouldn't – *couldn't* – speak about that day, not even from behind the curtain that stopped me seeing my father in the dock.

The defence barristers were relentless: 'Could there have been someone threatening your father, making him say what he said when he locked you in? The powerful people he believed were coming for him, coming for all of you?'

It was all his defence team had to go on: a mumbled, incoherent statement he gave in hospital where he was being treated for his bodged suicide attempt. He talked about being followed, being in trouble, then later he clammed up again. I think he must have realised how mad it sounded. And pride was important to my father, even when he'd destroyed everything else.

Yet the defence were only doing their job. I had told the police in my first interview that I thought I'd heard other voices while I was locked in my room. It was a distraction, of course; the oh-so-gentle detectives later told me there was no sign of a break-in, no DNA from anyone else in the house.

In court, each minute ticked by as slowly as it had when I was alone, in my room, staring at the key, unsure when to set myself free.

The judge let me stand down in the end.

'This young woman has already suffered so much. My condolences for your losses, Miss Ross.'

I was excused, but after my evidence was finished, I found I couldn't make myself leave. Part of me kept hoping there would be a moment of understanding, or revelation – that Dad would suddenly be able to prove it wasn't him who did this terrible thing. That he would somehow absolve me of the guilt I felt for what I did and didn't do that Saturday.

But there was no absolution: my father refused to give evidence.

Daniel Fielding did the same. All the journalists had been speculating the week of his own trial about what he'd say to defend himself. But instead of giving evidence, he got into the witness box and simply said he wanted to plead guilty.

Perhaps if Daniel had had the right help after his mother died, he might have been saved, as I was. And conversely, if I hadn't had Marion and Trevor, might I too have turned evil?

The Bristol traffic has cleared, and I accelerate onto the motorway. It's been raining all week, but now as I speed past, the bright sunshine makes the farmland glow emerald green, and the wild flowers on the embankments seem to grow before my eyes.

The familiarity of the landscape fills me with dread. Frome was surrounded by fields like these. An idyllic place to grow up . . .

I turn the radio to maximum, a rock station drowning out the memories. The car thunders towards the iridescent white struts of the Severn Bridge and then I'm crossing the water, away from my past.

14

The countryside thickens, inky green woodland encroaching on the road. In fairy tales, and tabloid stories, forests are where bad things happen. But I drive faster, because there are no memories here to trouble me.

'In two hundred yards, turn left. Follow the road for two miles.'

As I near Ashdean, the dashboard gauge shows the temperature falling: sixteen degrees, fourteen degrees, thirteen. The cerulean sky fades to silver, and the sunshine disappears behind the dense branches.

The sign as I enter the town reads ASHDEAN – THE ENGINE ROOM OF THE FOREST.

I've never been before: court artists only go to the scene of the crime if the jurors do too and at Daniel's trial, they saw videos of Jim's burned-out house instead.

This town is the colour of soot. As the car judders in and out of potholes, its narrow streets are deserted. In Brighton, Friday night draws everyone to the sea, the week's stresses over, the fun about to begin. Here, it seems, people stay home.

'At the roundabout, take the second exit.'

I've arranged to stay at a local pub with rooms tonight, but I've set the satnav to first take me to the house where Tessa and her baby died. I don't want to be a voyeur, but this commission is important to my career, and I want to get it right.

And I've not forgotten that Charlie was injured here, too.

Reflexively I check my mirror, in case he's appeared on the back seat. No. Perhaps now I'm well rested, I won't see any more hallucinations.

I drive past the old market square. On the left, there's a bus stop and a bay for two taxis – do they work for Jim, I wonder? He runs a cab firm, along with his construction business.

The road takes me past a war memorial, and a weathered brown statue of a miner and a forester, armed with axes and head-torches. That was what the men of Ashdean did, before they closed the collieries down.

Nothing looks open. There's a Boots, and a Greggs, and the inevitable former Woolworths, transformed into a pound shop. The other frontages are shuttered, but it's not clear whether they've closed for the night, or for good.

'At the junction, bear left.'

The road through the town splits. The right fork leads towards more rain-soaked cottages, but my route takes me towards a newer part of town, past a high school, squat and brown, flanked by a patchy playing field. Then rows of houses, the odd one derelict, drawing the eye like rotten teeth in a gaping mouth. The area is seedier than I had imagined.

'Turn left up Sycamore Road.'

As I take the turn, I see the sign, less rusted than the rest:

TO OAKLAND CLOSE, MAPLE AVENUE, CHERRY BLOSSOM LANE.

For a few weeks after Christmas 2003, number 9 Cherry Blossom Lane was an address everyone knew by heart. As I take the second right turn, I recognise the tall town houses. Number 9 is the middle house in a row of three.

It looks utterly ordinary, not a place you'd expect to find heroism. Or evil, for that matter.

I reverse to park, and in the silence of the deserted street, the clutch is shrill as a scream. I get out of the car and walk past the neighbouring houses. A lime-green paddling pool, half-deflated, sits under the window frame of the first. In the last driveway there's an old sports car with bricks in place of wheels.

In the days after the fire, the pavement here was carpeted by flowers. The same had happened at my house. I never went home, but I saw it on the news: the pile of rotting, pastel petals. My social worker brought me a selection of the cards left there. I only recognised two or three as coming from people who'd known us and I despised the strangers who'd appropriated my grief.

But now I'm the same as them.

I want to turn back, my cheeks red with shame, but something about the house catches my eye. Number 9 has been rebuilt, the concrete frontage whitewashed and dazzling, even with no sun. It almost hurts my eyes. But that's not what's strange. It's the windows: every one has newspapers taped to the inside of the panes.

Why? To stop people seeing in? Jim doesn't live here anymore. He said on the court steps after the trial that he could never go back, and tomorrow I've arranged to meet him at his new house.

I feel it again: the sense I'm being watched. I close my eyes, afraid suddenly that I will see young Charlie outside the house where he nearly died.

Except, I can hear footsteps and it makes me realise something for the first time: Charlie never makes a sound.

'Been a while since we've had a rubbernecker.'

I spin around. A ruddy-skinned woman in her fifties is watching me from behind the fence of the last house.

'Sorry, I—'

I shrug. There's not much I can say. What else would a stranger be doing here but coming to gawp?

I look towards the woman's neat house, the half-decent car in the drive.

'Is it empty now? Jim's house?'

'Last lot of tenants wrecked the place. Mr Fielding had to do it up again but no one else has rented it yet. Not like they're queuing round the block to live where some poor girl and her unborn kid died, is it?'

'Did you know them?'

'You a reporter?'

I shake my head.

'Didn't know Tessa except to wave at. She wasn't here long. Only after she and Mr Fielding wed and of course, that were only months before the fire.'

I look back at the blanked-out windowpanes. Was this a happy home?

'And did Jim live here before, with his first wife?'

The woman nods. 'Yeah. Sharon. She wasn't from Ashdean, originally. Trouble with a capital T.'

It seems a cruel judgement on a woman whose life became so unbearable she jumped off a bridge.

'In what way?'

'Oh, not for me to say. But she wasn't much of a wife. No one could have blamed Mr Fielding for looking elsewhere. Not that he had to look far.'

Is she insinuating that Jim had been having an affair?

'Good mum, though, give her her due,' the woman says, interpreting my silence as disapproval.

'You knew Daniel?'

She nods. 'He wasn't a bad lad, bit of a mummy's boy if anything. Her doing herself in hit him hard. His big sister, that's Amy, she was always the smarter of the two.'

I look up at the house again.

'You wouldn't have known anything had happened there.'

She shrugs. 'For a long while, even after it had been all replastered, painted, the lot, you could still smell the fire. Like a ruddy great barbecue.'

I shudder. 'And Jim? You knew him well?'

She narrows her eyes. 'Everybody in Ashdean knows Mr Fielding. I wasn't surprised when he did what he did that night.'

'Rescuing the children?'

'Loved those kids like they were his own.'

She gives me a sideways look.

'Did you know Charlie and Jodie too?'

She nods. 'By sight, yeah. They were always out in the garden, with their parents. Well, Emma and Sharon were chalk and cheese, but Mr Fielding was mates with the kids' dad, Robert, until he did a runner.'

'Did they work together?'

'No, it was when they were teenagers. Young Jimmy was a right tearaway. Spent a year inside for what he got up to.'

I didn't know that.

'What was that?'

'Joyriding, from what I recall.' The woman's blushing now. 'Our very own Jimmy Dean.'

'He sounds like a charmer.'

'I've always liked bad boys.' She smiles. 'At school, he was in the year below me and you know how it goes, usually girls only look at the older lads. But when Mr Fielding came back from his year in the nick, he was taller, stronger. Tough, you know? We all fancied him.' She blushes again. 'You sure you're not a journalist? You're good at getting stuff out of me.'

'I have one of those faces, people say.'

'Lose someone, did you?'

I turn back to face her.

'What?'

'Three kinds of people who come to places like this. First the reporters. Then the rubberneckers, desperate to have a piece of the action. But I've changed my mind, I don't think you're one of them. Apart from anything, you didn't bring a bunch of bloody carnations.'

'Who are the third kind of people?'

'The sad ones. You can see by the way they hold themselves, they're embarrassed. They didn't *want* to be a part of this, but it's like they couldn't help themselves. What happened here – not just the fire, but what Mr Fielding done, how he saved those kiddies – made them come.'

'People would tell you that?'

She nods. 'Used to make them tea. No charge, mind. It'd all spill out. Dead wives, kids, parents.'

'Do you think visiting helped them? The people who came.'

She shrugs. 'A brew makes most things a bit better. Want one?'

I'm tempted to go with her, to ask her more about Jim, and Daniel too. But she's clearly the local gossip and I don't want anyone to know about the commission until it's definite.

'Thanks for the offer, but I've had a long drive. You could point me in the direction of the Forester's Rest?'

'Just head back out and right onto the main road, until you're nearly out of town. If you get to the bloody great white house on the right, looks like a nuclear bunker, you've gone too far. Mind you. Maybe you'd like to take a look at that too.'

'Why?'

'It's where Jim Fielding lives now. Behind a very high wall. You can be sure *he* won't be inviting you in for a cuppa.'

15

A mile down the road, the last pebble-dashed houses peter out, and the Forester's Rest appears on the left.

But I see it too late, and have to drive on, looking for a turning place. Before I do, there's a long, high, plastered wall, painted in a textured white finish that looks too sticky to climb.

Jim Fielding's house.

I drive slowly, still trying to spot somewhere to turn. As the road climbs out of the dip, the landscape opens up again: rich green meadows and sandstone farm buildings. Sheep dot the landscape. After the unrelenting silence of Ashdean, it's a shock to hear the sweet-sour melodies of a blackbird.

Finally, I do a U-turn, and on the way back, I pass the walled house again, right-angled corners sharp as daggers. A reinforced metal gate, the width of a truck, is topped with razor wire. Twin CCTV cameras turn in opposite directions, even though the road here is deserted.

The security measures seem extreme, but Jim lost two wives and a child. I imagine he wants to keep those who are left as safe as he can.

The car jolts over something, and when I look back in my mirror, I half expect to see a vision of Charlie. But instead, I realise it's a dead animal – a large bird. I think there are hawks in the forest, and other birds of prey. I hope I wasn't the one who killed it.

I turn into the pub car park, where modern extensions dwarf the original Victorian footprint: there's a skittle alley, and a peach-curtained function room.

As I step into the pub, a large, brown dog with a broad, pink muzzle bounds towards me, growling and wagging his tail simultaneously.

'Rambo, easy.' The landlord appears from the same direction as the dog. 'Nothing to worry about, love, unless you're a burglar. But you don't look like a burglar.'

'I'm staying tonight.'

'Oh yes. I had you down. Single room, is it? I've given you a double. Singles are all above the bar, which would have been noisy as we've got a do in tonight.'

He gestures down the corridor – I can see the dark-varnished woodwork of a long bar, and beyond that, oak tables and chairs, all empty.

'A do? I've been driving through the town and it's deserted.'

'Getting dolled up. Ashdean lives for its Friday nights.'

He takes my overnight bag from me and puffs up the stairs with it.

'Rambo, no!' he says, sending the dog back down.

The animal lies on a tread, its long body spilling over the edge.

My room is huge: there's a king-sized bed with a fern-patterned duvet cover, textured walls painted apple green, and an old map of the forest.

'This is cosy,' I say.

'We redid the rooms. Hoping to get the ramblers in. Hasn't worked. This bit of the forest isn't chocolate box enough. You a walker yourself?'

'On my way up to see family.'

The excuse I'd made up feels phoney now. I've seen how Ashdean isn't really on the way to or from anywhere.

But the landlord is already on to the next thing.

'Oh, if you're planning to eat, you might want to do that now. You won't want to be fighting off drunks while you're trying to eat your ploughman's.'

'What's the celebration?'

'An engagement do. There *will* be drinking, that's for certain. But it's always good-natured. Like one big family, Ashdean. We live too cheek by jowl for it to be any other way.'

I take a shower, then go down stairs. The bar is tidy, with local ales and a basic menu of pies and pub grub. The landlord sets my table in the corner and I trip, not noticing the low step up to it. But at least, as it's slightly raised, I'll be out of the way.

Almost on the dot of seven, Ashdean arrives ready to party. The customers are all ages, a little dressed up: the women in tops with glitter panels or cut-out backs, the men in pressed shirts with short sleeves revealing tattoos and muscled arms. But it's a lot less outrageous than Brighton.

I look at a group of younger lads, in case one of them is Charlie. But I probably wouldn't recognise him even if he was there.

A few customers give me curious glances as they order their drinks, but soon it's so busy that no one looks my way at all. A DJ has set up in the other corner, where a few tables have been pushed out of the way to create a small dance floor.

I finish my dinner and am just about to buy another drink to take up to my room, when the main bar door opens and the atmosphere changes so instantly it's as if someone has flicked a switch.

Two women come in first: a skinny blonde, younger than me, with a fake tan so deep it's as though she's been dipped in linseed oil. The other woman is my age, and very heavily pregnant, with lank, sandy hair.

The pub holds its breath as a man hesitates on the threshold, his back to us as he tosses away a cigarette. Even before he turns, I know who he is. He enters like the lead singer on a comeback tour, grinning as he takes the hand of the pregnant woman, and circles his arm around the skinny hips of the other girl.

Jim Fielding.

Weather-beaten but ageless, eyes bright, smile broad. He must be in his early fifties, but he's not gone to seed. His clothes emphasise the flatness of his belly and the strength in his legs.

I wait for the furore of his arrival to die down, but it doesn't. The blonde girl must be twenty – no, even thirty years – his junior, but she gazes up at him as though he is Romeo to her Juliet. He sweeps a strand of golden hair away from her temple, then looks up at the waiting customers.

'Friends. Family members. Enemies.' He waits for the laugh, which comes as a wall of sound. 'Kidding! Thanks for coming here tonight to be with me, and my new fiancée, Leah.'

Fiancée? I hadn't expected that. After what happened to the first two Mrs Fieldings, it would take a brave woman to marry Jim.

'Despite all that's happened to our family, I feel like a bloody lucky man. Because this woman has agreed to become my third wife. Not hanging around to give her time to change her mind, either. So get August the twelfth in your diaries. I don't know what I did to deserve meeting this special person, but it must have been something good.'

He turns back to her. I've never looked at another person with such transparent desire. My discomfort at the age gap fades a little.

When he kisses her, I sense the women sighing. And when they break apart, the pub erupts in applause.

Only the pregnant girl doesn't join in. Her hands rest on the top of her protruding belly, and she tilts her head in my direction. I catch my breath. It's like seeing Daniel: the same high cheekbones, the same watchful eyes. This must be his older sister Amy, all grown up.

I wonder if she's still in touch with Daniel in prison, if she has told him he's going to be an uncle. If she misses her brother, as I miss mine.

'Not a bad lad,' the neighbour had said.

Was he a good brother? Despite everything he did?

'Thirsty work, getting engaged,' Jim says, and walks up to the bar. 'First round's on me!'

I plan to slip away when no one is looking. But as I cross the bar, I can see the other people at the table with Amy. A pretty, middle-aged woman with a salt-and-pepper bob holds the hand of a teenaged girl whose soft features make me look again. She has Down syndrome. And now I realise who she is, too: Jodie O'Neill, the tiny bridesmaid at Jim's last wedding, the child in bunny ears he rescued from the fire. The woman with the bob must be her mother, Emma.

Which means that even before he turns, I know who the last person at the table is. The laughter, the clinking of glasses, the electronic sounds from the fruit machine all fade away.

Mid-brown hair, soft and fluffed up. Broad shoulders, carrying a little too much weight. And a flat, shiny patch on his cheek, perhaps all that's left of that terrifying night fourteen years ago.

Charlie.

Our eyes meet. For a fraction of a second, I half-expect him to recognise me too.

But he blinks, then looks away.

I can't take my eyes off him. Charlie is a man now. Of course, I knew that in theory but even so . . .

A flash of red in my peripheral vision makes me turn. It takes me a moment to understand what – or rather, *who* – I am seeing.

It's the young Charlie – the lost child in a red football shirt. He watches his older self, hands bunched into small fists. His face seems so much clearer than the real man. And the boy is sobbing silently.

I try to look away or blink him gone. Tears run down his ruddy face, and there is nothing I can do.

A burning sensation in my palm makes me look down. The room key in my hand is biting into the flesh where I'm gripping it.

The last time I felt this scared, my bedroom key was in my hand and through the half-open door to the bathroom, I saw the aqua tiles splashed with the deepest crimson.

I blink again. The younger Charlie – *my* Charlie – has disappeared.

I stumble to my room and fall onto the bed. This cannot go on. When I'm back in Brighton, I'll do something about the visions – find help, talk to a counsellor or something. Whatever's the matter with me, it can't be as terrible as not knowing.

Sleep won't happen now, but I close my eyes to stop myself seeing a boy who isn't there. Party music drifts towards me. Jaunty songs from the seventies – for Jim, I suppose – and up-tempo contemporary tracks, for the woman who is going to be the third Mrs Fielding.

16

I must get some sleep in the end, because when I wake, last night's events seem unreal. I force myself to focus on today – this commission matters. I dress smartly and skip breakfast, knowing hunger will make me sharper.

Outside, low white cloud hangs over the forest like a blanket, though it's surprisingly hot as I walk towards Jim Fielding's house.

Guard dogs begin to bark when I'm still a good three hundred yards from the gate. The sound has none of Rambo's amiable gruffness. The perimeter wall is freshly painted, the border of green shrubs thorny and forbidding.

A slate sign is mounted on the wall: THE WHITE HOUSE.

I think of Jim's reception at the pub last night; perhaps he's being ironic.

I walk up to the gate without hesitating and push the intercom. As I wait for a response, I run through the flattering words I've rehearsed. Seeing him last night has made me more nervous. Jim is clearly no pushover.

The intercom rings and rings. I stare at the panel; a glass lens reflects my own image back at me, monochrome and blurred. Someone behind those gates can see me better than I can see myself.

The dogs have stopped barking, which makes me even more sure there's a person on the other side settling them.

'Hello.' I speak into the grille. 'I'm Georgia Sage. I am here to see Mr Fielding.'

The blast of static is so loud it makes me jump backwards.

'Didn't you see the sign? No junk, no sales.'

The voice is a woman's: young, scratchy. Leah?

'I've actually got an appointment with him. Arranged by Benjamin Rowland, he's a publisher in London.'

'Jim's out.'

'Could I wait?'

She tuts like a teenager.

'He never said nothing.'

'It's about a painting.' I wonder if I can flatter *her*. 'You might like to be painted yourself?'

Silence. Then a series of clunks as bolts retract into the steel casings. The gate whines as it moves slowly inwards. I'm impatient to see inside.

First, I see spikes: an island of cacti set in a sea of black gravel. Beyond the 'garden' sits a single-storey glass building, with bamboo growing up against the windows like prison bars. This is in another league from Cherry Blossom Lane. Jim Fielding's life has been full of sadness, but it hasn't done business any harm.

There are no dogs in sight.

The central wall of glass slides open, and a woman's shape is silhouetted against the light, her body as angular as the house. As my eyes adjust, I see she's wearing workout gear, black Lycra with flashes of red, moulded to her faultless physique. She reminds me of a sports car.

'You were in the pub last night,' she says accusingly.

Sweat blooms under my arms, while my mouth is dry.

'I stayed over before my meeting with your fiancé. It's about painting him for a book.'

I step into the entrance hall, and she glares at me. Why is she so hostile? Behind her I can see the building has two wings, surrounding a central courtyard full of even spikier cacti.

'*Painting?*' She says it as if it's the most awful perversion she can think of. 'My Jim doesn't even like having his photo taken. Why would he let anyone *paint* him?'

'May I show you?' I reach into my bag, and she steps back, as though I'm about to draw a weapon. I hold out an American book of court art I brought to show Jim. 'I'm a court artist. We go to prominent cases to illustrate the hearings, because cameras are banned. I was there when your fiancé gave evidence thirteen years ago.'

She takes the book from me, leafs through using the tips of her long nails.

'Ooh,' she says, stopping at a sketch of the trial of an actor accused of tax evasion. 'Do you get to meet them, then?'

'That was in the States, but I've seen a few stars in trials here.' I try to think of one that might impress her. 'Remember when the Echo Boys accused their manager of fraud? I was as close to them as you are to me now. And Tommy Echo,' I whisper, as though we might be overheard, 'kept farting all the way through.'

'No!' She giggles. 'That's rank. I had a poster of him on my wall and everything.'

'Leah, what's going on?'

Another woman's voice, low-pitched and slightly breathless, comes from further inside the building, followed by heavy footsteps.

Amy Fielding, her belly impossibly big on her bird-like legs, enters the room.

'Hello,' I say, holding out my hand. 'I was just telling Leah here how I've got an appointment with your dad to discuss painting his portrait.'

She keeps her hand to herself.

'How do you know he's my dad?'

I force a smile. 'Well, you do look very alike.'

Though she looks much more like her brother.

'I've been commissioned to do a similar book to this, but for the UK,' I say, returning to the script I prepared. 'A mix of famous people and well-known cases. As well as the original court sketch, I do a new painting. Yours to keep.'

'We've got loads of pictures already,' Leah says.

I can see them, behind her. Photos of the New York skyline, movie posters, a posed studio shot of the newly extended Fielding family – minus Daniel, of course.

'Yes, but a portrait is special. Much more lasting than a photograph. Your fiancé was so brave; people really remember what he did that Christmas.'

'I was too little to know anything about it, but of course, he's told me it all.' Leah slaps the book shut. 'Which is why I know he won't do it. It broke his heart, what happened to Tessa and the baby. But he's moved on from that night, thanks to me. He won't wanna go backwards.'

So why did he agree to see me?

I look at Amy, who shrugs.

'What Dad does is his business, but it sounds like a terrible idea to me.'

'I understand that, but I'd still love to explain it to him in person,' I say, trying to keep them talking. 'Readers would be thrilled to see he's found happiness. I could paint the whole family, maybe, ready for when the little one arrives. And there's the perfect space for it right here.'

I point at a blank section of wall.

'I'd rather stick pins in my eyes than have anyone draw me looking like this,' Amy says. 'Once the *little one* is here, I'm having my tubes tied as soon as I can.'

There's a wryness about Amy that I like. But Leah is completely humourless.

'I reckon you're wasting your time and your breath,' she says. 'But I suppose it is up to him. Now's your chance.'

Leah turns, and over her shoulder, I see the gates opening again, and an old London cab nudging through the opening, paintwork polished to a mirror shine. Jim Fielding smiles broadly as he gets out, and the gates lock into place behind him.

17

As I take Jim Fielding's hand, the colour leaches out of our surroundings. Nothing else is as vivid.

When he takes his hand away, I see a flash of scarlet on his palms, burns he sustained in the fire that have never quite healed.

'Miss Sage. Sorry, I got held up.'

'Georgia, please.'

'Georgia.' He makes the name last longer than usual, rolling the vowels around on his tongue. 'Lovely. And you have to call me Jim. I see you've met the two women in my life.' He kisses his daughter on the cheek, his fiancée briefly on the lips. 'Do you want to come inside?'

I follow him through the entrance hall again, and then to the right.

'Welcome to the White House. I bet you'll never guess how it got its name.' He laughs.

The first room is a spotless white kitchen. There's a stack of pizza boxes next to the chrome bin, and a glass jar full of protein bars next to the kettle: his and hers, at a guess. Bright light pours in through triple-glazed windows on both sides, so the air is thick and humid. Beyond them, a strip of lawn so dazzling it must be AstroTurf.

'Where do you keep your dogs?' I ask.

He chuckles. 'On a CD. They're part of the security. My bark is worse than my bite, whatever people say.'

The living area is next, den-like with cream leather, sunken sofas and a modern fireplace hanging from the ceiling like a steel teardrop. I realise Amy and Leah have gone, without Jim having to ask.

He gestures for me to sit down, and as I sink into the expensive cushions, he pulls up a chair opposite.

'Not what you expected?' he asks.

'I had no idea what to expect,' I say. 'But it probably wouldn't have been this.'

'You thought it'd be all horse brasses and kegs of scrumpy.'

I smile. 'It's an incredible space.'

Jim nods, satisfied. 'Something a bit special. Benefit of being a builder. I wanted nothing that'd remind me of the old place.'

I let a moment pass.

'I'm grateful that you agreed to see me.'

'Doesn't mean I'll do it.'

'Of course not. But I want to reassure you, there's nothing sensationalist about this.' It's the kind of thing I've heard journalists say over and over. 'What happened to your wife and unborn child moved so many people, including me. And now you are to marry again. I think everyone who followed your story would love to know that you've found happiness again.'

'You *were* there, in court, weren't you?' He studies my face, his gaze unhurried. 'I didn't think I recognised you, but you know what, I *do*. You were so young. Like him.'

Him. I wonder if he ever says Daniel's name aloud.

'I'd only just started work. But your evidence has stayed with me more than any other witness. It was incredibly dramatic.'

'Put on a good show, did I?'

'I'm sorry. I didn't mean to sound glib.'

He waves it away. 'It was a long time ago. I'm yesterday's news.'

'That's not true. What happened touched people. The time of year, your heroism. The loss you suffered.'

Jim sighs. 'They're always in my heart, Tessa and the little one. And of course, Charlie and Jodie are still in my life, they're some consolation.'

I decide not to mention I was in the bar last night.

'Your godchildren?'

'You've done your research. Though only Jodie is my godchild. Their piece-of-shit father left before she was even born. I've done my best to be a better dad to them than Robert ever would have. Jodie is going to be a bridesmaid when I marry Leah.'

I remember the photo of his wedding to Tessa. Jodie was a bridesmaid then, too.

'And Charlie?'

'Lovely lad. I tell him not to try to hide that scar on his face. Girls love a story, a rogue.' Jim smiles. 'He's learning. He's like the son I never had.'

Except you did have a son.

Though I suppose I can't blame Jim for not counting Daniel. I've tried *my* hardest to forget I have a father.

'Readers would love to know that you've been able to make a fresh start.'

He says nothing.

I look down at the book in my hands.

'Anyway, this American book is similar to the one the British publishers are bringing out.' I hold it out but he doesn't take it.

I try not to imagine how much Maureen will gloat if I fail. 'I'd paint a portrait that would be yours to keep, and we might be able to pay some limited expenses, to cover the time you spend sitting for me . . .'

'You can see for yourself, I don't need the money. And I'm no oil painting neither.'

'I generally use acrylics.' I smile.

But he's still frowning.

'Here's your chance then. Why would you do it, if you were me?'

I try to think of an answer.

'It could be a way of ending that chapter of your life. You're about to start a new one, with Leah. The painting would show the world that it's possible to recover, even from the most awful trauma.'

'Is it?' he says, and for a moment, it feels as if he knows what happened to me. Even though there's no way he could.

'A portrait can capture much more than a photograph. Pain as well as happiness. It's more honest. My aim would be to show the real Jim Fielding.'

His eyes widen. 'Not sure anyone wants to see that. We all have stuff we'd rather no one sees. Even you, Georgia, I'm sure.'

'Well, you control everything. We'd have sittings, ideally three or four. I'd take sketches. You could play music. Daydream. Or talk.'

He gets up, walks to the window overlooking the fake lawn and a line of bottle-green trees.

'I don't talk about what happened, to anyone.'

'And you won't have to for this either—'

He talks over me. 'It's not that I wouldn't have liked to talk. But everyone around me wants to press on. *Heroes* aren't meant to look back.'

He says *heroes* as if it's a curse.

I remember Neena telling me how often victims of terrible tragedies were keen to talk to her, to be on camera:

'You'd think it's the last thing they'd want to do. But they want to speak to someone who isn't involved, to help them work out how they feel. Even if that uninvolved person happens to be a reporter who is going to broadcast the whole lot to millions.'

Perhaps that's why Jim hasn't told me to piss off. He needs someone to talk to.

'It must be hard at times. Not feeling you can open up.'

He says nothing, but flexes his fingers, as though he's grasping for something.

'Maybe the painting could show it takes as much courage to live with grief, day in, day out, as it does to run into a burning building. Courage and grit.'

'With me, it was whisky and work. Until Leah came along, anyhow.' He turns back to me. 'What's in it for you, Georgia Sage? Coming to the back of beyond, painting my ugly mug.'

I smile. 'I spend my days drawing bad people, the stuff of nightmares. Just for once, I'd love to paint someone good.'

He laughs. 'Flattering an old man is an underhand way to get what you want. But can I trust you, Georgia? Are you sure this is just about a painting?'

I think of little Charlie, and the strange affinity I felt with Daniel in court all those years ago. Am I lying by not admitting I'm more invested than I said?

'What else would it be?'

'When the fire happened, the journalists used all kinds of tricks to try to get their tacky exclusives, to uncover things that weren't even there. It left me . . . suspicious.'

'This is a serious project with a serious publisher, Jim. There's no agenda.'

He sighs, opens up his hands. The skin that grew over his burned palms flashes scarlet again.

'Leave the contract for me to look over. I'm not promising anything. It's up to my family as much as me.'

I try not to let my disappointment show. Jim might agree to it, but I don't think I did nearly enough to convince Leah or Amy.

'Thanks for thinking about it at least. I know readers would take a lot from seeing you've rebuilt your life.'

'Phoenix from the ashes, that's me,' Jim says.

18

Monday morning, and the police medic is Oli's first witness of the week. How he handles this will make or break the case. Yet as I try to concentrate on the evidence, all I can think about is Ashdean – and Jim.

'How soon were you able to examine Miss Tranter after the rape took place?'

The doctor frowns, deepening the lines on her forehead.

'Unfortunately, it was a good thirty-seven hours. The young woman confided in her mother, who persuaded her to report what had happened.'

It's been two days since I met Jim Fielding, but I haven't heard from him. The longer I wait, the less likely it seems he'll say yes. Yet I *want* him to. He's such a fascinating subject.

And I want to paint a hero.

'. . . but this isn't uncommon, though, is it, after a rape?'

The doctor shakes her head.

'No. Reporting is often delayed, and we do what we can to preserve what is left. However, Miss Tranter had already showered multiple times. The skin on her legs and abdomen showed signs of being scrubbed. She told me that she had done that herself, but whatever she tried, she still didn't feel clean.'

Oli waits, to let those words sink in.

'Did that affect the evidence you were able to gather?'

'Yes. There was no semen or other DNA due to the delay and also the washing.'

In sexual assault cases, juries appreciate hard facts, solid data. The lack of it won't help Oli's case. Yet his body language stays confident.

'But we should differentiate between DNA and other *medical* evidence, shouldn't we, Doctor? Because you did find relevant injuries when you conducted your examination. Could you explain to the jury what you found?

'Although first, ladies and gentlemen, I must warn you that you may find some of the details – and photographs – distressing, but they speak very clearly to the violence the defendant used.'

Later, it's the medic I draw for the evening news. In my picture, she's holding up an evidence photograph of a woman's horribly bruised back and hips, Delft blue mottled with manganese violet.

Cruella's cross-examination was as bad as I'd feared, suggesting the victim was a drunk with a liking for 'rough stuff' in the bedroom. The doctor stuck to her guns, insisting that the external and internal bruising appeared too extensive to have been from consensual sex, or accidental injuries. But Cruella argued back: even the victim's own friends admitted she'd had too much champagne – surely the marks to her legs might have come from walking into furniture in an unfamiliar hotel room.

And as for the genital swelling: 'We are from a different generation, though, aren't we, Doctor? Cultural phenomena like *Fifty Shades of Grey* show that today's young woman is more . . . imaginative?'

'I don't see how that's relevant.'

'Could the injuries not be explained by experimentation with, say, domination and submission?'

'Only if it were very extreme.'

'Yet youthful passions are, by their very nature, extreme . . .'

Now, in Manny's storeroom, my anger at Cruella's tactics filters into my sketch, adding layer after layer of purple bruising, until I have to rein myself back and tone it down again with flesh tones.

Toby pokes his head through the beaded curtain.

'Ready?'

'Almost.'

As I step back to assess the final drawing, I jump. Charlie is sitting on Manny's sofa bed, the one he kips on when the cafe is quiet at night.

I blink, try to send the boy away. But when I open my eyes again, he's still there, his Teletubby at his side. Tears are streaming down his face though still he doesn't make a sound.

'Shhh,' I whisper.

I *know* he's not real. But it is impossible to witness a child's pain and not want to take it away.

What do I know about the real Charlie? That he survived the fire. That his sister was born disabled. That his father deserted both of them.

What can I say to make any of that better? I remember how my mother would always be there when I woke from night terrors. I picture her face, feel her soothing touch on my arm, but I cannot hear the words she would use to calm me down. So many details of my childhood have been erased by what happened afterwards.

Charlie's face is distorted from crying, his right eye now as puffy as the burned area surrounding his left. His T-shirt is tear-soaked, and his balled fists begin to scrub away at his sockets. Big boys don't cry.

My body yearns to reach for him. But I am too afraid – of feeling nothing, or even more of feeling *something*.

The kid looks so real, and despite my fear I feel completely normal. Not tired. Not stressed. Heart FM plays in the kitchen and I can hear every word of the ballad as Manny sings along. The smell of coffee drifts in as he makes my espresso.

'Charlie, go, please. You're not real.'

He breaks my gaze and looks towards the door, his arms stretching up towards someone I cannot see. The crying stops, and he puts his thumb in his mouth. My heart breaks. Pip used to do that when he was little.

'Are you here because I saw Jim?' I ask him. 'Are you trying to tell me something?'

He doesn't react. I cannot make sense of this: there is no reason for me to hallucinate. I'd planned to look for a counsellor, but maybe the cause is medical. A brain tumour? Cancer?

If it is, I should seek help, soon. I might be getting worse.

'Done?' Toby says, pushing past me to see the sketch, unable to see the sobbing child. 'That's bold. Very dramatic colours.'

I let him carry the board and my drawing out to where the cameraman is waiting. But I don't join them. Finally, when I look around, the child has gone.

I slump onto the sofa, right where Charlie was, and feel tears pricking behind my eyes. But they're not for him. They're for my brother, the child I really failed.

19

The walk-in centre waiting room is packed.

'It's our rush hour,' says the receptionist. 'You'd be better off going to your own GP.'

'I need to see someone tonight.'

She shrugs. I take my ticket from her and sit down. 432. As I look up, the electronic display flickers.

The red 420 turns to 421.

Like the minutes on my clock radio, the countdown to the moment everything changed.

I close my eyes, but the memories keep coming. The echo of half-heard male voices. A spray of blood across aqua tiles. The choices I made that make me share the guilt with my father.

I force my eyes open, look at the woman next to me, wincing as she flexes bleeding fingers to type a message into her phone.

I get mine out too. No missed calls or messages from Jim Fielding. He'd have called by now if he was going to do it.

To distract myself, I google my symptoms. The phone screen is completely knackered, but the results for *hallucinations, causes,* couldn't be clearer:

Schizophrenia
Parkinson's Disease
Dementia

My finger hovers over the words, but I already know too much about each one. A boy at art school was schizophrenic. At first, his eccentric behaviour gave him an edge, but then he deteriorated until only numbing medication kept him alive.

There's a judge in the Western region with Parkinson's but before he was diagnosed, everyone thought he was an alcoholic. I look down at my hands, which are steady. But what if it's happening when I draw? Maureen's snide comments – 'Not your best work, Georgia' – might be truer than she realised.

And dementia? My memory feels as sharp as ever, though often I wish it weren't. And anyway, surely it's a disease of the old.

Unless this is another legacy from my father; perhaps he's given me faulty genes, along with the money I never wanted.

There's another thing the three conditions have in common.

They are all incurable.

'Last chance, number 432, or I'm going straight to 433!'

A florid doctor in his sixties is scanning the waiting room.

'Sorry, that's me.'

I follow him into the consulting room, which smells of BO and disinfectant wipes.

'What seems to be the problem?'

He sounds weary – he must have asked this tens of thousands of times in his career.

'I've been seeing things.' He doesn't look up, and his indifference makes me brave. I couldn't have said this out loud to my regular GP. 'Things that don't seem to be there.'

'Hmm?' The doctor frowns up at me, as though I've only said it to annoy him. 'Things?'

'People.'

'What makes you think they're not there?'

'Other people don't see them.'

'You've asked them?' But before I can answer, he's checking my records on the computer. 'Georgia Sage, DOB 7 April 1986?'

I try not to flinch. For my NHS records, I had to keep my real birthday. Everyone else thinks I was born in November.

'That's me.'

'Have you had a fever?'

'No.'

He reaches across the desk with a claw-like hand and touches my forehead to check for himself.

'Are you using drugs? Heroin? Legal highs?'

'No.'

'How many units of alcohol do you drink a week?'

I try to remember how many I am supposed to.

'Is it twenty-one? I'm not a heavy drinker anyway.'

'It's fourteen. In a woman of your age, with no known medical conditions, drugs or alcohol abuse are the most likely cause of hallucinations. Unless there are other symptoms? Dizziness, vertigo, the shakes?'

I tick them off in my head.

'No. I feel normal. Tired but normal.' I take a breath. 'I'm afraid I might be going mad. Or getting dementia. Or Parkinson's.'

There's a moment of relief after the words leave my mouth: the release of sharing your worst fears.

But the doctor tuts.

'Diagnosis by Dr Google, I suppose? Look, you're clearly a healthy young woman. Stress, is it? Or burning the midnight oil?'

I stare at him.

'This clinic isn't equipped for mental health issues. You're registered with a GP. Make an appointment to see her?'

I feel attacked.

'And what would she do differently?'

The doctor sighs. 'Refer you for CBT. Or possibly an MRI, though personally, I think that would be a waste of NHS resources.'

'Could I get an MRI privately, to rule anything out? I have the money.'

He sighs again and reaches for a sticky note decorated with a drug company logo, to write down the name of a hospital.

'This place does them. Over in Hove. But it'll cost thousands and honestly, you're wasting your cash. Get early nights and cut back on the sauce. That should do it.'

He hands me the note, plus a leaflet, and presses the button for his next patient.

It's only when I'm back on Queen's Road that I realise the leaflet lists local addiction services. But my irritation gives way to a kind of relief. He's right: I am young, well, unaddicted. A doctor wouldn't let me walk away if he thought I had something serious.

I *will* book an MRI, to put my mind at rest. At least my inheritance means I can afford to do that. But I'm probably *physically* OK. Mentally? The jury's out.

Still, I keep my head down as I walk home, so I don't risk seeing the boy who isn't there.

20

Today the defence case begins, and Cruella calls the footballer. Sam Carr is immaculately dressed, and as he steps into the witness box, he reminds me of a bridegroom waiting at the altar.

'Perhaps you'd begin by telling us why you stayed at the hotel on that weekend?'

We hold our breath until he speaks. Like the girl, he'll have been well prepared for this.

'We were there for training.' Carr is known for his gruff voice, but these first words are softer. I wonder if he's reciting a script. 'We always go there. Time away from the ground, helps with teamwork.'

'With bonding?'

'Yeah. Hotel's very private, so there's no hassle from paparazzi.'

He glares at the press bench: is that fear, or scorn? I'd guess it's both. We have the power to make or break him, and he doesn't like that.

'So, that was your plan on the night in question?'

'Just chilling. We were knackered from training, plus there'd been team talk, tactics. My brain was full of it. We had a swim, to unwind.'

'And was that when you first saw Miss Tranter?'

Carr sighs. 'Don't remember. There were some girls splashing about in the spa pool. Giggling, you know. But I didn't take much notice. Wasn't what we were there for.'

'When did that change?'

The footballer half smiles. I hadn't understood before why he was such a pin-up. But momentarily, he's film-star handsome.

'They recognised us.'

'The young women?'

He nods.

'And this happens often?'

He can't help himself: he smirks.

'Yeah.'

I *want* him to go to jail. To see the smirk disappear – rapists and baby-killers are never allowed to feel safe. Even ones as charming as the footballer.

Did Daniel Fielding suffer for his crimes? I bet he had his share of revenge beatings.

'And when you said, *they recognised us*, did you mean all of you?'

'Me, I guess. Dunno why.' He turns to the jury, as though he's sharing a joke. 'Maybe because I'm *tall*.'

Cruella frowns. She doesn't want her client to come across as too full of himself.

'Every young man might dream of being followed by pretty girls. But, are there *negatives* to your fame?'

'Sure.' Carr smiles laddishly at the jurors. 'Honey traps. Girls who pretend to like you, but really they want the cheque they'd get for selling their story. Bunny boilers.'

'Are you currently in a relationship?'

'No. I'm too busy. I won't lie, there's been the odd girl, but I've always been sensible. Behaved myself.' He raises his hands in a gesture of bafflement. 'But look where *that* got me.'

I look at the jury, hoping they're seeing through him. I can't tell . . .

'Behaved yourself. What does that mean?'

'Some lads forget that we're never off duty. Lose control. Not just with women, but with drugs. Gambling.' He scoffs.

'But not you?'

'I'm a brand. I built that. Sure, the pundits take the pi— the mickey, call me a control freak, on the pitch, and off. But I'm looking after number one.'

Cruella nods. 'And this self-control extends to relationships?'

'Yeah. This is why this is all such bullshit.' For the first time, Carr's voice reverts to a threatening growl, as his frustration spills over. 'Like . . . Why *would* I make a girl do anything she didn't want? I know this is gonna sound arrogant but I don't need to force anyone to come to bed with me. I could go out any night and . . . Not because I'm God's gift. But right now, I got money, I'm in the magazines. Women can't get enough of that.'

So he is a pig, as well as a rapist. I sneak a glance at the gallery. No Charlie. I'm relieved – I don't want him to hear this kind of bullshit.

OK. Stop that right there.

He can't hear it because he's not real.

Cruella nods, as though Carr has just described something deeply traumatic in his past, rather than stated how rich and desirable he is.

'And that makes you vulnerable?'

'It . . . Yes. I'm not complaining about my life. But this? The stuff I'm accused of? This is not how it was. Not in a million years.'

* * *

I draw him handsome.

Too handsome.

Not that the footballer would ever see the difference. I wouldn't be surprised if his 'people' get in touch with me after this goes on air, to ask to buy my sketch.

Carr won't realise I've puffed him up, made his stance over-bearing, almost threatening, in the dock. His tan is amplified, a shade too tangerine. Still a good likeness, but with just enough arrogance to make you doubt his pleas of innocence that Neena will parrot in her piece to camera.

'Hope that's OK,' I say, handing her the sketch outside Manny's.

She holds up the drawing.

'Better than OK. This is great, Georgia. You're back on form! Fancy a drink to celebrate?'

I think about what the walk-in centre GP said about drinking. 'Not tonight.'

'Don't tell me. Vegan, tantric-sex evening class, or whatever the funky people are doing in Brighton these days?'

I nod. 'Something like that. See you in the morning.'

Walking home along the blustery seafront, my phone rings.

Jim Fielding Mobile

I cross my fingers as I answer, a silly childhood habit I've never lost.

'Georgia, I can hear the sea!' He sounds jovial.

'Yes, I'm right next to it.' I wait.

'I'm probably crazy for doing this,' he says, and I let my hopes soar like the gulls, 'because I'm an ugly old bugger. But I'm in.'

'That's fantastic.'

And it is, though I ignore the way my stomach lurches as I imagine going west again. Nerves, that's all. This commission is a big deal.

'Yeah, well, what you said made sense, kind of. A way to mark the end of one era, and the start of a new one.'

'That's a great way of seeing it.' I try not to scare him off by seeming too keen. 'When could we start, do you think?'

'No time like the present. Do you have any plans for the weekend?'

21

It took me years to understand the rituals, the costumes, the pomp of the courtroom.

But now I get it. The crimes we commit against each other are raw and savage. The ermine and the oak contain that savagery.

As Oli prepares to cross-examine the footballer, I want him to win. Cases don't get to this stage unless the evidence is strong.

'Would you describe yourself as spoiled?' Oli asks Carr, without preamble.

'I'm well off. But I've worked for that.'

'You don't have to delay gratification very often, do you? Whatever you see, you can have.'

Cruella stands up, rolling her eyes.

'This isn't a real question, is it, Your Honour.'

The judge agrees. I glance at Oli. When we lived together, we kept a Chinese wall when I was sketching a case where he was prosecuting. His idea. So I wouldn't be swayed to see the defendant as guilty.

He never knew I see *everyone* as guilty, deep down. He never had an inkling about why I do this job, even though he knows me better than anyone else alive.

Oli addresses the witness box.

'The point I want to make is about your life, and your expectations. Can you remember the last time anyone said no to you?'

Carr scowls, before regaining control and settling his features into that expression of injured innocence.

'Money doesn't buy everything. I still need to work hard. Do my training. I can't pay someone else to get up at the crack of dawn. Or stand here, with my whole life on the line.'

I try to gauge how that goes down with the jury. They're giving nothing away, their faces blank. But I sense Oli's frustration, as though there's something about this case that he can't bring up in court.

'You didn't answer my question.'

Carr shrugs.

'What was it again?'

'I asked if you could remember the last time anyone said no to you. I wonder whether the fact you can't suggests you wouldn't hear it if they did.'

Cruella is on her feet but Oli concedes before she speaks.

'Withdrawn.' But I can tell from the little flick of his wrist that he feels the jury got the point he was trying to make. 'Let us move on to the first time you exchanged words with Miss Tranter.'

At the break, I corner Oli near the toilets.

'What aren't you allowed to say about the handsome sportsman?'

'Careful, Georgie. Hopefully, it'll all come out when he's locked up.'

'He's got previous? There's nothing in the press cuttings. Not so much as a kiss and tell.'

Oli shakes his head. 'You know I can't—'

'OK. I won't push it. But I reckon you're doing all right this morning.'

He nods. 'Hope so. Oh, have you heard any more about the book?'

'Yeah. Fielding says he's going to do it. I'm going there for the first sitting with him tomorrow.'

'I was actually hoping he'd have turned it down. It's a murky old place. I don't like the thought of you getting tangled up in it.'

My hackles rise.

'I'm a grown-up now.'

'You always were. But what if I could think of another case, a better one?'

'It's already set up. Unless you can give me a stronger reason—'

Neena turns the corner, on her way to the ladies'.

'No fraternisation, you two. If the judge doesn't give you a bollocking, Imogen might. Pregnant women have hormones you shouldn't mess with, Oliver.'

Oli nods. 'Don't I know it?'

And he's gone before I can ask him what exactly it is that's troubling him about Ashdean.

22

It takes me five hours to drive to the forest, even though I set out first thing on Saturday. As soon as the West Country landscape becomes familiar, I switch on the most raucous music I can find, to leave no room in my head for memories – or hallucinations.

Instead, I think about the court case, and yesterday's evidence. Will the jury convict Sam Carr?

If I didn't know how justice works – and how hard it is to get a rape case to court at all – maybe I would be swayed by Cruella's innuendo. Yesterday she outlined the evidence she has in store next week: CCTV from the hotel's public areas, showing Julie Tranter drunkenly bashing into objets d'art, explaining away the external bruises. And a new medical expert to dismiss the internal injuries too.

Whatever happens, that young woman will never be the same. Something shifts inside when you become a victim. You realise the idea that we have any control over our lives is an illusion.

I'll never know *why* my father killed Pip and Mum, and spared me. But I do remember the instant I realised he was changing from my familiar, overworked dad, into a man full of anger.

It was a Sunday, a fortnight after Christmas. Abi Murray had been given a proper make-up set and had brought it round to my house for us to do each other over. The Spice Girls were being interviewed on the radio, and Abi was getting frustrated with me because I couldn't draw the kohl eyeliner on straight.

'I look like a badger. Let me show you how to do it, you nana.'

She held the mirror up in front of both our faces, and with her other hand, she guided mine along the curve of her lashes, so it made a neater stripe. Instantly, she looked five years older, or at least, she did to me.

'. . . you nag and you nag and I can't stand it anymore! You've no idea what I'm doing to keep on top of everything.'

Dad's voice but not as I'd ever heard it before, coming from their bedroom, the room next to mine. I heard my mother murmur something soothing back.

'They're blaming me, Deb. But all you care about is whether I'm home in time for your lousy meals, or whether I help the kids with their stupid homework. Don't you get it? This is trouble.'

My eyes narrowed in the mirror's reflection, and so did Abi's.

She blinked, reached for a brush, began to smudge the liner up across her lid.

'And this is how you turn it into a smoky eye,' she said. 'Very sophisticated. You try.'

On the other side of the wall, Mum's tone was pleading. I caught odd phrases.

'. . . look for something else. We can manage while . . .'

'I have to fight. See! You have no idea. No *fucking idea at all.*'

I dropped the brush. Dad never swore. I heard him stomp down the stairs, and out of the house, slamming the front door.

Abi picked the brush up and continued to smudge the black pencil, ignoring the sound of my mother's almost muffled sobs.

'Abi, I—'

'Shh. My parents argue. Everyone's parents do,' she said, placing the brushes back in their little plastic slots. 'It's better than divorce, though, right?'

Except my parents had never rowed before. Ours was a house where soft-soled slippers were worn indoors. Doors were never slammed, and no one but Pip ever raised their voice.

But after that day, a dam burst. My father's anger filled every space. I stopped bringing anyone home, and Pip did the same thing. Even Marmite began to whine and do a pitiful half-crouch whenever my dad passed his bed on the kitchen floor . . .

'Travel update now, and there's been an accident on the M5 between junction 11a and 12, causing tailbacks . . .'

I sigh: so much for distracting myself. I need to think about this afternoon, how to make it work. How to show Maureen and those snobby BBC bastards that I can create something worthwhile . . .

I run through what Jim told me when we first met: how he has no one he talks to about what happened to him. That's why he said yes, I'm sure of it. Well, I get it: the survivor's guilt; the fight not to relive the same events over and over, when there's nothing that can be changed.

And if he wants to use me as an unpaid counsellor, that's OK. Because I am using him too.

I'm on the outskirts of the forest at last. What did Oli call it? *Murky.*

Yet today Ashdean feels anything but murky. There's a brochure-blue sky above the spiky forest that surrounds the town. It feels less oppressive than the first time I came, as though someone has applied the cheeriest Instagram filter to every street.

I slow down as I approach the White House. The plastered walls reflect the sun relentlessly as I approach, blinding me momentarily. I park up on the grassy bank, and unload my easel, a canvas, pencils. No paint, not yet, though I have a box full of new, unopened oils in my suitcase. I haven't used oils since I was a child, but the publisher insisted in the end, for the sake of variety. I try not to think about the smell, but even the thought of it makes me nauseous . . .

The steel bolts retract noisily before I've reached the gate: Jim must have been watching me approach. He's waiting for me on the other side, dressed in jeans and a checked, cobalt-blue shirt with short sleeves that reveal two large tattoos. A crimson snake weaves around his right arm, while deep-green leaves grow around the left.

'Welcome back, Georgia. You like my ink?' he asks. 'My own design, a forest tattoo for a forest boy. Cost me a fortune and hurt like stink, but they cover up the ones I got in the young offender institution.'

Is this his first admission? At art school a tutor told us that portrait sittings often take on the air of a confessional:

'And like a priest, you must keep their secrets, except in the painting itself.'

I ignore the mention of prison – it's nothing the neighbour hadn't told me already – and step a little closer to look at the details of his tattoo. It's a little blurry, definitely not the best work I've ever seen, but the branches and roots intertwine, like a forest in a children's storybook.

'I'll try to do them justice in my picture.'

Jim nods, as though I've passed a test by not asking him why he went inside. He clicks a remote and the gate closes behind me. I don't like being locked in and my heart pumps harder, but I make myself focus on Jim's pale-denim eyes, and then the scarred hands that carried two children to safety.

That's better.

'We're alone, in case you're wondering. Leah . . . still doesn't completely agree with the painting. She knows how important my privacy is to me. But I told her you're sound. That you won't screw me over.'

I smile. 'I'm here to paint your picture, that's all.'

23

We pass through the white kitchen and the vast living room, into a fully glazed corridor. There's a door, a solid hunk of blond wood broken only by a keyhole halfway down.

My heart speeds up a little as Jim unlocks it, but there's something about him that's reassuring.

'Welcome to my lair. After you.'

Instead of floor-to-ceiling windows, the room has cedar-clad walls, the only light coming from a pane in the roof. His office is large, dominated by his desk, a vast, black leather swivel chair and a tan couch. There's no other furniture, no family photos, not even a bookshelf.

'Take a seat. Coffee?'

I sit on the couch facing his desk, a lump of oak that's been varnished so it shines like water.

'Black, please.'

He pushes a cedar plank and a cupboard opens, with a kettle, tea and coffee on a tray, as though we're in a hotel. I look more closely at his things.

'You're the tidiest man I've ever met,' I say, as he busies himself making drinks.

'Is that a sure sign I'm a psychopath or something?'

'Why – are you?' I say.

'Do you always start interrogating the people you're going to paint before you even pick up a brush?'

I laugh. 'Do *you* always answer a question with another question?'

Before he turns away, I see a half-frown cross his face. He stirs my coffee, turns back and passes the cup over the desk. He sits down; his office chair is much higher up than the sofa, so I have no choice but to stare up, like a child before the head teacher.

'I'm more into actions than words. But then, you know all about me, don't you?'

'Sorry?'

His voice is suddenly serious.

'You can see through me, right? It's what you do, in your job. You've got X-ray vision, can see all our darkest secrets.'

I shake my head. 'People always think that. I'd be worth billions if I could. The Human Lie Detector. But I do believe art can reveal more than a photo.'

'Should I be worried, Georgia?'

'Not if your conscience is clear.'

He stares at me. I break the gaze first, unsettled by his intensity. The room feels smaller, as though the walls are moving in.

'So is this the nerve centre of Fielding Construction?'

'I have an office in town, they handle the cab business there too. Though the *really* important stuff is either in here' – he taps his head – 'or behind these walls.' He pushes against another section of the wall, and it slides open to reveal dozens of folders. 'It's why I thought you might like to paint me in here.'

I flinch. It's a terrible setting. And the thought of being shut in here for hours on end turns my stomach.

'Maybe.'

'Or we can move the furniture around?'

'This is quite a . . . dominant space. Not much light. And all the wood panelling might make you look like you're posing in a sauna or something!'

He doesn't smile.

Shit.

It's not like the background even matters. What matters is making him so comfortable he can reveal himself.

'So where would you suggest?'

Colder, now, the chumminess gone as suddenly as the sun behind a cloud. This man is not used to people disagreeing with him.

'Is there somewhere that's more of a blank canvas? I didn't want to offend you, but for the picture, we want *you* to be the focus.'

'Not my cedar panelling?' The twinkle is back. He stands up. 'All right then. The atrium in the entrance hall enough of a blank canvas?'

I nod. 'That should work.'

'Good stuff. I paid a bloody bomb for the curtain walling, it'd be nice to see it immortalised for posterity.'

I set up in silence, and Jim Fielding watches me. *The artist at work.*

He sits in a brown leather armchair we've carried in from the living room. He chose this one specifically. It's slightly too small for him, so he looks . . . not fat, but uncontainable. I was going to point it out, but I think he already realises exactly how this will make him appear.

He smiles at me, as though he can read my thoughts.

'Better?'

'Yes, thanks, the light in here is really good.'

Though even in full sunshine, the details of his face elude me. Instead, it seems to be made up of angles and planes, like a Picasso made real. My pencil hovers over my sketchbook but doesn't quite make contact, as I prepare to make studies, imagine possible compositions.

'Always used to look young for my age, but now my misspent youth is showing. Will I be able to stick your painting in my attic so I'll stop getting old?'

I laugh. 'There's no attic here.'

'I loathe stairs.'

I think of his four-storey town house in Cherry Blossom Lane – the journeys he made up and down a burning stair-well as he tried to rescue his wife. The injuries he inflicted on himself, trying to open red-hot metal door handles, only to be beaten back by the flames.

'It's OK,' he says. 'You can ask me about that night. Get it over with. It's the reason you're here, after all.'

It feels too soon to be prying. But I may not get the chance again.

'I suppose I wonder what made you able to do what you did. I can't imagine being that brave myself.'

I know I'm not. I am a coward.

Jim looks at me steadily, and I tilt my head so I can get a clearer look into his eyes. For so long, I've searched the eyes of killers, rapists, abusers, looking for guilt. I'd like to see what goodness looks like.

But what I see is Daniel's eyes.

'I didn't think. Jodie and Charlie were in my care. How could I have told Emma if I'd let them die? Those kids were all she had.'

I remember the neighbour talking about the kids' father leaving. Emma and . . . Robert, that's her husband's name.

'But didn't you feel afraid as you went back inside?'

'Not at first. The fire didn't seem to be spreading that fast. The kids were too tiny to get themselves out and I thought my Tessa must be right behind me.' His injured hands turn into claws as though he's reliving it, grasping for something out of reach. 'But it was the smoke, see. She was unconscious by then. When I realised she wasn't coming out, I tried to get back in but the other neighbours dragged me away. I shouldn't have let them. For a very long time, I wished I'd died too.'

I let the space between the words grow, for him to fill, as I work.

'You know I lost my first wife too? My Sharon.'

I look up from the sketch pad; the page is already full of little studies.

'Yes.'

'Always knew I might lose her, right from when we first met. She was in the kids' home down in the town, and those places are pure evil . . .' He shakes his head. 'But we thought we could get past that. All the messed-up stuff from when we were growing up, we were gonna get right with our own kids. Whatever we did, whatever mistakes we made, they'd be loved.' He scoffs.

I sense that Jim doesn't want platitudes, so still I say nothing.

'I wasn't up to the job, was I? Failed two wives. Sharon jumped off a bridge right in front of me, and my Tessa died as I watched. Fuck knows why Leah wants to marry me when you look at what went before.'

Silence no longer seems enough.

'Jim. I'm so sorry.'

He stands up and leaves the hall. For a couple of minutes, I don't know whether I should pack up or go after him.

He returns with two glasses of water, and a small table to put them on.

'I don't know where that came from. Forget it.'

I look into his eyes. The blue has blurred, making them hard to read.

'My friend who works for the BBC says sometimes it's only possible to be honest with a stranger.'

He's about to say something else, when a clock chimes somewhere else in the house. He looks at his watch, a silver Rolex.

'Leah will be back in ten minutes and it's best if you're gone well before then. Just to keep the peace. I'm not scared of much, but my fiancée is a force of nature.'

'A few more poses would be great in the time we have left.'

'How does this work for you?'

He places his hands on the arms of his chair and leans back. I think he's acting, but I understand why.

'Very powerful. The godfather.'

He grunts. 'The rumour mill in this town at work already, is it?'

'No, I—'

'I know the gossip. Maybe I even start the odd rumour myself. Does no harm if people think you're a hard nut, does it?'

'I honestly haven't heard anything.' It's only a small lie, and the nosy neighbour's admission she had a crush on the teenage Jim hardly counts. 'Except what you told me yourself about being in jail.'

'Young offender institution. Not proper jail. Joyriding, and a few boxes of stolen fags they found in the boot of the car. Not mine. I didn't even smoke, not then. But I took the blame for a mate. No sense both of us serving time.' He laughs humour-lessly. 'Toughened me up. And that reputation's made life a lot easier. But I'm a pussycat compared to Leah. And she's due back in five minutes. That's your warning.'

'Understood. One last sketch.'

I turn the page to make a hurried first attempt at a composi-tion that might work for the final painting. My hand trembles, half-afraid of making the mark on the page, committing myself to the direction this painting will take, and the story it will tell.

I narrow my eyes, take in the shape of him, his head, his body in the space, as my art teacher first taught me to do. The pencil meets the paper. His shape dominating the space, as heroes – and villains – always should.

24

Outside, late afternoon smells of sharp sap and crushed leaves. My body feels tight and my mind full. I need to stretch my legs before the long drive home.

As I walk, I replay the last couple of hours. The Jim in the photograph, the Jim I drew in court, they're both two-dimensional. Can I capture all the contradictions – his guilt *and* his heroism, his hard-man reputation alongside the vulnerability?

Am I good enough?

My talent used to be the only thing I was sure of, but now it seems elusive.

The town is not quite deserted – a few women cross the square, bags of shopping weighing them down, and two drivers lean against their cabs at the taxi rank, one vaping, one smoking a roll-up. Maybe it's my imagination, but there's something predatory about the way they track me with their eyes.

I pass a small supermarket and a laundrette belching out heat and the itchy smell of soap powder. The road slopes downwards, towards the modern part of town, where Jim lived, and Tessa died.

Shit.

Charlie – or at least, a boy in red – is skipping ahead, in the opposite direction. There is nothing ghostly about this kid. I follow him, veering right, down an alleyway sandwiching together two strips of workers' cottages. The yards are mean and dark, space for no more than bikes and washing lines. A few spindly weeds grow in the shadows.

I've lost sight of him.

But when I get to the end of the alley, there's a different surprise: a green, large as a cricket field, and on the other side, an enormous, double-fronted Victorian house, stone-built, the sunshine giving it a spectral glow.

Now I see the high fence that surrounds it, topped with rusting barbed wire the colour of dried blood. Beyond the wire, the front garden has given up the fight against nature, with top-heavy plants that would reach my shoulder blades.

A peeling sign mounted on the fence reads:

DEVELOPMENT OPPORTUNITY: FORMER CHILDREN'S RESIDENTIAL HOME, 12+ BEDROOMS, PARKING, EXTENSIVE GROUNDS, VIEWS TO VILLAGE GREEN & FOREST SUITABLE FOR CONVERSION TO HOTEL OR BUSINESS HEADQUARTERS. POA

Is this the children's home where Jim's wife had lived?

As I walk the perimeter, I recognise the tell-tale signs of an institution. Blackened notices remind residents what's forbidden: ball games, smoking, noise after 7 p.m. RESPECT YOUR NEIGH-BOURS, one sign bosses in block capitals, as though the children here had less right to respect than everyone else.

I keep walking. There's a second sign as I face the front of the building. The same ageing advertisement, but a much newer board nailed over the top.

COPSE VIEW ACQUIRED FOR REDEVELOPMENT BY FIELDING CONSTRUCTION: NEW HOMES COMING AUTUMN 2018

Fielding Construction? I'm pretty sure that is Jim's firm. But why would he get involved here? *Those places are pure evil.* That's what he said.

I suppose he must be able to separate personal trauma from business decisions. But even so ... I hadn't realised until the sitting that he'd been there when his wife jumped to her death.

I shiver. Time to go.

I follow the fence round, back towards the sunshine. The grounds are huge: a summer house that must have been built when the mansion was, crumbles at the end of the garden. Next to it, there's an ugly modern garage block.

I see a flash of orange in the overgrown grass. A deflated netball. When I was in care – only for a fortnight – the thump of a ball against the wall of my room had seemed like a countdown. But I had no idea what would come next.

After I ran away from my grandad's, the social workers put me in the residential home as a stopgap, while they looked for a permanent placement. It wasn't like this place – the building was modern, the inside painted in pop-art colours – yet somehow it had the same abandoned air.

I remember sitting on a tartan-duveted bed, the door propped open, the care workers discussing my 'risk status' in the corridor. It was a couple of days after the funeral. I felt as though I'd been scoured out with wire wool, and all that remained was a girl who looked the same but had nothing left but bone and sinew, barely held together by skin.

The other kids tried to rile me on the first day, because that was the game with newcomers, but I didn't respond to their teases, kicks, a half-hearted punch. They nicknamed me *Suzombie.*

'You're a chicken!'

'Am not!'

For a moment, I think I am back there.

'You fucking are. Go on, it's not really dangerous, they just *say* that to keep people out.'

The voices are young, and they're coming from inside. I follow the sounds until I spot a small tear in the metal fence, barely big enough for a dog to squeeze through.

'There's a bloody great hole in the floor. Look!'

'Jump over it.'

'Goes all the way downstairs, see. I'm dizzy looking through it.'

'Don't look, then. You'll be all right, just—'

Boards creak a warning. Something heavy falls, followed by a gentler rain of rubble or plaster.

'Shit, what have you done?'

'You told me to jump. What the fuck am I meant to do now?'

I hear pain in the child's voice. I think it's a girl but I can't be sure.

I try to squeeze through the gap in the fence, but the metal spike catches my T-shirt, scratches the top of my arm. Tiny beads of blood surface on my skin.

'Oi. Who's in there?' My own voice sounds as reedy as the children's. I try again. 'Are you OK? Do I need to call an ambulance?'

For a few seconds, I hear nothing. I go towards the building. More rubble falls, followed by a muffled shriek. I hold my breath.

They burst through the rear fire door, dark hoodies sprinkled with ghost-grey plaster, like victims of an earthquake. Two of them. They clock me, and race towards the hole in the fence, tearing at the metal mesh, but I'm behind them, and manage to catch one by the sleeve.

'What the hell are you thinking? It's dangerous in there.'

The kid's hood comes off as he – no, *she* – tries to pull away: the other is already long gone.

'Get your dirty hands off me,' she says, her words spitting out, eyes defiant. The dust has turned her black hair grey.

'You could have been killed!'

She wrestles with me.

'Yeah, well, I bet there's tonnes of bodies in that shithole.'

'What?'

The girl sees her chance and pulls away, leaving the hoodie behind in my hands, like she's shed a skin.

'You're a dirty paedo too!' she calls back, as soon as she's far enough away to realise I'm not going to run after her.

My breathing is rapid from the tussle.

I bet there's tonnes of bodies in that shithole.

Institutions always attract wild theories, scary stories of bogeymen and wicked crones. But then again, I've sketched two cases involving abuse rings in children's homes: I know what can go on.

I scan the field. No one is watching.

I scramble across nettles and thistles and bits of fallen masonry. This building hasn't been occupied in years, even though it seems like a prime redevelopment opportunity. Why has Jim waited so long?

I pull open the fire door and step into the musty building. When the door closes behind me, I try to keep calm. Now I smell something rotten: as my eyes adjust to the darkness, I see the stripped carcass of a fox or a dog on the cracked white floor tiles. Did it seek shelter and get trapped?

The door immediately to my right leads to a row of toilets; a cracked basin sits upended on the floor, tall as a gravestone. There is one sign for Females but none for Males – perhaps the home was girls-only.

On the left, the door sign reads Laundry, and I can see a hulking tumble drier through the frosted glass. Ahead, the grandest of staircases: this building had another, fancier life before it became a children's home.

I step carefully, half-expecting the ceiling to come down on top of me.

Light comes through holes in the roof, highlighting the black-and-white mosaic floor. I reach out for the banister. My hand dislodges a layer of dust so thick it makes me cough, but underneath the wood is smooth.

When the tiles stop, the staircase starts. But there are only a few steps before huge gaps appear in the wood, the treads eaten away by woodworm, only darkness beneath. I can't go any further.

I glance up. A combination of old wallpaper and graffiti covers the wall on the half-landing. The writing is almost unintelligible, layers on top of layers. I try to unscramble what people have painted here. There are tags, and shapes that might be faces or something cruder. I scan the wall, looking for recognisable names or words. For a moment, I think that the loops in the corner seem to read CHARLIE, but when I lean a little heavier on the banister it creaks ominously.

Enough. I retrace my steps back outside. I fold the girl's hoodie, and lay it next to the hole in the fence. Perhaps she will come back for it.

Once I'm through the barbed wire, I look back at the building. Whatever happened here, it's a good thing most of these places have closed down. Children do not belong in institutions; even in the best, the environment encourages petty cruelties. And in the worst . . .

As I return to the car, past the fried-chicken shop and the boarded-up bank, I feel conspicuous. Even as the sun beats down, I find I can't stop shivering.

25

It's early evening by the time I arrive back on the outskirts of Brighton – the last part of the journey stop-start, as the week-enders queue to get to the coast.

I realise I've left my phone off, and when I turn it back on, a flurry of texts light up my screen.

Oli's wife has gone into labour.

Each round-robin message is more thrilling than the last.

First, **at the hospital, we think it's started a bit early.**

An hour or so later, **our baby already misbehaving by being breech, so Imogen is being prepped for theatre for a caesarean.**

In the next one, Oli explains he's going into theatre with her so will turn his phone off, and if there's no news, that's nothing to worry about.

And after that, nothing. I drop off the hire car, and instead of going straight home, I head for the beach. The tide is out, and the beach is still packed: a balmy evening that makes you want to linger. As I walk, dodging the kids playing and the mums with buggies, I cross-examine myself as rigorously as any barrister.

It could have been me, having Oli's baby.

Should it have been?

It's the main reason I broke off our engagement, or at least the reason I gave. Oli has always wanted to be a parent. I never felt that way.

Actually that's a lie. When I was a *very* little girl, I pushed a pram and nursed a doll which gobbled water from a bottle and emptied it out the other end. Pip's arrival showed me real babies were a lot messier and harder to soothe, but I loved to help bathe him, or rock him to sleep.

'I'm his big mum and you're his little one,' my mother would say.

I assumed one day I'd have my own family. Until I lost two-thirds of the one I had in a single afternoon.

Oli's fortieth birthday and my impending thirtieth brought the issue to a head, with our married friends dropping less and less subtle hints about getting on with it, 'while Oli can still play football without his knees giving out.' Then Oli's mum got cancer, and even after she recovered, he wanted to get on with producing the grandchild she was looking forward to.

I couldn't do it.

Everyone told me to think it through. Neena, who'd gone through three rounds of IVF and nine circles of hell to have the twins, was the most bolshie.

'Even if you haven't heard it yet, your biological clock will start ticking in the next couple of years, George. And you'll regret it if you let Oli go. He is *perfect* father material.'

'There's more to a relationship than kids.'

'Sure, if both of you feel the same way. But Oli actually cooed at my twins last week even though they smelled like farmyard animals and were producing litres of Day-Glo snot. He's broody. And if you can't give him what he wants, it's only fair to let him find someone who will.'

Three years ago now, but my biological clock is still on silent. I either never had the maternal instinct, or what my father did extinguished it.

I stop and stare out to sea. Did my father also pass madness on to me? There was something inside my dad that made two acts of violence possible. Or inevitable, even. That's the sort of thing you can't see in an MRI. It could be lying dormant in me?

I was right not to take the risk of having kids: my visions could be yet another sign of bad blood.

The weekenders are following the tide as it shrinks back, and the setting sun turns the pebbles a rich scarlet.

My phone buzzes in my pocket. Oli.

A girl. A beautiful girl with a full head of dark hair, 7lb 8oz, don't ask me what it is in metric. Imogen is a star, and mother and daughter are doing well. More than can be said for me. Am a bloody wreck.

Tears fill my eyes as I imagine Oli's face. I look up at the sunset and the colours take my breath away. I want to capture it tonight, in a painting for his newborn: her first sunset. I don't have to have had Oli's child myself to feel happy for him.

Better to have loved and lost? Maybe. But I can't risk it again.

26

My flat feels stuffy and stale when I let myself in, so I open up the shutters, make coffee, and sit in my armchair, bathed in the magenta afternoon light. There's two days' post on my lap to sort through, mostly junk: pizza flyers, letting agent ads . . .

The envelope is at the bottom of the pile: pale pink, with my name handwritten on the front in familiar block capitals. My heart speeds up.

Already?

I slip my finger under the corner of the envelope and tear it from end to end.

It's a birthday card, a photograph of two hairy pot-bellied pigs, rolling in rain in a filthy sty.

It's been signed by Marion and Trevor, with a row of kisses. And on the left-hand side of the card, there's a longer note from Marion. Her careful handwriting has shrunk with age, making it harder to read. She must be almost seventy by now. Every time I get her news, I fear something might have happened to one of them. I feel the usual dread as I go to the window, hold the card to catch the last of the sunlight.

Dear Georgia,

We never know whether to send a card. The last thing we want to do is remind you of bad times, but Suzanne was the person we first met and learned to love, so we still want to celebrate her birthday.

Guilt fills me. When I left their care for the anonymity of art school in London, I didn't think how much it'd hurt them. And by the time I realised, it felt far too late to reach out again. I send a Christmas card every year, with brief, perky headlines about my life.

> *I hope life down by the seaside is treating you well. I've seen a few of your incredible drawings lately. You always had a talent and even though we doubted your path a little, perhaps your work helps you deal with what happened.*
>
> *All is well here - we have the aches and pains of advancing age, but compared to many, we're lucky. We've had a lovely young man staying with us recently, the same age as you were when you first came to us. He's on track again. There's something about the farm that really does seem to heal.*

I smile. Marion always writes as though it's the place that is magic. In reality, it's her and Trevor who mend broken children.

> *There is one thing. We had a letter from the prison, requesting that we pass on the message that your father has expressed a wish to get in contact.*

I grip the card, wishing I could unread those words.

Why now?

My father has been out of my life for more years than he was in it. I never sought him out, and he has never made any effort to explain what he did, or why, other than the pathetic lies he told the police in the hospital.

So what can have changed – is he sick, dying? And if he is, am I supposed to care?

We'd never tell you what to do, you know that. But Ms Penney, who sent the letter, went to some trouble to track us down. Her email is h.penney@hmpservice. gov.uk

We understand why you keep us at a distance, sweetheart – we must be a reminder of painful times. But never forget there will always be a bed and a hug for you here if you need either. We are proud of the wonderful person you became.

With all our love,

M&T

Wonderful person? Hardly. Alone, a failure at everything except my work, and even that seems a struggle now.

I close the card. Every year the urge to pick up the phone to them is almost irresistible. I remember their number and I know that within seconds of dialling it, I could be talking to the only two people in the world who have known me as both Suzanne and Georgia.

Yesterday was thirty-one years since I was born. I wonder how my parents felt about starting a family? They could never have imagined how it would end.

If my father dies, then the reason behind what he did to us all dies with him. But however he might have rationalised it in the years since, there can never be a reason good enough.

I won't email Ms Penney. I won't give my father anything. He doesn't deserve to be in my thoughts, not now, not ever.

27

On Monday the footballer trial witnesses are so minor that the BBC don't cover it – Oli's baby couldn't have timed her arrival better.

I get the train to London late afternoon, at Oli's insistence. He greets me at the door to Imogen's private room. His eyes are bright but tired. He hugs me wordlessly, then lets me inside.

The room is a jungle of extravagant contemporary bouquets, their scent so thick I feel the perfume catching in my lungs. Somewhere in a clearing is Imogen, nursing her baby.

'Georgia, meet Millie Victoria Priest, aged forty-nine hours and . . .' he checks his Patek Philippe, his dad's old watch, 'twelve minutes.'

'Oh, Imogen, congratulations!'

I lean over the bed to kiss her on the cheek. Her hair has been blow-dried, but her skin is free of make-up, possibly for the first time since puberty. The baby's face is tucked discreetly under an exquisite crocheted shawl as she suckles, so all I can see is the tiny body in a dove-grey sleepsuit.

'Thank you. She's a hungry little miss, but she won't be long.'

'And how are you?'

'I feel great. High as a kite.' She waves at the drip. 'They're going to stop the drugs tomorrow, apparently. That's why we've tried to get everyone to visit today, while I am still on top form.'

There's no edge between us: Imogen came along a very decorous eleven months after I left Oli, and we're very different creatures. I've done what I can to paint over my past, but the tells of my middle-class upbringing reveal themselves now and then. Imogen is properly posh, a former chalet girl who can ski, ride and cook. The girl Oli should have fallen for all along.

He's behind me, watching his wife and daughter. I hand him a box of organic chocolate truffles and a knitted peach-coloured rabbit from a little shop in the Lanes. The sunset painting I started on Saturday isn't finished yet; I want it to be perfect.

'Thank God you didn't bring flowers, I feel like we're in Kew Gardens,' he says, gently touching the smile stitched onto the rabbit's face. 'Still can't quite believe it. We're parents. We're supposed to know what we're doing.'

Imogen laughs softly, so as not to disturb the baby.

'Thank goodness we have the maternity nurse or I'd be terrified of going home. Ah. I think Miss Millie might have finished for now.'

I look away while she rearranges herself. She doesn't need the nurse, not really – she has an air of utter capability. And boarding school doesn't seem to have messed with her head, as it did a little bit with Oli. Instead, I saw the very first time I met her that she radiates a very practical kind of love.

'Oh . . .'

It comes from Oli, a sigh and a benediction in one.

The baby faces me. The first thing I notice is her dark hair, lush and surprising. Her face seems indistinct – her features still unformed – so I step closer, leaning in. Babies aren't often beautiful, but this one is. Her lips form a perfect Cupid's bow, and her eyes are crescent moons.

Déjà vu.

'Hello, little Millie,' I say, feeling silly. I lost the art of talking to children a long time ago. 'Welcome to the world.'

Her arms rise towards me, hands open as though she wants to take hold of mine. She opens her eyes. They're almost black. I had expected innocence, perhaps the only time in life we have that quality.

But instead, they're incredibly knowing, and even though it's impossible, it's as if I've seen them before.

Pip.

My hands are tingling. My breath stops. A sparkling blackness fills my vision.

'Georgia. Georgia?'

Oli's voice. The scent of flowers, and disinfectant. Fingers digging into my shoulders, like tent pegs, the only things holding me up.

'It's all right. Sit down for a bit.'

I feel the edges of a chair against the back of my legs, my knees folding as I sit.

'I thought you were going to faint,' Oli's saying. 'It is terribly hot in here. But there are no bloody windows to open.'

I don't feel hot. My limbs tingle and my head throbs.

'I'm so sorry. What an idiot.'

'It's absolutely fine,' Imogen says, smiling her best head girl smile.

Millie is still watching me with those knowing eyes. It's good that I'm seated now because I'm experiencing it again: the sensation of being back in the moment when I first saw Pip in hospital.

* * *

It was very different from this: my mother in a ward with five other women, the babies in plastic moulded cribs, a smell of tea and boiled veg. No flowers, too big an infection risk. Instead, balloons and teddies and huge padded cards flanked each bed, the women competing to prove how much her new baby was loved. As if it would protect them in their future lives.

Mum had tried to cover her exhaustion with make-up, but it looked orange in the artificial light.

'Come here, Suzanne. Do you want to hold your baby brother?'

I was scared of holding him wrong, but Mum was insistent. As she passed the bundle to me, she winced from some unspoken injury. I took the baby then, to make her better.

He was heavier than I expected. The woollen blanket was rough against my arms and the baby scowled, skin deep pink, as though he'd been sunbathing.

'He's called Phillip,' my father said, and I thought it seemed too grown-up for this small person. Phillip was a name for men, not children.

'Pip,' Mum said. 'For now, we'll call him Pip.'

That was when he opened his eyes. Of course, he couldn't have recognised his name, though later I wondered if Mum had been calling him that when he was still in the womb, in those moments when I'd caught her stroking her belly, and whispering to herself.

'You're his big sister,' Mum said. 'It's up to you to look after him.'

Those big, newborn eyes locked onto mine: huge black pupils, ringed with a strange, slate blue. Babies all have blue eyes, and they can't focus at that age, I know that now, but I felt he was making a pact with me, to look after each other.

And I broke it.

'You do look a bit ropey, Georgie,' Oli is saying. 'Have you eaten? The food here is very good. Or we can share some fizz?'

I blink, to send the memories of Pip away, so they don't contaminate this room, this new life.

'Another time,' I say. 'I haven't been sleeping brilliantly. I ought to go, in case I'm coming down with something.'

That's enough to make Oli recoil slightly.

'Ah. Oh, yes. That's a point. Will you be OK to get home? Reception can call you a cab to Victoria.'

'The walk will do me good. Imogen, I'm sorry. She really is a beauty. And lucky, too. I can't imagine two better parents.'

She laughs. 'Let's see about that in a few weeks' time. Thanks for coming. We hope you'll be a big part of her life.'

I blow them both a kiss as I leave the room. Oli follows me into the corridor, but stays at arm's length.

'I wasn't sure whether to mention it, especially here, but . . . I heard something on the grapevine just before Imogen came in. I'd made a couple of calls when you got the book commission, and a mate sent me a text. About Daniel Fielding.'

The incongruity makes me light-headed again.

'What?'

'He's in the prison hospital. He . . . Well, he tried to kill himself. Nearly bled out before they found him. But he's going to make it.'

Cadmium red, sprayed across cold tiles.

I shake my head, banish the image.

'You thought he might have been paroled by now.'

'Couple of months to go, it turns out.' Oli sighs.

'What – he spent thirteen years inside, but waited until now to slit his wrists? It doesn't make any sense.'

Oli reaches out to hold my hand.

'Look, don't dwell on it. I only told you because of the portrait thing. In case it comes up when you see Jim.'

'Unlikely. Daniel seems to be the one topic that's off-limits.'

'Georgie, are you sure . . .?' He shakes his head. 'Forget it. On to happier things. We want you to be a part of our Millie's life. Maybe even . . . be her godmother.' He blinks. 'Shit. I wasn't meant to tell you. Imogen will kill me. When she asks you, act surprised, all right?'

Oh, how I'd love to be that person: the cool godmother with the funky seaside flat and the arty job, and the quirky advice that contrasts with Oli and Imogen's conventional lives.

But I am *not* the person they think I am. I'm a liar, as unpredictable and damaged as Daniel Fielding.

'Thank you. That's an incredible thing to offer. I'll – I'll need to think about it.'

It'd hurt Oli too much if I said no now. I'll let time pass and then let it slide. I cannot be trusted with a child. Because I promised my mother I'd look after Pip, and my promises mean nothing at all.

28

'I feel really grubby.' Neena says on Wednesday night, after filing her report for the six o'clock bulletin.

It's been a day of innuendo and tetchiness, as Cruella brought in her medical expert witness to dispute the prosecution's. Oli's junior did the cross, while Oli takes two days of paternity leave, and he did a poor job. I sense the case is slipping away from the CPS.

Worst of all, Charlie is back.

He shouldn't be. Last night, I paid for an MRI which found nothing wrong with my brain. I thought it was over.

But when I looked up from taking notes this afternoon, there he was, sitting in an empty seat in the press bench. He stayed for several minutes, by which time my concentration was shot to pieces.

'It's not been the most spectacular advertisement for British justice,' I say to Neena.

'We need several large gin and tonics to wash away the bad taste. And don't you *dare* tell me you've got a prior appointment with your yogi.'

She's crossing the road towards the Lamb before I have the chance to argue. In Brighton's sea of gastropubs and vegan burger joints, the Lamb is unique. It reeks of coastal damp and is only kept afloat by coppers and lawyers and hacks.

'I envy you living down here, George,' Neena says, bringing the drinks over to our booth.

We're boxed in by shelves of old books and dusty ships in bottles that would sell for a fortune to gullible tourists in North Laine.

'It's great. Apart from the killer gulls and bin strikes and the rampaging hen parties with their giant inflatable cocks.'

Neena holds up her glass and we clink them together. 'Do you miss London?'

Does she mean London, or the lifestyle I left behind? Neena and her husband were regular dinner guests when I lived with Oli. Kitchen suppers in Clapham, Augusts in Dordogne, ticking almost every box for a barrister with old-money parents and an artistically leaning partner. We had everything except the offspring.

I don't miss the suppers or the gites: I never wanted them in the first place. But maybe I miss London. My first refuge: a place where no one cared less, exactly what I needed when I was seventeen, and searching for an escape.

'George?' Neena is still waiting for my answer.

'I miss the Croydon IKEA, maybe. But they say we're even getting one of those, so there's no reason to leave Brighton except for the National Portrait Gallery. Or a juicy murder trial.'

'You have family down here, right?'

People assumed that when I announced the move, and I didn't bother to correct them.

'There aren't many of us left,' I say. 'Anyway. How are the twins settling in at Steiner school?'

'Oh, don't pretend you're interested,' she says. 'Even I struggle to fake any enthusiasm for the holistic curriculum. And don't change the subject either. I want to know what's going on. Ever since this trial started, you've been weird.'

'I'm sorry about the drawings, it's—'

'I don't give a stuff about the drawings so long as they look vaguely like people and are done by the deadline. But *you* do care. Your work matters more to you than anything. So when that goes tits up, something must be really wrong.'

I sip the gin: the peppery juniper reminds me of sundowners in Neena's garden, all the fears and confidences she shared after another round of IVF failed, or her bosses started moaning about the time off she needed for hospital appointments.

Now she's offering to be there for me.

'I . . .'

What would she say if she knew even a fraction of the secrets I keep hidden? I don't know if she'd forgive me for the lies I've told.

'Is it the commission?'

I frown – I haven't told her about it yet.

'Oli mentioned it. He doesn't think it's good for you.'

'You've been talking about me behind my back?'

'Well, obviously . . .' Neena grins. 'Look, I think he's being a bit of an old woman about it, if it's even politically correct to say that anymore. I think the project sounds fascinating.'

'I *was* planning to tell you about it, Neen. It's really interesting so far.'

So I tell her about the book, about Sharon Fielding's suicide, and Jim's need to tell me what a failure he is. I mention the derelict children's home he's now bought, the nosy neighbour, the oppressive gloom that hangs over Ashdean.

I don't tell her about seeing the young Charlie.

She comes back with another round of doubles.

'That sounds so Gothic,' she says. 'Hey, if Jim Fielding suddenly confesses to something juicy, I want the exclusive, OK?'

I smile. 'What would he confess to?'

Neena shrugs. 'I dunno. *Wicker Man* style rituals in the woods. Or maybe it was him who murdered both wives and framed his own son?'

'I don't think he's a psychopath. I would have noticed.'

'Isn't that the point about psychopaths, that you don't, until it's too late?'

She laughs and I join in, though it doesn't actually seem that funny.

'The whole thing *is* a bit off. Jim's son Daniel was convicted of starting the fire. But he's just tried to top himself, a few months before getting out. That's odd, right?'

Neena shrugs. 'Killers are unpredictable. What was the evidence against him like?'

'There wasn't anyone else who could have done it. Daniel was at the scene, prints on the petrol can. Though he did plead not guilty to begin with, then changed his plea for no apparent reason. No motive, either.'

Neena downs her drink, and grins at me.

'Why don't you just ask him?'

'Yeah. It's *that* simple.'

'It's what I'd do. I've got a few prison contacts who could probably find you an only *slightly* dodgy way to visit Daniel Fielding. I bet you could get him to say something interesting to use for publicity when the book comes out.'

I scoff. I leave the investigations to Neena. Georgia Sage is logical, methodical, unemotional. A spectator, not a player.

And yet, perhaps the visions have changed that, whether I like it or not. At least if I could see Daniel, it'd reassure me that what happened in court *was* justice, and that any connection between him, me and the visions is merely in my head.

'Just for argument's sake, if I did want to ... What would I have to do?'

'Well, there's the official way. Write to him, ask for a visitor's order, all that jazz. But even if he did want you to visit, it could take months, by which time I guess you'll have finished the painting.'

'And the unofficial way?'

'Smuggling you in the back of the laundry lorry?' Neena laughs. 'There are other options, especially if you can grease a few palms. Let me make a call. So long as a) you cheer up, and b) promise you won't go to Sky News when you get your scoop.'

29

'Woah, Dexter!'

Dexter the border terrier is no bigger than a cat, but he's got the strength of an ox when there's something he wants. And right now, he wants to be on the beach, and he's pulling me down the steps next to the bandstand, past the children's playground, towards the water.

A Motability scooter driver swears at me as she swerves out of the way.

'Sorry, he's not really my dog,' I call.

Dexter's too much for my elderly neighbour so I walk him as a favour.

We head towards the dog-friendly section of the sand, between the two cafes.

Families have taken possession of the entire beach from the Pier to the Lawns, staking little claims with buckets, spades and disposable barbecues that stink like jet engines. We won't get our city back until September at the earliest.

In September it will be twenty years since I lost my family.

Dexter is dragging me down the final steps, onto the cold grey banks of pebbles the sea has made. The tide is way out, revealing honeyed sand I never knew was there until I moved to Brighton. The dog patters across it, chasing lazy gulls twice his size, leaving prints that last only a second before they fill with water again.

I slough off my sandals and step into the water, so cold still that it almost hurts.

'Cheeky chappy, yours.'

A fiftyish woman is walking towards me, pointing further along the waterline.

I look up: Dexter is chasing a much larger dog in and out of the surf, silhouetted against the sun. I shade my eyes with my hands. Recognition makes my heart pound.

'Is he yours? The German shepherd?'

'She. Yes. Lena.'

I can't take my eyes off the dog. A shower of memories, images, good days, bad days, rains down on me.

I try to hang on to now: the icy water, beach huts in regulation red and jade, the smell of scorched sausages and beer.

'You don't see so many of them these days, do you?' I say.

'No. Shame, they're such lovely dogs.'

'We had one. When I was a kid.'

Lena's owner nods enthusiastically.

'So gentle with children. People who see them as aggressive know nothing about the breed. What was yours called?'

'Marmite. Because of his colour.' I laugh. 'It was the only name me and my brother could agree on.'

I stop. What the fuck am I doing?

'Lena's giving your little lad a run for his money.'

The two dogs are haring up and down.

'He's not my dog, I just walk him now and then. For my neighbour, she's not as mobile as—'

'Nothing against terriers, but once a German shepherd owner . . . You'll want another one eventually, when you have time. Did yours live long?'

'Sorry?'

'Marmite. Did he reach a ripe old age? People say pedigrees are susceptible to all these chronic conditions, but Lena's eleven, and look at her go!'

A coldness passes through me, even though the afternoon sun is as warm as it was a moment ago.

The sand under my feet shifts, and my head pounds. I remember when the police arrived and all I wanted to know was where Marmite was. They found him hiding at the bottom of the garden, catatonic with fear. My father had spared him as well as me. But I could hardly look after him: an eleven-year-old no one wanted, even without a dog in tow. The social worker told me he was rehomed but for all I know, he was put to sleep.

'Sorry, but I – I need to go.' I grope in my pocket for Dexter's lead. Where is it? Shit. 'DEXTER!'

The dog must hear something in my voice, because he responds for the first time, trotting back towards me obediently.

'Hope to see you again, it's nice to meet someone who doesn't run in the opposite direction when they see poor Lena, they've had such a bad press—'

'Yes. Goodbye.'

I fumble trying to reattach the lead to Dexter's collar, jam my sandals onto my wet feet, then pull him up the steep bank of pebbles, back towards Brunswick.

'Shit!'

I miss my footing and tumble back. The woman's dog is still striding along in the lapping tide, but a boy has joined Lena, the child's yellow flip-flopped feet slapping on the sand. He's throwing a bright blue Frisbee, right across the dog's field of vision.

The dog ignores him completely.

The boy turns.

He is grinning. He mimes throwing the Frisbee in one direction, to fool Marmite, a trick Dad taught us both.

We've done it ten thousand times, but Marmite falls for it every time.

'Pip!'

I *know* it isn't him. That it can't be. And yet . . .

When he throws the Frisbee again, Lena ignores him once more.

Only I can see him.

Oh God. Charlie was bad enough. But Pip too?

I stand frozen. So many years on, my little brother's absence still hurts the most.

I find myself walking towards him. I blink but he's still there, so vivid, sun in his face, crescent moon eyes, as though he's laughing at his latest silly joke. This is how I always remember my Pippin.

The sun disappears behind a cloud and, for just a moment, Pip's face changes as though he's glimpsed me.

He's gone.

My legs buckle, and I collapse onto the pebbles, only just holding on to Dexter. I blink, over and over, willing my little brother to come back, but there is nothing on this stretch of the waterline except the retreating figure of Lena the Alsatian.

I long to hold my brother, smell his boiled sweet smell, feel the energy pulsing under his skin.

As I try to summon the strength to get up, I scan the length of the beach again. Happy families as far as I can see. There's a buzzing in my ears and a sudden terror turns my blood to ice. Are some of them hallucinations too?

I know Pip can't be real.

I saw him dead.

But Charlie looked utterly real to me, until I realised no one else could see him.

I stare at the children playing, running, jumping. They look less real than my dead brother. But how many of them am I imagining – a handful, or every single one? Where are they all coming from? And what do they want?

Ahead of me, the old West Pier pokes out of the water, rusty foundations exposed by the low tide.

I struggle to my feet, up and over the pebble banks, back to the flat, carrying the dog upstairs with me, because I can't face the small talk from my lonely neighbour. I close the door behind us, pour water for him, and a brandy for me, and sit at the kitchen table, forcing it down like medicine. Dexter wedges himself between my feet, licking salt water off my skin.

'It's all right, boy.'

But it's not all right. I grab my phone and google the number of a counselling clinic I know does work with Victim Support. Denial has got me nowhere.

I need professional help to make sense of what I actually saw twenty years ago – and what I think I am seeing now.

30

'Happy Easter, Georgia!'

Jim is waiting for me on the other side of his gate, dressed exactly as he was a week ago. I didn't have to remind him. The brown leather chair and my easel are in position in the entrance hall, with the virgin canvas I had sent ahead propped against the wall. It's a muggy afternoon, and the lowest clouds seem close enough to touch the glass roof.

'Hi, Jim. It's great to see you again.'

I'm lying – the last thing I felt like doing today was driving from Brighton to the Forest of Dean and pretending to be OK. Since yesterday on the beach, I haven't been able to get the image of Pip out of my head. When I was driving fast, it was bearable. But whenever I've had to slow down, I watched the people on the pavements, wondering if they were really there.

Two mahogany side tables – the nesting kind my grand-mother had – are laid for each of us: tea for him, coffee for me, iced water for both of us. Next to the coffee, a bowl of chocolate mini eggs, and another of fruit.

'Thought you might be hungry after the drive.'

I smile: living alone, I miss tiny, surprise acts of kindness.

'Thank you. How long do we have?'

'A couple of hours? Leah's gone to the gym. I told her to take Easter off, but no, not with a wedding dress to fit into, apparently.

Today it's Bodypump, with weights. I said, "Leah, don't overdo it, I like curves."'

I don't remember Leah having very many curves.

'And what did she say?'

'She snarled. She's always that bit more aggressive before she's been to the gym.' He gestures to the chair. 'I'm all right to get in the hot seat, am I?'

'Of course.'

I pin a large sheet on the easel, ready to work more closely on the composition. My sketches from the first sitting look pathetically tentative, compared to the figure in front of me. I hadn't been in the mood for this, but now I'm back, I want to try to do Jim justice.

'Do you mind if I take a few photos as we talk? Just on my camera phone, to refer to at home.'

It's procrastination, really. After Neena's comments on my work, I'm low on confidence.

Jim nods and sits up a little straighter.

My phone makes a fake shutter sound as I take pictures.

Click.

'You've been having a good old nose around my home town, I hear?'

I freeze. Jim looks self-satisfied, as though he's caught me out.

I remember the taxi drivers watching me as I walked through Ashdean the last time I was here.

'Have you got me under observation?'

Click. Click.

Jim laughs. 'I wasn't kidding when I said this town runs on gossip.'

'I just took a walk after the first sitting. Stretched my legs before I drove home.' I think about Copse View. 'You bought the children's home where your first wife lived. I was surprised.'

He tuts. 'Not you as well, Georgia. I'm disappointed.'

I frown. 'I'm not criticising you.'

Click.

He peers at me, then sighs.

'Sorry. I'm so used to Ashdean's wagging tongues that I forget how normal people behave. I bought it to help the town. It's a beautiful building, but it's been empty for ten years now and it's turned into a magnet for graffiti and toerags.'

I picture the kids I followed inside.

The cold feeling comes back.

'You're going to redevelop it?'

'Yeah. Flats for young people across the main three floors, plus a couple of family houses in the grounds.'

Click, click, click, capturing his benefactor's smile.

'Sounds great.'

Though I can't imagine wanting to live there.

Jim looks at me. 'You felt it, didn't you? The misery creeps into the mortar – all those poor kids, taken from their shitty families into an even shittier place.' He spreads his fingers. 'But imagine toddlers playing in that big garden. Young couples starting new lives. That'd banish the bad vibes.'

'Very philanthropic of you.'

Jim shrugs. 'I won't lie, there's money in it too. Got the place for a knock-down price. But I don't believe in sitting on cash. My dad was the biggest bloody skinflint you've ever seen but counting money didn't make him happy. Never even lived long enough to enjoy what he'd put away.'

Suddenly, he stands up.

'You've done it again, Georgia, with your spooky ways. I told myself that there'd be none of that Jeremy Kyle crap today.'

I shake my head. 'I'm saying nothing.'

'And that's your secret, right? Ask questions, then stay quiet for so long I fill in the gaps.' He sits back down. 'From now on, I'm keeping it zipped.'

Maybe silence will help me focus. God knows I need to. I've taken enough photographs to paper the walls of my flat. Time to get on with it.

I tuck my phone in my pocket and square up to the canvas-sized sheet of paper on the easel. But the longer I stare at Jim's face, the less sense it seems to make. Perhaps I need to approach it differently. Start somewhere else. I step back.

Of course. His *hands:* the hands that saved two young lives. He's folded them, one on top of the other, so I can't see the injuries, and that feels the right way to paint them, wearing his heroism lightly. They're good hands, in proportion, with a couple of solid gold rings, but a gap on the left ring finger.

'Will you wear a wedding ring, when you marry?'

Jim looks up at me.

'Course I will. I believe in equality.' He nods at my hand. 'No ring. Do you have a partner, Georgia?'

I don't answer.

'Come on, if you're trying to get inside *my* head, it's only fair I should get a peek into yours.'

I play along. 'I'm single. I was engaged once, but it didn't work out.'

'No kids?'

'No.'

'Want them?'

'I . . . No. It feels like too big a gamble.'

Jim leans forward. I sketch in his arms against the sides of the chair, trying to capture that sense of a man who has outgrown it.

'A gamble how?'

'Whether they'll be happy. Healthy. So many things can go wrong for a child.'

Jim looks at me and something seems to shift in the room.

'Did something happen to you, Georgia?' His voice is gentle.

I shake my head. 'Working in my world, I hear so many terrible things.'

'It's easier going into it blindly . . . Me and Sharon . . .' But he stops himself.

He's fighting it. He *wants* to let out all the pain and regret he's been storing up.

'Are you brave enough to do it again?' I ask him. 'Have kids with Leah?'

'She's broody. Wants to give me a son, she says.'

You had a son. You still *have one.*

Does Jim even know Daniel attempted suicide?

'To carry on the name?' I say.

He laughs. 'Something like that. The Fielding dynasty, forever . . .' He stops. 'I don't want to make the same mistakes again. But how am I meant to avoid that, when I don't even know what the mistakes were?'

'With Daniel?'

The name hangs in the air between us. I half expect to be thrown out. But instead, Jim exhales slowly.

He nods. 'With Daniel.'

It's the first time he has said his son's name out loud to me. I stay silent.

'Every man wants a son,' he says eventually. 'Well, wants one of each. A daughter to spoil. A son to . . . be a chip off the old block.' He scoffs.

I sketch in his torso, neck, the shape of his head, and wait for him to continue.

'Amy was actually more like me. Danny was quieter but I loved that boy. And then Sharon was gone and . . . I should have realised how desperate he'd become. Done something.'

'I'm sure you did your best, Jim.'

'I did nothing.'

'Have you talked to Leah about any of this?'

Another bitter laugh. 'God, no. She thinks I'm as strong as she is. Funny. According to the gossips, I've sired little bastards all over the forest, but here I am, getting cold feet about the most natural thing in the world.'

I remember the gossipy neighbour's hints about Charlie and Jodie when I visited Cherry Blossom Lane.

Loved those kids like they were his own.

Jim shifts in his chair.

'Sometimes there's nothing anyone can do,' I say to him. 'But you got it right with Amy, didn't you?'

'Oh, yes, she's a belter. Went to uni and everything, until Tessa died and she dropped out to look after me. Who knows what she'd have been if . . . But she'll be a good mum. She's been wonderful with Emma O'Neill's kids.'

'There you are. And you're a father figure to them, too, aren't you?'

Jim swears under his breath.

'I'm not their dad, OK? Whatever you've heard.'

'I wasn't suggesting—'

'People always look for an ulterior motive. Me buying Copse View or keeping an eye on Charlie and Jodie. No one can believe that I want to *help*. I've got money, those kids need it. What's so fucking complicated about that?'

'Their real dad doesn't contribute?'

'Robert? They're better off without him.'

His tone has changed. I wish I could take out my camera and record the sudden ruthlessness, but instead I try to capture the set of his jaw on paper.

'I heard you were friends?'

For a moment, everything is still. Jim's knuckles turn white in his lap.

'That all you heard?'

'Yes.'

'I thought we were mates, too. But he was a user. I fell for it and I paid in jail and he got away scot-free. And then he came back and I fell for it a second time, until the fucker deserted his own family, his own pregnant wife.'

'Why did he go?'

'Search me. He always put himself first. I mean, we all do when we're kids, but we're meant to grow out of it when we become parents. Not Robert, though. He stayed a selfish twat and I was the one who picked up the pieces. It was me that drove Emma to hospital when she went into labour, me who held her hand when the doctors told her what was wrong with Jodie.

'And what did I get for being decent? The Ashdean gossips decided I had to have an ulterior motive. And that tells you all you need to know about this fucking place.'

'Jim, I'm sorry, I didn't mean to make you angry.' I put down my pencil. 'The point I was trying to make was that you've done your best for those kids, which means when you become a dad again, it'll be fine.'

He looks at me and I feel he's going to challenge what I said for being too glib. Which it is. But instead he sighs.

'Georgia, I swear, the next time we meet I'm getting too drunk to speak.'

'Not a word of what you've said will leave this room.'

He shrugs. 'No one would believe it anyhow. Jim Fielding, a soft touch and a headcase?'

I look at my watch.

'Time's almost up.'

'I hope you kept working while I was banging on. When does the painting bit start?'

I begin to pack up.

'Next time. I want to do some work at home and then we need to schedule another couple of long sessions, ideally soon.'

He sighs. 'This is harder than I thought it'd be but . . . I keep my word.' He gets up from the chair, stretches out his long arms and with it, he loses the vulnerability, becomes Big Jim Fielding again. 'No chance of a sneaky peek?'

'Like a bridegroom seeing the wedding dress before the big day. It'd be bad luck.'

He winks. 'You can't blame a bloke for trying . . .'

I leave, and as I walk through the gates, I feel him watching me.

He's right: I'm not progressing as fast as I should be. But Jim's pain is always there in the room with us. If you've been lying to yourself for years, you need a stranger to hear your confession.

Who will hear mine?

I load my stuff into the back of the car, and once I'm in the driving seat, I study the White House, with its cameras and pristine fortress walls. I start the ignition, set the satnav and put my foot down.

31

I ignore Easter. People are busy with their families, so no one calls me. But I'm not lonely. I use the court recess to work on the book commission.

I still don't feel I'm capturing anything about Jim that a photograph can't. Maybe I'm kidding myself to think I might be good enough for the cover, or to be in the book at all.

I see nobody real, and nobody imagined either. No Charlie. No Pip. That's a small consolation. When Tuesday comes, and I go back into the world, outside feels overwhelming. So loud and so bright I can't quite process it.

'Hey, I think I've got you a way in,' Neena says when we meet outside the crown court. When I frown, she adds, 'Into the prison where that Fielding boy is. You'll have to pretend to be teaching an art class, but it's better than going in and out with the dirty laundry, right?'

'I've never taught anyone in my life.'

'A bunch of lifers won't know the difference, will they? They'll be too busy staring at your tits. How much do you want to talk to this guy?'

I don't even remember saying I did.

'When would it be?'

'Ah. That's the only slight catch. My contact is changing jobs – I think that's why he's up for it – so it has to be this Thursday.

I checked the witnesses here and they're boring that day so we won't need you. It's all worked out perfectly.'

I shake my head. 'Yeah, except I don't even *want* to talk to Daniel Fielding.'

Neena tuts. 'Seriously? It wasn't easy to arrange.'

'I can't see the point.'

A taxi pulls up outside, and Maureen emerges, waiting for the driver to help with her cases and easel.

'*She's* the point, George. That talentless old bag has been boasting that she's going to be on the cover of the crime book. But if you can get even a few words out of Danny boy, to be released at the same time as the book, then you'll be the star turn. The publisher will have to put your painting on the cover.'

Maureen gives us a bright smile as she passes us.

'Morning Neena, Georgia. Lovely day for a rape trial, isn't it?'

'*See*,' Neena says, once Maureen has trotted into the building. 'She thinks it's a done deal already. You can't let her get the kudos that you deserve.'

'I'd like to think my work is good enough without having to resort to this sort of thing.'

I regret it as soon as I say it. I sound pious. Plus, I don't even think it's true anymore. Apart from the odd exception, my most recent work has been utter crap.

'And I'd like to think that I'd have climbed the greasy pole without schmoozing and sucking up. But I did those things all the same, just in case it wasn't enough.'

Toby, the producer, is walking up the road towards us.

Neena leans into me to whisper, 'You can have until the lunch adjournment to examine your conscience, George. Then I'll have to let my guy know either way so he can get the paperwork organised.' She reaches for my hand, gives it a squeeze. 'Look, there's still something about the Fielding case that gets the public fired up. I was googling the whole thing while I was at the soft play centre yesterday. It's a good chance for you to make your name.'

And then Toby is back, all bossy and thrusting, and I think about it. Neena *is* probably right. I do need to raise my profile, but do I really want to use someone else – even if he is a convicted killer – to do that?

'Perhaps you'd like to tell me what's brought you here to see me this afternoon?'

The therapist is in his fifties, pebble-grey hair, dressed to blend in with the surroundings. His name is Ed or Ted or Ned. I choose not to remember. I am not here to make a new friend.

We're in a counselling centre just off the seafront. An assessment session to see whether I can be helped, the appointment I booked after 'seeing' Pip. I've rehearsed this: a simple explanation, in my calmest, most rational voice, to show I understand only too well how crazy I sound when I explain what's been happening.

I have been hallucinating two children who cannot exist. I know they can't exist. I don't feel crazy. But that doesn't make them go away.

But now, in this bland, beige room, I'm dizzy with fear. Because once I start to tell him about why I am so scared, I'll have to share other things I've never told anyone about.

'Things are . . . getting to me. I'm not sleeping well. My work is suffering.'

The counsellor mirrors back with a nod of encouragement.

'Things. What kind of things?'

Silent people. Lost children.

I saw Charlie again while I was walking over here, as three-dimensional and vivid as everyone else around me. When I tried to stare him out, he just grinned, before running past me, towards the pier.

'I do quite a stressful job. It can be hard to switch off. Now and then I have . . . nightmares. Vivid nightmares.'

'Switching off we can help with. And sleep is so often the first casualty of stress.' Another nod, reassuring this time; the counsellor knows the territory. He's not my first. I know how they work. 'Tell me about your job, Georgia.'

'I work as a court artist. I sketch what happens in the big cases that are of most interest to the public. Cameras aren't allowed so I draw the murderers, rapists. Terrorists.'

The counsellor leans forward, professional interest replaced by unconcealed curiosity.

'The stuff of nightmares,' he says, when I've given him a potted history of my career so far. 'Anyone doing this work would be affected, I'd imagine.'

'Perhaps.'

I think of Maureen, scratching the surface with her acrylic nails, and I know it's not true. Some people are impenetrable.

'Has anything else changed recently?'

'I moved to Brighton a couple of years ago after a relationship break-up, but the . . . sleep problems have only started recently.' I try to steel myself to go deeper, but I can't. 'My work is suffering. And it can't, because they're cutting right back on court artists.'

Maureen will be OK if it ends, of course, settling into an early retirement of geraniums and geriatric wife-swapping. But me? I don't know what I'd do – who I'd be – without this.

'Aside from sleep issues, are you experiencing other symptoms?'

He has the same carefully non-judgemental expression as the counsellor and social workers I saw in 1997. I wonder if I could have been 'fixed' back then, if I'd admitted how I really felt.

'Sometimes it feels as though I'm being followed.' It's as close as I dare go. 'Does that sound insanely paranoid?'

The counsellor smiles. 'We'd call that hypervigilance. Along with physical symptoms, like racing heart, clammy hands, unsettled tummy. They're caused when the body misinterprets a benign situation as threatening. Does that sound familiar?'

I don't want to disappoint him.

'Maybe.'

'The body can get stuck into this fight or flight response, like a needle on a record.' He smiles.

'Right.' His glibness frustrates me, but then I've only given him half-truths to work with. 'Why does it do that, though?'

'There could be all sorts of reasons. Current stress. Unresolved feelings or traumas can manifest themselves in some fairly unpredictable ways.'

Manifest. As in, hallucinations.

'And counselling can make that better?'

'That's certainly our aim. But there are more practical ways to calm the body's responses, one by one, to make life more comfortable in the short term. Simple techniques. Relaxation. Breathing. How does that sound?'

Bloody predictable.

But it's my fault for lying.

'Useful.'

The counsellor nods again.

'Excellent. And who knows, if we make progress with this, perhaps you can tell me the real reason you're here.'

He doesn't *actually* wink, but he holds my gaze for just long enough to make me realise I've been rumbled. For a moment, I imagine telling him everything, unlocking that roomful of secrets.

Unthinkable.

'I'm sure you have enough to be going on with,' I say, and we share a smile that makes us both complicit.

As soon as I leave the consulting room, Charlie is next to me, mimicking my leaden walk.

For all the platitudes, the counselling has helped me see one thing clearly. These manifestations are definitely linked to my past, and – somehow – to the Fielding case, too.

I've decided: I will visit Daniel, even though the idea makes me feel sick. Because, as much as I've tried to bury it, there was always a deeper connection between us.

And I either have to break it, or it will break me.

32

On Thursday, I take the train to the West Country, setting out early to get to the jail on time.

I buy a magazine to read but toss it aside, unable to focus. Confronting a suicidal man, even one guilty of the worst crime, is not something I ever thought I'd do. And especially not in a place with hundreds and hundreds of locked doors.

I stare out of the window, and despite my anxiety, the rapid movement makes me nauseous so I let my eyes close.

When I open them again, I can glimpse the sea as the train speeds along the coast. A memory comes unbidden, unwanted but impossible to ignore. My family's journey to Cornwall, that final summer.

The holiday was terrible, but on the way there, Dad was still making an effort. Pip even got to spend the last leg of the drive in the front, and pretended to be steering the car. Dad played along, telling my brother to take his foot off the gas and slow down, because the police were going to give him a speeding fine.

And not long after we reached the coast, Dad suddenly yelped, and pointed through the window:

'Look, Suzie, Pippin! Dolphins! See them?'

I couldn't see them. But Pip did. He whooped and pointed and laughed.

'And mermaids!' Pip cried out. 'I see mermaids too, on their backs, going for a ride on the dolphins.'

And even though my father always frowned on Pip's imaginary friends, that afternoon he just smiled as my brother described their long blonde curls and their shimmering turquoise tails . . .

I dig my nails into my hand. It's somehow worse to remember the good times. So I force myself to think about the rest of the holiday: my father snapping at the slightest thing; that morning when he refused to leave our cottage, even though it was the only day when it didn't rain from dawn to dusk.

Mum had ignored him. She took the car keys – even though she hated driving – and took us to Porthcurno, just the three of us.

'You're not going to spoil everything! I won't let you!' she'd shouted, as he banged on top of the car roof, telling us it wasn't safe.

I chose that day to paint later when Miss Hamilton set us homework of 'capturing a good moment'. Not because of the argument, but because of afterwards – the beauty, the landscape lit up by that special kind of sunshine you only see after rain.

On the beach, my mother had asked me, 'Suzie-Soo, how would you feel about living with just me and Pippin? If Daddy wasn't with us anymore?'

I wasn't stupid. I had school friends whose parents had divorced. I knew how the news had been broken to them: with half-truths and *choices* that turned out to be anything but.

'Why?'

Mum leaned in closer. Pip was digging a network of canals in the sand, which kept filling with water.

'He's not happy at the moment, you know that, don't you? Maybe it'd be temporary. I just . . . Can you imagine living in a house with no arguments?'

'But no Daddy either?'

She sighed. 'Suzie, I don't want to do it, but – I can't seem to get through to him. We may not have a choice.'

'I'd hate it,' I said. 'If you threw Daddy out, I'd go to live with him. You can leave him, but I never will.'

I remember she nodded, as though she'd known my answer all along. After that, we had ice creams, and when we returned to the cottage, my father ordered pizza, and it ended up being the nicest evening we had that week. Even though I couldn't sleep afterwards.

33

I hadn't expected it to look so much like a prison.

HMP Moor Heath is in the most isolated place I've ever visited, and the building is clearly designed to put the fear of God – or justice – into you. The Gothic façade faces north, dark slates slicing through a cloudy sky.

'Got a reputation, this jail,' my escort Gary says, as he parks up. 'Even the government admit it's rough. Fights, suicides, drugs. The screws are even greedier than usual, though of course that works in *your* favour.'

Gary is pretty greedy himself. To get in, I've given a 'donation' to the prison education programmes he runs, though I'm sure he pockets most of it. I'm also going to deliver a sham art class, while Gary pays someone to ensure Daniel comes along. The rest is up to me . . .

Gary is an ex-con himself, a wiry man, forty or so, with over-sized dental implants. I don't think too hard about what happened to his real teeth.

We enter the jail through a high iron gate; it closes behind us with a chilling finality. Sweat prickles through the long-sleeved white blouse I thought an art therapist might wear. When Neena first suggested this plan, she made it seem so easy. Now, I'm in my idea of a nightmare, and I've forgotten why I even agreed.

'Everything in the tray.'

My heart pounds while the gate staff rifle through my art materials, and make me sign countless forms. The £500 I gave Gary is in the glove compartment of his car, but no one searches him anyway.

'You've come a long way,' the security officer says, gesturing at the form where I've written my address.

'This is important work,' I manage to say.

Gary gives me a dirty look. Perhaps I'm overplaying it.

Another officer takes over to escort us into the prison. More gates, more bolts locking into place behind us. My body sways. I reach out to steady myself before anyone sees.

I imagine Daniel Fielding arriving in jail on the first day of his sentence, knowing there'd be no way out for a decade or more.

But why try to kill himself when release was so close? I've been trying to work it out: laying out my notes and sketches from the original trial and my sittings with Jim, looking for something I missed.

The jail smells of disinfectant, boiled vegetables and something else. Testosterone? As we walk further into the bowels of the building, and I see the state it's in, I realise it's the stench of rising damp.

'Place is earmarked for closure,' Gary says. 'Too far away from the outside world and the men's families.'

The screw – young, and red-cheeked – turns around and glares at Gary.

'We're not here for their bloody convenience.'

Gary raises his eyebrows at me.

The prison is a vast city, but I haven't yet seen a single prisoner. I can hear them, though. I keep my eyes on the railings, the stone treads of the staircases. The straight lines seem to curve as though I am in an Escher woodcut.

From nowhere, I hear a loud drilling, smell sawdust and hot metal.

'Don't worry, they're not escaping,' Gary says. 'Metalwork. Government loves to let men out with practical skills.'

'Safe-breaking skills, more like,' the officer mutters.

The atmosphere changes. More light is entering the building; I can see a little better. We exit via two secure doors, back into the fresh air.

'The resettlement section is away from the main prison,' Gary says.

He doesn't explain what resettlement is, but I've done my research. Daniel had a life sentence, but life – as the tabloids always rage – doesn't mean life for most. The judge recommended a sentence of twenty-five years, which means Daniel can be considered for release on licence after thirteen. And it's the resettlement wing where prisoners prepare while they wait to hear if they'll be let out.

Resettlement is more relaxed than the Cat A regime – yet again, I wonder why he tried to end his life.

In a few minutes, I plan to ask him.

The red-faced officer buzzes us out of the main prison concourse, and I see my first prisoners, dressed in sweatpants and jumpers. We're handed over to another officer.

'I'm Mike.' He grins.

I reckon he'll be getting a chunk of my 'donation'. He shows me into a small room with blue padded chairs, school tables, a whiteboard, and a narrow window just shy of the ceiling. The light is flat, the walls blank and blurry with damp.

'This is the best we could do for your "workshop",' Mike says, eyebrows raised. He knows this is a sham. 'I'll round up your students. They've been looking forward to it.'

As the men troop in, they glance at me, without real interest. They'll already have been on short trips to the outside world as they prepare to rejoin it. Despite what Neena says, a woman is no great novelty.

They're older than I expected, one hobbling on a dodgy knee. They could be retirees at a council art class. Perhaps my father is taking a watercolour class, in his own jail. The more I try to focus on these men, the more I see Dad, older, greyer. Sicker? I cannot imagine how he's adapted to a prison regime. He always had to do things his way.

'And here's our straggler,' Mike says, stepping aside to let the final student into the classroom. 'Shift yourself.'

Even before I see his face, I know it's Daniel: that shuffling, defensive gait, like a dog always waiting for a blow. I grip the edge of the table.

Does he know he's the only reason for this charade? He moves painfully towards the back of the room, wincing. I look for dressings or marks on his wrists, but the skin appears to be unscarred.

His sweatpants rise at the ankle as he sits down and that's where I see dressings and realise why he was shuffling. He didn't slash his wrists. He cut through his *ankles*. Did he do it this way thinking that his attempt would go undetected for long enough to bleed out?

If I was apprehensive before, now I am afraid – of this place, of his story, and of what I might learn.

Gary sits down next to the door. Mike nods at him, then at me.

'Have fun!'

He leaves the room.

I let go of the table and look at the six men in front of me. Only Daniel stares at the floor; the others wait for me to speak.

I take a breath.

'Welcome, gentlemen. My name is Georgia, I'm an artist, and this afternoon I'm going to give you an introduction to the basics of drawing faces.'

34

In an hour, all my students but one manage to get *something* on the page.

Daniel simply stares at the blank sheet of paper.

I walk behind him.

'Sometimes it's hard to get started, but remember, it can all be changed later. That's why we work in pencil.'

He turns and I look at his face properly for the first time. The last thirteen years have been hard on both of us. His pale skin is still unlined, but his eyes are guarded, like a veteran who has seen too much. I smile, hoping he'll smile back, but instead he stiffens.

Does he remember me from court, all those years ago?

Before I can say any more, Mike walks into the room.

'Time's up, Da Vincis.'

As the other men leave – the oldest guy, my star student, thanking me on the way out – I don't move.

Daniel pushes his chair back. The metal chair legs screech against the lino.

I look up at Gary, hoping he realises I need more time. Despite my fears, I haven't got to this point to leave without a single word from the person I've come to see.

He studies me, and then Daniel.

'Your first visit to a Cat D, isn't it, Miss Sage? You need the tour of our nursery garden. Fielding, do the honours?'

Daniel scowls, but it's clear he can't say no. He shuffles ahead of me, into the lobby, then through a door leading to an outside courtyard zig-zagged with tiered troughs and lush greenery.

He is taller than his father, and more muscular than I remembered. But there's nothing menacing about him. In fact, I think *he*'s scared of *me*.

Once we're far enough from Mike not to be overheard, I speak.

'You recognise me, don't you, Daniel?'

He keeps his eyes down, but stops next to a raised bed full of young tomato plants.

'You're the art teacher.'

His soft Forest accent comes as a surprise. I barely heard him talk in court, except to confirm his name and then to speak three words. 'Not Guilty' on the first day of his trial.

And 'Guilty' on the last.

I stare at him until he can't stop himself looking up. When he finally does, the raw memory of the last time I saw him in court rushes through me, turning away from everyone to be taken 'down' to begin his sentence.

Justice being done.

Daniel leans over, pinches off the side shoot of a tomato. The sharp green smell is too fresh for this grey place.

'Why are you here?' His voice is hoarse. 'What the hell has this got to do with you?'

I knew the question was coming, rehearsed an answer. But now my mind is blank and mouth dry.

'Daniel,' I say eventually, 'yours was the first big case I drew. I've been asked to go back to it, to paint your father as he is now. But I feel like no one ever listened to you, to your side of the story. I came to give you a chance to talk.'

Daniel snorts. 'Do I look like I give a toss about *art*?'

He takes a few steps back towards the prison building.

'It's not about art, it's about . . . truth.'

'Truth. Like that picture of me you drew for the papers? The one where I looked like a monster?'

So he does remember.

'I . . . I drew what I saw.'

'Yeah. A psycho. Lock me up and throw away the key. So how much did he pay you?'

'Who?'

'My father. One day you drew me looking normal, the next . . .' He stops. 'Unless it was *love.*'

He laughs drily. He sounds exactly like Jim.

'My drawings showed what I saw, Daniel. I had no contact with your father. But I did feel sorry for you, on that first day. We were the same age. Out of our depth.'

'You looked right at home to me.'

I ignore him. 'And then you changed your plea and we never heard why.'

He groans. 'Look, there's an entire bloody prison full of men who'd swear blind they're innocent. Don't waste your time with me, it's too late.'

I glance at his ankles.

'Is that why you tried to kill yourself?'

He steps close to me, so his features blur. I smell stale coffee on his breath.

'What are those birds that feed off dead things? Vultures. That's you.'

His words are full of venom. For the first time, I see a fury in him.

'Daniel—'

'Tell my devoted dad I'll do the job properly soon, and he won't have to worry about me anymore.'

'Your dad doesn't know I'm here. I came because you never had a chance to tell anyone your side of things.' My words sound tacky to me, the false promises of a gutter journalist. I try to remind myself that it's about more than that. 'And if you're depressed, you can get treatment. You'll be free soon. Don't you want to start again?'

'No. I'm poison. Everyone I get close to suffers, or dies.'

I flinch. How often have I felt the same?

'You're not the only one who misses your mum. Your father still feels terrible about what happened. He told me.'

Daniel spins around, his eyes black.

'Told you what?'

'How guilty he feels that he couldn't save her – or you. He loved you, Daniel. I think he still does, despite what you did.'

His jaw hangs as he stares.

I keep talking. 'And as for your mum, it wasn't your fault. You were a child. There was nothing you could have done to stop her.'

I know these words, because people said them to me about my father. I never believed them either.

I look at Daniel. For a moment, I think he might be about to cry. But then he shakes his head.

'You don't have the first fucking idea, do you?'

'Maybe not. But I want to. I want to understand.'

He takes a step towards me, his hands balled into fists, and held rigid at his sides.

'Do you really think you're the first to try to nail him?'

'What are you talking about?'

'There was a woman copper saw through him too, she got bloody nowhere. And everyone who did know what my hero dad has done is dead. Except me. You know what kept me going inside? The thought that he might slip up. Get caught out. But he's like the fucking *Titanic*. Unsinkable.'

I try to make sense of what he's saying.

'Daniel, tell me what this is about.'

'He was *there*,' Daniel whispers, as though someone else might hear, 'on the bridge with my mother – there were witnesses. He fucking pushed her off, I know he did. But he still got away with it. You'd think that would put women off, wouldn't you? But no. First Tessa. Now this new girl he's going to marry. They all think they're the special one.'

I glimpse something move over his shoulder.

Charlie.

Not now, not when I need to focus.

'You think your father killed your mum?'

'Not just her. His best mate, too. Not that anyone ever seemed to see anything weird about him just *disappearing* one night. But you're just as blind as the rest of them. I bet you think he's in love with you too.'

He's backing away now, towards the unit. As he does, his ankle twists and he stumbles. His face contorts in pain.

'No, that's not why I'm here. Daniel, come back. Please.'

But he's already hobbling into the building, and my escort, Gary, is tapping his watch.

Charlie is heading towards me now, his thumb in his mouth, as though he's tired.

Then he walks right through me, and as I flinch, I realise. He wasn't heading for me after all. He was following Daniel.

35

I stumble onto the train at Plymouth, and when I look up, Charlie is there, chubby fingers tracing patterns on the table. I try to blink him away, but each time I open my eyes, he has moved to another seat, as though he's playing musical chairs.

Forget him. Think about reality, instead. Daniel was lying. He has to be. He's deflecting the blame for the unforgivable thing he did all those years ago. It worked so well that I never got to ask him why he started the fire.

But it's madness. Jim didn't kill Sharon, or anyone else. Why would he?

Except my father had no reason to kill *my* mother, and he still smothered her with a pillow.

My phone rings.

Neena Calling

'So what's the scoop, George?'
'There is no scoop. He didn't want to talk to me at all.'
My voice sounds edgy – I'm irritated by her thirst for a story.
'Oh shit. What – he refused completely?'
'I cornered him and he said a couple of things. But the upshot is, he blames his dad for his mother's suicide. According to Daniel, Jim pushed her off that bridge.'

'Woah. Now that'd be a scoop and a half.'

'Except he's invented it. There would have been an inquest into her suicide, right? The only useful thing it tells us is that Daniel's unhinged. It changes nothing.'

Neena doesn't reply and when I look at my phone, I realise the signal's gone.

As I wait for her to call back I replay what Daniel said in my head – *could* there be anything in it? Surely not. Jim is a hero. Haunted, yes, but by what he didn't do, not what he did.

My phone rings again.

'You still think Danny boy started the fire because he was an angry teenager who blamed his dad?' Neena asks.

'Pretty much.'

Charlie is on the other side of the aisle now, staring at me, his eyes dark and intense. I turn towards the window.

Neena sighs. 'That's not going to get you headlines for your book. Or get me off the road and into a cushy number in current affairs.'

'So *that's* why you press-ganged me into this.'

'Come on, George. You have to admit it was worth a go. I'll have to find another cold case to make my name.'

'Right now, your career is the last thing that's bothering me.'

'Sorry. I forgot you're not a hardened hack like me. That you still care about people. It must have been hard.'

I think again about the meeting. At the time, there was something so real about Daniel's fear.

'There was one other thing,' I say. 'Daniel claimed a policewoman had tried to investigate his dad for something. Said she got nowhere.'

'No name? Details of what she was looking into?'

'Sorry, Neena. I should have narrowed it down but . . .'

'You don't have the killer instinct, do you?'

For a moment, I consider telling her about the other person Daniel thinks his father might have killed. *His best mate* whose 'disappearance' no one ever questioned. He must mean Robert, Charlie's father.

But I hesitate. I don't want Neena to scent blood again.

'Never mind. It was a long shot. You're going to have to go to plan B.'

'Which is?'

'Trip Maureen in the corridor so she breaks her wrist. And paint Jim Fielding so . . . has to be the cover boy or . . .'

'You're breaking up, Neena.'

'Ah that's . . . Listen, I . . . tomorrow for the closing speeches . . . Cruella . . .'

The signal dies completely. I put the phone face down. Charlie has moved back to my table. He's still staring, almost accusatory.

The train picks up speed, the moorland blurring beyond the window. Suddenly, in the distance, without warning, I see the hills turning into flint walls, ancient, unbreachable.

It feels as though I am racing towards them. I *know* it must be another hallucination, but still my body braces itself for impact. *Nothing.*

I close my eyes. I can't bear this. I have to tell the counsellor the truth next time. Face up to what is happening to me.

When I dare to open my eyes again, the hills are simply hills. Charlie is still there, sketching invisible patterns on the window with his sooty index finger.

36

I have another six hours of travelling ahead, so I try to put the Fieldings out of my mind and doze. The landscape changes as we leave Dartmoor behind.

I find myself thinking again about that last family holiday.

We always left Cornwall before dawn, in case of traffic. Like every year, Dad and I loaded the car while Pip and Mum – the night owls, bleary-eyed and barely functioning – shuffled out once the engine was running. I got to sit in the front, playing I spy with my father in conspiratorial whispers and competing to spot signposts for the strangest places.

Mousehole, Plusha, Tregadillett.

We giggled together as though we were the kids. I loved my father so much.

The sun rose at half past five, and by six, we'd reached the edge of Dartmoor, and Dad was smiling, because we were making good time. It had been a bad-tempered holiday, with my parents barely talking. On telly, married couples had passionate rows and passionate kisses to make up for them, but before this, Mum and Dad had always had formal – but affectionate – conversations about the weather and chores.

This new silence felt dangerous, as though they were both fighting off the urge to say things they knew they'd regret.

There'd been that conversation with Mum, about living somewhere else, one that I'd punished her for by taking Dad's side even more than usual.

As we travelled east and north, I became hopeful home might mean normal again.

'Time to wake the lazy twins,' Dad said, cocking his thumb at Mum and Pip in the back, then turning the radio on.

'This is BBC radio news from London. The death has been announced of Diana, Princess of Wales.'

I looked at my father.

'Dad?'

He leaned over, turned the volume up.

'. . . in hospital in the early hours of this morning, after a car crash in central Paris.'

I twisted in my seat to see Mum coming to, stretching her arms, still unaware of this impossible news. Pip lay with his cheek against the upholstery, spittle marking the grey tartan fabric.

'Deborah. Deborah, wake up. Something's happened.'

She mumbled a complaint, but he shushed her as the velvet-voiced announcer said the Queen and her sons had been informed. A crash of what sounded like static turned into the roll of drums, and doom-laden horns began playing the national anthem.

'Who's dead?' Mum asked.

Dad said nothing as the music played, and I felt the pressure of tears in my eyes. I looked out of the window at the people in the cars we were passing, and if they weren't crying too, I envied them the few minutes before they heard.

'It's the Princess of Wales,' Dad said eventually, turning off the radio as the music headed for the crash and thunder of its close. 'They got her, Deb. Even she wasn't safe, in the end.'

The world grew hysterical. My friend Abi and I would weep until our eyes were dry as paper, and bought eye drops in Boots so we could weep some more. We had nothing in common with Diana, this doe-eyed woman older than our mothers, richer than we could ever hope to be. But the drama and mass grieving was irresistible for two girls on the cusp of puberty.

Meanwhile, my father shrank further into himself.

The night after the funeral, I watched those two lost boys on TV, walking away from viewing their mother's coffin. Dad was talking to Mum in the kitchen and his voice was getting louder.

'Don't bury your head in the sand. Of course it was murder.'

'But who would want to kill *her*?' Mum's voice was taut.

'Powerful people. Don't you realise what goes on under the surface in this country, Deb? We're pawns. If we do things the powers-that-be don't like, they'll get us.'

'Colin. Please. You've never talked like this before. Has something happened?'

He pushed open the kitchen door and strode from the house. I heard him drive off.

'Where's he gone?' I asked Mum.

She shook her head. 'Work maybe? Though what he's going to do there at this time I've no bloody idea . . .' Then she smiled at me, as if she'd remembered I was her daughter, not someone she could confide in. 'Christmas is coming, Suzie. I bet he's just getting in some overtime.'

After he killed them, when I saw a newspaper picture of the sparse handful of bouquets people laid outside our house, I thought of the flower mountain left for Diana. Why did her death matter more than my mother's and my brother's? She'd had a rich, full life. Pip's hadn't even begun.

But really, my anger was directed at myself.

37

Today it's the closing speeches: Oli's last chance to nail the footballer; Cruella's to clear her client's name. Neither will have slept last night.

I got home from Devon so late I could barely keep my eyes open. Yet I couldn't sleep, my head full of unanswered questions about Jim and Daniel.

Oli goes first:

'The man in the dock is, by his own admission, spoiled. But that's not only about being able to buy whatever you want, go wherever you please, first class. Spoiled means you've started to believe that your needs and desires count for more than anyone else's.

'That everything – and *everybody* – is there for the taking.'

I write notes on autopilot, knowing that I can draw all the characters from memory now. It's just as well – the only person I seem to see clearly today is Charlie. He is everywhere. By the door, in the empty witness box, mimicking Oli's movements.

Is he looking for his lost father?

No. It's all in my head. I've made another appointment with the counsellor, though he can't see me until Monday. This time I'll tell the truth and ask him to do the same. An expert will surely know if I am going mad.

Yet the question Daniel raised about Robert O'Neill's disappearance is troubling me. Men leave their kids all the time, but Daniel seemed so sure it wasn't that simple.

'Bringing an accusation of rape is never the easy option for a victim. The defence have suggested many motivations for Miss Tranter's allegation – money, attention-seeking, even morning-after regret over an uncharacteristic desire for violent sex.

'Ask yourselves: does any of that ring true? Or is the most obvious motivation also the true one – Miss Tranter was raped by Sam Carr and she wanted her attacker to face justice?

'This, members of the jury, is your role and your duty. To hear the victim's plea and to make justice happen.'

As he sits down, I scan the jurors' faces again but I don't glean anything. After a short break, it's Cruella's turn.

'Rape is a terrible crime. One that always deserves a harsh sentence. But this is not about rape. It is about two people with different expectations. And it should *never* have ended up in court.'

Cruella spends the afternoon painting her client as the victim, and casting more innuendo at the young woman who brought us all here.

For my final sketch of the week, I draw her in full, bitter flow, with Oli in the background, and the footballer's face full of either fear or contempt, depending on how you see him.

I know how *I* see him.

But again I see Charlie more clearly. It's a relief to leave court, to stop pretending everything is OK. Once my sketch is done, I ask Neena what her weekend has in store.

'Ferrying the twins between swimming, tree house adventures and meditation classes,' she says. 'Please tell me yours will be two days of unbridled hedonism.'

I force a grin. 'Don't forget the compulsory orgy on the beach. Though with all the pebbles, al fresco sex is not what it's cracked up to be.'

'Have an extra shag for me.'

She blows me a kiss goodbye so as not to smudge her make-up before her live broadcast.

And I walk back towards my flat, Charlie skipping ahead, breathing in fresh air while I can. I won't leave the house again until Monday, because I'm scared of what I might see.

38

On Saturday morning, I wake early. Today I need a clear head: I am going to look for Robert O'Neill.

I'm alone in the flat, Charlie keeping out of sight.

I have started to credit my hallucination with a mind of his own.

It's hard to know where to start, so I just type Robert's name and Ashdean into my dodgy old laptop. Nothing comes up, though there are thousands of men with his name when you take the town out of the search. I try adding Jim's, but that only gives me coverage of the fire and the court case, focusing on Charlie and Jodie, with no mention at all of their father, beyond describing Emma as a single mum.

He's been wiped from history.

Though maybe that's deliberate: if he's deserted his family, he may have changed his name to avoid paying maintenance.

Luckily for Emma, Jim was there to help.

I make another coffee to give myself a break, then I read sites offering advice when someone goes missing. It seems that if a person really doesn't want to be found, there's little relatives can do.

When I changed my name, I didn't have to go the whole hog – there was no family left to search for me. And anyway, becoming Georgia was about escaping my father's name – and trying to escape the guilt – rather than responsibilities. I had none.

But why would a father leave his son and pregnant wife? Men do it all the time, I guess. Grow tired of the burden and the boredom. Jim hinted as much about Robert.

If only Dad had left us. In my teens, I went through a phase of trying to understand what might have made him do it, reading everything I could get my hands on about family annihilation. How these men – and it's almost always men – crave control. How they cannot conceive of the idea that their wife and kids could exist without them.

None of it helped.

I stop myself: don't think of that now. This is not about me.

I try to find more of a connection between Robert and Jim when they were younger, but the internet didn't exist then, of course. There's no trace of the joyriding or the boot full of dodgy cigarettes Jim took the blame for.

Why would there be, anyway? It's hardly the crime of the century.

But murder is different.

I don't really believe that Daniel was telling the truth about his father killing Robert, or Sharon for that matter. Yet I want to be sure. I want the man I am painting to be a hero. I want to believe in courage and selflessness, though at times those qualities seem as improbable as the existence of Father Christmas.

Jim *seems* good to me, but I thought my father was, too. My judgement is not to be trusted. I keep going, just to prove Daniel wrong.

A missing persons' charity website lists the criteria for presumption of death, which have changed in the last five years. Now a family member can apply to have a lost relative presumed dead by filling in forms and advertising locally, even if no body has ever been found.

I look for the local paper near Ashdean and find its online archives. Nothing comes up. I have run out of other options, so I widen the search area to papers throughout Gloucestershire.

And then I see it: a small ad marking the possible end of a life.

In the High Court of Justice Chancery Family Division

In the matter of an application for a declaration of the presumed death of Robert Gerard O'Neill.

A claim has been issued in the High Court of Justice, for a declaration that Robert Gerard O'Neill, whose last known address was 22 Oakland Close, Ashdean, Gloucestershire, is presumed to be dead. Any person having an interest may apply to the court to intervene in the matter.

If you wish to apply to the court, you should do so at Gloucester and Cheltenham County Court and Family Court hearing centre as soon as possible, and if possible within 21 days of the date of this notice. Delay may harm your prospects of being able to intervene.

Maurice Brett

Brett & Tomlinson Solicitors, 2 Harrison St, Gloucester

The date is March 2015. The rules say if the application is unchallenged, a certificate will be granted. I follow another government link to see if there's any trace.

And then I find it. Probate was granted a few months later, with Robert O'Neill's date of death marked as 20 December, 2008, which must be seven years after the last time anyone saw him alive.

Jim lied.

He must know that Robert's family applied for a presumption of death, so why insist to me that the man did a runner?

Unless Daniel is right, and Jim knows exactly what happened to his old friend.

My hands are shaking as I apply for a copy of Robert's will, which should arrive within ten days. Maybe it's a dead end, but I must try, because I want to banish any doubt about Jim. Otherwise, the idea of going back to paint him seems foolish at best. And at worst . . .

I pour my coffee down the sink and reach for a brandy instead.

39

'I've been seeing things.'

The counsellor blinks. Whatever he'd been expecting after our first evasive session, it wasn't this.

'Seeing things?' he repeats.

'Things that aren't there.' It's easier than I'd feared to say it out loud, in this bland room, to a man I am paying to stay calm. 'Not things, actually. People.'

On cue, Charlie steps out from behind the counsellor's chair. He's been with me all today in court, as the judge did his summing up, and sent the jury out. The verdict could be back by tomorrow lunchtime, or it could take days. Rape cases often drag on, as the *he said/she said* nature of the evidence – and the life-changing nature of a guilty verdict – makes juries hesitant to convict.

'When did you first realise you were hallucinating?'

I blush. 'It began about a month ago. Before I started coming to see you. In fact, it was why I made the appointment. Sorry.'

He opens his hands out in a gesture of acceptance.

'It takes time to trust. Would you like to tell me more about what you see?'

So I do. I tell him that Charlie looks a bit like a kid from a case a long time ago. I don't mention Robert or Jim. I don't want to overwhelm the counsellor or sway his diagnosis.

Then I talk about Pip, but not yet about how he died. My voice is businesslike, as though we're fellow professionals trying to resolve a puzzling problem. I need him to know I understand this isn't normal.

'When you see the boys, do you know they're not real?'

'I didn't at first with Ch— the first kid, but then I realised because no one else seemed to see him, or his distress. If I'd seen my brother first, of course, I'd have got it immediately. For all I know, some of the other people I see aren't real, either.'

The counsellor nods. He's trying to pretend this is bread and butter for him, like the humdrum stories he hears of broken relationships and family feuds.

'What do they say?'

'Nothing. They're completely silent.'

The counsellor is silent too.

'That's good, isn't it? No voices in my head?'

He ignores my fishing for reassurance.

'How do they make you feel?'

Charlie smiles at me.

'I . . .' I hadn't expected the question. 'It depends. If the little boy isn't crying, then I don't feel too bad. But sometimes he's upset, and that's hard, because there's nothing I can do. And my brother . . . I can't put that into words.'

Again, the counsellor says nothing.

'They frighten me, though, because I know I shouldn't be seeing them, which means . . .' I am afraid to say this out loud but I promised I would. 'Look, I've seen a doctor, I've had a brain scan. There's no medical cause. It means I'm going mad, doesn't it?'

Next morning, I walk to the hospital for the earliest appointment they do. I take the lift to the private wing. The dusty silk flowers in reception are a step down from the arrangements at the maternity hospital where I visited Oli's new baby.

The counsellor was kind but firm yesterday. What I'm experiencing is beyond his area of expertise, so he got me in urgently to see a friend who is a full-blown shrink. My daddy's money comes in handy again. But I bet it won't fix my genes.

'Georgia Sage?'

I follow the consultant's assistant down a corridor decorated with soothing art: seascapes and still lives blur as we pass. She ushers me into a consultation room and closes the door behind me.

'Miss Sage. Please, sit down.'

The psychiatrist has bifocals that make his keen brown eyes bulge slightly at the bottom edges.

'I understand you're in some distress.'

Initially, his questions follow the same pattern as the counsellor's, until he begins to focus on details that obviously mean something to him. What exactly do I see, and when exactly do I see it? He asks me three different ways about the voices or sounds that accompany my visions, and each time I answer the same: they are children, they are silent.

'It would be helpful to know a little about your family background and history,' he says.

I tell him the truth – most of it. No one has heard it for twenty years. My mother and my brother are dead. My father killed them, and tried to kill himself. I am the only one left.

I don't tell him that I was partly to blame.

He looks up, eyes sad behind the magnifying lenses.

'I am sorry. Was he ever diagnosed with any condition?'

I don't know how to respond.

'Not as far as I know.'

'What was the finding of the court?'

'He was offered manslaughter on the grounds of diminished responsibility but insisted he was innocent. They found him guilty of murder.'

'This is what you're most afraid of? That whatever happened to him, is now happening to you.'

I nod.

'Let us go back to your own experiences.'

I answer more questions. Y*es, I think my past has probably affected my relationships*, but *no, I haven't felt depressed or desperate*. Until now.

When he asks a fourth time about voices, I am tetchy.

'They're not telling me to do anything bad. But I know there *is* something wrong with me.'

'I don't doubt you, Miss Sage. Not for a moment. But if you have time today, I'd like to call a colleague downstairs, see if she can organise some urgent tests.'

The hospital is only ten minutes from the court; if a verdict comes in, I can run back.

'Tests on my brain?'

He shakes his head.

'Actually, they're tests on your vision.'

40

I haven't been this frightened for twenty years.

The psychiatrist's colleague is an ophthalmic specialist named Lynn Nash. He phones her PA, and once they've established I have the necessary funds to have the tests privately, everything becomes surreal.

Machines puff air into my eyes, blind me with red lights, make me stare, and blink, and look this way and that, until I don't know my left from right.

And all the time, the fear grows. I'm escorted from room to room with light touches to my arm or elbow. I'm en route to an unknown destination, wishing I were back with the psychiatrist, because – and this is most terrifying of all – somehow it felt safer there.

I wait for the consultant to finish her NHS clinic. Some of the patients have eye patches; one even navigates his route across the room with a white stick. After an hour or so – checking in with Neena to make sure the jury hasn't come back yet – a nurse appears.

'Is there someone you'd like to call? To be with you when the doctor sees you?'

'I'm fine.'

'Are you sure? Only it can be helpful—'

'There is no one.'

She smiles tightly.

I pick up a magazine, but they warned me the eye drops would make it hard to focus, so I put it down again. Beyond the window, a fine drizzle falls.

'Miss Sage?'

Dr Nash says nothing as I follow her along the corridor to the consulting room. It's smaller and scrappier than the one in the private hospital.

She takes a breath and her perfectly straight, grey fringe lifts a millimetre or two as she breathes.

'Well,' she says, 'I appreciate you didn't go to meet my psychiatry colleague today expecting to end up here. What I am going to tell you is quite complex, and it will take time to process. I'll write to you as well, to explain your options.'

I nod, though I have no idea what she might mean.

'You came to seek advice on the visual hallucinations you've been having. Understandably, you were concerned these might be a symptom of a psychiatric issue. However,' the fringe shifts again, before falling as she inhales, 'these hallucinations are actually a result of *physical* changes.'

Her calmness riles me.

'Am I imagining them or not?'

'What you're seeing is not real. But equally, you are not mentally ill.'

It should be a relief. But I sense this is the good news, and the bad news is to come.

'The visions you're experiencing are due to what we call Charles Bonnet syndrome. It is most common in the older population, but even there, it is under-reported. Patients can be reluctant to share what they're seeing, in case relatives or medical staff jump to the wrong conclusions.'

'That they're crazy?'

'Exactly. But it can be seen as a more exaggerated version of what all of us do every day. For example, I'm sitting behind this desk. All you can see is my upper body, plus my feet resting on the floor. But your brain fills in the gaps. Just because you can't see my legs doesn't mean they're not there.'

'Right.'

The conversation is almost existential.

'Charles Bonnet syndrome produces visual hallucinations which can seem as detailed and real as what is actually there. More so. Typically, patients see figures – perhaps in unusual dress. Sometimes people they know. Often complete strangers. Children are very common indeed.'

'I'm not the only one to have this?'

She nods. 'It can be an enormous relief to know that.'

'Well, yes, but . . .' I think of Charlie and Pip. 'But the children move, they play—'

'But they never speak, do they, Miss Sage? You see, that's the thing good psychiatrists like my colleague pick up on, the ones who know about Charles Bonnet. The hallucinations are always silent.'

I'm not mad.

I am not my father.

'Why am I seeing them if I'm *not* crazy?'

'This is where it becomes more complex.' Dr Nash places her hands together on the desk. 'Charles Bonnet syndrome happens when there's a . . . deficit in visual information. That's why we've been carrying out these tests, to establish what might be causing that deficit.'

A deficit? I shake my head at my own stupidity.

'It's been on my list for ages, to get my eyes tested. I moved from London a couple of years ago and haven't got around to finding an optician.'

I'm almost euphoric with relief. It makes *perfect* sense – this is the cause of my visions *and* my substandard drawings. I look around the room. Yes, the details aren't as sharp as they should be, especially in the middle of my vision.

'Miss Sage—'

But I interrupt her. 'I guess most people don't notice if they need glasses as it's gradual. Can you prescribe them or is there someone you'd recommend?'

'Miss Sage, it's not really about glasses.'

I try to ignore the warning note in her voice.

'An operation, then?'

'Charles Bonnet is the cause of your hallucinations, but not the cause of your vision loss. The preliminary test results appear to confirm what I suspected, that you have a form of macular dystrophy, known as Best disease.'

'Macular . . . Isn't that what older people get?'

'Best disease is not age-related. It is a rare genetic condition, and the damage begins far earlier, often in childhood, though it's common to reach your thirties or forties before you notice. Our tests showed the distinctive egg-yolk like deposits at the back of your eye, and then the one where we placed electrodes on your face confirmed changes associated with Best. We generally confirm by taking a family history. Have either of your parents suffered from early sight loss?'

I'm about to trot out the lie about both my parents being dead when I realise what she's said.

'Sight *loss*?'

Dr Nash nods. 'You're managing incredibly well. You've developed adaptive strategies, as people often do when the loss is very gradual. Do you tend to look at things from an angle, for example?'

I nod. 'I always have. When I draw, or paint, tilting my head helps me to . . .' I stop.

'To see more clearly?'

'It's how I've always done it. I thought it was my . . . technique.'

Dr Nash says, 'I'm afraid you may need to find a new hobby.'

'Art isn't my hobby,' I snap back. 'It's my job.'

She shuffles her paperwork. 'I . . . I'm sorry, I didn't realise that.'

'You said loss. What does that mean?'

'So. The deterioration is affecting the central retinal cells, your right eye more than the left. From the initial tests, we'd place the left at Stage Five of the disease.'

'How many stages are there?'

'Five.' She pauses. 'Your vision is poor, but stable. But there is a further complication, which some specialists regard as Stage Six. It happens when new blood vessels grow through to the retina and cause bleeds. That is most likely responsible for the more severe deterioration in your right eye. It may also be what prompted the hallucinations, which typically happen only once the deficit reaches a critical level.'

I nod, trying to take it all in.

'Our aim now will be to avoid a similar crisis on the left side, which can usually be arrested with injections. We will monitor you regularly.'

I breathe and try to think positively.

'OK. OK. So will you treat me here, or in London? Funds shouldn't be a problem. I'm freelance too, so if it's surgery I need, I can clear my diary straightaway.'

Dr Nash sighs. 'Miss Sage, I'm sorry if I haven't been clear. With Best disease, I'm afraid there is currently no treatment. There is nothing we can do to turn back the clock.'

The breath catches in my throat.

I am going blind.

41

It is as though I am watching this happen to someone else.

Dr Nash's voice seems to come from a long way away as she explains that full blindness – the profound darkness we fear the most – is rarer than people think. Glasses won't restore all my vision, but they might make reading and other tasks easier. There are tools, software programmes, injections to stop further damage. I may be able to live a life that looks quite normal from the outside. If I'm lucky, there may never be a crisis in my 'good' eye, the one that is doing most of the work.

But I will never drive again. I certainly won't be able to draw for a living.

'Will you be all right to get home, Miss Sage? *Georgia?*'

My name isn't real. But this is.

'I'm going back to work, actually,' I snap. 'And I'm exactly the same as I was when I walked in. I don't think I need a guide dog quite yet.'

'I meant, after such shocking news?'

'Oh.' I shake my head. 'I'll be fine. I just need some air.'

She hands me a bundle of printouts from the internet. I glance at the first page. The font is huge.

Best disease: cause, prognosis, management.

I sign the forms for payment – Dr Nash reassured me I'll now be called back for further investigations for free under the NHS

– but as I leave the building, I realise what I said to her is a lie. I'm not the same person I was when I walked into the hospital. How could I be?

Cool rain veils my face. I look around me, trying to understand how I missed such a drastic vision loss. As I pass front gardens, I scrutinise the leylandii hedges that cushion the houses from the noise of the main road. The leaves should be green, but to me, they look black.

'Your colour perception may have been diminished by the dystrophy, and straight lines may appear to bend.'

All this time I believed my wild colour choices and claustrophobic compositions were a sign of my unique artist's eye. But really, they were symptoms of the disease leaching the pigment out of the everyday.

Dr Nash says the faulty gene could have come from my mother or my father; either way, it's a legacy I can't get rid of. Thirteen years as Georgia, but Suzanne has had the last laugh.

I remind myself how to put one foot in front of the other.

She told me there will be genetic counselling, to discuss the risk of passing on the disease to my children. I don't tell her that it's my father's actions, not my genes, that will stop me having kids.

'We make accommodations,' the doctor said. 'When sight loss happens gradually, we interpret it as the world changing, not us.'

One in five patients – because that's what I am now – get the severe form, which is affecting my right eye, causing the loss in the centre of my vision.

A black hole.

Though it's not a hole: more of a softening. As I wait to cross the road, I cover my left eye with my hand. Automatically, I angle my head, so that the cars that race past are in the periphery of my vision, and immediately clearer. Without realising, I've been doing this for years. There are so many ways to be in denial . . .

I step off the pavement and I see him waving at me. Charlie. Right in the centre of my vision, where nothing else is in focus. *Not real.*

An accommodation made by my brain to fill in the gaps left by the disease.

But why Charlie? It's the one question Dr Nash couldn't answer.

'What patients see is utterly random, according to the research so far. There's no hidden significance. One patient was documented as seeing Victorian child mourners processing through her garden,' she told me. 'Another looked at the New York subway map and saw flowers blooming at each stop. The visions *do* recur, but there is nothing to suggest they have meaning.'

Yet still I cross the road to join Charlie. He smiles up at me, his young face rendered in perfect detail. *This* is why he's seemed so much more alive to me than everyone else. I can see him face on, no need to tilt my head or look askance. It's so obvious, I cannot believe I never noticed it before.

He is vivid, colourful, *beautiful.* More real than the real world.

I should probably hate him, but I don't. I remember something else Dr Nash said:

'You may find it reassuring to know that once a diagnosis has been made and patients realise they are not suffering from dementia or other mental health issues, the hallucinations become much less alarming. Even comforting.'

As I near the courtroom, I see a cluster of sat vans parking up. I look at my phone and I see I've missed five calls from Neena. I listen to my message.

'Where are you? The jury is coming back, I need you here.'

I step up my pace, jogging, then running the last two blocks. I hope I'm wrong, but I don't have a good feeling about this. It's too soon for the jury to be back unless the verdict has gone the wrong way . . .

42

'It's going to be OK, sweetheart. It doesn't mean they didn't believe you.'

The girl's sobbing reverberates around the lobby. The footballer and his legal team sweep past her, and Neena glares at me as she moves to join the media scrum.

I stay inside, out of shot, as Sam Carr takes up his position on the steps to give his victory speech. What I learned in the hospital has turned my world upside down. This verdict is no surprise, yet it feels like another blow.

'This should never have happened,' he begins, when he's sure the cameras are rolling. The glass doors open and close so I hear snatches of his words. He's glad *it's all over* and relieved *justice has been done*, not to mention dying to get back to the squad.

When I turn away, I see Oli. He waits at a respectful distance from Julie Tranter and her family. He never runs away if a prosecution goes wrong. He's ready to take the blame, to soak up all the anger, if it'll help.

'Of course they *didn't* believe me,' the girl is saying to the policewoman who grips her hand.

I try to read either of their faces: the lack of definition in them now makes horrible sense. How did I not realise?

Despite the blurriness, Miss Tranter's distress is crystal clear.

'Not the legal system's finest hour,' Oli whispers when I approach him.

'It was never going to be an easy win,' I say, touching his arm. Like most barristers, he works to maintain an emotional distance, yet I sense this verdict *has* upset him. 'I'm surprised the CPS brought the case at all.'

'They wouldn't have. Except he's done it before.'

'What?'

'Carr paid off the others. This was the strongest case so far – he got sloppy. Or too carried away. She was stronger than he thought. Hence the bruises.'

'Shit.'

'The police told her about the other girls Carr had raped, appealed to her conscience.' Oli sighs. 'That worked out well for her, didn't it?'

We watch over the banister as the girl stumbles down the marble stairs, caught just in time by her father. She and her family wait in the lobby until the footballer's limo speeds away and the hacks head off to file their stories.

'Maybe he'll stop,' I say, though I don't believe that.

'Or maybe he'll just become even more careful when it comes to covering his tracks.'

'Keep it dead simple,' Toby tells me as we wait to cross the road to Manny's. 'Just Carr and a hint of the jury foreman and His Honour Judge Seriously Grumpy in the background, big smiles all round.'

'Sure.'

'You've drawn it all before, right?'

The traffic clears. As we walk over the gaps in my central vision make something I've always taken for granted suddenly terrifying.

'Sure. It's a doddle,' I tell him.

Of course, I am no more damaged than I was yesterday, but now I know what's wrong with me, everything is different.

'Triple espresso is on me,' he says, leaving me behind in Manny's storeroom.

I face the easel, the blank paper almost accusatory.

I am no longer the court artist. I am an actor, cast in a role I'm not equipped to play. When I saw Neena just now, I half-expected her to see the truth. But she just told me off for being late, before heading straight into a live two-way on the verdict.

Why couldn't she tell I am a fake?

Maybe because she's only ever heard lies from me, from my made-up name to my invented past. Even my 'unique' way of viewing a subject – obliquely, like a cat observing prey – turns out to be part of the deceit.

This drawing will have to be my swansong. Not a grand portrait to grace the cover of a coffee table book, but a workman-like sketch representing just another everyday miscarriage of justice.

I take a pencil, force myself to make a mark, sketching in the shape of the footballer, because he is the main event today. The innocent man.

Like hell.

There is no black hole in the centre of the page, but there is a softening of the line. I shift my body so that I'm seeing more with my peripheral vision. I have to imagine Carr's expression as the jury delivered its verdict when I was still at the hospital.

I temper his relief with a hint of gloating.

Maybe my picture doesn't quite paint a thousand words, but today three would be enough: arrogant; triumphant; *liar*.

'Done?' Toby says.

I step away from the easel and he surveys what I've done. Nods, picks up the mount and paper, calls back over his shoulder, 'Manny's just made your coffee.'

I got away with it.

More than that – knowing my weakness allowed me to hide it better.

In the cafe, Maureen and the other journalists are round the big table in the window, comparing notes before heading off.

'Another close shave, Georgia!' Maureen calls out. 'Still, we've got bigger fish to fry now, haven't we, darling?'

She's holding up a magazine and I sense her watching as I take it. It's *The Bookseller*, and I angle it towards the light so I can read the small type:

Art of Justice book to Geronimo

A full-colour illustrated book featuring the artists whose work influences the criminal justice system is to be published by Ben Rowland, non-fiction publishing director at Geronimo.

The book, described by Rowland as '*CSI* meets Portrait Artist of the Year', will be published in May 2019. It features specially commissioned portraits by artists who work on reconstructions, artists' impressions and courtroom sketches.

'I'm excited about the line-up, which will include a portrait of Santa Claus fire hero Jim Fielding, by up-and-coming court artist Georgia Sage, as well as a new picture of disgraced actor Daisy Moritz by veteran Maureen Lomax. I expect it to appeal to true-crime fans and portraiture fans alike.'

I force a smile, though I know I will never finish the commission. A terrible painting is not the way I want to end my career.

In some ways, it's a relief. I was never going to understand what really happened in Ashdean anyway.

I'll have to call the publisher to explain. I imagine Maureen cracking open the sweet sherry to celebrate her victory.

'Paintbrushes at dawn,' one of the journalists says, and everyone laughs.

'I don't appreciate *veteran* very much, but it's certainly going to be interesting,' Maureen says. 'I'm having tremendous fun with Daisy. I've had the nod that she'll be cover girl, too. Sorry if you were hoping for that slot, Georgia.'

Yesterday, I'd have argued. Now I don't have the heart. I hand back the magazine and go to meet Neena outside.

'Good job, sweet cheeks,' she says, after she's finished her broadcast. 'It's almost as if you were actually in court . . .'

'Sorry about that.'

I consider telling her where I really was. No. Not until I've come to terms with it, decided what to do. We air-kiss goodbye and then she's off to record her voice-over. As the other journalists depart in a swarm, I feel as though they're already in my past.

I walk home, and Charlie is back with me. Every now and then I close my eyes, taking blind steps, trying to prepare myself for the worst-case scenario.

Whenever I feel I can't go any further, I imagine Charlie's little hand in mine.

Dr Nash said the hallucinations sometimes disappear once Charles Bonnet patients adapt to their altered state. I don't want Charlie to leave me. He is the only one who understands who I am.

43

As a kid, I was always a planner. Saved my pocket money for paint and brushes, had calendars ticking off the days until my birthday, summer holidays, Christmas.

After it happened, I never planned again. Why bother, when something – or someone – could render it all pointless?

Now I know I ought to start planning for my new future: research what is happening to me; call the hospital to chase the next appointment; make practical adjustments to my routine; think about what to do with the rest of my life. But since my diagnosis three days ago, I've hidden from the world.

A normal person would call on those close to them – someone like Neena, or Oli, even my foster-parents . . .

Marion and Trevor would be here in hours. They were paid to look after me, but I know our closeness went deeper than that. They believe I have made something of my life, that they helped put me on that path. They are proud of me.

I cannot break their hearts by telling them how everything has gone wrong.

Instead I call someone who is paid to listen.

My counsellor is fighting to conceal his interest in his newly exotic client. Charlie lopes in behind me, as though I'm dragging him to a dentist's appointment.

'How are you feeling about the diagnosis?'

'Right now, this second, I'm angry. Before I left home to walk here, I felt overwhelmed. And when I woke up, I was terrified. I think the psychiatric term for me right now would be a total fuck-up.'

'Humour can be a useful strategy.' He smiles. 'A diagnosis like this must be deeply unsettling. But you're still the same person.'

'I'm an artist. I observe. Record.'

And judge and condemn.

Daniel's face flashes before my eyes; I haven't thought of him for days. Now that I do, all the questions about what happened in Ashdean fill my head.

'You're more than your job, Georgia.'

'I'm not me at all if I can't do that anymore.'

Though perhaps it's just as well. I may have helped convict an innocent man. Maybe Daniel isn't the only one who has suffered from my particular form of blindness.

'Did the specialist know how quickly your vision might deteriorate?'

I shrug. 'It's already bad in my right eye, but my left may be stable. One day, there might be gene therapy. But it's genes that got me into this mess in the first place.'

It's the closest I've come to mentioning my family. I wait for him to go in for the kill, but he doesn't.

'What sources of support do you have, Georgia?'

'I don't want to burden people. That's why I called you.'

He nods. 'Of course. Though people who love you are unlikely to see any cry for help as a burden. I'm sure they'd want to help.'

'How? My career as an artist is over – there's nothing my friends can do to change that.'

'I understand how important your work is to you. But there are other ways to find meaning in your life.'

Meaning.

I stopped believing that on the day I lost Pip and Mum.

'Do you honestly think that?'

The counsellor leans forward.

'This isn't about my opinions, Georgia. But I've seen countless clients change direction, and many do find meaning, yes.'

'But some don't.'

'You have choices. And in the short time I've known you, I've seen determination. Even if it's mainly directed at keeping me in the dark.'

I smile. 'Touché.'

I look up at Charlie, who sits on his haunches, back against the wall.

'Are you seeing a vision now?'

I blink. Charlie has gone. I'm relieved, because I promised myself I wouldn't lie to the counsellor anymore.

'No. I don't want to talk about that.'

He nods. 'Let's stay with work, then. Did you know what you wanted to do from an early age?'

'I always loved to draw. The idea of doing it at criminal trials came later. It's not exactly on the careers officer's list.'

'No. So when did you realise it might be an option for you?'

'I used to hang out around the law courts, after I moved to London for my art course. I pretended it was for a project but really . . . I'd been in a court before. As a witness.'

He says nothing, letting me choose how far to go.

'Isn't this the bit where you say "tell me about your childhood"?'

Again, he doesn't react.

'Would you like to talk about your family?'

'I have no family.'

'But once you did.'

'They're dead.'

I expect condolences but all I get is a sombre nod, and silence again.

'My brother, my mother. Both dead.'

'How?'

'Murdered.'

I hear him take a breath. He waits.

'Don't you want to know how?'

I'm surprised at how angry I sound.

'Would it help you, Georgia? That's all that matters in here.'

I sigh. 'I doubt it. It was twenty years ago.'

'You were very young.'

Only four words, but he speaks them with such compassion that I feel tears building behind my eyes.

'My brother was even younger.'

The counsellor nods.

'Twenty years can feel like a lifetime ago, or yesterday.'

'Sometimes it feels like both at once.'

Another nod. 'Have you talked to anyone about this before?'

'They all wanted me to *let it out*. Social workers. A psychologist. The police, too. But I couldn't, not then.'

'And now?'

'It's too late.'

The same words Daniel said to me in the prison garden, before he turned away.

'Perhaps it helps to recognise that, sometimes, you still feel like the little girl who lost her family?'

No. I'm the little girl who made it worse.

'We were too ordinary for what happened. Two point four children. Well, two plus a dog.'

'What's your definition of ordinary?'

'Ordinarily happy. My mother worked part-time in an office. My dad . . . He was a manager in an engineering firm. Never had the chance of university, worked his way up from the factory floor. He wanted more for us . . . Well, for me . . .' I stop. 'I don't even know where this is coming from.'

The counsellor glances at the clock.

'We have time.'

'Yeah, I have an entire pointless lifetime to fill.'

He lets my anger go.

'There *will* be a point, Georgia.'

'My father killed them, you know.'

The counsellor says nothing.

'My mother, my brother. He killed *them*, but he let me live. I wish he hadn't. I wish we'd all died.'

I've wondered for many years what it'd feel like to confess that to someone. But it's an anticlimax.

'I'm sorry.'

I want to change the subject.

'Do you believe in good and evil?'

'I don't know,' the counsellor says, at length. 'My training tells me all human beings have the capacity for change. But I've met a few individuals who . . . challenged that. What about you, Georgia? What do you think?'

'I think we all have the capacity to be evil.'

'It's a strong word.'

I remember the footballer glorying in his 'victory', and all the other guilty people I've drawn over the years.

'It's more common than you'd think.'

'What about justice? Rehabilitation?'

Now I think of Daniel Fielding again – not the boy I drew, but the man who tried to kill himself. Jail has achieved nothing. That's if he should even have been there in the first place. Maybe all the anger about what happened in Ashdean was directed at the wrong person.

But there is nothing I can do to put that right.

'Prison is about retribution.'

'And forgiveness?'

I close my eyes: I cannot forgive my father. Or myself.

'That only works if there's someone left to forgive you.'

44

If the counselling achieves nothing else, it does make me decide to research what the future holds for someone with my medical conditions.

Back home, I peer at the laptop screen. The blurry display, I know now, has nothing to do with the equipment and everything to do with me. One of the leaflets suggests a text magnification app I can download, and it helps, a little.

My searches return diagrams of the egg yolk effect Dr Nash mentioned, and research on which gene is implicated in Best disease. No cure, though.

Googling Charles Bonnet syndrome instead brings up personal accounts from older patients who've seen visions like mine – trippy patterns, as well as people, brick walls and mazes – all produced by a brain frantically trying to compensate for what the eyes are no longer seeing.

There's a video of an artist who captures his strange hallucinations as abstract paintings on large canvases. They're not very accomplished but he sells them to people wanting to do good. I don't want to become a charity case, an oddity. The point about my work has always been to capture people as they really are – to reveal the secrets they thought they'd hidden from view.

I have looked at the guilty, then looked through them. If my vision deteriorates even further, I won't even be able to recognise my own face in the mirror.

Enough of this. I am out of wine, and I want to get drunk.

I don't notice the envelope until I'm on my way back from the off-licence, my three-for-two bottles of red clinking against each other in the blue plastic bag.

It's A4-sized, couriered and addressed to me. But there's no flat number, and it has been signed for by a neighbour.

My contracts for the art book arrived like this and for a moment, I wonder if the publisher has somehow found out about my eyesight, and this is a letter terminating the contract. Even though I know I'll have to end it myself, I'm not quite ready to tell anyone the truth.

So it can't be that.

Back upstairs, with a large glass of wine at my side, I open the envelope carefully. I've never had hate mail, but Neena has had her share sent to work, including a Jiffy bag with razor blades taped into the flap.

I tip the contents onto the floor: there's a DVD with my name written on in black Sharpie, and an A4 sheet neatly folded into three. I open it. It's a word-processed list of names in frustratingly small type. I look closer, tilt the page. Women's names.

No. Not women. *Girls.* At the top of the page, the heading reads:

Female residents of Copse View Home for Girls, Ashdean, 1978-1980.

My heart beats a little faster as a yellow square of paper falls to the floor. I reach down to pick up the sticky note, which has just a few words scrawled in the same block capitals as those on the DVD.

I GOT NOWHERE. MAYBE YOU CAN DO BETTER. PLEASE TRY FOR THEIR SAKES.

Who sent this?

I scan the names – there are thirty or more – trying to make sense of the list. Is Sharon Fielding here? Her surname would have been different then, of course, but there are no Sharons at all.

I hold my breath as I put the disc into my computer and wait for it to load. A folder appears with eight files identified only by number. I double-click on the first one.

A photograph appears: it shows girls dressed for a party. The image is fuzzy, and not only because of my vision. It was obviously taken decades ago; the poodle perms and batwing jumpers give it away. The 1980s? There are a few Christmas decorations on the unfinished wall.

I click on the next file: another party, same place. In the background, I can see a breeze-block wall, a painting table loaded with drinks. Different girls, same era. I pick up the typed list. Anne, Cathy, Samantha? They raise plastic cups to the camera. They look too young to be drinking booze.

The next photo was taken outdoors, in spring. The girls – I can't tell if it's the same ones – are wearing a lot less. One is sunburned across the shoulders. Another has eyes half-closed – either she was caught unawares, or she's drunk. They're all smoking, lined up against a whitewashed wall. Above this, glimpses of treetops.

Were these taken at Copse View? I pick up the envelope and look for a return address. There's nothing on the outside, but someone has written something on the inside flap. When I manage to focus on the tiny letters, my mouth goes dry.

Sent on behalf of Sharon Fielding, Copse View, Ashdean.

Whoever sent this knows I've been painting Jim. Maybe they know I visited Daniel too.

But they don't know that it's all over, that this crime and those people no longer have anything to do with me.

I click on the last photo.

For the first time, there's a man in the image. No, not a man – a teenager. The photo has been taken indoors with a flash because his eyes blaze. His upper body is naked, and next to him is a short-haired blonde girl, and she's clutching a T-shirt to her chest, which doesn't quite cover her breasts. She's fourteen, fifteen at most. Her face is hard to read. Shock? Fear?

But it's not her I stare at. It's the young man.

And a defiant, unfinished Jim Fielding stares back.

45

The woman in the dock doesn't look like a child killer. She is neat, featureless. I have no idea how I'm going to draw her.

I shouldn't be working. But when Neena called about this case, I couldn't bring myself to tell her about my diagnosis over the phone.

And there's a more important reason: she's the only person I can think of who might be able to make sense of the photos from Ashdean.

I've spent the weekend poring over the faces, especially Jim's, and reading the girls' names until I know them by heart. I've googled them too but got nowhere; the names are too common, the girls lost in the Web. Jim was involved with one, maybe more, that much is obvious. Perhaps they weren't willing. Whoever sent me the pictures obviously doesn't think the whole story has been told.

I'll never actually finish Jim's portrait, but he doesn't have to know that yet. I can still carry on with the next sitting, ask him questions. Except I don't know *what* questions.

Neena will. That's why I'm here.

'This is not about a mother who snapped from exhaustion, or suffered postnatal depression,' the young prosecution barrister is saying. 'The defendant, Pamela Kirk, is a cold, arrogant woman who felt she'd given her children life, therefore she had the right

to take it from them. Which is exactly what she did. For her husband, the nightmare will never end.'

The more I stare at the accused woman, the less clear she
becomes. The words of the opening speech float in and out of
my head – 'an evil streak . . . feelings of resentment that couldn't
be controlled . . . complete lack of remorse' – but I can't seem to
match them to the defendant's unexceptional face.

Little Charlie stands in the empty witness box, yawning, and
the fact he's not really there makes him no less vivid.

On the packed train up to London this morning, as Charlie
played hide-and-seek between the commuters' pinstriped legs,
I convinced myself I might still get away with this sketch. After
all, I've had Best disease for years without knowing, and still
managed to build my *glorious* career.

I was lying to myself. I try to angle my head to see the defendant more clearly, but nothing about her seems to register. *Knowing*
has changed everything.

Neena taps her watch and leans in to whisper:

'Can you manage a quick one, for the lunchtime bulletin? It's
a quiet news day, they want to lead with it.'

Shit.

This is not meant to happen yet.

I'd assumed I wouldn't have to draw the defendant until tea-
time. My plan was to catch Neena at lunch – show her the list of
girls who were at Copse View and ask her to apply her twisted
journalistic perspective to it all. But she'll be a lot less receptive
if I've already let her down with a poor drawing.

My hands feel numb. When I try to scribble a final note about
the woman – how the boat-neck shape of her taupe cotton top is

perhaps the most exciting thing about her – my writing spiders across the page and my pen falls onto the floor.

Neena leans down with me to pick it up.

'You *are* all right, aren't you, Georgia?'

There is a warning note in her voice.

I follow her as we shuffle out of court early, our faces towards the bench, avoiding turning our backs on the judge. Charlie pokes his tongue out, mocking me and the whole pantomime.

Outside in the street, I set up to draw near the camera, while Neena writes her script. The sunshine is harsh, making my eyes water.

'What are you planning?' she calls over.

I stare at my easel. My mind is as blank as the paper mounted on it. I have no memory of what this woman looks like, except that boat-necked top and the limp, mousy hair just touching her shoulders.

'Um, it'll be . . . her watching as the barrister opens for the prosecution.'

'Fine. I'll be done in twenty-five, that should be enough time, right?'

Twenty-five minutes. Fifteen hundred seconds. I've done decent work in that time before. But I want to run away, down the Strand, to lose myself in the meandering tourists and the impatient office workers getting an early lunch. Anywhere would be better than standing here, feeling blind.

Come on, Georgia.

It doesn't have to be brilliant, it just has to be done.

I tried to find a picture of the defendant in advance, knowing this could happen. But, unusually, the papers had found nothing on her: no Facebook account; no office party snap sold by a former colleague for a quick buck.

One step at a time: I sketch in the square angles of the court; the black, prosecutor's gown; the back of his head, reddish hair just creeping out from under the scrolls of the wig.

Pamela Kirk remains formless in my head. I reach out with my pencil, hoping something will come to me. I begin with the neckline, then the rounded slump of her shoulders and plump arms – at least, I *think* they were plump.

But no. Perhaps they were skinny, bird-like. A flat chest follows, and then guilty hands that touch the front of the dock. No wedding ring anymore.

I must do this.

The hair is easier, a few lethargic strokes in yellow ochre.

But her face . . . Her face won't come.

I sense Neena's eyes on me, from where she's setting up ready for her piece to camera. There can't be long left. I check my watch. Eight minutes have already passed.

How?

I try to remember what any nose is like, any mouth, and as I force myself to put another line on the page, I'm as clueless as a child with brand-new crayons, trying to represent the world for the first time.

Charlie stands near me. I copy *his* nose.

I add lips with a pinkish pastel. I try to fill in Pamela Kirk's eyes with the pencil and then smudges of dullish green.

When I step back, it's worse than I thought – a series of lines that just about make a face, but not a recognisable one. Neena has finished recording her spot now; she's heading towards me, reaching for the picture.

'It's not working,' I say, trying to shield it from view.

'What do you mean? Anything's better than nothing, I can't afford black holes in the package. Come on.'

I shake my head. 'Please. Can't you do without, just this once?'

'George—'

Toby is striding towards us, frowning with impatience, and I know the only thing left is to step aside and let them both see what a mess I've made.

I look away; I can't bear to be pitied.

'Oh,' says Toby.

'Shit,' says Neena. 'We can't use that, can we?'

The producer is staring at my picture.

'I . . .' He looks at his watch. 'We don't have time to reshoot . . . I mean, if we did it as a fleeting pan across, so we don't linger on the face . . .'

He's losing conviction as he speaks.

Before he can finish the sentence, I turn and run.

46

I don't stop until I get to Covent Garden Market, fighting through the crowds, abandoning the cautious walk I've adopted since my diagnosis.

Suddenly all the strength that propelled me from the court drains away. I lean against one of the wrought-iron pillars as I fight for breath.

It's over.

Whether they use the image or not – *please don't let them use it* – word will spread. Journalists live to gossip: before the day is out, everyone will know that I have lost whatever gift I once had.

Maureen will know.

And the publisher. And Jim Fielding . . .

Goosebumps prickle up my back and neck. I turn slowly, half-expecting to see Neena or Toby behind me, ready to rage.

But there's no one I know. Only the humpbacked tourists with their daysacks.

I wait for my heart to slow, and my strength to return. But while my breath grows less ragged, my legs still feel like jelly. I can't imagine making it as far as the Tube, never mind all the way home to Brighton.

I reach into my pocket and with shaking hands, call a number.

'It's me. Could you come, please? I need you.'

* * *

Oli finds me after thirty minutes.

In that time, I've had four missed calls: two from Neena, and two from WITHHELD – almost certainly a BBC news exec. Voicemail messages show as a blurry reel-to-reel symbol in the corner of my phone screen, but I'm not brave enough to play them back.

'Let's get you out of here,' Oli says.

I let myself be led out of the market like a child. A black cab is waiting. Oli gives the address of his chambers, and I climb in, slumping against the back seat.

Oli passes me a bottle of water, and when I've finished drinking, he takes my hand and holds it until we get to Lincoln's Inn.

It's thirteen years since I first visited him here; he'd hoped to impress me, and it worked. But as he leads me across the manicured grass, this legal Disneyland seems so distant from real life – and real victims.

Once we're inside, Oli finds a small, oak-panelled meeting room and gently ushers me inside. He takes off my coat, sits me down, then places my bag and box of pastels on the heavy table.

'I left my easel behind,' I say.

'I'll arrange to have it picked up. It'll be OK.'

My sobbing takes me by surprise, and Oli too. He crouches next to my chair and lets me cry, my head resting on his shoulder. I spot short strands of horsehair on the dark fabric of his suit.

'Were you in court? Did I drag you out?'

He shakes his head. 'Your timing was good. Early adjournment.'

I try to apologise between the sobs but the sounds I make are nothing like words, and he holds my hands in my lap.

I don't know how long I cry for. Two minutes? Twenty? But eventually I'm empty. I sit up, my eyes raw, my ears buzzing.

'I don't know where that came from.' My voice is the croak of an eighty-year-old, and I laugh. 'I've never cried like that before.'

Oli nods. 'I've never seen you cry at all.'

I point to the sodden patch on the shoulder of his suit.

'The dry cleaners on Battersea Park Road will sort that. Get them to do the blue riband service.'

He smiles. 'I will. Do you want to tell me what's happened?'

I do want to tell him everything. But where would I begin? With today's sketch? My diagnosis? Or earlier still, with Pip and Mum and what my father did?

'Yes. But I'll need a drink.'

'That is never a problem in chambers. Give me two minutes.'

47

I nurse the brandy glass, the crystal warming under my fingers. *Dutch courage*. Where do I begin?

'Oli, I'm going blind. Or, at least, I've lost a substantial part of my sight.'

He doesn't move. He's close to me, his leg pressed up against mine, and our breathing has taken on the same rhythm.

'How?'

'It's a genetic condition. It probably started in my teens. I didn't realise until . . .' I hesitate. The next part is harder to confide. 'It sounds mad, but I found out because I'd started seeing things.'

Again, if he's shocked, he doesn't show it.

'What things?'

'People who aren't there. I thought I was going crazy.'

I look up, expecting Charlie to be in the room with us, but it's just Oli and me.

'Why didn't you tell me?'

'Because I was afraid of what it meant. And I'm not exactly good godmother material if I'm a fruitcake, am I?'

'We're all a bit crazy, Georgie. But how does it connect to your eyesight?'

I explain.

'There must be surgery. There's bound to be something in the States—'

I shake my head. 'Right now, the best they can do is monitor me. Glasses might make a few things easier, but the damage is done.'

'Oh, my poor Georgie.' His voice breaks. 'Promise me you won't keep anything from me again?'

I nod. But of course it's already a lie. I know I won't tell him *his poor Georgie* is no more real than my hallucinations.

'So you still went to work today?'

The memory of what happened outside the Bailey makes blood rush to my face, the humiliation as blunt as a cosh.

'Yes. For the Beeb.'

He frowns. 'You haven't told Neena?'

My face burns hotter. I've humiliated her, as well as myself. As far as Neena is concerned, missing a deadline is on a par with murder.

'I thought I could manage, just until I'd got my head together. But I screwed up. My sketch was laughable.' I shudder. 'I ran before I could see whether they used it on the lunchtime bulletin.'

'It probably wasn't that bad, you've always been your worst critic.'

'Believe me, it was.' I sigh. 'Could you look, see if they did use it?'

'If you're sure . . .'

He takes out his iPhone and finds the BBC homepage. Chances are it's OK. I can't see the image having made it to air. So at least my shame will be restricted to my colleagues.

I watch his face as he searches.

He tuts, then puts the phone face down on the table.

'What did you find?'

Oli opens his mouth but I can tell he's reluctant to share.

'Tell me, Oli, please, or I'll imagine the worst.'

'They did use it.'

'Shit.' I close my eyes. 'Did you see the drawing?'

'No, but . . . Look, it'll pass. These things always do.'

'What will pass?'

I pick up the phone and swipe the screen, but crying has made my vision even worse than usual and I can't see the search results.

'It's on social media. A few keyboard warriors. Have they never had an off day at work?'

I find the controls to magnify the text.

Did you see the news at 1? Are the BBC getting the local infants school to do their drawings for them now?

Another has drawn their own court sketch, a stick man with a judge's wig: my job application, reckon my chances are bloody good.

Already, people are retweeting with the hashtag #sketchfail, and adding more of their own drawings.

'I'm sorry,' Oli says.

'What for? It was my mistake. To carry on, thinking I could hide the fact I'm a fucking dead loss.'

Oli reaches over to take the phone out of my hands, then adds a good slosh of brandy to my glass.

'Will you be OK, Georgie?'

I shrug.

'You'll call me, won't you? Any time. If there's . . .' He hesitates. 'If you feel desperate. If you start thinking you might do something, um, drastic.'

I stare at him. 'You mean, top myself?' I shake my head. 'I'm not the type.'

But my father was.

I close my eyes and see his venous blood, sticky as port, splashed across aqua bathroom tiles.

And then Daniel Fielding, lying in a cell, bleeding out from his skinny ankles.

And Sharon, falling backwards into a ravine – whether she jumped, or was pushed, the terror is unimaginable.

But maybe for the Fieldings, the fear of life was stronger than the relief of death.

Why?

He nods, reassured. 'What will you do now?

'Back to Brighton. The publisher is bound to see this and cancel the portrait.'

Oli says nothing.

'I know you disapproved of my taking the commission, but it is . . . it was important to me.' And to whoever it was that sent me those photographs, and the list of names from the home. 'Oli, was there something else you came across on the case? Any suggestion at all that Jim was more than just a Jack the Lad?'

He turns away and pours a brandy for himself.

'Why do you ask?'

'Well, it's not like you to try to stop me doing something.'

'No, I learned the hard way that it never works.' He turns back. 'I didn't trust him. The rest of the team adored him, knew what a great witness he'd make, so I never said it out loud, but I always felt he was holding things back.'

'Just a feeling, or hard evidence?'

He shakes his head. 'Georgia, it's such a long time ago. You can't expect me to remember every detail of all the cases I've worked on. I'm getting old. And the sleepless nights definitely don't help.'

I groan. 'Sorry. I never even asked about Millie. How is she?'

He smiles. And then he's off, telling me how they're coping, and what it's like having the world's youngest diva under their roof. Despite the moaning, I can tell he's happier than he's ever been.

It's only after he's taken me to the station, made sure I'm on the right train, and waved me goodbye, that I admit to myself that Oli was lying. He has a photographic memory. He's known for it on the circuit.

So why pretend he can't remember?

48

The BBC are terribly nice when they call to sack me. As I walk on the beach, the day after the debacle in London, my phone rings again and again.

Time to stop hiding.

'Hello, Georgia,' the executive producer says when I pick up, 'how *are* you?'

The sounds of the newsroom fade. A door closes. He's gone somewhere private for our last conversation.

'I'm OK. Look, I'm sorry about yesterday, it's—'

'Please. Stop there. We're worried about *you*. Though everything we know about social media tells us the feeding frenzy will blow over very soon.'

'It's fine. I don't even have a Twitter account.'

'Sensible woman. Now . . .' I hear him take a breath. 'We've been reviewing our court coverage, as I believe Neena might have mentioned. We're cutting back on commissioning freelancers. Which I'm afraid means . . .'

'You don't have to dress it up, Phil. I understand why you don't want to use me again.'

'Well, we could possibly revisit the decision if things change,' he says, dropping the pretence. 'We're no strangers to burnout in the news world. Perhaps you need a little time off.'

'Yes,' I say, wishing I could fix my life with a bloody mini-break.

'You've done great work for us, Georgia. Seriously, your illustrations were some of the best I've ever seen. You had . . .' He coughs, 'You *have* a gift. You've got my mobile. Please do call me if there's anything I can do.'

After he rings off, I stare at the phone until the screen goes blank. When I finally look up, a chattering crocodile of language students are coming in the opposite direction. It's going to be a sunny day.

I lean against the turquoise railings to let them pass. One girl catches my eye: the others all wear hoodies and ripped jeans, but she's dressed for a party, in a short denim skirt and a low-cut white vest that doesn't quite cover the pink bra underneath.

If I were the tour leader, I'd have made her go back to change.

But as the group files past, the girl doesn't, and nobody looks back to see where she is.

'You'll want to catch them up,' I call out, though she may not understand English.

She doesn't smile, or speak. She stares at me, and her long, blue-black hair is still despite the breeze.

Oh God.

As I watch, Charlie runs out from between the beach huts where he'd been playing hide-and-seek. He grins and races towards the girl in pink, and she crouches down to pick him up.

He's too big to carry, really, his chubby arms thicker than her spindly ones, and as he rests his head against her flat chest, he puts his thumb in his mouth.

I blink and blink again, but the two of them are still there. The girl strokes Charlie's hair and then sets him down. Her legs are pale, a few bruises blooming on her calves, and she totters, fawn-like, because her flimsy white heels are so high.

Might she be his sister? No, Charlie's sister is younger than him.

His mother? No. They are not alike.

Maybe she's just someone my desperate brain has invented. Dr Nash said that's as likely as hallucinations being based on a real person.

Except there is *something* familiar about her . . .

I walk back to my flat as fast as I dare, craning my neck this way and that to make sure I'm not about to collide with a bike or a running child. When I get inside, Jim's painting stands on its easel in the bay, my unfinished business. I took the cover off this morning, trying to assess whether it's OK. And whether the subject is good, evil, or somewhere in between.

I ignore it, and go to my laptop, pulling up the folder of images that was sent with the list of names from Copse View.

I click past the picture of the young Jim. I've looked at it often enough to know the girl I just saw on the prom is not the one from that photo. I scroll through the images, but none of them are right.

And then I see her.

She's in the background of a shot taken indoors. I see the bra strap first, a blurry stripe of pink against a bony shoulder blade. The hair is a wild shock of black, and her face is in profile, as though she's just turning, aware of the camera pointed in her direction.

She could have walked straight out of this photo, and onto the promenade, into my path.

Who are you?

And what do you want me to know?

49

I pull out everything I have on the Fielding case – my original courtroom sketches, the cuttings, and my work from the sittings with Jim – and lay the materials out on the parquet floor. I print out each of the photographs to A4 size and do the same with the shots of Copse View and the house at Cherry Blossom Lane I download from the internet.

I can't change my own past, or my future. But something went wrong at Ashdean. Maybe I can still expose that. All these years I've wanted to make the guilty pay – this is my chance.

Jim's half-finished portrait looms over me, just as he lords it over that strange town. I tack together four sheets of A2 paper to create a canvas as large as a picnic rug and kneel next to it on the floor. And then I begin to draw . . .

Dusk comes, then darkness, as I work furiously, propelled by frustration. No. Anger. Most of it has nothing to do with Ashdean – I'm not so stupid. But all the fury around my own past, and my loss of vision, might now serve a purpose in the present. The meaning the counsellor wanted me to find.

The sheets fill up: with Daniel, now and then; his sister; his mother – a cipher sketch based on a fuzzy image of her in a press report.

Next to them, I put the O'Neill kids and as I begin to draw Charlie, he appears in my armchair.

'Is this what you've been trying to get me to do all along?' I whisper.

He smiles back, and when I've finished sketching him, he's gone. Next to him, I draw in little Jodie, and a figure, based on my vague memory from Jim's engagement party, of their mother, Emma.

And right in the centre, a silhouette to represent Robert O'Neill. Jim's *best mate*.

And his victim?

I move the pictures and documents around, trying to get the timing clear in my head. In the photo I was sent, Jim is fifteen at most. It must have been taken before he was arrested and jailed for joyriding and nicking some cigarettes.

Why did Jim take all the blame? It's a pretty enormous favour to do someone you end up hating. Did Robert promise to help him after he was released? Because they stayed friends for years, according to Jim's nosy neighbour.

I move the note that came with the photos:

I GOT NOWHERE. MAYBE YOU CAN DO BETTER. PLEASE TRY FOR THEIR SAKES.

Whoever sent this feels as I do, that there is unfinished business here. What did Daniel say? 'There was a woman copper saw through him too, she got bloody nowhere.'

It must be the same woman. I write **who is she?** in big letters next to the note. Underneath I write, **and how did she find me?**

Tracking down an anonymous policewoman isn't going to be easy. I daren't make too many waves in Ashdean, because whoever I talk to there might report straight back to Jim. The girls on the list are the key, not the person who sent it. If I could only find one of those ex-residents, I might be able to get somewhere. I did try searching for them on the night the photos arrived, but maybe I didn't try hard enough.

I finish laying out the evidence I have: adding the boxy shape of the burned-out house at Cherry Blossom Lane. Then a photo of Tessa on her wedding day.

I scramble to my feet and survey what I've done, looking for connections. Everything leads back to Jim. But I struggle to connect what he might have done in his teens to the deaths of his wives.

Sharon lived at Copse View, of course. Perhaps she knew what Jim did, was going to blow the whistle. But why would she do that so far into a marriage that produced two children?

I remember the poisonous neighbour's hints that Jim was playing away, might even have fathered little Jodie. Could he have wanted his damaged first wife out of the way? And, having got away with it the first time, could he have tired of poor Tessa even sooner, and done it again?

I think of what Oli said about disliking Jim. And what he didn't say. I saw Jim as a victim of awful circumstances, but perhaps that's only because he *wanted* me to see him that way. He charmed me, but kept an eye on me too – keeping tabs on where I went and who I spoke to in Ashdean.

Did he only agree to the sittings to check how much I knew? If he did harm Robert, perhaps he thought my portrait commission was a ruse to dig deeper into his background. Maybe he knows the policewoman, whoever she was, still hasn't given up.

I stare at the old photo of Jim aged, what, fourteen or fifteen? Handsome, powerful. Hard to resist.

There's movement in the room. The girl with the vest top is standing in front of me. She's in perfect focus, a reminder that everything else is soft around the edges. I don't flinch. She seems to belong.

'Which one of these are you?' I ask, gesturing to the list of names, but knowing she cannot answer. 'Jackie? Or Andrea?'

None of the names seem quite right, but I *do* want to name her.

'I can't share my house with someone I don't know. So I will call you . . .'

Her vest falls off her shoulder, revealing the bright bra strap again. It makes her look so young, so vulnerable.

'I will call you Pink.'

50

My phone wakes me; I'm slumped in my chair, the laptop still open. I scrabble on the table for it and see an unknown London number before answering.

'Georgia, hi, it's Benjamin.'

The publisher. Shit. I immediately regret not letting it go to voicemail.

'Oh, hi.'

'Hope I haven't caught you at a bad time – are those seagulls I can hear in the background?'

I'm racking my brains to find an excuse to get off the phone.

'I'm . . . in bed. With a fever.'

'Oh dear,' he says. 'Sorry to hear that. I promise I won't keep you long. I just wanted to check in, see how the Jim Fielding portrait is going.'

I sit up, feeling sick, and not only because of drinking that entire bottle of wine. Benjamin must have seen the #sketchfail stuff on social media.

'Almost done with it, actually. I've been waiting for a good time for the last sitting. He's a fascinating character.'

'Great, great. And you . . .? Everything is all right with you, Georgia?'

The girl – Pink – is sitting on my bedroom chair. She looks as wrecked as I feel, her mascara clotted, her lipstick partly bitten away.

'You've been on Twitter, haven't you?' I say.

A gull swoops down onto my windowsill, screaming like a child.

'Yes, I have seen the . . . hashtag thing. Look, I'm not worried about your work at all. And we *really* want the Fielding case in the book. But I don't want it to be an extra pressure. So I was wondering if you might want to, I don't know, *collaborate* with another artist?'

'Don't tell me. With Maureen?'

I can't let him do this – not now I've seen Pink, now there's another lead to follow.

'Well, she would be the obvious choice, but—'

'This was her idea, wasn't it?'

'She just phoned to let me know she'd finished her commission, and mentioned you appeared to be under stress. I'd hate the deadline to make it worse for you. I have a moral responsibility to my contributors.'

Fuck her. Fuck Maureen and her scheming and her greed.

I don't know where all this anger is coming from, but I use it.

'What would be far more stressful, Benjamin, would be to think you're not behind me. Especially after all the things you said about how much more talented I am than Maureen. Still, I suppose if we got together, she and I could compare notes on the book. And on our meetings with you.'

I let the implications of a tête-à-tête between his two court artists sink in. If both of us pull out, there's no one else for him to call on in the whole country. *We are it.* The benefits of practising a dying art.

Pink is smiling at me.

'Um . . . OK. Maybe it's not time for that yet,' Benjamin says. 'I'd feel more comfortable, though, if we could make sure we're both on the same page, image-wise?'

'You want to see what I've done so far?'

'Yes.'

I could go straight into the living room, snap the portrait-in-progress, and be put out of my misery before lunch . . .

I'm too chicken, and this is too important, especially now.

'All right. But after I've done my next sitting.'

He sighs. 'Georgia, we can't cover any more expenses until we know we're getting something usable.'

I remember how slick and sycophantic he was at that meeting in the riverside boardroom. This is how quickly the world can turn.

'Fine. I'll be in touch as soon as I've got something to show—'

'But—'

'Goodbye, Benjamin.'

I cut the call and then, without giving myself the chance to lose my nerve, I text Jim. As I type, my fingers slowly tracing out the words, I am imagining two versions of him: the charismatic, haunted man I've been sketching, and the murderous version his son believes him to be.

The painting is almost finished but I need one final session. Is there any way we could meet again? Ideally without interruptions.

Thirty seconds later, I jump when the reply comes through.

Let me see what I can do. JF

I shower away the headachy feeling, and return to work. Last night's notes and sketches make more sense to me than I'd expected. My gut still tells me justice has not been done.

I got nowhere again searching for the Copse View girls, so I decide to focus on Sharon instead, looking for reports of her death in December 2001. The archives are limited but eventually I find a story from the Bristol evening paper, with the fuzzy image of a young Sharon that I half-recognise from a couple of the longer background reports around Jim the tragic hero. Her kids are a lot like her: their faces thin and thoughtful.

On the page opposite is a photograph of the Clifton Suspension Bridge, showing the stunning architecture, and the terrifying drop to the open gorge below.

The headline reads: *Loving mum jumped from suicide bridge despite husband's pleas, inquest hears.*

I magnify the text and position the screen so I can just about read the newsprint.

A Gloucestershire mum-of-two, who travelled to Bristol specifically to commit suicide, ignored her husband's desperate pleas and jumped to her death from a ledge as he watched helplessly, an inquest heard yesterday.

Sharon Fielding, from Ashdean in the Forest of Dean, had been suffering from depression for over a decade, the coroner was told. Her GP first prescribed anti-depressant medication after the birth of her son, now aged 15, and the treatment was effective for some years.

However, Mrs Fielding, aged 34, became depressed again approximately six months before her death and refused to seek help. On the day of her death, she waited until her son and elder daughter had left for school, and then took the train to Bristol.

In a statement read out at the inquest, James Fielding explained that he came home mid-morning to check on his wife, as he'd been concerned about her mood at breakfast. He found the house empty, and a note on the kitchen table which alarmed him. Remembering a previous conversation where she'd talked about taking her life, he drove to the notorious suicide spot over the Avon Gorge and searched for her.

Mr Fielding realised she had climbed up onto a ledge on the buttress wall on the Clifton side of the bridge, without being noticed by passers-by. He abandoned his car and climbed up beside her to try to talk to her. They had a conversation, but she then decided to jump.

Details of the conversation were not revealed in court, but a cyclist witness told how he saw two figures holding hands. He called 999 but before police arrived, the female figure disappeared from view.

Mrs Fielding's body was found later that day. She had suffered multiple fractures and catastrophic injuries on impact, and was found to be twice the legal limit for drinking. The note Mrs Fielding left was lost in the struggle.

The coroner recorded a verdict of suicide. He noted that barriers newly erected along the sides of the bridge have reduced the number of attempts. The buttress walls are not currently protected in this way for architectural reasons, but this is under review.

I read the article three times. Poor Sharon was only three years older than I am now. And her life had been a struggle from the start. I remember Jim saying in our first sitting that they'd hoped to overcome all the – what did he call it? – 'messed-up stuff' from their childhoods to give their own children love.

It seemed so believable when he'd said it. Now I'm not so sure.

There's nothing here to support Daniel's accusation that his father pushed his mother to her death. But the photo of the bridge shows how hard it must have been for the witness or anyone else to get a clear view of what happened in her last moments.

And maybe it's because I've spent my career listening to liars, but it seems a pretty big coincidence that Jim found his wife so easily. And an even bigger one that the note that explained *why* she killed herself blew away in the chaos.

Daniel knows more, he must do. He wouldn't have set fire to Jim's house if he hadn't truly believed his father was a killer.

And that's if he even *did* set fire to it. I never managed to ask him during my visit. Everything seems to shift from my grasp, as unfocused as my vision.

I need to ask him outright, but I'll never get back inside the jail. Perhaps a letter could work – one that convinces him there could still be justice for his mother. I'll have to pretend I believe everything he told me. The idea makes me uncomfortable but I need to make Daniel see I am the only person who cares.

Apart from whoever sent me these photos, of course.

As I grab a notebook to draft a letter, my phone buzzes.

The coast is clear on Saturday morning. Will that work for you? JF

The timing of his text unnerves me, although of course he is just responding to my own.

Saturday would only give me two days to get my act together, to build the evidence, so I can ask him the right questions. I find the idea of being alone with him in that glass house, behind those impenetrable white walls, scares me now.

But I can take precautions. Tell the publisher and Neena. Place all my evidence somewhere for safekeeping in case . . . Well, in case Daniel is right and his father does believe he can get away with murder.

I've seen enough psychopaths in the dock over the last thirteen years to know it's their arrogance that makes them dangerous.

But I have one thing that makes me dangerous too.

I have nothing left to lose.

I'll be there.

Dear Daniel,

I know you probably don't want to hear from me again, but first of all, I wanted to apologise for cornering you after the art class. I thought you might have wanted to talk, but I should have realised how vulnerable you must be feeling.

So why am I not leaving you alone? Because what you said got me looking again at everything that has happened in Ashdean since your mother died, and before. And I think you might be right. There have been too many deaths.

I won't write more because I know you fear others are watching or listening.

At our meeting, you wanted to know what your case had to do with me?

The truth is, I know what it is to lose those you love, under horrible circumstances. My father murdered my mother and my brother when I was eleven. Even now, I don't know why he took them.

I'm not telling you to make you feel sorry for me. I just want you to know that I understand how impossible it is to put some things behind you. And it ought to be easier for me - my father is in prison, at least. Without justice, it must be even harder. You can't let him get away with this.

I'm sorry for the drawings I did thirteen years ago. If you give me a chance to help you now, I can put some of that right. Make him pay. Please call or write back. I won't let you down again.

Georgia Sage

51

Now I'm not allowed to drive – the thought of how dangerous I was behind the wheel makes me shudder – I take the train from Brighton to Bristol, a four-hour journey, leaving on the earliest route west. I'm travelling a day early: before I see Jim again, I have some research to do.

On the seat next to me is the canvas, already marked in pencil with a composition based on my initial studies and photographs: the ghost of the portrait to come. Not that it matters now, but I have to keep up the pretence.

In the painting that will never be finished, Jim Fielding would take up almost every inch of the space, with no more than a hint of the chair bearing his weight. Even for an artist with full sight, it would be a challenge to capture his complexities.

Can he be a hero *and* a psychopath?

I texted Benjamin the date and time of the next sitting, because I have no idea how Jim might react to my questions.

'We apologise for the breakdown of the air conditioning system in Carriages E and H,' the guard announces, sounding bored. 'Like the rest of us, it's struggling in the heat.'

My carriage fills up with a hen party travelling to Bristol. I'm shoehorned into a corner seat, facing backwards, and I have to put the canvas on my lap. The women laugh and pass around bottles of prosecco, even though it's not even ten o'clock yet. My loneliness feels absolute – even Charlie and Pink are nowhere to be seen.

As I let my eyes half-close, the rural landscape beyond the glass shifts from soothing to extraordinary. Bright green serpents coil and hiss between the rows of crops on a distant hillside.

I hold my breath, startled but also awestruck. Dr Nash had warned me that this is 'normal' for Charles Bonnet patients. It explains the brick walls I saw on the train back from Devon, before I knew what was wrong with me.

Now I am no longer afraid of madness, I can appreciate their psychedelic beauty.

When I blink, they disappear.

'We will shortly be arriving at Bristol Temple Meads, where this train terminates.'

Sweat drips down my forehead as I lift my backpack off the rack, hugging the canvas to my body as I leave the station. When I tell the taxi driver where I want to go, he gives me a nervous look.

'Not planning to jump, are you, lover?'

I smile. No. But I want to try to understand why someone would.

He drops me next to a green on the Clifton side of the bridge. I've never been here before and that makes me edgy: since my diagnosis, I've avoided unfamiliar places.

At first, the structure doesn't look impressive. But once I get past the modern toll booths and onto the bridge itself, everything changes. Giant piers made of huge stones rise up ahead of me, linked by white girders stretching the impossible gap between cliffs. We're higher up than I expected and already just the thought of a person falling onto those unforgiving sand-banks below is giving me vertigo.

There's a paved viewing area to the side of the pier: I can look directly into the void. The view is spectacular: little rows of rainbow cottages running up and down the hill like the keys of a child's xylophone. Down below, the water snakes through brown mudflats. It looks soft, but I think of the broken bones Sharon Fielding suffered. It is anything but a gentle death.

I've been depressed, but I cannot imagine jumping, and definitely not if it meant leaving behind two children who needed me. What kind of a mother could do that?

But if Jim pushed her, knowing it would leave their kids motherless, what does that make him?

It's such a long way to fall. There would have been enough time to think, to regret.

For a moment, I think I see two figures at the bottom – Charlie and Pink. I blink, and they're gone.

I step back from the edge, vertigo making me nauseous. The visit has achieved nothing.

But I still have two more people to see before I confront Jim. I need everything I can get.

52

I take a cab back to Temple Meads: my journey the reverse of the last trip Sharon Fielding ever made.

Pink sits across the aisle from me on the train and then follows me onto the bus from Gloucester to Ashdean. There are seventy-three stops before I arrive back in Jim's domain. Seventy-three chances for me to change my mind, turn back.

The road narrows and the forest encroaches on us so that the bus driver has to put his headlights on, though it's still early afternoon. Finally, the road dips, as we travel down into Ashdean.

'Your stop at last, darling,' the driver calls out.

I get off at the square and walk towards the pub. A cabbie watches me, fanning his face with a copy of the *Sun*. Will he be reporting back to Jim later?

When I arrive at the pub the dog scrabbles against the door.

'Rambo recognises you,' the landlord says as the dog leaps up, trying to lick my face. 'On your way to visit "family" again, is it?'

He winks, to show he's seen through me.

'I've come back to paint the landscape,' I say, making sure the canvas is fully covered.

He raises an eyebrow but says nothing. Has he been speaking to Jim too?

At the top of the stairs, he takes me right instead of left. My room is higher up than the first time, and in the distance,

I can just make out the blur of Jim's house, surrounded by white walls.

I shower to get rid of the stickiness from my journey, then head right out again, a baseball cap pulled down low on my face. I don't know if it makes me more obvious or less, but at least it stops the sun making my eyes even more useless.

The walk back towards Cherry Blossom Lane is unshaded and I'm soon as sweaty as I was before showering. When I arrive, the estate is quiet, as it was the first time I came. Then the nosy neighbour appears as though she's been expecting me, dyed black hair tied back, an apron tight around her belly.

'You again.'

'Me again.' I try to make out her expression. Can I trust her? A gossip is useful, but also likely to tell everyone about *me* as soon as I've gone. It's a calculated risk. 'I came to take you up on that cuppa.'

She chuckles. 'That all, is it?' But she turns back towards her house, and leads the way through the back door, into her kitchen. 'I'm Chrissie. You?'

'Georgia.'

Chrissie nods, and for a moment I wonder if she already knows that.

'How do you take your tea?'

Not at all, if I can help it.

'Weak. No milk or sugar.'

The room smells of minced beef and vanilla air freshener, sweet and cloying. She's making a lasagne. I look around. It's a tip, but homely. An imposing oak dresser stretches across one wall, covered in photos and postcards. There's a wicker basket stuffed with children's games and soft toys on the floor, and a battered high chair next to the wooden table.

'The grandkids,' she says. 'Last one's all but grown out of that now, but I can't quite admit it to myself. Kept it in case one of my boys has another. Anyway, I think you told me a fib, last time.'

'I'm sure I didn't.'

'You said you weren't media. But you're painting him, aren't you?'

The room is airless.

'It's not for the news, it's for a book.'

She gives me a long look.

'Splitting hairs. Gonna be a pretty picture, is it?'

'Not pretty, but interesting.' I clear my throat. 'I'm trying to build up some more background on . . . how Jim is seen. In the town. To make it a rounded portrait.'

She places a large teapot on the table, wrapped in a hand-knitted pink cosy with piggy ears, then returns to her work, spreading an earthenware dish with the last of some grey-brown mince.

'Thought you'd get more gossip, you mean?'

'I—'

'I was surprised he let you do it, when I heard. He's not a fan of snoopers. But I suspect you can be quite persuasive. He likes pretty things. As long as they stay pretty.'

I hear the innuendo.

'Do you like Jim, Chrissie?'

She smiles as she arranges lasagne sheets so they form a solid layer, then pours over a thick white sauce.

'What kind of a question is that?'

'Because I'm not sure if I'm . . . safe with him.'

I hold my breath. I'd planned this as a gambit, but it *is* a risk. She could have a hotline to Fielding.

'Safe? Well, are you planning to fall in love with him?'

She stops scattering grated cheese over the top of the dish while she waits for my answer.

'No.'

'Then you're probably all right. It only seems to get dodgy for the women he cares about.' She laughs. 'Or their husbands.'

Robert O'Neill.

I picture my drawings, my mind map. I have to get her to say more.

'I have heard rumours that Jim finds it hard to take no for an answer.'

'You worried he won't be able to resist you, Georgia?'

She turns away and puts the food in the oven: the door snaps shut.

'He's been very kind,' I say, 'but I've heard people say stuff about him. Sometimes I think, no smoke without fire.'

Chrissie snorts. 'Not the most delicate way of putting it, is it? When you think about what happened to his house. And his second wife.'

As I look up, embarrassed, I spot Charlie sitting next to the toy box, feet tapping on the tessellated vinyl floor. The burn scar on his face glows crimson.

'But I hear you,' she continues, taking off her apron and sitting down to pour herself a tea. 'Truth is, the only people who really understood Jim Fielding are long gone.'

'Dead?'

'Or disappeared in a puff of smoke . . .' Chrissie giggles at the unintended pun. 'You got me putting my foot in it now.'

'Who do you mean?'

'His parents are dead, of course. And his wives. I don't think poor Tessa knew much, mind. Sweet but not the sharpest knife in the drawer. But Sharon understood her husband better than anyone. Which means you have to ask yourself – what made her jump?'

'Why do *you* think she died?'

Chrissie glances at my ring finger.

'Ever been married?' When I shake my head, she carries on. 'Every marriage has its own rules. Not the ones you agree to in church. I watched them for years, Sharon and Jim Fielding, and I always thought they loved each other more than most.'

'Watched them?'

'Well, heard them, really. The walls in these houses are made of paper and glue. He'd be rough as you like outside the house, but inside, what I heard, he did his best to cope with her moods.

'But then Robert showed up. Jim's long-lost pal, come to raise a family round the corner from his old mate, with his new wife and little boy in tow. And Emma was cute as a button. What man wouldn't have his head turned?'

Cute as a button? The woman I saw with Robert on the night of Jim's engagement party looked washed out.

'When was this?'

'A year or so before Sharon topped herself?' She stands up. 'I've got a picture of them all somewhere, let me see if I can find it.'

She goes to the dresser and starts pulling out photo albums.

'You think Emma and Jim had an affair?'

'Well, you have to ask yourself what pushed Sharon over the edge.'

Or *who*? I think. And it's the second time she's asked the question. Before I've worked out how to reply, she thumps a big photo album on the table.

'Found it!'

She riffles through – I catch glimpses of children, parties, groups. Chrissie seems to have taken it on herself to document the life of her street.

She must have had offers from the papers for these after the fire, and I admire her a little more for not selling. One of my dad's colleagues showed no restraint and flogged my father's pallid ID card mugshot. It's the media go-to on the rare occasions they revisit the case – in it he looks every inch the killer in waiting.

Chrissie slips a large photo out of its cellophane pocket. I try to hold it at my best viewing angle without her noticing. It shows a summer barbecue in somebody's back garden. Everyone has lined up together, ten or so adults, holding up bottles and glasses. Kids at their sides or playing in a lime green paddling pool behind them. Chrissie is missing: I imagine her behind the camera, bossing people into position and insisting they 'say cheese!'

Jim is at the centre of this picture. To see him, I need to position it to my left. Next to him, not Sharon, but a pretty young woman with coppery hair in a twenties-style bob, wearing a striped cotton dress. It takes me a few moments to recognise her as the careworn woman I saw in the pub on the night Jim got engaged.

'Is that Emma?'

She nods. 'Yes. this'd be, what, the summer before Sharon took her life. That's Robert, on the other side of her.'

The one that got away.

He's barely taller than his wife, and a head shorter than Jim. I tilt the picture towards the light. His face is pleasant, and his suit – a bit OTT for a barbecue – fits him so well it might have been tailor-made. But he's not handsome the way Jim is.

'He left town, didn't he?'

'Around the time Emma started to show with her second kid. Jodie. Poor little lamb. But men do that, sometimes, don't they? Get cold feet. They're never the ones left holding the babies.'

'Do you think Robert suspected he might not be the baby's father?'

'Nothing gets past you, eh?' Chrissie shrugs. 'Who knows. Only time I had much to do with him was when he built that.' She points at the dresser.

'Robert made that?'

I hadn't thought about what he did for a living and seeing this rather beautiful thing he created makes him seem more real.

'He was a chippie. No, more than that. A craftsman. Spent hours in here making sure every detail was right. Before then I'd thought he was a bit up himself. Too good for round here with his fancy car and his aftershave. He always wore buckets of it. What kind of a man does that?'

One who likes to smell good, I think. Hardly a crime, except in the eyes of the judgemental Chrissie. I can't wait to get out of here, but I need to keep pushing.

'Awful,' I say. 'But the dresser is lovely.'

'Yeah. He was good company, as it turned out. Not a snob, like I'd thought. The car and the rest, I think he wasn't well off as a kid. Wanted things to be better for his family, his boy.'

Yet he abandoned them, what, six months later?

I look again at the photo and I notice something else: Charlie sitting at Robert's feet, the child's podgy hand reaching up towards his father, who smiles back. The kid can't be older than two. His round face is unblemished – of course, the fire hadn't happened yet.

There's an intimacy about the moment that makes it more compelling than anything else in the photo.

'They look sweet together, Robert and Charlie.'

'He talked about the kid a lot . . .' Chrissie takes the album from me and closes it with a slap. 'I thought this was about Mr Fielding trying it on with you?'

'It was,' I say. 'But I'm curious about the O'Neills, too. They are part of the story. And Robert doesn't look the type to do a runner?'

Chrissie says nothing. Then she shakes her head.

'I hate to break it to you, Georgia, but some men aren't very nice. Now, I need to be getting on.'

The mood has changed. I'm sure she knows more but she's closing down. Honesty is my last throw of the dice.

'Please, Chrissie. Help me understand. I've spent hours with Jim and I feel like I know less about him now than when I started.'

Chrissie returns the album to the dresser. Her blouse is sticking to her back, a line of sweat darkening her spine. The lasagne is beginning to cook, and the meaty smell makes me nauseous.

'What *do* you talk about when you're painting him? You and Mr Fielding?'

'Family. It seems to be everything to him. He's gone out of his way to look after others, including Jodie and Charlie. He even wants to create affordable homes. He's one of the good guys, isn't he?'

Chrissie opens her mouth and I wait.

'If I were you, love, I'd finish your painting and move on. Everybody has secrets. I'm not saying his are worse than anyone else's. But whatever they are, they're nothing to do with you.'

I'm being dismissed.

'You're right. Thank you, anyway.'

I stand up and as I do, I see Charlie on the floor again. His pose is exactly the same as it is in the photo: he reaches up, to me, or to his unseen father. Something happened to deprive this kid of his dad.

'One last thing. Do you have any idea where Robert might have moved to?

Chrissie sighs. 'For Pete's sake. How should I know? It was chaos, back then. First poor Sharon. Next thing, Emma mooning round town, asking everyone if they'd seen her husband. No one had a bloody clue. Least of all Jim. He was in pieces after Sharon died, hardly capable of doing up his shoelaces, never mind . . .'

I wait for her to finish the sentence.

'Never mind what?'

She stares at me for so long that I wonder if she's heard me. Then finally she speaks.

'Like I said before, anyone who might really know what went on that Christmas, is long gone.'

She shakes her head, and ushers me towards the back door.

53

I walk down Chrissie's drive, and out of Cherry Blossom Lane.

Once her house – and number 9 – are out of sight, I lean against a tree, glad to be alone again.

Long gone.

Chrissie contradicted herself with everything she said. Implying that Jim drove his wife to despair, then insisting he was the perfect husband. Suggesting Robert was a weak man who was tired of fatherhood, but showing me a photograph that seemed to demonstrate the opposite.

I look at my watch. Ten to five. There's one last conversation to have before I see Jim again.

Little Charlie is walking ahead of me, keen to make tracks.

'Let's go and see how you turned out, eh?' I say.

The streets are still quiet. Sometimes, in Brighton, I long for the absence of voices. But here, it doesn't feel peaceful. As I pass rows of houses, the blank eyes of the windows reflect my blurry image back at myself. I think of all the secrets behind them.

The garage where Charlie works – or where he's a *wage slave grease monkey* according to his Facebook profile – is under a line of old railway arches, though the town's station closed decades ago. A man – forties, rail-thin – stands outside, talking to someone on his mobile.

'Is Charlie here?' I ask.

He nods towards the garage.

The young man has his back to me, as he sweeps the floor. I glance around, looking for *my* Charlie, and am relieved the child has gone. I'm going to need all my concentration to handle this.

'Hi,' I call out.

Grown-up Charlie doesn't hear me. The fluid way he moves as he drags the broom across the concrete is so familiar.

'Hello?' I say, louder. Too loud.

He spins round, tearing earbuds from his ears. Even without *my* Charlie here, finally being face to face makes me dizzy.

'We're closing for the weekend, sorry.'

'I don't want my car fixed. I want to talk to you.'

His hand darts to his face and he wipes it across the area of his cheek which was burned in the fire. He leaves a smear of oil behind.

'About what?'

'About your godfather.'

'Yeah, no. I gotta leave now. Mum's working tonight so I'm minding Jodie. Can't be late, she gets upset.'

It's a relief Emma won't be around. I daren't risk talking to her, because she has so many reasons to be loyal and report back to Jim.

'It's important.' I trot out the lie I've planned. 'It's about a surprise for Jim. For his wedding. It won't take long.'

Charlie shrugs. 'You could walk with me, I s'pose.'

'Great!'

'All right, I just gotta—'

He waves down at his blue overalls and I realise he wants me to leave while he changes. I step outside and wait. His boss is off the phone now, and I hear him ribbing Charlie when he emerges.

'Hey, toy boy, don't do anything I wouldn't do, eh, kid?'

Charlie is blushing when he steps alongside me. The first time I saw him, he was with his mates, cocky and laddish. Now he just seems terribly young.

'Did you hear that Jim is having his picture painted for his wedding?' I ask.

He shrugs and keeps walking.

'I'm the artist who is doing it. I've spent a couple of days drawing him. But I also want to talk to other people who know him well.'

'What for?'

'A portrait isn't like a photograph. It's layered. Every time you look at the painting, you see something new about the person. Their kindness, sense of humour, their sadness. That's why I want to know how other people see Jim.'

He crosses the road towards a brambly bank with a path worn by decades of people taking the same short cut.

'Right.' He sounds dubious. I don't blame him.

'I hear he's been good to you, since your dad . . .' I leave the sentence unfinished.

'Fucked off and left us to it?'

Charlie sounds defiant, as though he's expecting me to tell him off for swearing.

Instead I say, 'I know what that's like. I haven't seen my dad since I was twelve.'

I hate using my own past this way.

'I don't really remember mine. Except that he left at Christmas.'

'I'm sorry.'

'Don't be. Best present he could have given us. If he couldn't even be bothered to say goodbye, why should I care?'

I think of the little boy in the picture, reaching up for Robert. If Jim did kill his friend, he broke his child's heart too.

'You have no idea why he left?'

'Thought you were here to help you paint Uncle Jim better?'

Charlie is cannier than I thought. I consider whether he might be Jim's son, but the dates don't fit: Chrissie said Robert moved here with his son already in tow. Charlie looks wrong, too: his features are too rounded and pleasant, with none of Jim's power.

I pull myself up the last part of the bank by a branch. Something pierces my palm.

'Ouch.'

I look down and a thorn is embedded in the centre. I hadn't seen that they were roses.

Charlie comes back to me and inspects my hand.

'That's gone deep.'

He reaches over and pulls out the thorn. A bead of blood appears and he passes me a clean tissue from his bag.

Ahead of us, there's a new estate, the small houses built in little clusters. I sense Charlie's nearly home. I'm running out of time.

'Your dad is a carpenter, isn't he? Is that how he met Jim, working on site?'

Charlie shakes his head. 'They knew each other way before that, when they were my age. Uncle Jim even went to jail for him. My dad is a selfish shit.'

'It sounds as though Jim was more of a father to you than Robert.'

Charlie glares at me. 'Wish he was my fucking dad. He wouldn't have left Mum with no money and nothing to flog but a bunch of fancy suits he never even wore.'

'Maybe your father didn't have a choice?'

'Course he did. I know why he left.'

'You do?'

'He knew Mum was having Jodie and he couldn't handle the idea of a disabled kid. Not good for his image. Even though my sister is worth ten of him.'

But Jim said Emma didn't know Jodie had Down syndrome until delivery.

'How do you know that?'

'Jim told me.'

'But . . .'

Has Jim lied to me, or to Charlie? Maybe he's lied to everyone.

'Jim won't like it, you asking all these questions. Hates gossip.'

'It's not gossip. Everything you say helps me to make the portrait richer, but I want it to be a surprise. So please don't mention our chat.'

I want to ask even more questions – like, do you know Emma has had your father declared dead? But that's something I'd never do.

Charlie shakes his head and stomps off, conversation closed. As he approaches the cul-de-sac opposite he stops and, for a moment, I think he's going to come back, to shout at me, maybe. Or tell me something else?

But then he waves at someone in the garden of the furthest house and breaks into a jog. *Jodie.* She comes running towards him and as they meet in the street, he lifts her up as though she's five, not fifteen, and I can hear her giggling from here.

54

In my room, I bolt the door and lay out my big sheet of sketches on the floor. I take out a pencil and begin to draw. Robert is now a person, not a silhouette: a carpenter who wears too much cologne. A loving father.

A victim?

Charlie hates his dad, but then he never really knew him. All he has to go on is his absence, and what others have said about him.

Especially what Jim has said about him. And maybe Jim has strong reasons to stop Charlie – or anyone else – ever trying to find Robert O'Neill. But why has no one warned Charlie that his father has been declared dead?

A hard copy of Robert's probate paperwork should have been sent to my flat by now; perhaps it's waiting for me at home. I go to the records office site to check the despatch date.

You have one new download waiting to view.

I hadn't realised it'd be online too. I only have my phone with its tiny display, but I want to read it. The PDF opens quickly: it's two pages, the first a covering note giving details of where and when it was filed.

The second page is handwritten: three paragraphs. It's hard for me to read, though I *can* see how painstaking his script is. It fits what I know about this careful man with his good clothes and his detailed craftsmanship.

I magnify the text, to read just a couple of letters at a time. The will is dated the year before Robert's disappearance, and the address at the top is 22 Oakland Close. The first paragraph must have been copied from a book or the internet: *I declare this is my last will and testament.*

The second lets just a little of this man's personality bleed through.

> *I wish I had more to leave her, but everything I own goes to my beautiful wife, Emma Caitlin O'Neill. I hope that we will have many decades together but I trust that she will care for our cherished son, Charlie, and that perhaps one day he might take up the carpentry tools I've used to make a living for my small but perfect family. Whenever I die, I will have been a lucky, lucky man.*

Jodie wasn't even conceived then, I suppose.

> *As to my funeral and the disposal of my remains, I leave the arrangements to Emma, whatever makes it least painful for her. But I would ask that I am cremated, and my ashes scattered by the playground in our special place here in the Forest, so she and Charlie can visit me, and he can play, while she enjoys the peace, knowing I am at rest too.*

The will has been witnessed by a couple of people whose names I don't recognise. But the unexpected sweetness of the words actually makes me catch my breath.

Charlie should have seen this, should know how his father felt about him. Yet no one in Ashdean even seems to have told him that Robert is presumed dead.

Perhaps because the man they fear was behind it could come after them too?

The canvas of Jim leans against the wall, the box of new paints beside it. I bought the oils the publisher wanted me to use before I knew about my vision, before I understood this last sitting was all going to be a charade. I haven't used oils in twenty years – even the slightest whiff of that tarry smell along the corridor at art school was enough to send me gasping out into the street, the olfactory memory of the last time I used them literally nauseating.

The painting will never be finished, whatever happens at the sitting. I couldn't care less. All of it – the book, the publisher, and my rivalry with Maureen – seem trivial now. Even Oli and Neena feel like characters from someone else's life.

They are of course, in a way: because they are part of Georgia's.

As I pick up the tubes of oil paint, I can almost feel myself becoming Suzanne again, the girl who tried to capture the world – and the people around her – as she saw it. The girl who loved faces, and the stories they told.

The girl who hasn't dared to look properly at her own face in the mirror for twenty years.

'I want you to paint all our faces,' Pip had demanded, as we discussed the plans for his eighth birthday. It was going to be the best ever.

'A portrait of you and your friends?'

I remember feeling pleased. My first commission.

'No! Paint *on our faces*. Like superheroes. I will be Spider-Man.'

Of course I said yes. No one but Dad ever said no to Pip. He'd already bought his outfit on a trip to Bristol with Mum. He knew exactly what music he wanted too – 'Tubthumping' played on a loop, so all his mates could throw themselves at the sprung floor of the church hall, screaming *And we get up again*', at the top of their voices.

As well as the face paints, I was saving up to buy him a Tamagotchi, though I had a bet with Abi that I'd end up taking care of it – Pip was as flighty as every other seven-year-old.

Being a big sister was equally brilliant and irritating. But are you still a sister when your brother is dead?

For a while, I had to be. The hearse picked us up from Grandad's house, in a drab town a hundred miles from home, where no one knew me in person but everyone knew what I was: the tragic survivor.

First, we went to the funeral home. I didn't want to see my mother's body, but I did ask to visit Pip before they closed the coffin, because otherwise I thought I'd believe he was still out there, giggling and playing tricks.

They'd asked me what his favourite clothes were, and I'd told them they'd find his birthday outfit in his wardrobe. And that's what they dressed him in, the wide-legged black sports pants, and a rainbow hoodie from The Gap. They'd pulled the hood up over his head and I thought it looked strange, until I realised he probably had injuries there. I wanted to paint his face like Spider-Man's, but I knew no one would understand.

Even though I'd never seen him so still, a part of me expected him to leap up.

I get up again.

But he never would. And that was down to me.

None of Pip's friends, or mine, came to the church: it was too far for them, and anyway, what responsible parent would let their child experience something so unbearable. Instead, the congregation was made up of my grandfather's elderly friends, and weeping thirty-something women who'd been at school with my mother.

I wore a black party dress with a lace hem, too young for me, but the mourners treated me as an adult, with their hugs and handshakes and *sorry for your loss platitudes.* And I began to see myself as an adult too. I had chosen to come to the funeral and that made me realise I could choose not to stay with my grandfather. A couple of days later, I ran away. When the social workers held a family meeting – me and Grandad all that was left – I knew he was relieved that he wouldn't have to look after me.

'I doubt I'm up to the job, to be honest,' he'd said, as though he was being asked to do gardening that might hurt his arthritic knees.

Just because two people are mourning the same souls, doesn't mean they can offer any comfort to each other. My grandfather died before the anniversary of Mum and Pip's death. Another life my father ended.

The relationship between Pip and me remains frozen. He is buried with Mum in the family plot, but I've never been back. Knowing he is supposedly 'at rest' does nothing to assuage my guilt.

But it might still help Charlie and Jodie to have somewhere to visit *their* dad, to know they were not deserted. Another reason I have to make tomorrow work.

55

It's too hot to sleep properly. I wake, hoping the weather has broken, but instead the morning sun rises white-hot and relentless.

I don't bother with breakfast. The landlord offers to store my stuff for the day 'while you go off painting the woods', but I take everything with me. I hope I won't have to run, but it's good to be prepared . . .

Approaching the White House, I smile, in case Jim is watching me on CCTV. Fear is good, it'll keep me sharp. And I need to be sharp, to make the most of this last chance.

My steps falter.

Admit it, Georgia. You're afraid.

I could still turn back. Why is this *my* responsibility?

Because all I've seen – the girls in the photos, Robert's will, and my *companions* Charlie and Pink – make it so. Because I know no one else will fight for them.

The gate doesn't open early this time. I have to press the intercom.

I say, 'Hello, it's me, Georgia.'

There's silence.

It's a few seconds before the bolts are released.

No one is waiting for me as I cross the white shingle – the dazzle makes my eyes sting – but when I enter the hallway, everything is as it was the last time: the brown leather chair; the two mahogany side tables with coffee, water, biscuits. Before today, that seemed courteous and considerate.

Now it seems controlling.

'Hello, stranger.'

I turn. He's dressed the same – jeans, checked blue shirt revealing his forest tattoos – and he's the same person. But I'm not. I know about my failing vision, and I know about his lies.

'Hello, Jim. Thanks for having me back.'

He's carrying a bottle of white wine, and puts it down on one of the tables, before stepping forward to embrace me. He's never done that before.

I let myself be held, though his touch makes me want to run. Are these hands that have killed?

Finally, he lets go. I place my rucksack close to the easel, facing towards the chair. Hidden inside the front pocket, my phone is already recording everything we say. I've tested it three times.

Jim unscrews the wine cap and pours himself a large glass.

'Dutch courage. To tell you the truth, Georgie, after the last sitting, I'd decided to pull out because of all the memories it was bringing back. But then . . .' He looks up at me. I can't read his expression, but his voice is kind. 'I saw you'd had a bit of bother. I didn't want to let you down.'

'The Twitter thing? Have you been googling me?'

'Well, you know so much about me and I was curious about you. Got to say, I was shocked at the stick you got. I don't understand this modern way of hitting someone when they're down.'

'I appreciate your support,' I say, though I am wondering what else he found out about me. 'I know the publishers were very pleased when I told them I was coming here today.'

It's a really heavy-handed way to let him know people know where I am, but Jim just nods.

'Right you are.'

I begin to set up.

'Anyway, Georgia, let's keep it light. None of your interrogation today.' He sits down in this chair. 'Alexa, play Classic FM.' Music fills the room. 'My new toy. My daughter got it for me. I can play whatever you fancy. Jazz. Songs from the shows. Whatever will help you to make me look handsome!'

I nod, but I know the music will make it harder for my phone to pick up what he says. Is he doing this on purpose?

No.

He has no reason to suspect me.

'They say they're listening all the time,' I tell him as I place my canvas and lay out my paints. 'The companies. Recording your every word.'

He shrugs. 'Good luck to anyone having to wade through my ramblings, but I can turn it off if you'd rather.'

'Can we keep it off to start with? Actually, before we get going . . .' I decide to jump in. 'I do have some news for you. You might know already but I think it's only fair to check.'

'Know what?'

'A barrister friend of mine told me that Daniel's being considered for release under licence. I wasn't sure if the Prison Service would have informed you.'

It's a lie. I have no new information. But I want to see Jim's reaction. I look up, tilting my head to try to read his face.

'I – No. I hadn't heard that.'

'With the wedding coming up, I thought you'd prefer to know. I don't know if you could be worried he might . . .'

'Try again?'

'Well, yes.'

Jim doesn't move.

'I'm sorry. I shouldn't have mentioned it.'

He sighs. 'You've seen how we live? Inside, we're safe. But I can't hole up in here all the time, and neither can Leah.'

'Surely they wouldn't release him if he is still a threat?'

'It's not like I thought he was a threat *before*.' He sighs again. 'Thanks for the warning. I'll get one of my guys to make a few calls.'

I regret the lie now, in case it's put Daniel at risk.

I open my paintbox. The lids on the tubes are squeezed on factory-tight. Once upon a time, I craved the intense colours of oils the way other little girls craved sweets. But after that day I was locked in, blood and paint became inseparable . . .

My heart is beating so violently I'm sure Jim must hear it. I choose Viridian green for the background of blurred leaves beyond the glass roof. Unscrew the cap, pierce the metal seal. Let the scent unfurl, like a new shoot on a pine tree.

I try to breathe away the panic, the way the asthma nurse taught me, all those years ago.

I am here. I am not there. I never have to go back there.

Jim takes a slurp of wine, grimacing.

'You think I'm to blame, don't you?'

I meet his eyes, the centre of his face blurring. Is this the moment when it all comes out?

'For what?'

'For what happened to Sharon and Tessa.'

His voice is flat, but his eyes are soft-edged circles of Prussian blue.

It's not a confession: Jim wants me to reassure him there was nothing he could have done. Or he's testing me.

'No. But you've told me already, Jim, that you do blame yourself.'

The smell of the oil paint reminds me Jim is not the only one to carry that burden.

Jim sighs. 'I know. We weren't going to talk about any of this, were we?'

He takes another gulp of wine and stares resolutely ahead. Conversation closed.

I blend other colours: Cobalt for his shirt, Payne's for the fading tattoos. The paint smell grows stronger, a potent cloud of memories. Jim stares into the distance, and I move my head so I can study his face.

Hero or villain?

My head says he's guilty. My heart sees a lost man.

I try to focus on simply capturing him as he is at this pre-cise moment, my brush creating the broad shape of him on the canvas, vivifying the feeble pencil marks I'd made before. Time becomes irrelevant. All that matters is the two Jims – the one sitting there, and the one I am remaking in paint.

'You had a moment, just now. Didn't you?' Jim says. 'A light-ning strike or whatever artists have. I saw it in your face. Lit up from the inside, like a candle.'

I angle my head towards the canvas. His eyes stare back, keen and challenging. A few moments ago, this was no more than an outline; now there's no doubt that this is Jim Fielding.

I can still paint.

I'm half-blind, but I still have some talent left.

'Yes.'

'What's that feel like?' he asks.

'I . . .' No one ever asks me this. They're all too obsessed with the people I draw to care how I feel. 'It *is* like you said, Jim. Brightness. For a moment, there's just me and the work. A bomb could go off right next to me and I wouldn't notice.'

'Have you always had a talent for drawing?'

'Painting more than drawing. I loved colour, as a kid. My mother always said I spilled my dinner on the tray of my high chair just so I could draw faces in it.' *I'd forgotten that.* 'Though maybe all children do that?'

'Never fed the babies,' Jim says. 'Though my Amy is about to pop. So I'll get my chance with my first grandchild. Unbelievable. My baby, a mother herself.'

I go to ask him the usual questions – what day she is due, does she know the sex – when I stop myself.

That isn't why I'm here.

The painting, the chit-chat, are irrelevant. But him talking about family is an opening for me.

'Where does Amy live?'

'Up on a new estate I built a couple of years ago. Closer to the other end of town, to where we used to live.'

I seize my chance.

'You've changed the face of Ashdean. And now you'll do the same with Copse View.'

He says nothing.

'It really stayed with me, what you're doing there. To transform a place that must have bad associations for you personally . . .' I tail off.

'How so?'

'Well, poor Sharon. And isn't that where you two met, at the home?'

'I met her at school, after I got out of the nick.'

'Oh, I thought ... Well, I thought it must have been quite a draw for the young men of Ashdean.' I know I'm getting into dangerous territory, but there's no alternative. 'A house full of teenage girls.'

'You thought wrong.' His voice is steely. 'Never set a foot in the place until long after it closed, and then only with my architect.'

I know you're lying.

The photographs prove he was there. But he's losing patience, and I am running out of time.

I'd planned to tease him into revealing pieces of himself, enough to give Oli, Neena, the police, something to pursue. But instead I'm just making him angry. I should stop this before it gets dangerous. Feign illness, leave the bloody picture behind.

Movement in the corner of my eye makes me turn: Pink stands outside in the courtyard, her worried face clearer than anything else around me. Perhaps she doesn't want me to give up.

'Sometimes I wonder if I'm going to do you justice,' I say, returning to the script I planned out. 'So many aspects to your personality. Bravery. Strength. Generosity.'

He raises an eyebrow. 'Why are you buttering me up?'

I laugh. 'No. Seriously. Most people I draw are . . . small. Even the cruel ones, the criminals. They do terrible things because they're inadequate. You're different.'

As I say the words, part of me believes them. Despite all the lies, I want him to prove himself a hero.

But Jim shrugs it off.

'I'm as inadequate as the next man, Georgia.'

I shake my head. 'No. I think you've always had courage. Look at what you told me about taking the rap for your friend. Richard, was it?'

'Robert.'

'You didn't have to do that.'

He is motionless.

'Why did you do that, Jim?

He opens his mouth, and I will him to unburden himself – to tell me he was blackmailed, that he'd done things he was ashamed of.

'You know what, let's call this a day,' he says, very quietly.

He stands up and I sense his power. Over his shoulder, I look at the open glass doors that lead out to the driveway.

Calm down. It's OK. People know where I am. And he knows that they do.

I don't have long left. I have to switch tactics. Plan B.

'Jim, you let me come and paint you for a reason. I think it's because there are things you haven't been able to share for so long. Things that have been crushing you.'

'Who the hell do you think you are?'

He's coming towards me now, knocking over the bottle of wine. His rage is sudden and intense. I brace myself for a blow. But instead he picks up my bag, rips open the zip, and empties the contents onto the floor.

'Where is it?' he's asking. 'Where have you hidden the fucking thing?'

'What?' The mind map drawing falls out, but he ignores it.

'Whatever you're using to record me. I trusted you, Georgia, I wanted to *help* you. Christ knows, I am a sucker for a girl in distress but—'

'I don't know what you're talking about.'

He has emptied everything onto the marble floor now: art materials, toiletries, my laptop.

'Where's your phone?'

Instinctively, I reach out to grab back my bag. He spots the front pocket and unzips it, pulling out the phone.

'You little bitch! Have you recorded everything I've said?'

He throws the phone at the floor and I hear the battery fly off.

I manage to grab the handset and battery, and scrabble around to throw whatever I can back into my bag. I need to get out of here before Jim turns on me.

As I head out into the courtyard, I pass Pink, who is watching, expressionless.

'Open the gate, Jim.' I hold up my useless phone, 'or I will call the police and tell them what you've done.'

'What? What am I meant to have done except help you?'

I am by the gate. The metal against my back is scorching though my T-shirt fabric, and Jim is panting from heat or rage or both.

My mind races: my last chance to get him to say something, anything, that I can tell the police. Just one fact that'll make them look into what happened at Copse View and to his supposed best friend.

Otherwise, what has this all been for?

'I wanted to believe in you, Jim. But too many bad things have happened to the people around you. Sharon? Tessa? Even Daniel has suffered.'

Jim's on me, now, his fingers gripping my clothes, holding me against the gate. Our faces are inches apart, his skin pale with anger, pupils black.

'You think I haven't suffered?' He spits out the words. 'I loved them and I lost them and still everyone thinks it was down to me. Can't any of you get it into your heads – I didn't hurt anyone!'

I am teetering. Do I run, or jump?

Jump.

'Not even Robert O'Neill?'

He flinches.

'Jim. Did you kill Robert?'

It feels as though I am falling, waiting for the impact as I hit the ground.

56

His eyes don't even seem to see me anymore. I try to find the bolt to the gate behind my back, to work out if there's a manual release.

Before the blow falls.

'That piece of shit is what this is all about?'

'It's about all of them,' I say, my voice a whisper now. 'The girls at Copse View. Your wives. And this guy who supposedly abandoned his kid and pregnant wife without leaving so much as a note.'

I close my eyes and wait for pain.

But instead, his grip on me loosens.

'Why are you doing this? Do you get a twisted thrill from messing with people's lives?

'You can't be allowed to get away with it.'

'With what? You've decided I'm a murderer based on what . . .? Gossip from an old neighbour, and the ramblings of my sick son?'

So he *has* been keeping track of me.

'You lied to me about Robert. You said he'd left of his own free will. But he's been declared dead and—'

'Robert deserved to die.'

I stare at him. There it is: a confession, of sorts. But I've no recording, and he knows it. It'll be his word against mine.

If I even get out of here.

'What did Robert do to you, except get in your way because you wanted to be with Emma?'

Jim scoffs. 'You think you get it but you really don't. I should have known from your drawings – you've a warped view of people, of the world. You shouldn't be let anywhere near people who've suffered.'

He takes a step back towards me. I cringe.

'And what about Copse View? You've lied about that too.'

'Don't you fucking dare judge me. You weren't there.'

And you swore you were never there either.

But I say nothing.

'One painting. That's all you had to do. My Amy had her suspicions about what you were here for, but I felt sorry for you. I could tell you were lost and I gave you the benefit of the doubt. Never again.'

'I did only come here to paint you. I *wanted* you to be good. I never expected to find out—'

'Find out what?'

Pink stares at me from over Jim's shoulder.

'That you're as bad as the rest of them. Worse, because you pretend to be a hero.'

'I've never claimed to be anything special,' he says. 'It's everyone else that decided I was someone they should look up to.'

He's less angry now. Could I call for help? Not without a battery.

He nods. 'Go ahead, Georgia, call whoever you like – the cops, the media. Use my landline, be my guest. But what will you tell them? You came *here*, remember. You badgered me for this last sitting. And, seriously, if you want me to unlock the gates, I will. But first, let me explain what happens after you leave here.'

He's going to let me go.

'You are never to come back. The commission is off, and you'll leave the canvas with me. Don't worry, I'll burn it, so your artistic reputation won't be harmed. What's left of it, that is. All right?'

I nod.

'And you forget me and Daniel and Robert fucking O'Neill. For your own sake as much as mine. Stop hijacking other people's pain, and deal with whatever makes you so bloody damaged.'

I stare at him.

'All right. I'll go.'

But already I'm thinking of how I can take what he's said and use it to fuel the next online search for evidence, to track down the people who know what he's hiding.

He comes closer, his face a blur, his breath acidic with white wine.

'Don't think I won't know if you keep asking questions,' he whispers. 'I've stayed on top this long by knowing what people are going to do before they do it. And if you don't stay out of my life, I will *ruin* yours.

'I'll tell people that you harassed poor, damaged Charlie and visited the spot where my wife killed herself. That you spied on me. And for what? To get a story that doesn't exist. To build your career.'

I say nothing.

But I don't even have a career. I only have this.

'One last thing you should know: I don't hurt women. Never have, whatever you think. But if violence is what it will take to protect the people I love, that's what I'll use. Do you believe me, Georgia?'

My body feels limp. Behind Jim, Pink has turned her back on me and is walking away. I thought I was brave – that being hurt was something I could endure. But the fear I feel now shows I was lying to myself. I was a coward before, and I haven't changed.

'I believe you.' I breathe. 'Open the gate and let me go.'

'You agree?'

I nod.

He turns and goes into the house without speaking. I feel a metallic whirr behind me. The bolts retract. The gate opens.

I lean down to grab my bag and wait until the gap is just wide enough for me to squeeze through. Once I am on the other side, I don't look back.

I run to the town square. Only when I see people again do I slow down, though God knows, I shouldn't be reassured by that. No one in this town has ever borne witness to what Jim Fielding did.

My breath returns and finally my heart stops thumping, as sweat runs down my back. He's not coming after me. Why would he? I have nothing on him except one old photo, a few unsubstantiated rumours – and my hallucinations.

But I don't feel relieved that I got away. Because I've failed.

I sit on a stone seat underneath the greying war memorial, the only place with any shade. My hands tremble with energy as a taxi pulls up next to me. I could get in that cab, tell it to take me home to Brighton, sod the cost, but how do I know the driver wouldn't report straight back to Jim with my address.

He probably has it already.

The next bus leaves Ashdean in thirty minutes. It's time to admit defeat.

* * *

It's after midnight when I get home. I tried to sleep on the train, but Jim's story and my own twisted through my thoughts like tree roots. We have guilt in common.

He doesn't know who I am, but he senses *what* I am. A coward who hid behind a door when I should have faced my father, whatever the consequences. And, yes, a vulture who picks over other people's dirtiest secrets instead of facing her own.

57

I knew from the day of the murders that I'd failed my brother once. I didn't know about the second time until my father's trial.

Every day I went into the public gallery, next to the rubber-neckers who turned up, rain or shine, for their free entertainment. They knew who I was, even though I'd been hidden by a screen while I was a witness. Each morning, they shifted along to let me take the one seat where I wouldn't be able to see my father, and he wouldn't see me.

I remember watching the pathologist swear on the Bible. He seemed too young and ordinary to spend his working life coaxing secrets from the dead.

'And would you describe your impressions when you first attended the house?' the prosecutor asked him.

'I arrived at just after 7 p.m. on the Saturday, after receiving a call from the coroner. The scene had been cordoned off and a forensics team was already in attendance. The layout of the house itself was standard. I grew up in a similar private estate myself.'

The pathologist knew I was in court. He glanced up at me in the gallery, as though he was asking permission to carry on. I nodded.

We'd both seen the same things, but with different eyes. The family bathroom, the first room the pathologist was shown to, had blood spatters across the bath and tiles, 'consistent with venous flow'.

That was the first room I entered too: the place where my father had attempted to take his life. To this day, it's the only thing he's done that suggests he regretted his actions.

The next room was my parents' bedroom, where the pathologist found my mother's body on the bed, dressed in her slouchy weekend jeans, her 'I Heart Falmouth' T-shirt and her cooking apron.

'There was no obvious sign of injury. I noted however that her partially opened eyes had petechial haemorrhages – usually a sign of asphyxiation by suffocation.'

The next room was mine – empty by then, of course. The pathologist noted 'a large fresh solvent stain to the carpet, which I noted but later disregarded as irrelevant to this case.'

The first secret I kept: the argument over that spill was what set everything in motion.

Pip's room in the loft was the last one the pathologist came to, the smallest in the house.

'The scene here was rather different, due to the resuscitation efforts made by members of the ambulance service.'

'Can you describe what you saw there?' the judge asked.

'In the centre of the room, on the stripped pine floor, there was a male child I estimated to be around eight years old. He was deceased. His T-shirt had been cut open to facilitate access for chest compressions and other interventions. But the child had sustained some injuries prior to medical attention. There was blood pooling on the floor surrounding his head – see photograph A372 in the jury bundle, and further stains on the duvet cover, item A388. I didn't form an immediate opinion about how these might have been caused, but certainly, there had been trauma.'

Trauma.

There had been some comfort in knowing my mother's death had not been brutally violent, and that she was already gone by the time Dad pushed the key under my door.

But now I sat rigid on the fold-down seat, my fingernails biting into my palms, as the pathologist described my little brother's final minutes on this earth.

'When the paramedics arrived, they did detect a faint pulse. However, the child went into cardiac arrest and though there were extensive efforts to restore spontaneous circulation' – the pathologist looked at the jury members – 'that is, to make the heart beat again, alas these failed.'

As the pathologist went on to describe the post-mortems, I heard nothing more. Instead his words repeated in my head.

A faint pulse.

It meant that while I was staring at the key on the floor, wondering whether to disobey my father, and imagining I could hear men arguing outside, my brother was clinging on to life in the room above mine.

Second by second, beat by beat, Pip was bleeding out. His heart was trying to pump oxygen to dying cells, but instead making him weaker and weaker until . . .

I couldn't hear any more. I thought I might be sick. I rose, the seat of the chair slapping up, making everyone look towards the gallery. As I turned to close the door, I glanced down and saw my father for the last time.

He saw me – I know he did – but he didn't even acknowledge me.

In the street, Marion held back my hair as I vomited bile into the gutter – I hadn't eaten for days. As we drove back to the farm, I decided that as soon as I was old enough, Suzanne would be gone. No one would know who I'd been before, what I'd done. What I hadn't done.

After the trial, I began to recreate myself, layer by layer. The executors of my mother's will did the same to my old house: it was steam-cleaned and redecorated, ready for a buyer who could overcome squeamishness in return for a bargain family home. The money raised was carefully invested by trustees and it's what enabled me to become new: it paid for me to go to art school, to *find* myself. It paid for most of this flat.

But deep inside Georgia, there's always been Suzanne.

I'll email the publisher tomorrow, finally admit that I can't finish the portrait after all. I expect he'll be relieved. He'll find Maureen another celebrity case to paint. She will be the star of his book. His *cover girl*.

And Jim will get away with everything: whatever he did to the girls, to his wives, to Robert. The photos and cuttings are on the floor, from the work I did before my trip, but they're not evidence. They just led me into a place of even deeper darkness.

Wine isn't enough. I pour a huge slug of gin into a glass. No tonic. I'll have to find a more permanent way to forget about the Fieldings, and what they did to each other, but for now, this will help.

Except the worst thing Jim showed me has nothing to do with the Fieldings. All these years, I thought I could see evil, make justice happen, make the bad people pay.

When really there was one guilty person who would never be brought to justice.

Me.

58

I don't wake until after nine, and the residual taste of gin is cloying. The temperature is already in the high twenties. I push the sash windows open with a screech, letting even hotter air into my living room. What now?

I pick the Ashdean papers off the floor and cram them into a box file. Then I fetch my rucksack and tip everything into the same box: the sketches, the crumpled sheet of mind mapping, the lot. I close the box, put it in the armoire, slam the door shut and lock up.

Done with.

Just like my career.

I'm wired, restlessness coursing through me. What am I meant to do now? Today, tomorrow, for the rest of my life? The Ashdean stuff helped me to put off facing what my disease means. But now I can't do that any longer.

I go to the beach. The tide is out, so I turn right and walk along the sandy stretch where the water meets the shore. It doesn't matter if I can't see properly here. With the sea on my left, at least I won't get lost.

I walk faster than I have dared to since my diagnosis, not caring if I trip and fall. The waves splash against my bare legs, the cool water welcome when everything else is relentlessly hot.

People glance at me suspiciously as I pass. It's not normal to rush in this weather.

'Where's the fire, love?' a man calls out as I stride between him and his son, playing football together.

I only begin to feel tired when I reach the cranes and warehouses of Shoreham Harbour. I once covered a murder trial that revolved around these vast docks: an everyday love triangle only made interesting by the fact the victim died a slow death in a storage container that was meant to go to sea but was held in port by a strike in another continent.

The killer claimed the victim had done it to commit suicide: locked himself in, so he couldn't change his mind. The jury didn't believe him, of course: suicide should be fast, allowing no time for regrets. It's only murderers – and particularly vengeful ones at that – who want to prolong the suffering.

I think of Sharon, on that bridge. Did she change her mind after she jumped? *If she jumped at all.*

Don't.

It won't help.

I've run out of beach, so I turn to go back the way I came.

How did Sharon feel as she fell? I wouldn't do it that way. Drowning is better.

My feet look shrunken and bloodless under the shallow water. This part of the beach is empty. I could lie down now and let the sea first cool, then take me. No one would miss me.

Right now, I can't think of one good reason why I shouldn't. No more questions or memories. No more guilt. It's so tempting . . .

But then I realise: there is one thing I must do first.

* * *

At home, I gulp down a pint of water, and unlock the armoire again. There's a folder right at the back that has nothing to do with my cases, and everything to do with my past.

I take out this year's birthday card and reread Marion's carefully measured note. I could pick up the telephone right now; I know her voice would make me feel everything can still turn out OK.

But I turned my back on them. It's not fair to burden them now.

I open my laptop, the font on the screen now set to a larger size. I copy the email address of my father's prison worker into a document, then lock the birthday card away again.

Among all Jim's lies, he told one truth: it's time for me to stop hijacking other people's pain. Facing up to my own isn't something I relish, but once I've done it, I will have fulfilled the last duty anyone could expect of Suzanne Ross.

And as for Georgia Sage . . . She died the day she lost her vision.

I get the gin ready. When I've finished this, I intend to drink myself to sleep for a second night running.

Dear Ms Penney, I type. I believe you've been trying to contact me on behalf of my father . . .

59

I am being shaken awake, not violently, but firmly.

In the last tumbling moments, I feel hands on my arm. And then I am awake.

'What? Who are you?'

The touch is gone though I am sure I still sense warm breath on my cheek. I remember: I'm in my own bed, in Brighton. Alone. I dragged myself in here at 2 a.m. after passing out on the couch.

The room is so hot.

Fire?

No, I can't smell burning. But something does feel very wrong.

Now I see her.

'Pink.'

She has her back to me, tiptoeing towards the door. She holds her finger up to her lips.

It was her that woke me, I'm suddenly sure of it. But how could she have? She is always silent. She doesn't exist outside my head. She can't have touched me because she isn't here.

I look for my phone. I'm sure I left it on my bedside table, the battery taped on after the clip broke when Jim threw it at the floor. My eyes adjust to the darkness enough for me to notice something else.

My front door is ajar.

'Who's there?'

Pink's eyes widen; glitter sparkles on her cheeks. She slips through the door into the hallway and I follow.

I turned the lights off last night but a sickly green tinge leaks into my flat from the FIRE EXIT sign in the communal stairwell.

My instinct is to shut the door.

But what if I shut an intruder inside with me?

Pink is tiptoeing past the kitchen – I glance inside but can see nothing out of place. I follow her. The door to the living room is closed. I never do that: the last time I closed it was when I brought the teacher back.

A lifetime ago.

Goosebumps cover my skin, despite the heat. Is there someone on the other side of that door?

'I'm calling the police,' I shout.

I can hear something. *Someone.* Rustling, and then footsteps on the parquet.

I look around for something to defend myself with. A knife? But fear has paralysed me.

Pink leans her head against the door. She turns and nods at me.

'Is it safe?'

She nods again.

As I creep forward, I wonder whether I should trust a hallucination. And when my hand tightens around the Victorian door handle, I flinch at the memory of another door I hesitated before opening. Another choice I had to make.

That time, I got it wrong.

I fling the door open. There is nowhere to hide in here, no furniture big enough to conceal a person.

I run to the windows. They've been pushed open as far as they'll go. Did I leave them like that? I can't remember.

I hear the sound of a car door slamming. A revving engine. Down on the street, there's movement. A saloon car – black? navy? – speeding away from me the wrong way down the square towards the sea. No lights. No way to see the registration number, even if I did have full vision.

Now, everything is still again. Did that even just happen?

I walk back across the room to turn on the lights.

The parquet is littered with cuttings and sketches and files, the doors to the armoire open. I didn't leave it like that: I'd packed everything about my old life away last night. I've been burgled.

Jim?

Who else?

I slump down onto the floor and try to work out what's gone. It doesn't take long. The folder for the Fielding case is missing, and all the newer sketches I'd done, including the taped-together mind map that tried to make sense of everything that has happened at Ashdean.

But what about the DVD with the photographs?

My stomach drops as I realise my laptop has been taken, too. Whoever broke into the flat must have been here for some time.

My teeth start to chatter. The intruder must have come into my bedroom. Taken my mobile off the bedside table only centimetres from my body, checked for anything else he wanted.

Pink looks sad, as though she wishes she could have woken me earlier.

'It's OK. It might have been dangerous if I'd interrupted them.'

Them? Jim, or most likely one of his men – driving the threat home.

I see they haven't taken Marion's note, at least. But all it'll take is a look through my latest search history to see not only that I'm going blind, but also how I feel about living with that. Or not.

I run through what I remember looking for . . .

How to make a will; how to leave property to a charity.

And the last search of all:

What it feels like to drown.

60

I don't report the break-in to the police – I'm certain Jim's people left no evidence behind. What they took makes it easier to ignore the outside world. I don't even bother to buy a new phone or laptop. I record an anodyne message on my home phone:

This is Georgia. Sorry I'm not around right now. I'm taking some time out, everything's fine, just need to drop out for a bit. Do leave a message and I'll call you as soon as I'm back.

A woman from the hospital ophthalmology department leaves a stroppy message, asking why I missed an appointment. Oli and Neena leave voicemails too, but nothing they can say will help.

Once a day I go out: collect my post from downstairs and check my emails at the internet cafe on Western Road, blinking and peering and magnifying till they make sense.

I doze in the day, and at night, I walk from room to room, looking for somewhere to settle. My head aches constantly, and everything tastes metallic. Except coffee, which I mainline.

The caffeine gives me the energy to get my affairs in order. It's not a huge job, but no one needs to be burdened by this, afterwards. There is perverse pleasure in choosing charities that could do good with money I didn't earn and never deserved. I draw up a list – a local refuge, animal welfare, an art therapy trust. I consider guide dogs, but it seems too neat. Instead, I find a small charity that aids genetic research into Best disease.

All my donations will be anonymous.

It's liberating, imagining a world without me. And maybe I might find another world where my brother and my mother are waiting. Though nothingness seems more likely. The handwritten draft of my new will is ready to send to the solicitor who handled my flat sale. As I put it in the envelope, I think of Robert O'Neill's will, and how he felt when he wrote it. The careful words and handwriting seem to fit what I know about him now. A perfectionist.

What went wrong between him and Jim? I try to put it out of my mind, but it keeps creeping back. Was it just that Jim wanted Emma to himself? It doesn't ring true that Jim would kill for that. Yet Jim virtually admitted to murder in our last moments together.

What if Robert knew something about Jim? They were friends as teenagers. Could Robert have known what Jim did at Copse View and tried to blackmail him? That could be why Jim took the blame for the joyriding and the thefts.

But perhaps that's why Robert came back to Ashdean years later – to ask his friend for money? And Jim decided enough was enough.

I have to stop this, accept I'll never know for sure.

Charlie comes, sometimes. He is a soothing presence, perhaps because I know he's done OK in real life. But when Pink appears, it reminds me I never found out her real name or what Jim did to her.

Pip stays gone. That I am thankful for.

Each night I hear noises that might or might not be there. Check the locks on my doors and windows over and over: more as a tic than because I think someone wants to get in. There is nothing left for Jim – or whoever he hired – to take from me now.

At least my to-do list is getting shorter. Only the two tasks I dread remain.

See my father.

And one other thing. Something I can't expect anyone else to do after I've gone.

'Can you help me? I have the key, but I don't know where unit 347 is.'

The guy on reception doesn't even look up from the game he's playing on his phone.

'Third floor, turn right out of the lift.'

The building is all echoes and clanging metal doors; it reminds me of the prison where Daniel has spent the last thirteen years. The storage facility is in an old warehouse, the corridors painted a shiny grey, the hammered aluminium cubicles bolted in place. Hard even for a sighted person to navigate – for me, it's a monotone maze.

I eventually make it to my unit. The padlock is pristine but stiff – it hasn't been opened since it was first used, I suppose – but eventually it gives, and before I pull open the door I wait for my heart rate to slow.

I've avoided facing this stuff for twenty years. No more putting it off.

It's emptier than I expected. Two-thirds of what I've been paying for is unoccupied space. Dead air. The unit is three metres square, equally high and deep and wide, a perfect cube. In my nightmares, it was stuffed with old furniture and pots and pans and suitcases full of dead people's clothes. The mattress my mother was smothered on, the rug where paramedics fought to save my brother's life.

I was most afraid of the smell of home.

Instead, order reigns. The removal men who shifted the boxes from Frome to here have stacked them neatly to the ceiling. It reminds me of a police evidence room. I move my head this way and that to read the labels on the dozen or so brown storage cartons:

Living room, kitchen, office . . .

Toys.

I had nothing to do with what was taken from the house. A friend of my mother's took on that grim task, after the police left. She came to visit me at Marion's to give me a few items in person: my paintbox; some clothes and school books; my duvet cover; plus an album of photographs and my Daler zippable art folder.

'It has the painting you were working on inside,' she'd said, 'and also the one Pip had been painting the morning when . . .'

She broke down and I patted her back as she sobbed. I was used to adults crying by then. When she'd gone, I threw everything but the album and folder in the bin. The album just fit inside the vinyl folder, which I've taken with me whenever I've moved, but I haven't looked inside once. I don't need to. I remember every detail.

Enough. This job won't get done if I spend my time looking back.

I set up two areas: one corner for charity donations, one for rubbish. In the centre, I put a plastic bag for things I will burn. I put my earbuds in and turn on a rock playlist, full volume, to drown out any emotion.

There's an old metal stepladder next to the boxes, I move it into position and climb beside the first stack. When I look at my hands gripping the rail, I see dried splashes of paint against the aluminium.

Ladybird red for Pip's room.

Bumblebee yellow for mine.

I blink away the memories, and take down the first box of kitchenware. Mostly electricals – the toaster, the kettle, Mum's Moulinex. For a moment, I picture them in their rightful places on the white melamine kitchen counter, next to a loaf of sliced bread always ready for me or Pip to make a snack.

I push the entire box to the rubbish corner and write ELEC-TRICALS FOR RECYCLING in black marker pen. Every box will be clearly marked by the time I am finished, ready for the clearance firm I've specified in my will. My father would be proud of my rediscovered skill for planning.

The next box is more KITCHENWARE. It's mainly textiles: tablecloths, napkins. I wonder why Mum's friend kept these, but not the plates or glassware.

They smell musty, though I am sure they were freshly laundered before going into storage, and little envelopes of moth-proofing chemicals have been tucked in at regular intervals. I imagine Mum's grieving friend packing them for me, as though she was creating my 'bottom drawer'. I hope she never finds out that I failed to have the future she thought I deserved to have.

When I take the tablecloth out, I remember: my mother made this at school, in needlework classes. The detail is hard for me to make out under the flat strip lights, but I can feel the care that went into it with my fingertips. There are summer flowers and bluebirds surrounding my mother's name, embroidered in satin stitch in a pale lilac.

Deborah

I put it down.

I don't need to save anything sentimental. After I am gone, none of this will mean anything to anyone.

My mother's tablecloth has some value, though perhaps only for rags. But I hope the charity shop might price in the work she put into it. Vintage embroidery is fashionable with the boho set in Brighton, and it would be nice to think of it having another life.

Don't think.

I lift the whole box and dump it in the charity corner.

Work faster, be ruthless.

As I go up and down the ladder, I try to pretend I am doing this for someone else. A box of my father's books and files goes into a new bin bag without a second glance. The police already went through them, looking for clues to his state of mind. They found nothing but order.

My mother's perfumes, handbags and costume jewellery give me an emotional jolt, but I refuse to give in to self-pity, to spray her scent onto my wrist, or wallow in nostalgia for dressing-up games. I have her few pieces of valuable jewellery at home, which will be sold. I'd considered giving her engagement ring to little Millie, but I changed my mind instantly. No kid deserves a victim's things.

The effort makes me sweat. Behind the first stack of boxes is my woven Lloyd Loom nursery chair. I could sit down to get my breath back, but I am afraid of space to think, so I keep going.

Now, my own things surface – the Enid Blyton books I loved, *Home Alone* and *The Lion King* in impossibly chunky VHS boxes, and the sparkly pink TV-video combo that must have seemed valuable to Mum's friend two decades ago but is now just a lump of cheap landfill.

I always had twice as many things as my brother.

The temptation to look in Pip's toy box is almost over-whelming but instead I immediately shift it with my foot into the charity pile. That one, the charity shop people can sort through. Maybe another child, or more likely, a nostalgic hip-ster, can play his games, do his jigsaws, cuddle the second, pristine version of his favourite rabbit Mum bought in case he lost the real, ragged one.

The last box is just marked PIP and finally, my resolve hits rock bottom. I sit on the floor next to it and hold my breath as I take off the lid. Photographs in *Toy Story* frames have been protected with bubble wrap; thankfully, it obscures the images.

But underneath is what I knew had to be here. I push the photos to the side and pull out the sketchbook. One of *my* sketchbooks, but donated to Pip when he told me he wanted to learn to draw, and I said I'd teach him.

On the front, he'd written PIP'S MASTER PEICES. I remember telling him, '*I* before *e* except after *c*.'

Like that *mattered*.

I grab the rubbish, the bag of stuff for burning, and Pip's sketchbook and pull the metal door shut. My hands fumble with the padlock. On the way out, I tip the sack full of my father's stuff into a skip.

One step closer to being ready.

61

Each night the sunset is more of a heartbreaker. Tonight's boasts a rosehip-red sky, the sea turning from mercury to navy. I watch it with a glass of wine in my hand.

I feel an urge to do a fresh painting: not for Millie, but for myself.

I set up my easel near the window. The sun has almost disappeared, but it doesn't matter. The colours have burned themselves into my memory.

I take out a watercolour palette. Really, that was a sunset to be captured in oil paints, but I left those in Ashdean. So instead I will go with dreamy, misty colours: a fading light.

At first, I don't quite register the buzzer, because I'm lost in my picture. When I do realise it's for me, I step away from the window. It's dark now, past nine. Probably a Deliveroo driver with the wrong door.

The buzzer sounds twice more, but the third time is less emphatic. I take a tentative step back towards the bay.

'Georgia! Georgie, answer the bloody door!'

It's Oli. I pause, hoping he hasn't seen me.

'I know you're there. I'm not going until you let me in.'

Shit.

I wouldn't put it past him to camp on the doorstep.

I run my hands through my hair, check my face in the mantel mirror: just this side of acceptable. I approach the window and stick my head out.

'Which part of "I'm taking time out" is so hard for you to grasp, Oli?'

He's red in the face and sweating, his suit jacket folded across his arm, briefcase resting between his feet.

'I'm worried about you.'

'I can take care of myself.'

'Really? Your phone's dead and no one has heard from you. I talked to Neena. I even called the publisher.'

'You shouldn't have done that.'

'I was worried. I *am* worried.' He sighs. 'Look, Georgie, I came down from London. It was murder on that bloody train. The least you can do is let me in. Just show me you're OK and I'll go. Plus, I'm dying of thirst. I might faint in the street.'

'Western Road is full of pubs. It's literally just up there.' I point. 'You'll get a much warmer welcome.'

He sighs. 'I get the hint, hurtful as it is. But at least let me in so I can tell you something about the Fielding case.'

I can't stop myself.

'Why? What's happened now?'

'I'm not going to tell you unless you let me in.'

'That's blackmail.'

He smiles. 'I prefer to call it . . . mutually beneficial. Come on, Georgie.'

I've been outmanoeuvred. I fling a cloth over the easel, not wanting him to see how badly I am painting now. I never gave him the sunset picture I painted for his daughter, either. Why burden a child with something so flawed?

His face seems blurrier than before, but I can see grey shadows under his eyes. We hug and I soften towards him, realising he must have given up time with his baby to come here.

'How's Millie?'

'Knackering. Life-changing. All the clichés.' He nods at my glass of wine on the side table. 'Can I have one?'

I realise he already smells of booze.

'Not your first today, from the state of you.'

'Nor yours. Some of the set took me out for lunch. Wet the baby's head. Not that the actual baby was there, obviously.' He sighs. 'And then I couldn't stop worrying about you and I got a bit maudlin—'

'As you always do.'

'As I always do, and I got on the train and, well, here I am.'

'And you want to keep going?'

He hesitates.

'It'll probably finish me off, but . . . yes. Have you got gin?'

Oli follows me into the kitchen, and I sense him watching my movements.

'I'm no more blind than last time I saw you, you know.' Though as I've not been back to the hospital, I have no way of knowing for sure.

'Oh, Georgie. I can't bear to think of you facing this on your own.'

His voice cracks. If he's like this about my illness, what will it be like after . . .? No. I won't weaken.

I hand him the tumbler and make one for myself.

'I can still see the essentials, like how much gin and how much tonic to add.'

I squeeze out of the front window, onto my strip of balcony, and Oli joins me.

He puts his arm around my shoulder.

'It's so bloody unfair, G. You don't deserve any of this.'

'There's no such thing as natural justice. We both know that, the years we've spent in court.'

'Hmm.'

He takes a swig of his drink, then unfolds the little metal patio chair and sits down, reaching into his jacket pocket and pulling out a pack of Silk Cut.

'Would it be OK if I . . .?'

'Sure.'

'I'm not allowed to at home, for obvious reasons. But there's something about sitting outside, in the sunshine, with a G & T . . . with you. Happy hour.' He lights his cigarette and then holds his glass up to mine. 'Chin chin.'

'Chin chin.'

I'm back, for a moment, in Sri Lanka, and the ridiculous hill station where we'd stayed, a colonial relic with white-coated waiters and stuffed animals staring down at us from the walls. A pianist playing 1930s show tunes. And the pudding dome coming off and the engagement ring underneath, nestling in the hollow of a rum baba.

Maybe I'm not seeing him as he really is now, but am using thirteen years' worth of memories to create an image of his beautiful face.

Smoke, juniper, ruby-red sunset.

His lips are on mine. The familiar taste of him, of lust and love and hope that life could be different . . .

I pull away at exactly the same moment as he does.

'I'm sorry,' we both say.

The physical gap between us widens as far as the tiny balcony allows. I don't even know who made it happen, but I know it was wrong.

'Sri Lanka, right?' he says, and I smile. 'Just because we split up, I didn't stop caring, Georgie.'

'I know that.'

'I came to make sure you were still alive—'

'No escaping that.'

I laugh, but it sounds like a lie.

'But also, I knew how important the Fielding thing was to you. Without it, I was worried something might have gone . . .' He looks for the right word. 'Well, wrong.'

I flinch. Has he guessed what I want to do?

'It's a painting, that's all. Worse things happen to people than losing a commission.'

'They do. They really do.' He takes a drag on the cigarette, breathes out of the side of his mouth in a long plume, a trick that's always made him look more like a hustler than a barrister. 'I wasn't entirely truthful about why I didn't want you to go to Ashdean.'

Oli looks out to sea, and I know he's doing what he always does in court – rehearsing his sentence. I tilt my head but I can't read his expression.

'As junior counsel on the case, I visited Gloucestershire to liaise with the prosecutor's office, and go through evidence with the police. Perfectly normal. But while I was in Ashdean, this other police officer came to look for me. A beat copper. She'd arrested him, but wasn't involved in the case anymore. I don't know how she even got to hear I was there . . .'

I think of Danny: *A policewoman tried before.*

'It's not a big town. I think it runs on gossip.'

Oli nods. 'Anyway, this officer, Jeanette, asked to meet privately. Suggested a place in the woods, bit of a trek. Did you see the children's home while you were there?'

I don't want to get involved.

'Look, Oli, this isn't anything to do with me anymore.' But when I glance down at the garden square, a girl sits, staring right at us. Pink. I nod. 'Yes, I saw the home. Copse View.'

'That's it. The police officer asked me to meet her in the copse behind there. I nearly didn't go, but ... Well, I'd read a couple of John Grisham novels back then, fancied myself as a hotshot. I was intrigued.'

I smile, despite myself.

'It was pissing it down and the mud was going all over my suit trousers. But she made me keep walking until we couldn't be seen. She tried to suss me out, asked me about why I'd become a lawyer. I was full of it, back then. Truth, justice. Perhaps my idealism made her trust me.'

'Trust you how?'

'She told me Ashdean was sick. She said they'd only stationed her there after training because they'd assumed she was a pushover. I thought she meant, I dunno, turning a blind eye to lock-ins, or letting people with the right handshake off the odd speeding charge. She told me I had no idea. She pointed at the kids' home – we could just about see the whitewashed walls through the trees – and said that she was convinced something bad had happened there.'

I hold my breath. 'What kind of something?'

Oli shrugs. 'She was evasive. But she hinted that it was all linked to Jim Fielding.'

I don't want to hear this.

But still I ask, 'What did you do?'

Oli sighs. 'I thought she was a flake. Reminded her that Jim wasn't on trial, that there weren't many men who'd have gone into a burning house to rescue someone else's kids. She told me that the girls at the home were someone's kids, too, and no one had been looking out for them.'

'Did she have any evidence?'

'I don't know. She stomped off before I could ask. I was cross, too. My best shoes were ruined from the mud, and for what?'

I try to process whether what he's said changes anything.

'Did you know then that Sharon had been in the home?'

'No. But what difference would it have made? It didn't affect the case. Daniel Fielding was at the scene of the fire, he had a motive. When he changed his plea, it was all over. Plus, if you remember, I was pretty distracted at the time by a certain young courtroom artist . . .'

We half-smile at each other.

'It was only afterwards, when the Operation Yewtree abuse stuff started emerging, that I wondered if Jeanette was on to something. I did a case with the same Gloucestershire coppers a couple of years back and asked where she was now. They said she'd left a few months after the Fielding trial. Had a breakdown. Left the service.'

While we've been talking his cigarette has burned down to the stub. He looks down, surprised, and lights another.

'I should have told you straight out, when you first asked about Ashdean. I never thought Jim would agree. But I feel bad I didn't protect you from all that nastiness. You pretend to be tough as old boots but we both know it's not the whole story.'

I turn away from Oli. On the square, Pink's gaze holds steady, her arms crossed, as if to say *I told you so*.

Would it have made any difference if he'd told me this on the pier that day? I'd probably have been even more determined to get involved. And knowing it now doesn't really change anything. Unless . . .

'Georgie? Are you angry with me?'

'No, of course not. But if the police ignored what was under their noses, then I *am* angry with them.'

And myself. I gave up too easily. Unlike the policewoman, still trying to do what's right, thirteen years on. Because she has to be the one who sent me the photos and that list of the residents.

'Do you remember Jeanette's surname?'

'Thorne. Look, she probably *was* a fruitcake. I came to tell you you'd had a lucky escape from the whole Ashdean mess.'

There is no escape from the whole Ashdean mess.

'You don't have to worry, Oli. With the commission off, I have no reason at all to go back.'

Oli nods. 'There are better times ahead for you, Georgie. I know there are.' He leans in for a final, brief hug. 'I ought to go home to my girls. Now I know you're all right.'

'Safe journey,' I say.

I watch him walk along the buttermilk terraces and then disappear. I *must* let him go, for his own happiness, and Imogen's, and baby Millie's.

But Ashdean isn't quite ready to let go of me.

62

Jeanette Thorne isn't that hard to find.

It takes me one Turkish coffee and less than an hour of squinting and swearing in the all-night internet cafe. I contact all the women by that name on Facebook, without saying what it's about.

Almost immediately, my friend request is accepted and a message pops up:

Took you long enough.

I type a reply:

Why didn't you tell me who you were?

The response is almost instant.

I had to know you cared enough to find me.

Jeanette works as a shop security guard and suggests meeting in her lunch break. I don't sleep at all overnight. Copse View, Sharon, Jim, Daniel, Robert – everything might make sense after I talk to her. I keep having to remind myself that Jeanette can't have enough evidence to take it further, or she would have done it already. Yet I have to know for sure.

When I board the train to Reading, the world seems louder and brighter after almost a week of self-imposed exile.

I find her in the furniture department of the store where she works.

'Jeanette? I'm Georgia.'

She nods. 'I know.'

She radios through to a colleague to say she's going on her break and leads the way towards a cafe outside the mall. It's a cheap place, all plastic fittings spray-painted in peeling chrome. When she goes in, the office workers and students clear a space for her to sit down – Jeanette has authority, with her over-embellished uniform and matronly figure.

But when she sits next to me, and I angle my head to examine her properly, I see her face is soft and unlined – though perhaps that's my vision smoothing out her skin. Her huge brown eyes lock on to mine.

'I didn't think you were ever going to get in touch,' she says.

'Why approach me in the first place?'

'I've got an alert set up, on email. If there's any mention of Ashdean or Jim Fielding on the Web, I get a notification. I hoped one day it might bring a news story about him finally being nailed. Instead, I got a story about him being *painted*. It gave me the idea. I found your address with one call to an old mate.'

'But how did you know I'd look into it?'

'I didn't. But journalists are even more suspicious than coppers. Another reason I left my name off. Added to the drama; like Watergate or something.'

I smile. 'I'm not a real journalist. But I *do* care.'

'Counts for a lot.' Her stare is intense: at first I thought she was afraid, but now I think she's bursting to talk to someone about this and has been for a decade. 'What do you think of him?'

Interesting that she doesn't want to say Jim's name . . .

'At first, I thought he was a tragic hero,' I say, 'and that he agreed to the picture to get the past out of his system. In Ashdean there's no one he could talk to honestly.'

'Huh. Honesty isn't his thing at all.' Jeanette picks up the sandwich I bought for her. 'So, what was troubling his so-called conscience?'

'Not preventing Sharon killing herself. Not realising Daniel was dangerous. Not saving Tessa.'

She unwraps her sandwich but then puts it down.

'When the fire happened, I was one of the first on the scene. There was no doubt Fielding was distraught. I've never heard a man howl like he did when he was trying to get back in to rescue his wife.

'It was me arrested Daniel, too. He stank of petrol – he was definitely there when the fire started. But when we were unloading him at the nick, he stumbled – on purpose – and pulled me down with him. While we were on the floor, he whispered, "Don't let my dad fool you, this is all down to him."'

'You think Jim started the fire in his own house?'

Jeanette shrugs. 'It did seem far-fetched, but I couldn't ignore it. I went to the cells later, to see if I could get in to see Daniel, but they'd already transferred him to Gloucester for court in the morning.

'I tried to put it out of my mind but it wouldn't leave me alone. One dead wife is a tragedy. Two starts to look like more than coincidence. And once I started tuning in to the whispers about Jim, I heard all sorts. Robert O'Neill disappearing, for one. Oh, and about Jim's dad.'

'What about his father?'

'He was the local bobby until he died of a heart attack. On the surface, Ashdean was this crime-free oasis while he was in charge. I realised it was only because no crime got reported or recorded.'

'You think his father was on the take?'

'Or lazy. Maybe both. Anyway, back then, I was stubborn, thought I could change the world.' She scoffs. 'Started going through the old files at night, when there was no one else around. Felt a bit daft, like some American gumshoe, with my torch and my notebook. But then I realised that apart from the heroic Mr Fielding, one other thing connected Sharon and Robert O'Neill.'

'What?'

'Copse View.'

I blink. 'I know Sharon was there. But Robert?'

Jeanette looks surprised. 'I thought you knew. That's why Robert came to Ashdean first of all. He lived in Gloucester, but he used to do handyman stuff at the home for the company he was apprenticed to. Old building like that, something was always going wrong. He was there most weeks.'

'You think that's where he became friends with Jim?' I realise something else. 'And was it him who took the party photos?'

She nods. 'Yes. So when they were both nicked for joyriding, he had a way to get Jim to take all the blame. Better a few months for taking without consent, than years for . . . Well, whatever Jim had done at Copse View.'

I remember our first sitting.

'Jim said he took the blame because there was no point both of them serving time.'

'Pretty big favour, right? Plus, why didn't Jim's father pull strings to get his son off the hook? If anyone was going to be made to carry the can, you'd expect it to be Robert. He was older, and he wasn't the son of a copper.'

'Where did you find the photos?'

Jeanette reaches into her messenger bag, pulls out a manila wallet.

'At the nick. It was down the back of one of the old cabinets. Old man Fielding died before retirement. I don't imagine he ever *meant* to leave this behind.'

I take it from her: inside are the prints of the eight photos she sent to me on disk, plus the list of residents' names.

'What do these prove?'

'You have to see them in context.' Jeanette leans in and lifts out two pages torn from a notebook, and a copy of a document. 'Read these.'

I hold up the page, angling it to the light.

'Sorry,' she says. 'Jim's dad had terrible writing.'

On the top of both torn-out sheets, there are dates in 1979, five months apart. In both cases, the note underneath is the same: CALL TO COPSE VIEW, ASHDEAN. ASSAULT REPORTED BY RESIDENT. NFA.

'It means no further action,' she says. 'So maybe they were just cat-fights between the girls, but it's the *lack* of detail that made me wonder. If it had been scraps, then I'd have expected it to be mentioned, a throwaway line. A note of the girls' names, maybe, in case they got in trouble again. But what if it was a girl trying to report *sexual* assault?'

Everything around me seems to go still. Even though I'd suspected abuse, it's still shocking.

'So perhaps a girl who'd been attacked asked for the police to come twice and both times the officer who turned up was her attacker's *father*?'

'Or it might have been two different girls,' Jeanette says.

It's hardly a comforting thought. I look at the third page, my eyes so tired now I can barely make it out. But I persevere and realise it's a document recording that James Fielding was charged with burglary and taking a car without the owner's consent, on the morning of 2 August 1979.

'You found this in the same file as the reports about Copse View?'

Jeanette nods. 'And the photos.'

I spread the documents over the raised cafe counter.

'I'm struggling to make the connection. What do *you* think happened?'

Jeanette sighs. 'What if old man Fielding knew what his son had done at Copse View and tried to deal with it himself? But then both lads were arrested together and, Robert threatened to expose Jim's assults unless his dad organised for his son to take all the blame. Sergeant Fielding might even have thought a short spell inside would teach his son a lesson?'

A group of people at the next table burst into giggles at someone's joke. I want to snap at them to be quiet.

'Robert left Ashdean after that. Why come back?'

Jeanette stirs the coffee with a plastic spoon; it looks like the grimy water that goes down the plughole.

'What do you know about O'Neill?'

I think about the one picture of him I've seen, in the neighbour's photo album.

'Not much. A craftsman. Nicely turned out. I have a gut feeling he loved his son.'

'Maybe. Loved nice things, too. He'd gone before I came to Ashdean, but everyone I asked remembered his clothes better than they remembered him. He had all the labels. Top-of-the-range

Sierra. But he was a chippie. A new dad. Where did he get the money from? I think he heard about his old mate doing well, and decided to blackmail Jim a second time.'

I think it through.

'But he got too greedy and . . .'

Jeanette raises her eyebrows. 'Have we reached the same conclusion about Robert's sudden disappearance?'

'I think the whole of Ashdean reached that conclusion. Jim could kill two birds with one stone, right? Get rid of his blackmailer, and send a message to anyone else thinking of causing trouble.'

She drains the last of her coffee and packs her uneaten sandwich into her bag.

'I never realised, until I was stationed there, that a whole town could keep a secret. What a hellhole.' She looks at her watch. 'Talking of hellholes, I need to get back to mine. They dock me an hour if I'm even a minute late.'

'Was that why you left the police?'

'I . . . I had a breakdown. It wasn't what I had expected of policing.'

Jeanette closes her eyes. Bronze eyeshadow has settled into the creases between her lids. I want to hold her hand, to tell her at least she tried.

As we walk towards the store, Jeanette pulls her plastic epaulettes straight, and tucks stray grey hairs into her bun.

'What now?'

'Over to you. I'm out of ideas.' She stops. 'There's no body. No proof of what happened to Robert. And I did try to match the dates on the photos with the paperwork about the assaults and the names on the residents list, but I didn't get anywhere.'

I stare at her. 'What dates on the photos?'

She shrugs. 'On the back. It was the latest technology, then, to mark the date and time when the pictures had been taken. But you've seen the names. Copse View was mostly used for short-term placements. There are dozens of girls in the photos, and dozens of names on the list. I got nowhere.'

'Could I borrow the photos?'

'I already sent them to you.'

Telling her about the burglary might freak her out.

'I need the originals, with the dates on the back. It's a long shot but I'm willing to try.'

Jeanette looks dubious.

'Needle in a haystack but if you think there's a chance, then do all you can.' She hands me the folder. 'Just . . . promise me not to let it drive you mad. Fact is, some people just get away with murder.'

I travel back to Brighton where I buy a replacement phone and the cheapest second-hand laptop I can find.

Once I'm home, I open the envelope and find the photograph with Pink in the background. It's the only clue Jeanette hasn't had access to. For all I know, it's not a clue at all. Except . . .

When I look up, Pink is there in the flat.

'What did Jim do to you?' I ask her. 'I wish you could tell me.'

I turn the picture over. The date is faint, but it is there, in red ink across the back. 29 May 1979.

I check the list of girls living at Copse View in May. It had a fast turnover, just as Jeanette said – but a few stayed as long as six months. I draw an asterisk next to their names; there are twelve girls in all.

Now I check the dates of the two police visits. I don't know for sure if those visits are connected to Jim, or the girl I know as Pink. Whether Jim's father attended for the same reason on both occasions.

But this is the very last thing I can try.

The date of the first visit is 20 February. That narrows it down: now I am left with four girls who were there when the police were called *and* lived at Copse View when the photo of Pink was taken.

The second police visit was 29 July. I hold my breath as I scan the list of residents with stinging eyes. Three of the girls had left by then. But one remained.

Rosanna Chapman.

I look up, and Pink is smiling at me.

'Is that you?'

She keeps smiling.

'Hello, Rosanna. It's nice to know your real name at long last.'

63

My sense of triumph doesn't last. When I search, there is no trace of Rosanna online. It shouldn't be a surprise – so much time has passed. She's probably married. Hopefully she's left Ashdean behind her.

But there is news of my father. A new email has arrived.

Dear Ms Sage,

She's respecting my new identity. I suppose it's not uncommon in her world.

Thank you for your recent email. I appreciate the contact after so many years of silence must have been shocking. I'm sorry to have to break the news that your father is unwell, and the prognosis is terminal. Although his specialists are unable to give a precise timetable, they're talking months rather than years.

He's dying. My father is dying.

He is not yet hospitalised and is able to live a relatively normal life within the prison system.

As I understand it, he has never attempted to contact you before. Nor has he cooperated with any suggestions

KATE HELM | 319

of applying for parole, although he is no longer considered a risk. However, recently, during conversations with the pastor, he expressed the desire to speak to you. I would not want to put any pressure on you. However, if you are undecided about whether you ever would like to communicate with him, time is not on our side.

He's dying *soon*.

My reflection in the laptop screen is fuzzy enough for me to see him in it. The last of the Ross clan, with our fair hair and our wide-set eyes.

Please do call me to discuss it if you wish. If you do decide you'd like to see him, I have some discretion to process a visiting order quickly, given the circumstances.

I am numb.

Do I ever want to see my father again?

If I'd been asked that a year ago, there's no way I'd have considered it.

But now I realise why I emailed the prison officer: I want to make him suffer. Just like Jim Fielding, my father thought he had the right to take life or spare it, on a whim.

My father, at least, is no longer a danger. I click reply to the email. I *will* go to see him, if only to take away any shred of comfort he might feel from 'saving' me.

And as for Jim? Jeanette's theory about Robert blackmailing him makes sense, though it also makes O'Neill less of an innocent. He must have known what Jim had done when he took those photos at Copse View, and when he used them as his own get-out-of-jail card.

But it doesn't mean he should have died.

With him gone, the only hope of finding out what really happened at Copse View in 1979 lies with this Rosanna. There must be a reason she is in my life, and Charlie too. I feel as though I am so close. And I have money. Now I have a name, there are other ways to find her.

Jim thought I was weak, and for a while, I was. But it's different now: no past, no future. I can devote the present to making a difference for the first, and last, time.

I hang up four times before I let my call to Neena connect.

I am such a bloody coward.

'George? George, are you OK?'

Oli will have told her about his visit, but I trust him not to have told her about my vision loss.

'Yes. I'm sorry I've been avoiding you. I felt so terrible about the sketch.'

'Oh, screw that. I was pissed off for twenty-four hours but then I got worried. I can't believe I didn't spot you were burning out. You're my mate. I should have known.'

'I'm pretty good at keeping stuff hidden when I want.'

'True. Listen, do you want me to come to Brighton? I could come this weekend. Bring the kids. Mind you, that'd be enough to send you right off the deep end. So I'll come alone. Except for our mutual friend, gin. How's that?'

She's such a whirlwind, I almost say yes. But then I pull back.

'Not this weekend, but soon. Actually, I called to ask a favour. I've been using my time off to do some admin and I'm owed some money by a private client, who has gone AWOL. I know you have all sorts of nefarious freelancers working for you. I wonder if you could give me the details of a private detective?'

'Oh.' She sounds a little hurt. 'Oh, yeah. OK. How nefarious do you want to go? On a scale of one to ten?'

'Ten. It's quite a lot of money.'

She laughs. 'Fair dos. The best one I know for people-finding is refreshingly unscrupulous. I'll text you his email address.' She pauses. 'Next weekend, though? Or any night during the week? I don't want to lose you as a friend, whatever's happened with work.'

'Me neither.'

When the call ends, I stare at her name on the screen until it vanishes. I wish she hadn't forgiven me. It makes it so much harder to live with knowing I will never see her again.

I email the private detective, and within a couple of hours, he emails me back, asking for details of the person, and spelling out his fees. I reply with what little I know about Rosanna, warning him she might have tried to hide her identity.

The reply comes later in the evening.

Pretty much impossible to really disappear these days, if you know where to look. Usually get a hit on someone this age within a couple of working days. As soon as you send my retainer, I'll get cracking.

I transfer £300. It's a long shot, but what else do I have to spend my money on?

Pink is with me this evening. I can't think of her as Rosanna yet but her presence is reassuring, as though she wants me to know I am on the right track.

All weekend, I hear nothing. But on Monday my new mobile rings, an unfamiliar number flashing on the screen. The private detective must have news.

When I answer, there's a long wait before someone speaks.

'Is that Georgia Sage? This is Daniel Fielding.'

I'm so shocked, it takes me a few moments to find the words to respond.

'Daniel? Are you all right?'

'You want to talk to me about my dad.'

'I didn't expect—'

'Expect me to call? Me neither. Life's full of surprises, right? I didn't expect to still be alive.'

He sounds different: still belligerent, but also more animated.

'Can you talk safely?' I remember that prisoners aren't allowed mobiles inside. 'Did you borrow someone's phone?'

'I'm out.'

'What?'

'Free at last.' His voice is sarcastic. 'Once I was all patched up, they sped things along. Apparently I'm not a danger to society anymore.'

I wonder whether Jim knew this at our last sitting, when I lied about his son being up for parole.

'Are you OK, Daniel?'

'Yeah. But it's different. Everything is different.'

'I bet.'

I close my eyes, imagining how the world looks to him. All the things I've done and seen, since he was sent to prison: the technology, the world events.

But I won't feel sorry for him.

I don't know for sure he was innocent of arson. Murder. Jeanette said he was there, after all.

'I need to meet you, Daniel. Could we—'

'Were you lying, Georgia? About *your* dad, what he did? Because I looked up your name and there was nothing connecting you to any murder case. Except the ones you draw.'

'I changed my name,' I said.

In the call's background, I hear city sounds. Wherever he is now must be overwhelming after the isolation of the jail on the moors.

'Prove it.'

I hate the idea of telling anyone who I was, but I understand this is a test. And I also understand why a man with a father like Jim would find it hard to trust anyone.

'My name was Suzanne Ross. We lived in Somerset. It happened . . . twenty years ago. You'll find me if you look for that.'

There's a pause.

'I still don't get why you give a shit about us.'

'For what it's worth, I care about justice. About people like Jim paying for what they've done.'

I can hear his breath.

Don't hang up, Daniel.

'I'll call you when I've checked you out, *Suzanne*. If that's who you really are.'

He ends the call. I sit, looking at the phone. I have no idea if I just spoke to a murderer or an innocent man.

I used to think I could tell the difference.

64

There've been three periods in my life when I've woken up thinking about creating, and fallen asleep with the brush in my hand. The first was when I fell in love with oil paint, aged eleven.

The second came when I went to art school as Georgia, trying to lose my old self in my new identity.

And now, I paint as I wait for the endgame. Hours turn into a day, then two. I hear nothing from Daniel. When I summon up the nerve to call the number he rang me on, no one answers. But the private detective has emailed to tell me he has leads on Pink – on Rosanna. Enough for him to request another payment. And the prison officer has arranged a visiting order for me to see my father next week.

I've found my own way to prepare for that. Yesterday, I went to the art shop in the Lanes and bought new paints: oils, from the same budget range I used when I was eleven. I recognised them from the colours, because the print on the tubes is now impossible to read.

I spread them thickly on the palette – I don't need to worry about being sparing – and I purposely breathe in the fumes, making myself remember, so I feel angrier and angrier, ready for when I see my father.

And they fuel my anger against Jim, too. Anything to give me the energy to pursue this to the bitter end.

My phone buzzes in my pocket. It's a video text. I click on it, and a baby appears. My vision makes it blurry, but as the video plays, I hear a gurgle that turns into a laugh.

It's Millie. And Oli has sent a message to go with it:

I know you're feeling low. I am here for you, and so is your prospective goddaughter. Please say yes.

I play the clip again, trying to make out more detail. The walls in the background are painted primrose yellow. The nursery was once my art room, where I kept my sketches, my own private library of hate and suspicion. Thank God I never had a child with Oli. I don't deserve one.

I text back:

Thank you, but I'm not at all godly, never mind worthy. But I love the video. Millie will break hearts. Love G x

I pour some wine, and stand by the window, looking out at the dark, out-of-focus square. It's only six weeks since I stood here and saw Charlie for the first time.

That feels like another person's life – a carefree one. But it was only ever that on the surface. I was kidding myself. Georgia, Suzanne – what's the difference?

Shame is like oil paint: it doesn't fade with time.

On Wednesday afternoon, the private detective sends me an email marked urgent. I open it to find the address, email and phone number of Rosanna Chapman. Pink *is* still alive, and living with a partner, a son and a daughter. Surprisingly, she still lives in the forest, though not in Ashdean.

This completes my work for you. My invoice is attached.

I settle the last part of his bill. It's cost me £600 of my father's blood money for a few details with the power to shatter someone's life.

While Pink sits in my armchair by the window, bathed in the early evening sunlight, I try to work out the best way to approach Rosanna.

Visiting her – Neena would call it doorstepping – is the one way to be sure I will get a response. But it may not be the one I want. I imagine someone turning up at my address to ask me about what my father did.

I'd slam the door in their face.

No.

An email seems too . . . casual, but a letter – on her doormat, the shocking reminder of something she wanted to forget – feels almost as intrusive as a visit. And a phone call out of the blue perhaps the worst of both worlds.

If I email her, at least I know it'll go to her only, and won't involve her family.

I draft something in a notebook. Pink is dozing in the sun, and I try to picture the woman she has become.

'What do you care about, Rosanna?' I say. 'What could persuade you to revisit what might have been a terrible time in your life?'

I can only answer for myself: justice.

And I begin to write from the heart, with none of the sense of manipulation I used in my letter to Daniel.

Dear Rosanna,

I need your help and I know what I am asking isn't easy. But I believe you were assaulted when you were at the Copse View residential care home – or if you weren't, then you might know who was.

So many years have passed that perhaps you've tried to forget it. But I promise you, this still matters and there are people out there who still care about justice, who want wrongs to be righted. So if there's even the tiniest part of you that still remembers and hates what was taken from you, then please get in touch. There could be ways to speak out but stay anonymous, if that is what it takes.

And it's even more important now, because he's about to marry again. There have been other girls. There may be more.

It's not too late to make things right.

I hit send before I change my mind. When I reread the email, it occurs to me I'm writing as much to myself as I am to Rosanna.

When I see Daniel's mobile number appear on my screen later, I am almost scared to answer it.

Before I can say a word, he whispers:

'I believe you. You really are Suzanne.'

'Hello, Daniel.'

'Your dad's as big of a shit as mine is, right? Worse. To kill his own kid as well as his wife.'

He sounds drunk or stoned. I guess if I'd spent thirteen years in jail, I'd spend a lot of my time getting wrecked myself.

'Daniel, is everything OK?'

'Yeah, yeah. Life's hunky-dory. I'm gonna get him, the fucker. Tomorrow. Like you said.'

'What are you talking about?'

'In your letter – you said I can't let him get away with it.'

'That's not what I meant—'

He laughs to himself.

'He's not gonna see me coming. But I'll make sure he knows it was me before it's all over. I'll be the last person he ever sees when the knife goes in.'

No.

'This isn't what you want, Daniel. What about justice? Making him face up to what he's done?'

Daniel scoffs. 'Bullshit. Won't happen. He's bulletproof.'

'That's not true – I'm working on getting evidence. You can help me.'

'Fuck that. I want him to be as scared as my mum was.'

His speech is getting more slurred, and I am afraid he might drop the phone, or end the call before I can calm him down.

Maybe it is just the drink talking, but what if it's not?

'Daniel, where are you?'

'Night shelter in Gloucester kicked me out a few days ago for being pissed, so I decided to come home.'

It takes me a moment to realise where he means.

'Ashdean?'

'It's a shithole, but you know what they say. Home is where the heart is.'

The probability of him being serious just increased by a frightening degree.

'You've only just got free, Daniel,' I say, in the calmest voice I can manage. 'Think this through. You don't want to end up inside again.'

'I'm done thinking.'

I try to work out what to do. It's too late to get a train to Ashdean but I could maybe get a cab. It'd cost hundreds, but who cares?

'Where are you sleeping tonight?'

He laughs. 'Take a guess. I'll give you a clue. It's very grand, though it has seen better days. It's got a lovely view. And I feel extra close to my ma.'

Shit.

'You're at Copse View?'

'And guess what happens here tomorrow?'

Before I can reply, he says, 'Daddy is giving the press a special tour and showing them all the amazing things he's going to do here. I'm going to give them an even better story.'

'Daniel, think it through—'

'It's all I've thought about for days. *Years.*'

'I want you to tell me everything. Tonight. If you kill him, they'll put you away again. Say you were mad. But if you talk to me now, I can speak for you. Tell the press what your father did to deserve it.'

'You're not gonna talk me out of it.'

'I know but . . . I bet you're hungry. I could bring food.'

Silence. But at least he's stopped arguing.

'You want to talk. You wouldn't have called if you didn't.'

I hear something between a yes and a grunt.

'Good. Stay where you are, don't drink or smoke anymore and I'll get you sorted. All right?'

Silence.

'You trust me, don't you, Daniel? You know I'm the only one who knows how you feel.'

I hear a mumbled yes.

'Good lad. It'll take me a few hours, but I promise I am coming. I'll phone you when I'm nearly there.'

'Curry,' he says. 'Bring chicken curry.'

When he hangs up, I log onto Uber, hoping someone is desperate enough to drive me 180 miles.

I have to try to stop him.

Though, if this doesn't work, I become an accessory to murder. And there's a tiny part of me that thinks if justice can't do its job, then maybe murder is exactly what Jim deserves.

65

The driver is silently resentful, despite the premium fee he's getting for the trip.

Suits me: conversation is the last thing I need.

On the journey, I try to use my bag as a pillow, but I can't sleep. I packed in a hurry, throwing in a sleeping bag for me, a few toiletries for Daniel, cash. And, as an afterthought, the photos from Copse View, and a kitchen knife. The photos, in case they trigger any memories for him, and the knife . . . Well, I still don't know what Daniel did and didn't do the night of the fire.

I cannot ever imagine using a knife. But who knows what I am capable of, if it comes down to him or me?

And, of course, I am going back into Jim's territory, against his orders. If I can defuse the situation with Daniel, Jim will never know I was here. I can get the driver to drop me on the other side of the copse, where no one will see me. And hopefully, I can talk Daniel out of what he wants to do.

I call Daniel on the hour to check . . . I don't know, that he's still alive? That he hasn't changed his mind and gone straight to the White House. I keep reminding him I'm bringing food. I hope he's too hungry to do anything before he gets the take-away I've promised.

As we drive, I stare out of the window at the cars and lorries and the cat's eyes marking the lanes on the motorway. My world seems to be getting fuzzier, but I can't tell if that's real or simply because I have lost interest in most of it.

I doze eventually, and when I wake, Charlie is in the front of the car, grinning at me, as though he's delighted to be up front like a grown-up. Pink sits at my side, hugging her long, skinny legs to her chest. Her shins are pale and bruised.

We're going back, Pink, to the place where bad things happened. I hope it's going to be worth it.

I check my phone to see if there's been any response from Rosanna. My heart leaps as I see her name in the sender line of my inbox.

The email is blank: it's a read receipt. But still – *she's read it.*

How must that have felt, to read my message? I imagine it like a bomb exploding in the middle of the life she's built for herself. I'm going to ask her to go back in time to pursue something – someone – she's probably spent thirty years trying to forget. And I don't even know for sure it'll work, that any evidence would be admissible after so long, even if she wants to give it.

Oli would know, but I can't ask him. All I can do is tell her, when she replies, that she might still be able to make a difference.

If she replies.

We stop at a wealthier-looking town five miles outside Ashdean, to buy Daniel's curry. The car fills with the sickly, spicy smell of the food, as I direct the driver to the woods.

I tip him – for the first time, he smiles – and let myself out. It's a sultry night and the moon has a red cast. Now the adrenaline has subsided, I realise that after days of numbness, I am afraid. I've seen two Daniels – the vulnerable, teenage defendant with the air of a victim, and the prison inmate whose unpredictable temper made me think he did kill Tessa after all.

But even if he did, hasn't he served his time?

Pink and Charlie are no longer with me. Maybe my brain is too full to summon them up.

Copse View looms beyond the trees, its whitewashed walls tinted red by the moonlight. I try not to trip on roots or stumps I can't see. Can I talk Daniel round? Give him hope that there could be more to his future than another brutal killing?

I weave in between the damaged wire fencing that surrounds the house, and enter through the door I used the first time I came.

Is this where the story begins?

The smell of alcohol and urine stings my eyes. Perhaps there've been parties here. It's gloomy, though some moonlight comes through the missing windows and the open roof above the rotting staircase. I use my phone as a torch, to make sure the floor in front of me isn't missing.

'Daniel?' I call out. 'Daniel, it's me, Georgia. Where are you?'

Silence.

Has he gone already? Jim's house is only fifteen minutes' walk.

'Daniel, come on. I know you're here.'

I hear someone moving behind me.

Could I have been set up? Daniel's call might have been a test by Jim, to see whether I was still trying to find out the truth.

I turn. In the half-light, I see Daniel, and smell him, too: booze and neglect. He's lost even more weight since I saw him in prison, and the skin on his face clings to his skull. He wears new jeans, an old bomber jacket and filthy trainers. It's thrown together, the outfit of an ex-con with no option but to take what he's given.

He doesn't look at me.

'Thought it was a wind-up. Never thought you'd actually come.'

'Well, we both want the same thing. Let's eat first, then talk.'

'Watch yourself,' he says, as he sidesteps the rotting boards next to the grand staircase, moving towards the back of the building.

I follow him into what must be the largest room in the house. It would have been the drawing room for the first family who lived here. The fireplace has been removed, leaving a gaping brick hearth. At the back of the room, ornate glazed doors might once have led on to a manicured lawn. Instead, half are boarded, and the others mostly cracked. Through the panes, I can see building materials stacked up against the breeze-block garage.

There's no furniture. In the corner furthest from the French windows, Daniel has unrolled his sleeping bag. I can smell it from here, the sourness of fabric that has been soaked hundreds of times and never quite dried out. Despite the muggy night, this space is chilly and damp.

I spread out my own sleeping bag in the opposite corner, pocketing the knife I'd rolled into the centre and slipping it back into my holdall. Where is Daniel keeping the knife he intends to use to kill his father? Will he use it on me if I try to stop him?

I take the lids off the takeaway boxes and Daniel sits next to me and starts to eat. I wait until he's finished – no, devoured – his food, and hand him a bottle of Coke to wash it all down.

'Why did you come here, Daniel?'

He shrugs. 'Told you on the phone. It's time.'

'But why here? This building?'

'Slept in the copse the first night after I hitched from Glouces-ter. Then worked out there's no security here so moved in. There's been no one else here until today when some of my dad's guys came in, talking about the big launch tomorrow. He's gonna show the press how he's gonna change the face of this place. Such a *good bloke*, right?'

'What did he do, Daniel?'

'You've got a fucking short memory. I told you.'

He's volatile. I need to take it more carefully.

'I know you think he killed your mum, and Robert O'Neill. That's who you were talking about in prison, wasn't it? But why do you think something happened to him?'

He swigs the last of the Coke.

'Got eyes.'

'You saw something?'

'Might have.'

'When?'

'Few days after Mum . . . After she was on the bridge. Dad was drunk. Robert came round. A big row kicked off. I could hear them from my bedroom.'

'What was the row about?'

He shakes his head. 'I could only hear the noise, not the words. But Dad was louder. I heard Mum's name. Then the back door slammed, and Dad's big pick-up reversed out of the drive. He was gone . . . dunno, an hour. I was scared because I knew how drunk he was. I thought he'd crash. I didn't want him to die too.'

Daniel stands up, goes to his rucksack and comes back with a roll-up, which he lights, taking a huge gasp like an asthma sufferer using an inhaler.

'When he came back, he was swaying all over the place, but he still managed to chuck everything in the washing machine before he passed out.

'I stopped the machine, pulled out the dripping clothes. Everything but his big coat was soaked with blood. So much of it. Mud, too, up his trousers, like he'd been digging.'

'What did you do with the clothes?'

Another drag on the roll-up.

'Put the wash back on. What else was I meant to do?'

'Go to the police?'

'I was fifteen. Mum was dead, and I *loved* my dad. He was all I had. I thought if he'd . . . hurt Robert, well, Dad must have had his reasons. Robert was a twat. Up himself, acting like he was a big deal. And I didn't think he was *dead*. It was only when Charlie's mum started looking for him, when I wondered . . . but not for long. My dad was my *hero*.'

He scoffs at his own naivety.

'What about your mum, Daniel?'

He nods. 'For two years I believed she jumped. Hated her, some days, for leaving us. When Dad married Tessa, I was angry with her too and . . .'

Daniel stubs the roll-up out on the wooden floor.

'The autumn after they got married, I ran away. They were all lovey-dovey. Couldn't hack it. I kipped on mates' sofas, smoked a lot of weed. But Dad never gave up on me. Gave me cash. Told me I could come back whenever I wanted. Then he got firmer, telling me I shouldn't spend Christmas alone, and he had news. It was two years after Mum had died. I wanted to be with my family again. Even took them a present, showed up early on Christmas Eve, let myself in with my old key. I wanted to be there when they got home. Surprise!

'It was so nice. There was a Christmas tree and all these presents.' He blinks. 'It was . . . homely, just like it'd been when Mum was . . . happy.'

He is silent for a minute.

'I stuck the kettle on, went through my post. I was waiting for my provisional driving licence, one of the things Dad had sorted for me. He was gonna teach me. That hadn't arrived. But there was a letter.'

'From who?'

'It wasn't signed. Fuck knows.' He shrugs.

'What did the letter say?'

'That Dad had killed my mum by driving her to the bridge and then pushing her off. That he'd murdered Robert O'Neill and buried him in the woods. All to get them out of the way so he could be with Emma.'

Isn't that what the neighbour hinted at? Could she have sent the letter? I imagine the young, grieving Daniel reading it, in the house where he grew up, letting graphic images of his father's actions form in his head.

'What else was in the letter, Daniel?'

'It told me everyone in Ashdean knew what he'd done but they were too chicken to do anything about it. That I should man up . . .'

He spreads his fingers. I realise I recognise the gesture: his father does the same thing.

'Now, I wonder if it meant, come forward, be a witness. But that afternoon, I couldn't think straight and . . .'

I look at his pinched face, and I see the boy he was much more clearly than the man he is now.

And I see the truth.

'Oh God. It *was* you, wasn't it?' I whisper. 'You did start the fire that killed Tessa.'

66

Daniel turns away from me, shoulders hunched as though he's expecting a blow.

'Tell me the truth. What did you do?'

He keeps his back to me and begins to speak.

'I . . . I ran out of our house. Bought two litres of cider and went to the woods. Got drunker and drunker while I worked out what to say to him . . . You really want to hear this?'

I realise it might be the first time he's ever told anyone what happened that night.

'Go on.'

'I was gonna confront him alone. But when I walked back, I could see him through the window in his fucking Santa outfit, reading to the O'Neill kids as if he'd had nothing to do with killing their dad, or my mum, and I . . .' He begins to cry. 'I swear I didn't know about Tessa being pregnant. But I can't say for sure it would have stopped me.

'All I could think was – Mum's dead, he killed her, he doesn't deserve to live. And I thought about all the nights I'd cried because I'd let her down, or hated her for leaving me. The betrayal of knowing Dad caused it all . . . It was like my head was going to explode if I didn't do something.'

I wait.

He steps towards the French windows. The darkness outside has an amber tone.

'I went into Dad's garage, and got his petrol can and then I crept out the door and up the stairs, dribbling a trail along the carpet—' He stops. Takes a breath. 'I didn't put any on the ground floor.'

'You thought the kids would be able to get out?'

Daniel turns towards me, but he still can't meet my eye.

'They were downstairs. I thought Tessa was too. She was a party girl. She never went to bed early.'

I fill in the gap.

'Except she was pregnant. Tired out.'

Daniel makes a choking sound.

'I should have made sure. But I was so angry. I wanted the house gone, the lie of it. I didn't care if me and Dad died. Maybe I wanted that. An ending.'

He scrubs at his cheeks.

'Almost as soon as I saw the flames going up the staircase, I . . . It was like waking up except the nightmare was in front of me. It was me that called 999. I ran to the phone box and when I got back, Dad was outside, with the kids but no Tessa. It was only when he went back in that I realised she was still inside—'

'Stop crying,' I snap. 'Why not own up to it straightaway, if you felt so bloody guilty?'

'I had to lie. To tell the truth.'

'Bullshit.'

'No. Believe me. I couldn't tell the detectives what I knew, because they were in with Dad, and if they'd told him, he'd have found a way to shut me up before court. But I knew he couldn't stop me once I got in the witness box, with journalists and the public there. So I kept my gob shut all through remand, but pleaded not guilty so I'd get my turn. Tell them what he did. And what I did too. I wasn't going to lie.'

'But you never gave evidence.'

He returns to his backpack and pulls out a battered photo.

'This was on my bunk, in an envelope, the night before I was going to go in the dock. I knew it was from Dad. I put my hand in, expecting a razor blade or, I dunno, a bullet. It was just a photo.'

He passes it to me and though I can't make out the details, I know what it shows. It's the picture of the Cherry Blossom Lane summer barbecue. A copy of the one Chrissie showed me.

'Turn it over,' Daniel says.

When I do, I see the names written on the other side, the way people used to on old pictures. But this is different. Three of the names are crossed out: Sharon's, Tessa's and Robert's. Next to Amy Fielding's, there's a red question mark, and a scrawl. I angle it to read:

It's your choice, Dan.

I look up at Daniel.

'He'd kill all of us, don't you see?' he says. 'Even Amy, his favourite. He'd even kill Amy to save his own fucking skin.'

The favourite.

I try not to think of my own father, sparing me.

I force myself to think about Jim instead: a psychopath who sees everyone as disposable.

'So you changed your plea to keep Amy safe.'

'It was too much of a risk. I thought, when I was free, I could try again.'

'And now you are free.'

He shakes his head. 'Amy's not. She writes to me, once a year, on my birthday. The last letter, she told me she was pregnant. That's when I realised she'll never get away from Ashdean or Dad.'

As I watch, he leans down to scratch at his scarred ankle.

'You tried to kill yourself after that last letter from your sister, didn't you?'

He sighs. 'I wanted to die. But now I'm glad they found me before I bled out. It means I can finish it. Set her free. It's the only way to stop him.'

He's not pretending: he really is capable of murder.

'Daniel. Listen to me. It might not be the only way.'

'More bullshit.'

'It's not. There might still be a way we can make him suffer. Something that'll take everything from him.'

He looks up.

'I believe your dad abused girls, right here, at Copse View. Maybe your mum, too. It goes back that far.'

He frowns and then turns slowly, looking round the once-grand room, as though he is seeing it for the first time.

'Abused?'

'A long time ago, I think your grandfather knew as well, that he helped to cover it up. Robert knew too. That's probably why he died.'

Daniel's fists are tight against his thighs, as they were when I saw him that time in prison. Perhaps it's a strategy they taught him to control his anger.

'Changes nothing.'

'Except I think I've found one of the girls he hurt. I'm going to try to talk to her, tomorrow. If I can persuade her to talk, then it'll *all* come out. Your father will go to prison. And you *know* how they treat sex offenders. If you want him to suffer, that's going to be worse than a quick death.'

His features are difficult for me to read.

'This woman he . . . hurt. Why would she talk to you now?'

'I have to be honest. I can't be sure she will. But if I can make her understand that it didn't stop with her, that Jim has hurt so many people since, and still could, maybe that'll be enough to get her to talk.'

'And if she doesn't want to help?'

Jim doesn't deserve mercy. And if the system can't deliver, maybe rough justice is the only option remaining.

'If she can't help, then I promise I won't try to stop you doing it your way.'

67

I try to persuade Daniel to move back out to the copse to sleep tonight, but the food has made him tired and tetchy. So I let him lie down on my sleeping bag. We'll move at six, before the media circus begins.

He is a killer, but he's a victim, too. That anonymous letter came at the worst possible time. Whoever wrote it, whatever their reasons, they created the spark that made Daniel start the fire.

But who would do something so reckless? Chrissie, the neighbour? A friend of Sharon's? I even wonder about Jeanette. But she only began to suspect Daniel *after* the blaze.

Daniel cries out in his sleep. I crouch next to him.

'It's OK, Daniel. You're not in prison. I'm Georgia – Suzanne – remember?'

His eyelids snap open, pupils dilated. For a moment, I think he's going to attack me, but then he blinks.

'Yes,' he says.

Lying down, his slack face reminds me of the addicts I see begging around Brighton station.

'Daniel, are you on drugs?'

He gestures at the discarded takeaway containers.

'No! How many junkies do you know who could polish all that off and still be hungry?'

I smile: he's never said anything lighthearted to me before, and it gives me a glimpse of the person he might have been, or might still become.

He falls asleep again, becoming rigid as a corpse in a coffin, limbs straight and unmoving. I suppose years in a prison bunk will do that. In his jacket pocket, there's the outline of a knife.

Could I reach over, disarm him?

I made him a promise – try it my way first, but then let him do what he wants.

As soon as the sun's up, I am going to call Rosanna. Now she's read my email, she knows what this is about. I have to persuade her to talk to me about what happened. If she won't help, I am out of ideas.

And out of time, too.

I sit on the floor, back up against the wall, facing the door. Begin to rehearse the words I will use to persuade Rosanna that now is the time for justice.

'Georgia. *Suzanne.* Wake up.'

I smell Daniel's sour curry breath before I open my eyes.

'They're here. Dad, and Amy.'

Now I'm awake. There *are* voices coming from somewhere else in the house: a woman's and a man's.

Getting louder – heading towards this room.

I gesture towards the French windows, and scramble up, grabbing my things. Daniel looks as though he's going to pick up his stuff too.

'There's not time,' I whisper.

The truth is, it won't matter if he leaves his sleeping bag and gear. It's indistinguishable from the other rubbish left by previous rough sleepers and partying kids.

The glass doors are bolted but not locked; when I turn the handle, I hold my breath, half-expecting one of the loose panes to fall out and shatter. But they hold, just, and I inch through, followed by Daniel.

I'm relieved he's following. Though it doesn't mean he won't still hurt his father, only that he wants more of an audience.

I flatten myself against the outside wall, close enough to the room to hear what is being said. Daniel does the same, on the other side of the windows.

'. . . sure you don't want to tidy up a bit?' Amy says in a low voice. 'It stinks.'

'That's the whole point, sweetheart, we want this to be the before. Like on TV.'

Jim sounds affectionate, but his voice makes my hackles rise.

I glance over at Daniel. I can't make out his face, but his body is rigid.

'All right,' Amy says. 'So I thought after this, you could lead them out through the French windows, towards the summer house, and the garaging?'

They're walking towards us. I can't shrink back any further. We didn't close the doors behind us.

I don't dare breathe.

'No. I don't want them anywhere near there.'

'Come on, Dad. You're being daft. It's not like it has any architectural merit. Like I said, we should bulldoze it. We could even squeeze in an extra dwelling if Brian does something clever. Wheelchair accessible bungalow. Even the council couldn't say no to that.'

'I won't tell you again, Amy. It's staying.'

His tone has changed. Is there an unspoken threat underneath the fatherly tone?

I hear Amy sigh. 'All right. So just a quick glance in here, then, and then back out the front to give the . . .'

Her voice fades as they move out of the room. I dare to look over my shoulder, and catch a glimpse of Amy, her belly even bigger than it was when I saw her the night of Jim and Leah's engagement.

But Jim hasn't left the room. I freeze. He's staring out of the French windows and for a moment I am certain he's seen me. I brace myself. My bag is at my feet. Inside it is the kitchen knife I brought.

Jim isn't seeing me. He's focused on something outside, yet when I look ahead of me, there is nothing moving, nothing different. Only the materials, the summer house and the garage block.

Jim sighs and turns around, leaving the room.

I exhale.

When I look over at Daniel, he seems smaller, younger. Without saying anything, we creep back into the room, sensing they won't come back here. I hear a car start and drive away. Then, silence.

Daniel doesn't move.

'Was that the first time you've seen him since . . .?'

'Since I was sent down. Yeah.' He shrugs. 'He's exactly the same. Like none of what's happened to me, to Tessa, to Mum, has affected him at all.'

I could tell him the things Jim confessed to during the sittings: the guilt about not saving his wives; the missed chances to help his son. But everything he told me was untrue, designed to manipulate me, find out what I knew.

'What is this place to him, Daniel? Do you know?'

'Apart from Mum being here . . .'

I catch a glimpse of movement outside, but I already know who it is, and that Daniel won't be able to see her.

The sight of Pink leaning against the garage's breeze blocks reminds me of one of the photos.

Could that have been where Jim hurt her, and where he took other girls, to do what he wanted? And is that why he doesn't want it touched?

As another figure moves to join Pink – Charlie, throwing his ragged Teletubby toy as though it's a ball – an even more sinister thought occurs to me.

Is that where he buried Robert?

'He doesn't deserve to live,' Daniel says.

'You promised to let me try to make it right my way first.'

He says nothing.

I look at my watch. It's gone seven. It's just late enough for me to call Rosanna, and keep calling until I get an answer.

'When is the tour meant to be happening?'

'Noon, from what the blokes I heard said.'

I nod. 'Give me until then.'

As I step back outside to make the call, I realise that a girl Jim abused is now the only person with the power to save his life.

68

I walk to the far side of the garage block, facing the copse. Pink stands next to me as I prepare to make the call.

I try to picture this woman – Rosanna – as she goes about her morning routine. Fixing breakfast, getting the kids up – I don't know how old they are, but she's Jim's age so I imagine them as teenagers, oversleeping, ignoring her increasingly irritated calls up the stairs.

Whenever I picture a family house, I still default to thinking of the one where I grew up, despite what happened there.

Now, I guess another family occupies the space that was ours. Two or three families might have come and gone since we did. Do they ever sense what happened to my mother, my brother and me?

Stop putting this off.

I take a deep breath, rehearsing what I want to say, and then dial Rosanna's number.

The line rings.

Picks up.

'Hello, Mrs Chapman, my name is . . .'

Her voicemail talks over me.

'Hello, I can't come to the phone right now. Leave a message after the beep.'

An adult woman's telephone voice, carefully enunciated. Not the voice I expected but then, I picture her as Pink, a teenage tearaway. I take a deep breath before speaking.

'Mrs Chapman, my name is Georgia. I emailed you and I know you've read the message. Please, let me speak to you just once. I'm ... visiting the area and I could meet you anywhere. But soon. Today even. I wouldn't ask if it wasn't really, really important.' I hesitate. Is there anything else I can say? 'Just call me back. Thank you so much.'

I leave my number and when I hang up, I wonder if it's enough.

The garage wall is already warm against my back, from the morning sun, or perhaps still retaining the heat of the sultry night. I close my eyes. I don't smoke but I wish I had one of Daniel's roll-ups.

My phone buzzes. The screen is hard to read in the bright light but it's from her.

Don't call me again in case someone else picks up. My family don't know. They can't ever know.

I'm formulating a reply apologising and promising discretion when another message follows.

Text me instead of calling.

She's not saying no.

Adrenaline floods my system, making up for the lack of sleep. I don't want to pressure her so I wait for her to send a third message.

A minute goes past. Two. My resolve falters as I try to plan some persuasive words.

The phone buzzes.

> I didn't sleep last night for thinking about your email. I know the home closed down. I thought it would have stopped then. Are you sure he's been doing it again?

I type:

> I think he's done worse. I think he's killed someone. Maybe two people. He has to be stopped.

When she doesn't reply immediately, I type:

> You're the only one who can make it happen, Rosanna. And maybe your family don't need to know. I have lawyer friends who can advise on staying anonymous. But first, please let us meet. I can come to you. Whatever you want.

I wait. Three, four, five minutes. I wonder if I've pushed too hard.

> Not at home. It's too much of a risk. Let me think of somewhere.

Any time now, she could get cold feet. But I cannot say any more. I look up at the decaying old mansion, wondering what secrets it holds.

There's a place in the forest, Little Pike. Eight miles from Ashdean. A visitor centre with a cafe and a kiddies' playground, I take the kids there at weekends. But weekdays it's quieter. Safer.

I recognise the name: the bus stopped there when I came here from Gloucester. I'd imagined her with much older kids.

When?

My fingers are trembling as I type.
I could be there this morning. 10.30?

Enough time to persuade her before the press launch.
I remember one last thing, and text, *How will I recognise you?*
She doesn't reply, but Pink is here now, smiling at me.
I whisper, 'You'll show me who you are, won't you?'

69

Daniel agrees to walk with me to the bus stop two miles out of Ashdean, lured by the promise of a bacon roll from the petrol station opposite. We both have good reason to avoid Ashdean itself.

There's an edginess between us as we sit back from the road, hidden by the bus shelter, him eating his sandwich, me with a coffee I don't actually want in this heat.

What Daniel did – the murderous thoughtlessness of it – is shocking. But it doesn't stop me seeing he's a victim, too.

'This woman, Rosanna. You reckon she'll talk?'

'I don't know, Daniel. She seemed keen to meet, which has to be a good sign. Right?' I need reassurance.

He shrugs. 'I wouldn't. If this wasn't my blood, I'd walk away. You still could.'

'I know.'

Daniel finishes eating and rolls the sandwich wrapper into a ball, throwing it into the bin.

'We used to go there when we were kids. Little Pike. Me and Amy. Mum and Dad.'

I imagine him as a kid. Think of what Jim said about him and Sharon trying to raise their children happy, to overcome 'all the messed-up stuff from when we were growing up'.

Another lie designed to gain my sympathy? Or a rare glimpse of the truth?

'You sure you want to go back inside, Daniel?'

It's my way of asking the bigger question: can you really kill again? Starting a fire that spreads too far is one thing. Sinking a knife into the father you used to love is another.

He doesn't respond.

'Think about it, Daniel.'

'Phone me after you've spoken to the woman.'

I could always take it out of his hands. Report him for breaching parole – I'm sure being caught with a knife would get him arrested again within hours, taken back inside.

We hear the bus approaching and I step forward to hail it. As I board, I glance at the other passengers, assess if any of them might know Jim. They're all women, mostly pensioners. One fans her face with a magazine, a red, tartan shopping trolley taking the space next to her. An ordinary day.

The bus pulls away. Daniel stays mostly hidden, but I wave at him through the window, and I think he waves back.

There are only twelve stops to Little Pike. Each one feels like a countdown.

The next stop is Nailbridge.

As the bus trundles along the forest road, I will my brain to come up with a hallucination to distract me. But the greens and browns stay blurry and everyday. Charlie and Pink have deserted me. Though perhaps I am so close to an answer that I don't need my little guides anymore.

The next stop is Steam Mills.

What can I say to Rosanna to persuade her to do the right thing? I mustn't lie by promising her she'll be happier, or safer, if she speaks out. Whatever she asks me, I owe it to her to tell the truth . . .

Outside, branches reach out to strike the metal sides of the bus. I feel shaky. But how scary can a kids' adventure playground be? I imagine Neena's answer – 'fucking terrifying, you better believe it' – and it makes me smile.

The next stop is Little Pike.

I press the stop button.

The bus pulls up next to a rusting iron shelter, incongruous against the wild forest backdrop. I step off and watch the bus retreat over a hump towards Gloucester. Gone. Now I turn away from the road, towards the woods and the visitor centre, looking for a signpost.

It's quieter than I expected, but that's the reason Rosanna suggested it. A wide track opens up, big enough for cars and coaches, and I follow it. Despite the heat, the earth under my feet is springy and damp, the canopy of trees creating a rainforest climate.

The track leads to an empty car park. I look again for signage, and finally spot a wooden arrow. I get close enough to read the carved-out words, and have to push ivy out of the way to make out:

LITTLE PIKE ADVENTURE CENTRE – TAKE A WALK ON THE WILD SIDE!
PLAYGROUND, CAFE, WCS >>>

I follow the arrow down further into the woods. It's the first time I've been into the forest proper, and though I've seen it from the road, everything is very different on foot: there can't be anywhere else in England that's as green, as primeval. I picture the memorial statue in the centre of Ashdean: the forester and the miner with their torches and their axes to help them fight their way through the woods, and plunder the riches under the earth.

My small backpack rubs against my shoulders, making the skin sore. I left my sleeping bag for Daniel. Though if he does what he plans, tonight he'll be back on a prison bunk.

As I walk, I listen for the sound of children playing, but all that comes back is the rustling of leaves far above, and the soft padding of my own feet on the forest floor.

Sweat soaks through my cotton shirt. I lean against the trunk of an oak, grateful for its shade, and look up. The tree's leaves vibrate against a white-hot sky, a colour chart of different greens: Hooker's, Alizarin, Sap. One day, perhaps, I might paint this as an abstract, the absence of my central vision represented by the sun.

Who am I kidding? There is no 'one day'. After next week, when I meet my father, there will be nothing but absence.

Stay focused on now.

The temperature has dropped. Overhead, charcoal clouds stutter across the sun.

I walk slowly, wary of the roots and branches that are reclaiming territory from human trespassers. The further I go into the woods, the more it resembles a Tolkien landscape. Root balls stand tall as cars, and are covered in moss. Trees twist and warp and I have to use the roots to clamber up and over without tumbling back down.

I peer ahead, hoping Charlie or Pink might suddenly appear to show the way. But I'm alone. It's still early, though.

I send a text to Rosanna anyway. I don't want to be here any longer than I have to be. If I can't persuade her by noon, it'll all be over.

It's me, I text: no names. I'm walking up from the road. It seems very quiet, are you here yet?

It gets wilder. Rust-coloured lichen and moss make it hard to get a footing. Every now and then, there are timber planks sticking up, perhaps old walkways, which collapsed long ago. There's a smell like the dying embers of a bonfire.

'Ow.'

My foot strikes a root and I begin to topple. I reach out, up, grab a branch. It snaps off in my hand and I think I'm falling. But I right myself, just in time.

As I catch my breath, I glimpse primary colours through the trees: the playground. I'm desperate to get out of this wilderness, but I force myself to walk carefully.

'*Georgia!*'

I spin around, but there's no one in sight. Did I imagine that?

My phone buzzes, but when I check, it's a notification to tell me my message to Rosanna hasn't been sent. There's no signal – when did I lose it? – but at least I'm here now, at the playground. Behind it is a large chalet which must house the cafe.

I listen. Silence. I step over the low log fence into the play area itself. The metal roundabout is rusted; I push it, and it moves stiffly, with a screech. All the equipment here is old-fashioned. Even Pip would have pronounced it *soo boring . . .*

Don't think about him now.

Something lands on my face. I jump. I realise what it is, and I laugh.

Rain.

We've been waiting for this.

I look at my watch. It's 10.30.

'Hello!' I call out. 'Rosanna?'

My own voice echoes back to me.

I walk across the greying wood chips, towards the chalet. A faded metal sign for ready-made ice creams and lollies gives prices twenty years out of date. Next to the closed hatch, a piece of laminated paper has been nailed into the wood, rust spreading like blood round a bullet hole.

I squint, moving my head so I can just read the type:

DESPITE OUR BEST EFFORTS, LITTLE PIKE ADVENTURE CENTRE IS CLOSED. PLEASE CHECK OUR WEBSITE FOR FURTHER UPDATES, AND REFURBISHMENT PLANS.

THANK YOU FOR YOUR SUPPORT OVER THE YEARS.

The date, at the bottom: DECEMBER 2005.

No. I must have misread.

But no matter which way I twist my head to see it more clearly, the date stays the same.

Blood rushes in my ears. Could Rosanna really not have realised this place closed down *twelve years* ago?

And something else about our text conversation niggles and I get my phone out.

The message still hasn't sent. I try to ignore the panic rising through my body and look at the message history instead.

I take the kids there at weekends.

If Rosanna has young kids, they must have been born *after* this closed down.

I don't know what's going on, but I don't want to be here any longer. I begin to retrace my steps towards the road – the earth already a few shades darker, as the rain starts to penetrate the dried-out layers. There are two paths ahead of me, and I can't remember which I took. But both must lead towards the road. I take the one that feels right.

'*Georgia.*'

I turn towards the whisper. Still no one.

'Is that you, Rosanna?'

There's movement to my left but as I spin round, I can't tell if it's animal or human. A rabbit? No, bigger than that. A fox?

'Over here.'

The whisper is coming from the same direction. I take a few steps towards her. Part of me wants to run, back to the road, far away from here. But I haven't come this far to get spooked by a few trees or a bloody rabbit.

A shriek pierces the air: it's the sound of a child in distress. Perhaps Rosanna brought her child with her?

Now sobbing, just audible beneath the splash and hiss of raindrops on parched vegetation. The scent of the earth reminds me of graves. I walk towards the voices. The sound of more pain is unbearable. I pick up the pace, starting to run.

And the earth falls away and I am falling too.

70

I am weightless just long enough to fear the impact.

The back of my head smashes against solid ground, my teeth crash together, and pain sends a slice of bright, burning heat through my bones.

At last, I'm still. I take stock: a sensation like broken glass inside my right ankle; the smell of sap and soil; the taste of rust.

Blood in my mouth. My tongue darts around my gums, exploring. No teeth missing. But my bottom lip stings where I've bitten into it.

I'm in a hollow, thin tree roots forming a network like blood vessels through the earth beside me. The space is wide enough for me to lie full-length, like a deep bath.

Or a coffin.

Except it's deep too: deeper than I am tall. I'm lucky I didn't break my neck.

I push myself up and reach over to inspect my ankle.

Fuck.

It's bent at an unnatural angle, and when I try to move it, the blowtorch pain is so intense I can't bear it . . .

I must have blacked out, because suddenly my face is sopping wet from rain, or tears. Maybe both. I try to manoeuvre myself to the shallower end of the pit, grasping at the sides, but the earth crumbles between my fingers. Perhaps, if the rain keeps falling, it'll be easier to dig away at it. But it'll also turn slippery, harder to get traction.

The blood in my mouth tastes like fear.

OK.

This is OK.

Rosanna is coming to meet me and I *did* hear someone, didn't I? An adult *and* a child? I must shout as loudly as I can, so they find me.

'HELP!' The earth surrounding me deadens the sound. I prop myself up further, ignoring the pain, and tilt my head towards the sky to try to make myself heard outside. 'Help me. Rosanna! I'm here. I'm HERE.'

My voice sounds feeble. I find my phone in my pocket. Still no signal. Maybe I should try 999 – I read once that the signal needs to be minimal to do that, but I feel like a fraud for even considering it.

Except this *could* turn into an emergency. I am hurt, in the woods, and no one except Rosanna knows where I am.

I dial 999, but the call doesn't even try to connect.

Focus.

Rosanna will find me. She *must*.

'Help!' I call out again.

My throat is dry from that coffee – so long ago now – and I swig from my water bottle. How much should I drink? I could be here for a long while yet . . .

I can't think like that. And I can't let her leave.

'ROSANNA!'

I remember that people hear their own name better than any other word. Or was it fire?

'Fire!'

The pain in my ankle surges in time with my heartbeat. The back of my head starts to sting too. I touch it, and when I look at my fingers, they're covered in blood.

HELP!
FIRE!
ROSANNA!

Have I called the words a hundred times? Five hundred? They've lost all meaning.

I could be here for hours. Days. Except I won't let myself believe that. *Someone* must come this way. Dog walkers, or . . . In so many murder cases I've covered, a body is found by an excited dog let off the leash.

I could die here.

No. Someone will come to look for me.

But the only people who know I'm here are Rosanna – who must have got cold feet, it's ten to eleven now – and Daniel, who will assume I've failed unless he hears from me. Who will likely be arrested before the day is out.

Don't panic, I tell myself. But the fear is drowning it out.

I think I hear something. *Someone?*

My breathing and pulse are so loud. I strain to listen to the forest. Twigs snap, somewhere in the distance.

'*HELP!*' I call out, as loudly as I can. 'ROSANNA! Is that you? Help me!'

The pain subsides, as though every one of my cells is needed to hear if someone is coming. Yes. Those are *definitely* footsteps. But there's no reply, no acknowledgement that someone has heard me.

'PLEASE!'

'Hello?'

A man's voice, from some way away.

Oh, thank *God*.

'I'm here. I've fallen,' I call. 'Please help.'

'I'm coming,' he says. 'Don't worry, I'll find you.'

For a moment, he sounds like Jim.

But it's just the local accent that's familiar. Jim couldn't know I'm back, could he?

My mind races. Was I being followed? I hadn't seen anyone. Though can I ever be sure of what my damaged eyes tell me?

'Hello?' the man calls again. 'Where are you? Call out, so I can follow your voice.'

Not yet. Not until I am sure.

'Love, I can't help you if you don't tell me where you are.'

Instinct tells me it isn't Jim. That this is my best chance.

I call out: 'I'm here. I'm here. Please come.'

The footsteps get faster, louder, closer. It's stopped raining now. The skies are clearing too, as though the man is an angel sent to save me.

'I'm coming, love. I know where you are, I'm nearly with you . . .'

And suddenly he's right by me, and his shape blocks the light, and I know it's not Jim: too slim, too fair, too *small*.

He crouches down, next to the hole, and pauses as though he's trying to make sense of what he's seeing.

'Everything is going to be OK, now, Suzanne,' the man says, and at that one word – that *name* – my guts turn to water.

He shifts so that the sunlight bathes the left side of his face, and I can finally make out enough to know who my saviour is.

Not an angel, after all.

A ghost.

71

He smiles at me. I can't make out the look in his eyes, but his teeth are too white and straight to be his own.

'You know who I am, don't you, love?'

'You're meant to be dead.'

Robert O'Neill shrugs his shoulders. 'Looking good on it, eh?'

I close my eyes, hoping this is just a new Charles Bonnet symptom, brought about by extreme stress or pain. But it can't be, because the one thing that makes Charles Bonnet stand out is that the visions are always silent.

I open my eyes again. He's still smiling, dazzling as a toothpaste ad. My brain tries to process how he can be alive, why he's found me, how he knows my real name.

But my thoughts are slowed down by a paralysing dread.

'Are you badly hurt?' he asks.

'I think I've broken my ankle. I can't climb out on my own.' I try to sound as though I am still expecting him to help me. 'But if you lie down at the edge, you could help pull me out of the hole.'

Robert looks as though he's considering this. I notice more about him now: despite his slight frame, he has muscular arms. He wears dark jeans and a shirt. His face is youthful, though that might be the blurring effect of my vision loss.

'It's not a hole. It's a scowle,' he says. 'The hollows look natural but mostly they're man-made, from prospecting for iron. The area's riddled with them.'

I try to think how to reply, but I sense he doesn't want me to.

'Great place for hide-and-seek.' His accent is broader than Jim's, his speech so slow and calm that it's almost disturbing. 'When we were kids, I always half expected to find a skeleton. Closest I got was a rabbit's skull once.

'Brought my Charlie here, too, when he was a toddler.'

For the first time, there is some warmth in Robert's voice.

'And Jodie?'

I know Robert was gone before she was born, but mentioning her might build our rapport.

Robert scoffs. 'Not my kid. Knew it as soon as I saw a picture. Freak of nature.'

His tone makes goosebumps rise on the surface of my skin but I try to ignore that. I need to focus on why he's here instead of Rosanna.

'Are you . . .? Did you come with Rosanna?'

The smile is back. 'Oh yeah. Rosie couldn't make it. Sends her apologies.'

My mind feels foggy. He must know her from Copse View. Did he stay in touch as part of blackmailing Jim? Did she call him when she got my message?

'I need to speak to her.'

'Might be tricky, Suzanne.'

'My name is Georgia.' I try to sound light, but my voice trembles. Despite the heat, I keep shivering.

'No, it's not. I know everything there is to know about you, Suzanne Ross. What your daddy did. How much that nice flat of yours cost. What you've got in your fridge. You should lay off the gin, it'll kill you, you know.'

His words pinball around my brain.

He knows where I live.

He knows what's in my flat.

He was the one who broke in.

Coffee-tainted bile rising in my throat makes me gag. I gulp it back, the acid burning.

'What do you want from me, Robert?'

'What I *wanted* was for you to stop digging around.'

I think about what was taken in the break-in.

'You stole my laptop. My phone.'

He nods. 'Technology is brilliant, isn't it. Texts, emails, search history. Closest thing you get to actually reading someone's mind.'

It feels like a punch to the belly when I realise: Robert has seen every email I've sent and all my searches on my laptop, and every text I sent on my old phone.

And he'll also have seen the disc Jeanette sent me, the one with photographs of the girls from Copse View.

'What have you done to Rosanna?'

'Ah, forget Rosanna. She's long gone. Though I bet she'd have been very moved by your email. I mean, who doesn't believe in justice?'

He must have intercepted the emails I sent. Except she *did* respond to my texts. I heard her voice.

'She's got my number. She could still be coming.'

Robert reaches into his pocket and takes out a phone. He throws it down to me.

'No. *I've* got your number.'

It's a cheap pay-as-you-go, for texts and calls only. No signal, but I've got the call and message history. I try to scan it in the gloom.

'Did you steal her phone too?'

He sighs. 'Not exactly.'

I manage to see the messages: the only ones here are from me. There's nothing about school runs or domestic errands.

'But the private detective gave me her mobile number . . .'

'Oh yes. The private detective. Thanks for the £600, by the way. It came in very handy. All this organisation costs a few quid.'

I exhale as I realise: he must have intercepted my emails to the private detective, and sent his own fake responses instead. Even the money I sent must have gone to him.

'Why trick me, Robert? What Jim did had nothing to do with you.'

But even as I say it, I see that might not be true. Robert is alive, so clearly there was no murder. What else *didn't* Jim do?

Push his wife off a bridge? Abuse Rosanna?

Sweat blooms under my arms, on my back, up and down my legs. A very animal reaction to fear.

'You're starting to get it now, aren't you?' he says, mildly. 'I mean, it's possible you would have let it go. But I couldn't take the risk. You've already got a lot further than anyone else has.'

As he talks, I'm trying to play catch-up. He can't have started the fire that killed Tessa – Daniel has already admitted to that.

But he could have been the spark.

72

The bile is back in my mouth.

'You wrote the letter. The one that made Daniel burn down Jim's house?'

Robert nods. 'People get so emotional at Christmas. And I admit I was emotional, too. Jim had sent me away from my only son. You can't blame me for wanting to deprive him of his son to even the score.'

I look at him: I may not see every detail of his face, but I do see evil.

All that time I was trying to convince myself Jim was a psychopath, it didn't sit right. He was too empathetic. Too attentive. Even when he turned on me, it was as if he was only doing it because he had to, for both our sakes.

But Robert is different.

'Your own kids nearly died because of that letter.'

'Kid,' he corrects me. 'Told you already, Jodie's nothing to do with me. I was surprised at how dopey Daniel responded. But it was OK. Everybody's hero Jim Fielding saved my Charlie. Though I had to think fast when I realised Danny was planning to parrot the letter in court. I was perfectly happy being dead.'

'You sent him the photo threatening his sister?'

'It wasn't threatening. It was . . . suggestive.' He leans in a little further. 'That's the key, Suzanne. Get other people to do the work. So much more satisfying than mucking in yourself.'

Everything has started to hurt again – my ankle, my head, my split lip.

'I need help, Robert, I'm injured.'

He steps back. A moment later, he throws something on to the damp earth next to me: a carrier bag. I open it: there's a plastic bottle of vodka, and three large blister packs of Paracetamol, plus a smaller brown bottle with eight tiny pills inside it. I can't read the label.

'That'll help with the pain. But make sure you take it all with the vodka. The little bottle, that's diazepam. Valium. Chill pills.'

'There's enough here to kill someone.'

He chuckles. 'No flies on you, are there? Not yet anyway.' The chuckle turns into a full-blown laugh. 'Sorry, I'm always being told off for my black sense of humour, so it's not often I get to let rip.'

'I'm not going to do this.'

He picks up a stick; for a moment, I think he's going to aim it for my head. But then he starts to pick at the bark with his fingers.

'I've seen your computer search history. *Death by drowning*. And you've rewritten your will. Your friends will be sad when you're gone, but not surprised. Though I'm afraid I can't guarantee you'll ever be found. These woods hold on to their secrets.'

The vodka and the pills lie in my lap. It's an easier way out than I'd planned. My last walk into the sea would still have taken resolve to avoid fighting the water as it filled my lungs.

But that was supposed to happen *after* I'd made everything right.

I'm nowhere near that. I don't even understand why this is happening.

'What did I ever do to you, Robert?'

'Nothing. But it's what you've started. Winding up Daniel and that police bitch. Digging around about those loser girls at Copse View.'

'You've left Ashdean. How did you know?'

'I've an old mate on the cabs, keeps me up to date on my boy. He told me you'd been hanging round Jim. I checked you out and unfortunately . . . here we are. I don't get a kick out of hurting women.'

The way Robert says it makes me certain he does.

'It wasn't just Jim hurting those girls, was it? You joined in.'

He's completely shredded the branch with his fingers now, and pieces of cream-coloured wood litter the dark earth like confetti.

'They weren't hurt. Bit of attention. They were all craving that.'

I feel even more sickened. 'But you made sure Jim was the only one in the photograph. That's how you blackmailed him into going to jail for you?'

He scoffs. 'Jim never got past third base. Not even the night I took that picture. They'd been kissing, that's all, though I told him the girl had reported him for that. Jim was a virgin when he went to prison. Silly fucker. None of the girls at my parties were. OK, so Rosanna pretended she was, but she'd obviously been the town bike.'

All this time, I'd been focusing on Jim.

The real predator was *behind* the camera.

'Where is Rosanna now?'

He laughs. 'Not a million miles from here. Though I can't be sure exactly where. This part of the woods has changed a lot over the years.'

Oh lord. I think he means he killed her. Buried her. Here.

'But I heard her voice. The answerphone message.'

'Like I said, that £600 you kindly sent the investigator went a long way. I found a woman in the pub more than happy to record that in exchange for a bottle of cheap and nasty white wine.'

I close my eyes. I must not let fear win. Must keep him talking, till I work out how I can get out of here. 'Did Jim know you were having sex with the girls?'

Robert shrugs. 'Yeah, I was his role model. Even did him a favour and broke in Sharon for him, ready for when he got out of the nick. Silly little cunt. If she'd kept her gob shut, I'd still be in Ashdean. I'd have been a *real* father to Charlie.'

'You slept with Sharon too?'

'Now, she *was* a virgin. A really lazy fuck. Not worth the bother back then, and certainly not worth all that's happened since.'

It clicks, like a key in a lock.

'You raped Sharon before she met Jim?'

'It wasn't rape—'

I ignore him. 'Why did you come back to Ashdean after you were married?'

'Jim got rich. Why wouldn't I have wanted to be friends again? He didn't bear a grudge for the jail thing. Not then, anyway.'

'But it was too much for Sharon, wasn't it? You there, all the time, with her kids, her husband . . .' I remember the witness statement at her inquest, about her and Jim talking before she jumped to her death. 'But she told Jim what you did. Didn't she?'

'Such a shit-stirrer, that woman. But even when he got me into the woods, Jim couldn't stop being the hero. Another couple of dings with the wheel brace and I'd have been worm food. But I begged – *no, don't kill me, I have kids, don't make them suffer for my mistake.*'

I look up at him, hearing the fake wheedling tone, imagining how Jim must have felt.

'He let you go.'

'Told me he *would* finish it if I ever came back. I was pretty bashed about, but I managed to hitch to Gloucester, slept rough for a bit. But I started over, with the help of some accommodating lady friends.'

I replay the conversations from my sittings with Jim: the hopes he had for his marriage and kids with Sharon. The way that ended. And then the second tragedy: losing his son, his new wife, their new baby, in a single night.

His sadness was real.

And one person was behind all of it.

'Are you going to help yourself, Suzanne?'

I look at the vodka and the pills. The walls of the dark pit seem to grow taller with each breath. But it can't end here.

'What if I don't take them?'

Robert tuts. 'I'll have to get my hands dirty. Rather avoid that, if you don't mind, brings back a few bad memories. Rosanna was skinnier than you but she clung on to life for far longer than you'd have expected. Mind you, I wasn't fully grown back then. And at least *your* body won't need moving.'

I look up: his face is calm, despite his confession. Rosanna is dead. Robert is a murderer as well as a rapist.

'Your choice, Suzanne.'

73

My choice.

The choices you agonise over aren't the ones that change everything. It's the split-second ones that alter the course of your life.

'Pip, is my nose really that enormous in real life?'

My brother is lying on his tummy on my carpet, painting my portrait on a page from my sketchbook. I've found my old poster paints – he's a messy worker, but at least if he spills some of those, there's no harm done.

'You are my ugly sister!' Pip giggles. 'Like in *Cinderella*. Ugly sister, ugly sister! Now I'll put big green bogey spots on your chin!'

I laugh along. Teaching him to paint never quite goes the way I planned, but when I'm feeling serious, his silliness cheers me up. The door is closed so the giggling won't disturb my father.

Pip picks up the big brush and dips it in brown paint, then spreads it over the blank part of his page to make a snake shape.

'Look, Suzanne, you've done a poo! A great big, brown, smelly poo! Stinky!'

He's hysterical now, thumping his fists against the purple carpet so hard that I worry Dad will hear. He made breakfast for us all this morning, but it was so bad no one wanted to eat it. And that made Dad furious.

'Shh, Pip.'

My scolding makes him naughtier and now my brother's legs are kicking the floor. I grab for his ankles to calm him down but he shimmies out of the way like a baby commando, still giggling, and . . .

It happens in slow motion. His bare foot kicks out and it just catches the leg of the easel, which gives way. I think my painting is going to fall face first onto the carpet, though thank goodness it falls the other way. But the turps . . . The lid isn't on the bottle and clear liquid spreads over the new carpet. The smell of turps fills the room. Already Pip is on his haunches, patting at the stain with his messy little hands. He looks up at me, trying to smile his way out of it.

'I'll make it better, Suzie. I'm tidying already, see!'

The turps has splashed onto the new canvas I got yesterday at the art shop in Bath. I saved up for a month to buy that.

And the carpet cost so much more.

'Get out of my room, Pip! You ruin everything.'

Soft footsteps on the stairs, my mother racing into the room, drying her hands on her apron, shushing me, even before she's seen what Pip's done.

'Look, Mum, he's ruined my canvas and my paints and spilled my turps on the carpet. The carpet I chose.'

'Shh. You should have locked him out, then, shouldn't you, Suzanne? That's why we gave you the key.'

'I shouldn't have to!'

'Be quiet while I think, Suzanne. Pip, don't touch anything else.'

My brother freezes, paint-stained palms in the air.

'It's ruined,' I say.

'Suzanne,' my mother says quietly, 'I'll buy you a new canvas and new turpentine.'

'When? It cost all my pocket money and we won't be going to Bath again for ages and—'

'Shut up, Suzanne! If your dad hears, we'll all have a miserable day. I'll find a way to work it out if only you can be quiet for—'

Downstairs, the back door slams.

'Deborah! What is that racket? They can hear you halfway to Bristol.'

My father thunders up the stairs towards us and I smile at Pip, because I know I'll get a fresh canvas from my dad straightaway, maybe even two, and if Pip has to stay at home while we go to the cinema, well, it serves him right.

He needs to learn to leave my things alone.

A little later, when Dad's sent him to bed and I've set my easel up again, I'm working on the Cornish picture when there's the gentlest knock on my door.

'Suzie-sue, I'm sorry.'

It's Pip.

I don't answer. Shall I let him in? He *sounds* sorry. But I want to get the painting finished. I want it to be right to take to school on Monday.

'Please let me come in. Dad is cross and I know I've been naughty, but I'll pay you back from my pocket money. Just let me come and give you a cuddle.'

Later, I think.

I push the door closed, and ignore his pleas, until he stops and I hear the creak on the landing that tells me he's given up and gone back to his room.

I had a choice, I could have let him in. Instead, I chose to turn him away.

74

I made the wrong choice then.

And now?

When I close my eyes, trying to block my fear, it's not Pip or Mum I see, but Oli and Neena. They pushed past the barriers I put around me. They cared. They still care.

If I surrender now, they'll never even know where I died. They'll replay the last conversations we had, blame themselves. They don't deserve that.

I take stock of what I have in my backpack: a handful of old photographs.

And a kitchen knife.

My brain is finally up to speed.

Robert is holding the branch above my head, ready to strike.

'Are you going to do the right thing?'

Before I can answer, I see the branch coming towards me. I duck, but it catches my left ear.

The blow makes me cringe like an animal. It's like fire ripping through my skin.

I feel blood trickling down my neck.

The branch is coming towards me again.

I find my voice.

'They'll find me,' I pant. 'And you.'

Robert scoffs. 'You're bluffing.'

'You sure about that?'

I reach into my bag, pull the knife as close to the opening as possible, but hold up the Copse View photos so he sees those instead. I need him to be down here, with me. Face to face.

Robert stares at the pictures. He'll want to get them from me. Then I'll get my chance.

But he just laughs. 'You know, I'd ruled this out for being too . . . gratuitous. But let's go back to Plan A. The good thing about burning someone alive is it burns paper at the same time.'

He disappears from view, and returns with a red plastic canister.

'No!'

He's opening the top of the petrol can. I can smell the vapour from here.

'The forest is too dry,' I call out. 'You'll end up with half the fire brigade here. If you want these, Robert, you'll have to come and get them.'

He drags something across the top of the pit – a rope ladder. Another blow smashes against my forehead, then he begins to climb down.

There is another smell now. Aftershave. Cloying and spicy, with a hint of clove that makes me think of the dentist.

As he navigates the rungs, I will him to stumble, fall.

Even just to look away.

Now.

As I thrust my left hand into the backpack next to me, groping for the knife, his fist strikes my chin.

Something cracks. My jaw. My teeth? Pain follows. Dazzling, light-splintering pain.

Another punch.

So shocking I cannot breathe.

He makes a grab for the photo in my right hand. Claws at my shoulder, wrenching it so hard I scream through bloodied lips, letting the photograph go. Now I begin and end with pain.

But there is something else, too.

Rage.

Rage at what he's done to all those people.

I will not be buried with everything I fought so hard to understand.

As he tips the contents of my bag onto the earth, I fling my body towards the other side of the pit, where he climbed down. My ankle screeches in agony as I drag it behind me.

'Come here, bitch!'

I grit my teeth. 'No, you come here.'

I know what I have to do.

He launches himself at me. As he does, I raise the knife.

We tumble back and for a moment, I think he's somehow avoided the blade; his face, close up, is still blank with fury.

I'm almost relieved – that I haven't hurt him, that it'll soon be over.

But now his eyes are widening and his lips are parting. As he falls away, the knife pulls out of his chest with a strange slurp. He lands on the dark, wet earth, gasping. And then I see the blood.

So much blood – a circle blooming on his chest, dripping onto the ground.

Vermillion. Lamp Black.

Can I watch someone die?

Do I have another choice?

Robert looks outraged. He rasps, 'You . . .'

But he's too breathless to articulate what he's thinking.

His T-shirt is soaked now. My own pain comes back and all I can see when I look down is more blood. Blood from my own wounds, covering my skin and clothes. Blood in my mouth, mingling with the taste of aftershave.

Robert's movements are slowing now, like a toy whose battery is running down.

He is dying.

I scramble towards the ladder and, ignoring the pain, pull myself up to the first rung. My shoulder doesn't work properly, and my ankle throbs as I drag it behind me, but the fear of looking back – at him, at what I've done – keeps me going. There are five rungs to go.

Time slows. I hear my own laboured breath.

Am I dying too?

But now I can just see over the top of the hole, I know I can do it. I reach up and pull myself along the damp earth to where Robert tethered the other end around a tree trunk.

Out.

Above me, the leaves rustle, and the white sky is like bleach in my eyes.

I try to reorientate myself. Through the trees, I glimpse the deserted cafe and playground and, turning my back on it, move a few pain-filled steps at a time, stumbling and leaning against trees. Checking each new section of earth with my foot to ensure it's not about to give way.

The world is darkening. Fireworks flash across the sky – my brain shutting down? – and I sense my last strength leaving me.

But ahead of me, Pip is beckoning, and beyond him the road is visible, though it might as well be miles away because I have no reserves left and I don't even feel pain anymore as I sink onto the hard, soft, forest floor, the bracken sighing underneath me.

Rosanna is here, too, somewhere close.

As I feel insects scuttling around me, I imagine them working their way through layer on layer of vegetation, soil, leaves. One day, millennia ahead, all of this will be compressed and carbonised. We will be forgotten, merely another seam of coal.

As I let go, it is almost a comfort.

75

Cold. So cold.

Am I dead?

The pain returns in a hot wave – first ankle, then back, shoulder, head, jaw, everywhere – and that's how I know I'm not. That, and the figure of Charlie who sits next to me, cross-legged, looking impatient.

A lorry flashes past along the road ahead – white against green, a thundering sound echoing long after it's gone. I am *so* close to the road, but when I try to move, my body doesn't respond.

I listen for another car and when I think I hear something, I call out:

Help me . . .

But it is no more than a whisper.

I blink and I am alone again. No Pip, no Pink, no Charlie.

I listen, because it is all I can do. Then I realise I am holding something. My phone?

No. It's the knife.

My phone is in the pit. With Robert. What happened – what I did – seems less real than my hallucinations.

No. I remember his face, his chest, the blood.

I am a killer.

I strain to hear more wheels against the road.

Instead, I hear footsteps, breaking twigs. A man, walking through the forest.

Robert?

Fear makes me curl up, like an animal, trying to make myself as small as I can, despite the pain.

Did I leave a trail of blood?

I am tired of everything being a fight. I have nothing left.

Robert is getting nearer, I hear him breathing. I should have stabbed him again. Made sure.

But alongside the fear: relief. At least I am not a killer. I am not my father.

Georgia! GEORGIA!

Not Robert's voice.

'I'm here.' My last scrap of energy.

Try again.

'Here.'

The man lifts me up. He's running now. My ankle jolts, burns, jolts, burns. My cries muffled by his chest. The dirty smell of him is familiar.

Daniel.

I want to know how and why and when but I can't form the words. In my head I am thinking *don't slow down but watch out for pits and mines and scowles . . .*

He knows that already because he belongs here.

'He's dead,' I whisper.

But he can't hear me.

He holds me tighter. Am I going to live?

Here comes the dark again, to swallow me up.

76

Before I open my eyes, I know where I am from the sharp smell of disinfectant.

A place of safety.

But there is no relief, because I know something else too: I am a killer.

Now other things register: the quicksand feeling of sedation and the numbness in my ankle; the burning around my ear that the drugs don't seem to be touching.

I am a killer.

Someone is in the ward with me. Close. When I open my eyes, the strip light overhead is so aggressively white that I instantly want to close them, but I fight against it, and my visitor comes into half-focus.

'You're back again,' Oli whispers.

He stretches, his arms and legs too long for the hospital chair.

'I've been awake already?' My voice is hoarse, my throat dry as paper.

'Three times now. But you haven't noticed me before. You remember who I am, though, right?'

'Of course.'

But still the *then* is sharper than the now. What I saw.

What I did.

He nods. 'Why didn't you tell me?'

'Tell you what?'

There have been so many lies and secrets.

'About coming to see Daniel. And the . . . stuff in the forest.'

The light beyond the ward window is dawn-coloured, the palest rose madder behind the grimy pane. I try to do the calculation in my head. Is it the day after? Twelve, sixteen hours since Little Pike?

Since I killed a man.

I see him again: Robert, the ghost. His eyes as he realised what was happening. His slowing motions. The stillness.

He didn't deserve that.

And now I remember exactly what he did: to Rosanna, and Sharon, and maybe to other women since.

No. He deserved worse.

'Am I under arrest?' I ask.

I can't make out Oli's expression, but I know he will find a way to break it gently.

'They *do* want to question you. They . . . found the knife.'

It'll be the word of a dead man against mine. I try to work out which of the things he admitted to me might be verifiable somehow.

'And the bloke, too. But he's in ICU so I'm guessing you'll get to tell your story first. I can be with you, if you want. Apart from anything else, I really want to know what the hell has been going on. And who he is.'

'He's *alive*?'

'He's had surgery but they don't know if he'll wake up.'

'It's Robert,' I say. 'Robert O'Neill. Charlie's father.'

Now he leans forward. '*What?*'

'I was meant to be meeting this girl – Rosanna. From Copse View. But she's dead, Oli, Robert told me he killed her. But the police won't believe me unless I can find evidence and I can't—'

'Shhh.' Oli reaches out, grasps my hand. 'Don't get upset. Whatever's happened, we'll sort it. I know you'd never hurt anyone unless you had no choice. You're safe, now.'

He smiles, and I try to smile back.

'Daniel. He found me, right?'

Oli nods. 'Yes. He's back under arrest.'

Oh God. 'He didn't . . . Is Jim all right?'

'As far as I know. Shouldn't he be?'

I open my mouth to explain, but I don't know where to start. Yet I want Oli to know before I talk to the police.

'Georgia, don't worry. I won't let them talk to you until you're in a fit state.'

'As my lawyer?'

'As your friend. Your very cross friend. You were lucky. Your ankle is knackered, you've got two rows of stitches in your head, but you'll mend.'

'Will you be struck off or something, if I tell you? Before the police?'

'No. You're not a suspect.' He pulls the curtains around the bed, even though the rest of the bay is empty. The sound of the rings against the metal rail reminds me of court. Of me on one side of the fabric, my dad on the other. 'You tell me whatever you want to.'

'There are so many things,' I say. 'But this part begins at Copse View.'

77

After lunch, the police come to talk to me. An older man and a younger woman, like this is a TV crime drama.

They set up a video camera to record what I say. Their faces are indistinct, but I try to read their body language as they get organised, to work out if I am a suspect or a victim, or both.

Even as the male detective states the date, time and place, I can't tell. But Oli sits next to the bed, ready to step in if they push me too far.

'Miss Sage, can you tell us why you went to Little Pike?'

'I went there to meet a girl,' I begin. 'A woman. But it was about what happened when she was a girl. I thought I knew something. As it turned out, I knew nothing at all.'

'Who was the woman?'

'Rosanna Chapman. But she wasn't there. Instead, it was a man who was supposed to be dead.'

As I speak, it feels as though those few hours happened to someone else: crossing the deserted playground; falling into the hollow . . .

Fighting for my life.

'Do you know the man's name?' the woman asks.

'I believe he is Robert O'Neill.'

She writes it down.

'How do you know this Robert O'Neill?'

'I don't.' *Nobody does,* I realise. Not really. He's as illusory as my hallucinations. 'But I knew of him. He's the father of the children Jim Fielding rescued from the fire in Ashdean. O'Neill was gone by then. I don't know what he's done since. But I think I do know what he did before.'

'Can we return to what happened in the forest yesterday?' the woman says.

But the older officer holds up his hand.

'Go on. Tell it your way.'

So I do, trying to stick to verifiable facts: Robert working at Copse View, meeting Jim; the photos; the incomplete police notes about being called to the home; the lack of action.

I can't see the police officers' faces all that well, but I notice their body language change as they realise this is even bigger than the attempted murder they thought they were investigating.

'Did you find a bag? My bag, in the scowle, where you found Robert?'

The male detective nods.

'The photos are in there. I believe Rosanna Chapman – the only one I could identify – is dead. That Robert killed her, when they were both teenagers. Buried her in those same woods. But there will be other girls who knew what happened there. Who might talk if they think you're taking it seriously this time.'

'Tell us how you got your injuries,' the woman says.

As I describe what happened, I experience the pain again, and the hopelessness, the certainty that it would all end there, in the woods.

And then I tell them about the moment I decided I wanted to live. About the knife going in and coming out, and the struggle to climb for my life.

I don't tell them about Pip guiding me towards the road, or that, when I was finally faced with death, I understood it wasn't what I wanted.

Whatever they might charge me with, no one can take that clarity away.

I am more than a survivor. I want to live.

On the second day, while I'm still in hospital, Robert wakes up. He claims not to know who he is, or what happened.

But the police are starting to fill in the gaps.

The female detective comes to see me on the morning of day three, to tell me what they know.

Robert has had half a dozen identities since Jim left him bleeding in the forest all those years ago. He's charmed himself into the homes of a series of women, leaving them with bones and spirits broken and bank accounts empty. None of them reported him to the police. It seems the women were simply relieved he had tired of torturing them.

'We've spoken to a few of them now, following the trail of his previous addresses. They all say the same – to start with, they thought he was too ordinary to be a threat. They thought *they* were the ones in control.'

'Do you think the women you haven't found yet are . . .?' I try to find the right words. 'All right?'

She says nothing. 'We're on it.'

'And Rosanna?'

'So far, we've found nothing on Rosanna since July 1979. It seems the staff at the home assumed she'd run away – she'd done that before – and as she was a few months from her sixteenth birthday, no one looked very hard.'

I half-expect to see Pink when I look up, but instead there's only me and the officer, and, across the ward, an elderly lady who came in yesterday after breaking her hip.

'He suggested he'd buried her at Little Pike.'

The officer nods. 'We are looking for disturbed ground.'

I nod and wish I hadn't. Everything is hurting now they've reduced my pain medication.

'He's a liar, isn't he? But I think he was telling the truth then. It felt like he was boasting.'

She sighs. 'It's a bit like untangling string. When we think we've found the end of one story, we realise it's the start of some-one else's.'

I know how that feels.

Oli comes back to Gloucestershire to drive me home.

'You look bloody awful,' he says.

'One of the benefits of being half-blind is at least I can't see that.'

I need him to laugh. I can't bear pity.

He manages a half-hearted chuckle.

'It explains a lot about why you shacked up with me.'

Weak jokes and mild insults will get us through.

He leads me out into the unexpected heat of the May afternoon, towards his new Dad-equipped 4x4, and moves the seat back so there's room for the cast on my ankle.

I turn to grasp the seatbelt. Charlie sits in the back. His presence startles me for a moment – I haven't seen him since I woke up wounded in the forest with him at my side – then makes me smile.

I've missed you.

'Some supplies for the journey.' Oli passes me a striped carrier bag. Inside, there's chocolate, nuts, Coke, a small bottle of brandy. He nods at the latter. 'For emergencies.'

As he starts the engine, I open the Coke and take a tentative swig, in case the bubbles hurt my gum around the tooth they had to remove. Oli sets the satnav, and the screen shows we have over three hours of driving ahead.

'OK, Georgie. You can sleep, or talk, or I can put the radio on—'

'Talk,' I say. 'I want to talk. To explain.'

'You already told me what happened in the forest.'

'Not about that. About me.'

As we travel out towards the motorway, I try to decide where to begin. I know telling the truth is the only way, but I'm scared he might hate me for it. For all the lies I've told.

'You have to know that I've deceived everyone, Oli. But I've felt worst about lying to you.'

'Like I said. I understand why you met Daniel.'

'The secrets . . . They're bigger.'

He sighs. 'Maybe they only feel big because you don't share them. It's not like I haven't always known there were things you hadn't told me.'

I close my eyes. When I open them again, I am ready.

'Oli, my name isn't Georgia Sage. My name is Suzanne Ross. My father murdered my mother and brother when I was eleven years old. I've been lying ever since. I don't want to lie anymore. I want you to know who I really am.'

I hear a sharp intake of breath. Then he reaches over and places his hand over mine.

As we drive, I tell him about the girl I was, the invention I became. And finally, I'm ready to tell someone exactly what happened that day in September when I told my brother he couldn't come in, when my father locked my door, gave me the key and told me not to use it.

Oli keeps his hand on mine as the car coasts along the motorway. He lets me chip away at the layers of lies at my own pace, like stripping paint, without knowing if what is underneath has rotted away completely.

When I come to the part about being spared that day, he says, 'Oh, Georgie,' and then shakes his head. 'Or do you want me to call you Suzanne?'

'No. Maybe now I'm more Georgia than Suzanne. Because what matters is the people who know me now. You. Neena.'

My story is done. The air in the car feels sour from it.

'I'd love to know about you, then, if you want to tell me,' Oli says eventually. 'Your brother. Your mother. There is more to your childhood than that one day, isn't there?'

And now he's given me permission, it comes out. The good, as well as the bad: memories of Pip, and Mum. Thousands of journeys up and down our front path with school bags and lunchboxes and swimming gear. Games of Swingball, Marmite leaping up, always the third contestant in our furious games.

The screech of Pip's recorder. The smell of my mother's chocolate cake. The ordinariness of our lives, our quarrels, our home.

I remember a day the colour of this one: picking honeysuckle and freesias to fill a jam jar, taking the bouquet to my room, capturing its delicacy in watercolours. Back then, when I thought I'd go on to paint the big wide world. The memories feel as vivid as my hallucinations.

I want to feel, smell, see that very small world again.

Before I can work out who I want to be next.

'Could we go somewhere else on the way home? I don't think it'd be a huge detour. I know the postcode.'

He glances at me. 'Of course.'

For the first time in twenty years, I say where I am from, and where I want to go.

78

There is one last layer to be stripped away.

'You sure you don't want me to try to come in with you?' Neena asks. 'My press card could go a long way in an open prison.'

I shake my head. 'No. I need my getaway driver to be ready to take me to the pub immediately afterwards.'

She nods, though I'm guessing the journalist in her is dying to see what happens next. When I told her about my past, she was the opposite to Oli: asking endless questions, not even trying to conceal her fascination.

'Aren't you the dark horse?' she'd said.

If she was hurt by my lies, the drama of my revelations cancelled it out.

I open the car door and twist to get my ankle and cast out first, then the crutches. Two days out of hospital, and I am still not used to it.

I could have delayed the prison visit, I guess. But I wanted to finish this. Going to my old house with Oli was something I did on a whim, but it has made me see I cannot move on without understanding that final day.

Twenty years in denial is too long.

The place where my father is serving his sentence – where, I suppose, he will die – is the opposite of the Victorian jail that held Daniel. It's low-rise, surrounded by a wall that's more decorative than deterrent.

The furniture and the security processes are still rigorous – they even X-ray my crutches, and run a metal detector over my cast – but buttermilk-coloured light pours in through modern windows.

'Miss Sage?'

I turn to see a small, powerful woman in a prison uniform.

'I'm Heather Penney. Thank you for coming.'

She looks me up and down when we shake hands but says nothing about my injuries.

I think she's younger than me – her features aren't quite clear – but she holds herself in an old-fashioned way, as though she's been trained to walk correctly by pacing with an encyclopaedia on her head.

As she closes the door behind me, and I hobble into the main building, I notice that an 'open' prison still has plenty of locks.

She escorts me to a bland room with a table and three chairs, helps me to sit down, my ankle stretched out. A fluted plastic jug of water and two cardboard cups are already laid out.

'Is there anything you'd like to ask before I bring him in?'

I glance at the door. Right now, I really want to leave. But my fear has kept me locked in for twenty years. Yet again, the key to getting out is in my hand. I've waited too long to use it.

'Is he . . . well?'

'He is relatively pain-free. One of the reasons he wanted the meeting sooner rather than later, was so that his appearance would not be too shocking.'

She thinks he wants to spare me. I bet it's all about his own pride.

'Would you like me to stay? We're confident there's no risk to you, and I have permission to wait outside, with the door ajar if you want privacy, but it's your choice.'

'I'd rather you were here.'

How does she know I'm no risk to *him*?

She goes to fetch him and the door closes itself behind her. My throat tightens and my head pounds. I'd give anything to see Charlie now, my little partner in crime. But he's contrary, will only show up when he feels like it.

The door handle shifts. I stare at it. I was kidding myself. I'm not ready. I will never be ready—

Heather comes in first. She steps out of the way and there is my father.

Still tall, though stooped.

My father's hair is titanium now, grandfatherly. I'm not ready to look at his face, so I focus on his clothes: proper trousers, not the baggy sweatpants everyone wore at Daniel's prison; a pale-blue shirt over bony upper arms, with sharp lines pressed into the short sleeves.

He's hovering beside the table, waiting. I don't think either of us know what for. Surely not an embrace.

'Shall we sit down?' Heather asks. I nod.

She moves out the chair, and ushers my father into it with a soft touch to his elbow. When I look at his face, he's staring straight ahead.

That's when I understand.

He can't see properly.

He has Best disease too.

Now I know that, I can study him: rail-thin, except his face which is chubby – from steroids, maybe? – so his once sharp features are undefined. Loose skin hoods the top halves of his eyes, but the blur of his pupils is the same grey-blue as my own.

He looks up and I don't look away. How much of me can he see?

'Suzanne.'

There is a longing in his voice. My throat tightens.

'Don't call me that.'

'I'm sorry. You sound the same.'

I don't know how I am meant to respond to that.

'I'm dying,' he says.

'Heather told me.'

'I don't expect you to feel sorry for me.'

But I think he does. Again, I have nothing to say.

'I got in touch because once I'm gone, you might regret not having the chance to ask me questions about it.'

It.

'You mean the day you killed your wife and your son? Our family?'

He inhales sharply. 'Yes.'

'Are you hoping for a deathbed reconciliation?'

'I don't blame you for being angry.'

I smile. 'Is that how you've spent the last twenty years? Doing therapy?'

He shrugs. 'I've talked to people. But mostly I've been alone. Thinking.'

'Thinking up excuses?'

I sound petty now but I don't care.

Heather shifts in her chair.

'Do you know why I came, Dad? I came to tell you I hope you suffer, that the pain relief stops working. And to tell you that no one will mourn you.'

But as the words tumble out, they don't feel as good as I'd hoped they would.

'Georgia,' Heather says gently, 'it might be best if you let him speak.'

I look at my father: did he know I'd changed my identity?

Dad nods as though he heard my unspoken question.

'It's a pretty name. I can understand that the one we gave you was a burden you prefer not to carry now.'

How polite he is. How restrained.

But I want to upend the table and wreck this room, smash my fists against the walls until my knuckles are bleeding.

'I want you to know that I always loved you, Su—' He stops himself. 'And Pip, too. It was just . . . different with him. I don't know if you have children yet, but you were my special one.'

'Lucky me.'

'When you were born, it was instant. The love I felt. And as you grew up, with your talent and your quickness. You were just . . . a kindred spirit. But Pip wasn't like us: I didn't understand him.'

Us.

I loved being the favourite: the little treats, the praise, the glow. I was guilty, too.

Except he was the adult. And I've remembered over the last few days that I *did* try to change things sometimes. That last summer when Dad changed, I observed him closely to try to understand what set him off, so I could warn Pip before it happened. So that we could be happy again, like other families.

'You were our father. You should have tried to treat us equally.'

'I know.'

He reaches over the table towards the water jug. Heather tries to help but he brushes her off. He spills some of the water when he pours, and gulps down what he's managed to get in the cup.

'Is that why you killed him? Because he wasn't the perfect son?'

He looks up sharply. 'No. Of course not.'

'Why, then?'

'To protect him from *them*.'

I scoff. 'Them? There was nobody else there.'

But even as I say it, I hear the voices on the landing again and my certainty wavers. What if he *was* telling the truth when he gave his first statement to the police?

'I know that now,' he says. 'But back then, all I knew was that the men had come back. Into our house, this time. And that I could no longer keep you all safe.'

79

'I'd never seen any of them before that summer. Then there were two of them, sometimes three. To begin with, I thought they were local guys, hired to rough me up. So I paid one of the men from the production line, bit of a thug, to watch the house. Reckoned he saw nothing, even on the nights *I'd* seen them on the street from my bedroom window. He laughed at me. But I knew it meant they were professionals. Dangerous.'

My father's breathing quickens, but it's not until Heather passes him a tissue and he uses it to scrub at his eyes, that I realise he's crying.

'Why would there be men after you?' I ask.

'I'd been having . . . trouble at work. I'd been making mistakes. Big errors. People were displeased. People you didn't want to displease.'

'What the hell are you talking about? You worked for an engineering firm, not the bloody Mafia.'

'That's why I knew no one would believe me. But I also knew I was seeing them . . .' He sighs. 'I shouted at them to go away, but they ignored me. They never said anything, they were just there. Menacing. Following us everywhere.'

Suddenly, I know what's coming. But I don't want to hear it.

'I felt like I'd put you all in danger and so it was my responsibility to protect you now. Then, after Cornwall, I realised we would never get away.'

'What?'

'Pip saw them too, in Cornwall. That's when I knew they were real. That I couldn't protect you.'

For a moment, it makes no sense. But then a memory comes to me.

We're in the car, on the way to Cornwall. Pip, staring out of the window at the sea, telling us he could see mermaids and dolphins and even the Loch Ness monster.

Of course my eager-to-please kid brother would have agreed if Dad had asked him if there were men around. But my father never bothered to get to know his own son well enough to understand this.

Wild thoughts fill my head like birds trapped in a tiny room. Even Heather is sitting bolt upright; I'm pretty sure this is new to her too.

'I came home after the trip and I started to plan,' my father continues. 'I saved your mother's sleeping pills. I ground them up and added them to her tea. And yours. And the milk on Pip's cereal.'

'You *drugged* us?'

I replay that last morning. I remember how unusual it was, Dad making breakfast, and I feel sick now, knowing why.

'No one ate it. Pip was in one of his crazy moods. I was tense. Even Marmite refused to touch it.'

I remember.

'What happened then?'

'You and Pip were painting, until he made a mess . . . I sent Pip to his room, your mum made the burgers for later and then went for a lie down, she had a migraine coming on . . .' He hesitates. 'Actually, it all made things easier.'

'You *planned* this. It had nothing to do with Pip spilling the turps.'

My father looks astonished. 'Of course it didn't. And I promise you your mother knew nothing about it. She was dozing and . . . There was no struggle.'

'But Pip *did* know, didn't he?'

He nods. 'If only he'd had breakfast.'

I say nothing.

'Pip was drawing you a picture. He'd written *I'm Sorry Suzie-Soo* in letters so big even I could read them. There were flowers—'

'And clowns and trees and dogs.'

'You've seen it?'

'They gave it to me.'

'He was crying, saying he was sorry. I told him it wasn't his fault, that he wasn't in trouble. But he . . . wouldn't stay quiet.'

'*Oh, God.*'

'I didn't want the sound to scare you, Suzanne. So I had to quiet him. Just one blow and he was out cold. I took the pillow and—'

I stand, throwing back my chair.

'I can't listen to this.'

'Pip saved you, in a way. I looked at him . . . At the blood and I knew, instantly, that I'd got it terribly wrong. I was supposed to protect you all from violence, not . . .' He bangs his fist against his head.

'But you left Pip alive. They said so in court.'

He shakes his head. 'No. I held him after. I knew he was gone. I was his killer but I was also his father. The paramedics can't have found a pulse.'

I close my eyes.

'When I came out of his room, I heard you humming to yourself. A pop song. I stood on the landing and my hands were shaking and there was blood on my shirt and the men were there. Right in front of me. I locked your door to stop them getting in.'

He hesitates. 'And I locked it to stop myself, too. Because you needed to be protected from all of us.'

I am back there, in my room. Hearing the key turn. Realising only one of my parents could have done it, that it wasn't another of Pip's jokes.

'I tried to sound calm, when I told you what to do. I knew I couldn't live with what I'd done. And I thought if I ended my life, at least you'd be safe. What would they have to gain by coming after you?'

The metal key glints on the purple carpet.

'I begged them to leave. I shouted. I hissed.'

The voices on the landing: not several people, but one, my father, trying everything he could to send the visions away.

'And when they said nothing, I tried to kill myself. But I couldn't even get that right.'

'Why didn't you say any of this in court?'

'My lawyer told me I could probably plead manslaughter on the grounds of diminished responsibility. No one but me believed the men had ever been there, so I must have been mad. I'd have been free by now, if I'd taken it. But I thought staying silent was the last thing I could do to protect you.'

'Protect me? No. You were too bloody proud to admit what you'd done, to let anyone know you might be going mad!'

He bunches his fists. 'I still thought the men were real. That if I spoke out in court, they'd come back for you.'

'Fuck you, Dad,' I say, trying to manoeuvre myself towards the door.

'Please. Let me finish. There's one more thing to tell you.'

I wait.

'It was only after I was sentenced, that I got a diagnosis. I know you can't forgive me, Suzanne. God knows, I can't forgive myself. But the other reason I wanted you to come here was to warn you. Because the visions? The people I saw, who weren't there?'

I nod, because I know what's coming.

'They came because my sight was failing. My brain ... It created the men to compensate. And it was caused by Best disease, which is genetic. You need a test, Suzanne ... *Georgia*. In case—'

'In case I go on to kill my family too?'

I look my father in the eye, expecting to see evil. But instead, I see only weakness and arrogance.

If only he'd asked for help, everything would have been different. Then again, I was in denial for years, too, ignoring my vision loss. Another thing that I inherited, perhaps?

And there's another quality that defines the man sitting opposite me: he is haunted. Do I really need to make it worse for him by telling him I have the disease too? His own vision is so damaged, he hasn't even realised I might be affected too.

'Thank you for the warning,' I say.

I take my crutches and manoeuvre them into position, ready to go.

There has been no apology. I suppose I shouldn't have expected one.

'Suzanne.'

I look at my father. 'What?'

'I haven't said I'm sorry, because it doesn't change anything. But I am. I really am.'

He can still read me, even after all this time.

'I didn't mean it,' I say finally. 'About the pain and everything. I hope they take care of you.'

I leave without looking back and the door snaps closed behind me.

September 2017

I am painting a picture. A seascape. The sky is turning crimson, melting into the horizon rendered in a steely Davy's Grey.

The beach is quiet, but also full of *my* people. In the distance, children play in the late September surf. One or two are real: I hear them calling out. But there's also a little girl of six or seven splashing at the shoreline, seawater dripping from the bottom of her modesty-preserving Victorian swimsuit.

A dragon, or perhaps it's only a wave, writhes in and out of the struts of the pier. The haze around it is sea spray, but I am painting it as smoke.

Pink runs along the pier, chasing someone I can't see. I half-expected that after the police found Rosanna's remains the hallucinations might stop, but in fact she and Charlie still dance in and out of my vision, even more vivid than before.

The difference is that now my life is filling up with real, blurry, *wonderful* people too.

'How much longer do you need?' Marion asks me.

My foster-parents have come to Brighton, their first visit. She and Trevor can't stop beaming at me, and I at them. I was mad to keep them away.

'Almost done,' I say, holding my brush in the air.

Robert has been charged with Rosanna's murder, and my attempted murder. They are reviewing the sexual offences: two girls from the home are willing to testify that they were raped. They both say the garage block was known as Robert's 'party place'. That's why Jim didn't want a house built there.

One of the girls shared a room with Rosanna. She will testify that Rosanna tried twice to report what was happening, but no one took her seriously. After the first time, Robert tried to buy her off with booze and jewellery.

After the second time, she disappeared. The girls hoped she had run away. It was easier to convince themselves of that than the alternative.

The police haven't found her body so it's hearsay, but some of it should stick. Once Robert is jailed, his fellow inmates will know enough of what he did to make his life as miserable as it can be. Though, from what I know of the man, it's the lack of control that will be the worst punishment.

I heard from Jim a month ago. Actually, it was just a photograph of a small wedding, featuring a skinny, bronzed bride in an enormous dress. Next to her, Jim looks half-embarrassed, half-delighted.

I turned the picture over, and on the back, Jim had written:

Thank you for leading the police to Robert.

Daniel has called me, too. He's met his father once, and though it's a long way from happy families, they're trying. I was wrong about them both, and about so much else. For too long, I viewed people through a strange prism, believing everyone had a streak of cruelty or evil that only I could see. But I was wrong: I cannot see through anyone, I only see what they choose to reveal.

Perhaps a tiny handful of people have no good in them – Robert O'Neill, and a few of the other unrepentant killers I've seen across a courtroom. But mostly, we all do the best we can, with what we're given.

And as for me, I'm learning how not to be lonely. It is like learning to read or write. Plus, I'm learning to see and to paint the world in a different way. As a brighter, more surprising place. My specialist has told me that Degas and Monet both suffered vision loss as they aged, yet their later work is still appreciated by millions. People say my landscapes are good. Perhaps I wasn't only born to paint faces after all.

I have things to look forward to. Oli wouldn't take no for an answer, so I intend to be Millie's coolest godmother, to make up for the lack of religious instruction.

Neena has had a couple of scoops out of the Ashdean stuff, and more to come. There's talk of a documentary after Robert's trials are over – she wants me to be the star.

'The blind artist amateur sleuth. Honestly, it's going to be an award-winner, George, it'll make our careers.'

She deserves her success – but she's going to have to keep *me* out of it. And anyway, I am not blind. My vision is stable and my other senses are exquisitely sharp, compensating for what is in shadow.

My father is still alive, just. I may visit him one last time. I no longer hate myself, and perhaps that means I can forgive him too.

'Who are they?' Trevor asks now, looking over my shoulder.

My new paintings always feature three figures that aren't really there. Mostly, they're in the distance, but in today's picture, they're in the foreground.

Mum, Pip, me. I reach over, add a smudge of rose madder to my mother's cheeks, and my own.

'People I remember.' I smile at him. 'Shall we gather everything up before the light goes?'

I am still a little afraid of the dark. My eyesight is stable, but there are no certainties.

As I scramble up from the pebbles, I glimpse a group of men down at the water's edge. One turns and stares right at me, then waves. It's only as he begins to walk towards me that I recognise his walk and remember who he is. The teacher, Niall, from the pub quiz, and the first night I saw Charlie, all those months ago.

I feel myself blushing. But instead of ignoring him, I make myself wave back. Perhaps he could teach me my latest lesson: how to let nice things happen.

'Look!' Marion shouts.

From nowhere, starlings are flocking around the skeleton of the old pier. At an invisible signal, they begin to soar, forming impossible patterns against the reddening sky. On and on they go, swooping, regrouping, making shapes that have never been made before, just for the joy of it.

Now I no longer look for evil, there is so much more to see.

Acknowledgements

From the first magistrates' hearing I attended as a 19-year-old trainee reporter, I've been fascinated by the justice system. In fact, it goes back even further. I longed for occasional afternoons off sick from school, watching *Crown Court* with my mum and pretending to be a juror. And on Sunday evenings, Dad and I were utterly addicted to *Rumpole of the Bailey*.

The idea of writing about a courtroom sketch artist was partly inspired by the Pen and Paper episode of the genius podcast *Criminal* (www.thisiscriminal.com) and my story grew progressively stranger when I read about Charles Bonnet Syndrome.

I'd like to thank Dr Amanda-Jayne Carr, Sensory System and Therapies in Stem Cell Biology Research Fellow at the Institute of Ophthalmology at University College London for advising on Best Disease symptoms and treatment.

A big thank you to author and lawyer Neil White (whose legal thrillers I love: neilwhite.net) for advising me on cross-examination and legal habits. However, all errors and inventions are mine, including the creation of a Gothic courtroom in Brighton, rather than the more mundane Hove Crown Court building, where I reacquainted myself with the delays and occasional dramas of everyday justice. Thanks also to Steve O'Gorman for the most thorough copy edit ever.

Many lovely writer friends have read, commented and encouraged along the way. Vin rouge and hummus came courtesy of Janie and Mickey at Chez Castillon. Thanks especially to Cally Taylor, Julie Cohen, Rowan Coleman, Miranda Dickinson, Tamsyn Murray, Angela Clarke, Araminta Hall, Sarah Rayner and Laura Wilkinson, for brainstorming plus virtual and actual gin.

Friends and family members have kept me going – big love to Geri, Jenny, Toni, my dad Michael, and my partner Richard. My mother Barbara died a few months before this book was published but thrillers were always her favourite genre – Mum, I hope I've done you proud.

Huge thanks to Hellie Ogden for seeing the potential in the very messy manuscript and helping me make it much more thrilling. Also thanks to Rebecca Carter and the rest of the Janklow and Nesbit team.

Sophie Orme was the very first editor to read the opening chapters, and it feels like synchronicity and serendipity that she's gone on to publish the book with such passion, insight and all-round brilliance. Thanks to her and to all the other fantastic folk at Bonnier Zaffre including Katherine Armstrong, Francesca Russell, Kate Parkin, Jennie Rothwell, Sahina Bibi, Felice McKeown and Stephen Dumughn.

Finally, thank YOU for taking a chance on my thriller debut. It means a lot! If you'd like to get in touch, find out what I'm writing next *and* win signed copies of thrillers by *my* favourite authors, join my club at kate-helm.com or say hi on Twitter or Instagram where I am @katewritesbooks and post pictures of books and of the beach in Brighton that Georgia and I both love so much.

Kate x